VOICES OF THE SOUTH

FLOOD

A Romance of Our Time

ROBERT PENN WARREN

Louisiana State University Press   Baton Rouge

Library of Congress Cataloging-in-Publication Data:
Warren, Robert Penn, 1905–
    Flood / Robert Penn Warren.
        p. cm. — (Voices of the South)
    ISBN 0 8071-2918-6 (pbk. : alk. paper)
        1. Dams—Design and construction—Fiction. 2. Tennessee Valley
Authority—Fiction. 3. Tennessee—Fiction. I. Title. II. Series.

PS3545.A748F4 2003
813'.54—dc21

                                                        2003054344

TO

Albert and Marisa Erskine

And I will plant them upon their land, and they shall no more be pulled up out of their land which I have given them, saith the Lord thy God.

Amos IX:15

Book
ONE

Chapter

1

IT HAD TO BE THE PLACE. There was the limestone bluff jutting abruptly up, crowned by cedars. It was bound to be the place.

Long back, when he had passed this way, it had been that sudden jut of gray stone above the trees that gave him warning in time to avert, unconsciously, his face; and then, as he whirled on, with eyes fixed down the road, he would know, in conscious shame, that once more he had done it. He would stare down the road and wait for the shame to thin out, to be absorbed colorlessly, like a drop of ink in water, into the general medium of his being.

In those years the road had been blacktop. Now it was concrete. New concrete. Now, after so many years, he did not have to avert his face. Quite consciously, he looked. Hell, he could look now.

The big sycamore by the creek was gone. The willow tangle was gone. The little enclave of untrodden bluegrass was gone. The clump of dogwood on the little rise across the creek—now that, too, was gone.

But the trouble was not so much what was not there. It was what was there. The creek was there, but it flowed decorously between two banks where stones were mortised into the earth; and on a boulder a cement frog, the size of a young calf and the color of Paris green, with a mouth gaping as richly bright as a split liver on a butcher's block, crouched. On another boulder a gnome, dwarf, brownie or some such improbability, with a cement beard painted snow-white, sat studiously fishing. The line with which the creature was fishing was a real line. It wavered with the motion of the stream. The water in the stream looked real. But the water lilies were definitely cement.

Bradwell Tolliver wished that the water did not look real. What always worried you was to find something real in the middle of all the faking. It worried you, because if everything is fake then nothing matters.

Throttling the white Jaguar down, he gazed at the big billboard there, anomalous in the blaze of day, the now un-lit neon as irrelevant as those needs that, with evening, would make a glance linger here. The sign said:

THE SEVEN DWARFS MOTEL

RELAX IN HAPPY DELL

Beneath the sign was a picture. A young woman whose endowments were not obscured by a virginally white night-dress was waking to the kiss of Prince Charming. The blouse of Prince Charming ambiguously suggested a pajama top.

Below the picture was another sign, the words ballooning from the bloated, minstrel-show-white lips of a benignly grin-ning black face painted to one side of the enormous billboard:

BREAKFAST SERVED IN COTTAGE
TENNESSEE SMOKED HAM AND RED GRAVY
YASSUH, BOSS!

Beyond the main structure of the motel there was the sec-ond billboard, and there Prince Charming again appeared,

leaning from one side to smile in ecstasy at a bed with
the covers neatly turned back. Opposite him, appeared the
well-endowed young woman, smiling too. Then, below, the
words:

FIRST IN THE SOUTH

LAZ-EE MAN'S DEE-LIGHT

ELECTRIC MASSAGE MATTRESS IN EVERY ROOM

HEALTHFUL—RESTFUL—ZESTFUL

NEW RELAXATION—NEW SENSATION

TRY IT, PAL!

Drifting on the slab at some five miles an hour, Bradwell Tolliver now studied the main structure of the motel.
The structure was done in the style of fairy-tale illustration,
plaster and cranky timbers, with a semicircle of appropriate cottages beyond, each set between two small, conical,
bright green, non-indigenous and non-thriving conifers. A
mulatto—no dwarf, but in the attire of nursery fantasy:
brown jerkin serrated at the bottom, with little bells at the
points, and tights with the right leg red and the left yellow
—was leaning on a gasoline pump, with a cloth dangling
motionless at the end of a limp arm.

Bradwell Tolliver thought of people stopping in those
little huts of fantasy. He thought of the fairy-tale waking.
He slammed the throttle to the floor, and the Jaguar bolted
like a thoroughbred ignominiously stung by a horsefly. Then
he braked it down. Yes, he could manage some gas. He would
be damned if he was scared of stopping there for a little gas.

He backed down the slab and crunched off to the pumps.
"Fill it," he said to the man with brown jerkin and mis-
matched legs, "high test," and he began to study the cottages. He tried to summon up some emotion, but could not.
Now he had stopped, and there was no emotion.

"Must be some high old times in Happy Dell," he said to
the man in the jerkin, who was now wiping the windshield.

"Yassuh," the man said, "mought be," and kept on wiping.

He had expected the man to grin. He had known the
kind of grin it would be. The chamois would pause on the
windshield and, in that moment of male connivance, of animal camaraderie, the face would grin through, servile but sly,

across the transparent, but real, barrier of History, as though through the windshield. But there had been no grin. Jingle Bells had not grinned.

So Bradwell Tolliver said: "They have to pay you much to wear those trick pants?"

"Boss," the man in the trick pants said, "was a time I had to wear me some cover-hauls said *Gulf* on the back. 'Nuther time my cover-hauls said *Sam's Service*. I don't feel no diff-urnt now, boss."

"Guess you got something there," Bradwell said. "What's on the pump?"

Handing over the ten-dollar bill, he thought idly that one time he would have made a story out of this.

The man had gone into the office for change.

Yes, once he could have made a good story out of this. He could make one now if he wanted—the chance encounter, the blank moment becoming charged by forces never specified, the cruel little prod he had given the man, the sudden recognition of unconscious courage, of the pathos of the lost man, the common man, clinging to some dignity in the midst of personal ignominy, loss of identity and general social wreckage.

"Christ," he said, and twisted his mouth. Right out of that lead review in the *New York Times Book Review*—that part down to the word *courage*. Right out of the lead review in the *New Republic*—that second part winding up with the *social wreckage*. Yes, that was the lingo of a long time back. You didn't talk about social wreckage now, you talked about conformism, about other-directedness, about the failure of nerve, about fall-out. Yes, that other crap was a long time back, twenty-five years back—but he was remembering it, every word, word for word. He wished he couldn't.

The words he wished he could not remember came from the reviews of his first little book of stories. There had been only seven stories in the book. The title was *I'm Telling You Now*. It had come out in 1935, in the fall of his senior year. For a while it was exciting to have written a book and seen it really published. But by February something was wrong. After not being able to sleep for three nights he went to the Dean of Men.

The Dean of Men was a large, big-brotherly sort of man with still splendid shoulders and suède patches on the splendidly disreputable tweed jacket. He leaned back in his swivel chair under the oar that hung on the wall—a blue blade with the Dean's name, a date, and the arms of the Oxford College where a stout back on the river and a thirst in the buttery had made a name for him. He moved the pipe from his jaws, and said: "I think you are making a mistake, Brad my boy."

Brad my boy got up courage enough to say that maybe he had to make that particular mistake.

"What will your father think?" the Dean asked.

Brad said that his father was dead.

The Dean flushed. Somebody had, obviously, been messing with the filing system in his head. Hell, he knew all about that squirt. It was just a slip. Sure, the squirt's father had died last year and the squirt had gone down South for the funeral. The squirt was from some place down in Tennessee. Hell, he could, suddenly, even remember the name of the place, and he felt better about his filing system. The place was Fiddlersburg, Tenn. In his mind he carefully made it that way: *T-e-n-n.*

He wondered how anybody from Fiddlersburg, Tenn., ever got the money to come up here to Darthurst. Or the shoes to come in.

Then he remembered that there were two squirts here from Fiddlersburg. The other pair of shoes belonged to a guy who was even named Fiddler. Calvin Fiddler of Fiddlersburg, oh Jesus. But this one was named—oh, yes, Bradwell Tolliver.

The squirt was staring at him.

So the Dean, suddenly coming to himself, said, somewhat acidly: "Of course if you're getting so rich. But even then, I should advise—"

"I haven't even paid off the advance," the boy broke in. "Five hundred dollars and it hasn't even paid off yet. It's not that, it's—"

"Well, if your mind is made up," the Dean said, his voice trailing off, his hand reaching out to toy with a pencil. But he brightened. "It's not as though your record here were so ferociously distinguished, is it?"

The boy stood there.

The Dean looked at him. The Dean himself had once written a novel. He had waited until after his Ph.D. to begin work on it.

"Well?" the Dean demanded.

The boy didn't manage to say anything.

"Well?" the Dean repeated.

"It's just that I wanted—" the boy began, then stopped.

"Wanted what?"

"To talk—I guess," the boy said, and felt foolish.

"You came at me with a flat statement. That you were leaving," the Dean said. "And a flat statement is, my dear fellow, a hell of a way to start a conversation of collaborative inquiry."

"I guess it's just that I—"

Then he stopped.

"Just what?"

"That I'm afraid," Bradwell Tolliver burst out, feeling more foolish than ever.

He had stood there, not knowing what he was afraid of.

Now, a quarter of a century later, sitting in the white Jaguar, in Happy Dell, he thought: *Afraid?*

He asked himself what the hell there had been to be afraid of.

He looked down at his right foot lolling by the throttle under the dash, waiting to tap that power. The foot was shod in a tattered huarache. The ankle was bare. He looked down at the Levis, pale with launderings and needing one now. He looked down at the pair of dark glasses on the other seat, and at the beat-up seventy-five-dollar panama lying beyond them. He looked at the glittering instrument panel of the Jaguar XK-150, in which, three weeks back, across mountain and desert and swelling prairie and the black soil of Arkansas, he had come rolling from the Coast. He looked up at the blue sky, for on such a day as this the top was down. He looked up at the beautiful sky of April, and sunlight washed over Tennessee, and somewhere an old man by an unpainted picket fence would be leaning crookedly over to gather jonquils to surprise his old wife when she woke up from her nap, and somewhere, in an empty field, boys would be throwing a baseball and uttering distant cries sad and sweet as killdees, and somewhere a boy and a girl, hand in hand, would be walking up a path into the green gloom of woods, and somewhere an old Negro woman with a man's felt hat on her head, the edge of the hat cut in not too careful scallops by a pair of scissors, would be throwing a fishing line into a creek; and bird-song filled the ears, and heart, of Bradwell Tolliver, and he tried not to feel anything.

Why didn't Jingle Bells come on with his change?

Jingle Bells handed him a five, a one, a quarter, and a dime.

"Listen," Brad Tolliver said.

"What's dat, boss?"

"I'm sorry I said what I did. About the trick pants." He hesitated. "Hell, you know what I mean."

Out of the very handsome café-au-lait face which, except for an expression of idiotic innocence, reminded Bradwell Tolliver of Belafonte, the brown eyes, which showed strange golden glints, stared out in confusion and, it seemed, supplication. "Boss," the man was saying in a voice that got softer, more furry, "I doan know whut you mean. True to de Lawd, I doan, White Folks."

"Damn it," Bradwell Tolliver said, "I didn't mean to—to be offensive."

He hadn't meant to put it that way. Twenty-five years ago he would have known how to put it.

"Huh, boss?" the man in the trick pants was saying, and the brown eyes stared at him, enveloping him in their softness, suffocating him.

Bradwell Tolliver remembered reading how a jellyfish devours an oyster: it smothers it with softness, the oyster gets tired in the softness, the shell relaxes. Bradwell Tolliver felt like an oyster.

"What I mean is," he burst out, "excuse me!"

"But, boss," the man was saying, "boss, I laks ma pants!"

Bradwell Tolliver touched the starter. The Jaguar quivered luxuriously. He looked at the money in his left hand. With his right hand he took the five, the quarter and the dime and slipped that into his T-shirt pocket. His left hand thrust the dollar bill out at the Negro.

The Negro stood there holding the bill. His face looked veiled.

"Goodbye," Bradwell Tolliver said, and the car slid away.

And in that instant the man said: "Thanks, Mac."

Bradwell Tolliver was sure he heard him say that. But he couldn't believe it. It was as though a ventriloquist crouching behind the pumps were doing a trick, throwing his voice there, there where it couldn't possibly belong, not in Tennessee, not in that mush-mouth—a sharp, hard voice that, deliberately, gratingly, said: "Thanks, Mac."

Bradwell Tolliver, even as the car slid away, whipped his head around. The man stood there, holding the dollar bill in his hand. He was grinning. But that grin was nothing like the grin which, a little earlier, Bradwell Tolliver had expected to have offered him through the windshield. It was a very different grin.

Bradwell Tolliver snatched his gaze away. He looked forward. Then, for an instant, he again met that grin—tiny in the rear-view mirror. Then it was gone from his sight. But in his mind he was still seeing the man, in his trick pants, standing there on the sun-glittering gravel, grinning victoriously after a new white Jaguar that fled away toward Nashville.

The car had taken a curve. Brad Tolliver could no longer see the Seven Dwarfs Motel or Jingle Bells standing there, holding a dollar bill and grinning victoriously. So he took his foot off the accelerator, the speed fell away, there was a faint, prickly crunch of gravel as he drove the car off the cement, and the car stopped.

Still gripping the wheel, he put his brow down against the upper rim. He thought: *I don't know what is happening to me.*

He reviewed the whole episode at the Seven Dwarfs Motel.

He could not understand why anything that had happened had happened. He thought: *It's not me.*

Then he remembered *The Dream of Jacob,* and how great the reviews had been, and how, right now, even in these times of blank screens and padlocked houses, it was in lights on a million marquees. He remembered why he was going to Nashville.

He felt much better.

The man in the trick pants stood on the gravel by the pumps and grinned after the Jaguar in which Mac was fleeing away toward Nashville. He wondered what had made Mac lay on that fake Southern accent. Hell, the Jag even had California plates. Who did Mac think he was kidding, try to be so God-damned Confederate?

The man in the trick pants shrugged. Let Mac have his fun faking the accent. He had his own fun faking it. Even experts didn't give him a queer look any more. Maybe nobody was expert enough to detect any flaw in your accent if you were saying what they wanted to hear.

"Yassuh, boss," the man in the trick pants murmured, and looked up at the enormous black face on the second sign, with the bloated minstrel-show lips; and winked.

He folded the dollar bill and slipped it into the pocket of the trick pants. A dollar was a dollar. He was doing all right out here, working Friday afternoons, Saturdays, and Sundays —Sunday night was usually rough, for he doubled as a bellhop—and getting into town early enough Monday for his ten o'clock class in Corneille and Racine at Fisk University. In good weather he could make the trip in forty-five minutes on his Lambretta. He had come all the way from Chicago to Nashville on it in less than two days.

Happy Dell was all right. The tips were good. He had even got one piece of tail thrown in for, he guessed, a tip. Maybe he should have told Mac about it when Mac asked him about high old times in Happy Dell. Yes, he thought now, standing in broad daylight by the highway slab, he should have told Mac, just Yankee to Yankee, how Yankees get together down in Tennessee.

Not that it had been anything to brag on. He would never have bothered with it back home, but being here in Tennessee had given the situation an added relish, or at least a challenge, even if the car, a three-year-old Rambler, did have Indiana plates and not local ones.

Nor had she been anything to brag on, getting afraid of forty, long in the tooth *peut-être*, and with glasses. But when, at 1:00 A.M., he had carried in her order of ice and Seven-Up, the character hadn't been wearing her glasses, and the face promised to be acceptable, especially with the only illumination that from the pink-silk-shaded bed lamps cunningly arranged by the management of Happy Dell. The character, too, had exhibited an attractive candor in popping the question, a candor that suggested a willingness to do her share.

She had done her share, and as he was buttoning his jerkin, had said graciously that he looked like Belafonte.

"I'm not," he said, "I'm Ralph Punch."

"Who?" she demanded.

"Didn't you ever hear of Punch and Judy, Judy?"

"My name's not Judy," she said fretfully, and sat up in bed, clutching the pink chenille counterpane.

"Oh, yes it is Judy, Judy," he said, and went out the door, out into the predawn dark, hating the world and himself.

Whirling toward Nashville, hearing the tires sing on the flawless surface, Brad thought that he should not have stopped there.

But, at the moment of stopping, he had been proud of himself for stopping. Nearly twenty years it had taken, but at least he had stopped there. Stopping there, he had felt good, for he had thought that never again would he, consciously or unconsciously, avert his face as he drove past this spot.

But this was not what now, as that wonderful, expensive piece of mechanism fled whitely down the slab, he felt. He now felt that he had taken a new defeat there. He boasted grimly to himself that at least he possessed enough honesty to admit that he had let himself in for a second defeat on this same field. Even if he didn't know precisely what kind of a defeat.

He had, at times over the years, even pretended to himself that that first defeat here, nearly twenty years ago, had been a victory. He had given her what she asked for, and she had wept. Yes, a victory. That was what, walking down a sunlit street or perched on a bar stool, he had sometimes been able to tell himself. But waking in the night or sitting at the worktable unable to work, he had always known that it had been a defeat. He admitted it now, whirling down the slab, even if he still did not know the exact nature of that first defeat here, a thousand years ago, back in 1941, when the world was young and gay.

She turned. She is turning her face toward me. She is smiling.

He saw a road sign. Twenty-five miles, it said, to Nashville. He glanced at his watch. Even after he made town he'd have to get through the traffic, out to Berry Field. After all the years since he'd been there, he might not even be able to find his way through town any more, they might have changed things so much. He watched the needle of the speedometer touch sixty-eight. Then he thought: *What the hell if Yasha Jones does have to cool his heels ten minutes in an airport?*

He let the needle drop back nearly to legal.

Chapter

2

EVEN AFTER MESSING UP the passage through town, he hit Berry Field by two-thirty, time enough to scan the glittering blue of sky westward for the first sign of the DC-7 from Los Angeles, and time enough to wonder what Yasha Jones was really like. All he had was an image in his head, and that image was not based on any acquaintance. For Yasha Jones had notoriously few acquaintances.

The image of Yasha Jones was not even based on sight, for Yasha Jones was never known to appear in those places where successful people go to be seen and envied and to reassure themselves that they, themselves, are truly successful, and that the night fears may, indeed, be ignored—the sort of place where Bradwell Tolliver went only rarely because he told himself that he did not need exactly that kind of reassurance, and because a man could spare himself, he had long since decided, the obscene and ambiguous pleasure of watching some notorious failure courting the headwaiter. So when he went to such a place it was for the purely practical purpose, the world he lived in being what it was, of tactfully indicating to some girl that he himself had the respect of the headwaiter.

For a moment, standing there at Berry Field, in Tennessee, he thought of himself seated before a gleaming expanse of damask with a girl's face smiling at him in candlelight. But the moment was so short he did not identify the face. And suddenly, beyond that vision, drawing across it out of the distance of blue sky, was the black dot that would be the DC-7.

With that he again summoned up the image of Yasha Jones, an image based on the few published photographs, photographs somewhat reminiscent of André Gide and Dimitri Mitropoulos. For the head of Yasha Jones, the Boy Wonder, was bald, bald as an egg, agelessly bald, and in those few photographs the face exhibited the same sense of profound inwardness and fastidious intensity found in the photographs of the old Gide and the aging Mitropoulos. The head of Yasha Jones was always, in those few photographs, slightly bowed, the gaze was veiled and the head seemed to float, with its exotic intellectuality, bodiless.

Exotic—the word occurred to Brad Tolliver as he stood there by the gate waiting for the plane to grow and assume shape in the sky. Yes, exotic, with that exoticism of Jewish intellectuality. He knew, of course, that neither Gide nor Mitropoulos was a Jew. But he said comically to himself that he was enough the true-born son of Fiddlersburg to carry the image of a Jew in his head as the archetypal image of all exoticism, especially of that exoticism of secret wisdom and slightly sinister learning which might prevail beyond the common, robust satisfaction of life, and which, in fact, might make ordinary men, wedded to their ordinary satisfaction, feel confused, depressed and, of course, angry.

So the image that came into his head now, after that of Yasha Jones and Gide and Mitropoulos, was the image of little old Mr. Israel Goldfarb, crouched in his tailor shop on River Street, in Fiddlersburg, his pale brow and paper-thin nose and dark, pained eyes bowed over the needle that moved slower every year as the arthritis did its work. Now and then he would cough.

Mr. Goldfarb—Old Izzie—had had a shelf of books over his sewing machine, not many, some ten or fifteen, and not one was in English. On good evenings in spring, when the light began to hold late, Old Izzie might sit out in front of his shop reading, interrupting himself now and then to gaze across the great bend of the river, which would be sliding past like molten copper, copper-colored with the spring burden of clay coming up from Alabama and with the reflection of the red sunset. Sometimes when the old man's gaze had lifted, it did not return to the page. He would sit there staring over the stained water, toward the western sky.

Several of Old Izzie's books were in a language which occasioned some debate in Fiddlersburg—was it Yiddish or real Jew or German or what? But the others were in French. When Brad had been studying French in the Fiddlersburg High School, Old Izzie once or twice asked how he carried himself or had remarked that it made beautiful time, was it not. People now and then might point out Mr. Goldfarb to some visitor and remark that he spoke French, this in the tone one used in showing the high-water mark on the bricks of Mr. Lorton's hardware store on River Street, or the new gates of the cemetery, or other items of local pride and interest. The French teacher, one of the three teachers in the High School, a young man recently out of the University of Tennessee, at Knoxville, was known to have remarked that Mr. Goldfarb spoke French, yes, but his accent was not very good; it was not Parisian. It was observed by some, however, that the young man tended to avoid the lower end of River Street, especially at seasons and hours when Mr. Goldfarb might be sitting out and might ask him how he carried himself. Young Brad Tolliver, for one, had noticed this.

Brad had always liked Mr. Goldfarb. He would give you a lemon jawbreaker and at the same time, in his soft careful voice, speak to you as though you were a man. Later he played chess with you and did not let you win. When Brad went away to prep school in Nashville he had gone to tell Mr. Goldfarb goodbye. But when, two years later, he went up East to Darthurst he had not gone to tell Mr. Goldfarb goodbye. Up at Darthurst he remembered, more than once, the omission, and felt bad about it. He felt even worse, the next summer—he was visiting a classmate up in Maine—when he heard that Mr. Goldfarb was dead.

Mr. Goldfarb, he heard later, had got a bang-up funeral. On the wall above the cot where he slept in the back of his shop they found an address pinned to the wall, some Goldfarb in Cincinnati, and the Methodist preacher, there being no Jews now left in Fiddlersburg, had telegraphed. The answer had been prompt:

PLEASE HOLD BODY TILL ARRIVAL ALL EXPENSES GUARANTEED
MORTIMER GOLDFARB

And Mr. Lorton, who had furniture and undertaking as well as hardware, had held it. The relatives, a son among them, had arrived, in a big black car with a polish that gleamed even through the encrustation of Kentucky dust accumulated in getting there, a car so long, people reported, that you had to drive out in the country to turn around.

They had even brought along a rabbi. The funeral, with Mr. Goldfarb in Mr. Lorton's most splendid coffin, was Jewish, but it was attended by all. Everybody said how dignified it all was. Everybody was pleased, too, that the deceased had left written instructions that he should be buried in Fiddlersburg. They said it was something to remember, how Jesus himself was a Jew. They all shook hands with the bereaved family.

The family took the books from the shelf, ascertained that no rent was in arrears, and, with the rabbi, got into the big black car and left. They left everything in the shop as it lay, but hired somebody to come in and clean up for the owner. Later, the Methodist minister reported to his stewards that he had received a substantial contribution for the church, by way of courtesy, from the Goldfarb in Cincinnati. Aloud, somebody wondered why, if the Cincinnati son was so all-fired rich, he hadn't taken better care of his father and not let him die of old-folks' TB. The preacher said that the son had intimated that his father had wanted to live his own way; and the preacher added that it was not theirs to judge. Then somebody remembered that twice a year Mr. Goldfarb had gone gallivanting off somewhere. He must of gone off to Cincinnati. The son must of sent him the ticket. The preacher said that to the best of his recollection the times the old man used to go to Cincinnati must have been Jewish feast days. He said he respected people for being true to their religion.

Standing there at Gate 3, at Berry Field, waiting for the DC-7 to trundle up, Bradwell Tolliver told himself that he would hunt up the grave of Old Izzie. It was, he knew, off in the old part of the cemetery—no doubt off in a corner where, long back, a few Jews had been buried, some of those cotton speculators who had trailed General Grant southward into Tennessee and Mississippi, had failed in their enterprise, and had got stranded as peddlers or storekeepers, left lonely and lost in the backwash of war. The graves of this last remnant were long since forgotten in blackberry bushes and love vine, but the nice stone erected by the order of the Cincinnati Goldfarb (and subsequently photographed by his own hand when the big black car had appeared for an hour on this pious mission) would probably even now, some thirty years later, show where the little old tailor lay. The stone, Bradwell Tolliver remembered, though put there by the order of the Cincinnati Goldfarb, had not been paid for by him. Old Izzie had left a note saying that the stone should not cost more than one hundred and fifty dollars. Old Izzie had left one hundred and fifty dollars for that purpose, in a brown paper grocery sack marked FOR TOMBSTONE.

But even if the stone was not big, Bradwell Tolliver thought, he ought to be able to find it. Yes, he would hunt it up. He could do that much to pay whatever debt it was he owed, or make up for whatever it was he felt he ought to make up for.

He wondered if the Cincinnati Goldfarb was still alive. He wondered if now they would come and dig up what was left of the little old tailor and take it away. Or was Cincinnati Goldfarb dead too, and nobody cared now about Old Izzie any more than about those cotton speculators whose dreams and avarice and fortitude had failed into peddling and death in Tennessee?

That little man, with his TB cough and tattered books, who had turned up alone and mysterious so long ago in Fiddlersburg—would he be left under the weight of water when the big new dam was finished to back up the river and the flood came in? Would that be another death, a drowning, an eternal drowning, a perpetual suffocation, a crushing weight on the chest that would never go away? Bradwell Tolliver, with

a sudden swelling of the heart, thought that he himself, by
God, if nobody else did, would take care of Izzie Goldfarb.

The plane was trundling up now. Bradwell Tolliver
had a thought that he must jot down. He got a stub of pencil
and an envelope out of his coat pocket, and scribbled:

> *Old Goldfarb—anybody move body?—*
> *Att'de of town toward exhumation?—theme?*
> *NB check program of exhumation?*
> *gov subsidy? General? Selective?*

Gosh, he thought, *a man forgets things.* You would have
thought a man would check this long back. You had to sense
possibilities, but things slip by. There were, in fact, so many
possibilities.

And he suddenly thought, with a cold flash of terror:
My father is there. Will the water come over my father?

Of course it wouldn't. Not unless he wanted it to. He
himself could get an exhumation, with or without bureau-
cratic aid.

At this point in his meditations the door of the plane
was opening.

The head of a stewardess—perky head, perky gold hair,
perky blue cap—poked out. Would she fly off and bring back
an olive branch in her beak?

Flood, he thought.

The DC-7 spawned out a languid spate of passengers,
blinking in the sun, but there was none, Brad was sure, even
remotely resembling Yasha Jones. But a last figure was coming down the sun-glinting chrome stairs.

At the foot of the stairs the gray-clad figure paused,
blinked in the sun-glare, set a briefcase on the cement, and
with a book still in the left hand, fumbled to adjust a pair of
dark glasses. But no: this couldn't be Yasha Jones—not this
figure in the tousled nondescript gray suit, nondescript gray
hat jerked down, overcharged briefcase that pulled the right
shoulder down a trifle, book still in left hand with a finger
stuck in to mark the place. This was clearly some prof from
one of these colleges around here, and not the Wonder Boy
of the Coast.

But the man approached, again set down the briefcase,
removed the dark glasses, removed the hat, and with a

quickly appraising glance like a doctor's, and an even smile, thrust out his right hand. The instant the hat came off, it was, of course, Yasha Jones.

The skull was not merely bald, with the slick surface of baldness. On the left side, beginning below where hair must once have been and reaching upward, was a strange irregular shape, outlined in the faintest pink tracery on the tan skull, lying there on the bulge of the skull to suggest a pale, bleached-out, pink, ghostly continent on a somewhat elongated parchment-colored globe. Within that continent, almost imperceptible lines ran crisscrossing, faintly crazing and hatching the surface, making it look like some piece of precious china that has been shattered, then painfully and scrupulously reassembled and glued. Bradwell Tolliver could see that the rest of the skull was not bald, at least, not entirely bald. It was merely shaven. In the glint of sunlight you could tell that.

The hand that grasped Brad's was not large, but the grasp was unexpectedly strong, and feeling that strength, he remembered, fleetingly, the one photograph he had ever seen of Yasha Jones that did not show the bald head. In that photograph a beret had covered the baldness and you could make little or nothing of the face—a lean but very muscular figure, taut and painfully muscled like a distance runner's, wearing only the beret and a bathing G-string, standing on a beach at Cannes—or was it Antibes?—and staring out over the fabled Mediterranean, toward the sunset. No other figure was in the picture.

"You're Tolliver," the lean, tallish man was saying, with the smile even and steady, the teeth very white against the very brown, very fine-grained, Morocco-leather-looking skin.

Consciously smiling, Brad was saying: "Well, you beat me. Man bites dog. I didn't recognize you. Thought you were a college professor."

"College professor—that's a fair guess," Yasha Jones was saying. "I almost was. A brand snatched from the burning."

Brad made a movement to pick up the bulging briefcase, but was forestalled. "Oh, no," Yasha Jones said agreeably. Then hefting the weight of the case, added: "So that's it! The professor's bulging briefcase—it gave me away. Elementary, my dear Watson."

They moved into the building.

Again Yasha Jones hefted the briefcase. "Books," he said. "Poetry, to be exact. A most useful therapy."

"Yep," Brad agreed, not knowing, quite, what he was agreeing to. But, hell, you couldn't ask a man, at least not on a three-minute acquaintance, whether he was referring to the human condition or a personal kink.

"Baggage is this way," Brad said.

Chapter

3

BY THE TIME THEY HAD CLAWED through the Saturday traffic in the now unfamiliar grid of one-way streets, and broken out into West End, the afternoon was wearing on. They passed, on the left, a considerable assemblage of buildings, in institutional red brick, set back beyond reaches of clipped institutional grass with the vacant black asphalt of parking areas proclaiming the melancholy blankness of institutional weekends in the spring. Above the whole, a clock on a tall square tower, gold hands on black face toward them, indicated 4:10.

Brad jerked a thumb toward the tower. "You being, as you say, an academic near-miss," he said, "that is Vanderbilt University."

Yasha Jones turned his cool gaze on the institution, turning his head to look back, even as they whipped beyond. "Ransom," he said, "Crowe Ransom—he was there once, wasn't he?"

"Who?" Brad said.

"Ransom," Yasha Jones said, "the poet."

"Yeah," Brad said, "yeah—I guess I heard tell."

"Have you read his poetry?" Yasha Jones asked.

Brad shook his head. "Nope," he said. "I don't guess I read much poetry."

"His is very beautiful," Yasha Jones said.

He sank into silence.

"Centennial Park coming up," Brad announced, with a parody of the tone of the bus-tour guide, nodding to the right.

Yasha Jones turned his head but said nothing.

"Yeah," Brad said, "when this town was a hundred years old they had a celebration for their longevity and powers of survival against Indians, smallpox, pellagra, Federal gunboats, a pork diet, Methodist theology and each other's society. They laid out a park, put in an artificial lake, and built an exact replica, only in much better repair, of the Parthenon, of Athens, Greece, this community being, as of that moment thenceforward, the Athens of the South. It is also the world capital of hillbilly music. Also it was, during the Civil War, the clap capital of the universe. The whores of Nashville, it was officially stated by Federal authorities, did more than the matchless cavalry of Nathan Bedford Forrest to stem the tide of human freedom and hard money. The United Daughters of the Confederacy ought to have a monument there in the park to those gallant girls of the VD Brigade who gave their all to all. But no—all we find is the Parthenon. Now if you want to drive in and see the Par—"

Bradwell Tolliver suddenly stopped talking. The Jaguar was little more than drifting now.

Yasha Jones said nothing. With detached politeness his gaze remained toward the right.

Brad slammed his foot on the throttle. "Hell, no," he said. They were well past the park anyway.

Yasha Jones was looking straight up the long street, into the leveling light, the glitter of afternoon traffic. Brad stole a glance at him, in their silence. *Damn it*, he thought, *I ought to go back and take him in the park. I ought to rub his nose in the God-damned Parthenon.*

Then he wondered what was the matter with him. Not with Yasha Jones—with Bradwell Tolliver.

It was stopping at that God-damned motel.

They moved on, in silence.

In silence, at least, until Brad said: "This is where the stately homes of the Old South are. Anyway, the Nashville version of same." He nodded toward the left. "This is the Belle Meade section. This is where, back in the days when enlightened people talked like that, my first wife said the Captains of Second Class Industry and First Class Extortion lived. But they were not that. They were good Americans trying, under difficulties, to maintain the American way. But my wife, she was a Commie. By that time, in fact, an ex-Commie. She was an awful well-dressed Commie, and ex-Commie, with an impressive trust fund. Her father had set it up for her when she was just a little girl, when, for what I gather was good and sufficient reason, he walked out on her mother. Later on, in 1929, he walked out of a window, a high one."

He paused.

"Well," he resumed, "if it hadn't been for Baby Girl's trust fund—well, things might have been—"

He heard his own voice trailing off. You didn't have to spill your guts. It was just that the kind of silence this guy created sucked you in. It got you to gabbling. It was a kind of treachery, that silence. That guy had started out smiling and putting out his hand. He had even made a joke. Then he pulled this silence on you.

Well, he—Bradwell Tolliver—could be as glum as anybody.

He drove along, glumly.

It was a lie, he thought, that business about the trust fund's having anything to do with what had happened. It was just something that had come into his head. A man didn't have to cook up explanations. Anyway, not lies. He thought: *At least I have tried to live without the lies.*

He heard the voice of Yasha Jones saying: "I knew you were married to Suzie Martine."

"Yes," he said. Then, after a second, added: "But a lot later. Long after the war. She was definitely not a Commie."

"A very fine designer," Yasha Jones said. "Did beautiful work for me in *Sands of the Sea*."

Brad said nothing. He had loathed the picture. For his money the Wonder Boy had sure dropped a two-headed calf that time. Even if it had grossed five million. It stunk.

"It stunk," Yasha Jones was saying, cheerfully. It was as though Yasha Jones had opened a flap in the side of his head and, like reaching into the glove compartment, had taken out the words. He felt defenseless.

"I ruined it," Yasha Jones was saying. "When I had finished my devoted work, the only good thing in it was Martine's sets." After a moment he said: "I enjoyed working with her. I like her."

"I do too," Brad said, evenly.

But he didn't, he admitted inside himself. Nor did he dislike her. It was that he simply didn't care. Had he ever cared? He asked himself that, watching the land swell into hills now.

It is a problem in semantics, he said to himself.

"Too bad we didn't make it," he said out loud.

They hadn't made it. Maybe if she hadn't cared so much they would have made it. They might have had a decorous charade with a handsome joint income-tax return and long experimental Sunday mornings in bed, and been quite happy in it. But she had cared.

Yasha Jones said nothing.

Brad felt the silence beginning again. He settled into it. He gave a little more throttle. He stared ahead at the road winding into the hills. The hills were wooded. They yet showed, in April, a delicate paleness of green, some gold yet left. The cedars looked dark and solid against that paleness.

Had she cared? He wondered if she—but he was no longer thinking of Suzie, but Lettice—

That preposterous name!

He wondered how he, even lying in the dark with the silky hair over his face, had ever murmured that preposterous name.

Her mother had been so God-damned Anglophile. She had been so God-damned Long Island Anglophile. She had loved the English so much she had doomed her daughter to a name that no true-born son of Cowpens, King's Mountain, and Fiddlersburg could, even in the silken dark, murmur without feeling absurd.

Lettice.

And Lettice had hated nicknames. "My name is Lettice, God damn it," she would say, and give a characteristic quick challenging little toss of her high head. She carried her height like a challenge, too. She was almost as tall as he was. Five feet nine and a half. With naked heels—narrow, clean-tendoned heels set straight on the carpet—she could almost look him straight in the eye with a look that said: *This is me.*

He had taken her height as a challenge. When she wore high heels, an issue on which she never compromised, and stood a fraction above him, he held his own head well back and felt proud. He was the guy up to that slim-waisted, high-headed, high-bosomed lusciousness.

But now, all at once, nearly twenty years later, whirling westward out of Nashville, he wondered, coldly, if things would have been different if she had not been tall. Suppose she had been, for example, five feet four. Somewhat cuddle-some, perhaps. Would there have been a mystic difference?

Hell, you didn't have to have explanations. Hadn't he lived past explanations? But suppose she had been five feet five, and her name had been Sallie.

But it had been Lettice.

He looked at the wooded hills of Tennessee in spring. Then he knew. Of course! It was that pale succulent vernal green—

One thing led to another. *Lettuce* to *Lettice* to *Let's.*

"Let's," she would say, and it would be all she would need to say, for he would know exactly—oh, precisely, precisely, as she used to be in the crisp habit of saying—what she meant.

Everything was always tangled up like that. Everything you remembered was like those long strands of lights for the Christmas tree you take out on Christmas Eve and can't for hell's sake untangle, and half the bulbs are busted any-way, and when you start following a certain strand it will cer-tainly take you into a new snarl you hadn't anticipated.

Not that he, himself, had ever owned those yards and yards of small green electric wire and a thousand God-damned little colored bulbs to put on a God-damned tree, but now and then, after the war, during the off-and-on periods of bachelorhood he had got asked in to help decorate the tree for somebody's tots and then get drunk by one A.M.

Sometimes you got drunk earlier and that made it harder to unsnarl the wires. This was one of the differences between unsnarling Christmas-tree lights and unsnarling your personal recollections. For if you were drunk, or about to be, you could unsnarl the strands of recollection more readily than when you were sober. But, of course, they would all get snarled up again, and probably worse, with perhaps a new strand or two, by the next morning.

Well, he had about quit any serious drinking now. That was something, he guessed. To score a KO on John Barleycorn. He was certainly sober now, this minute, sober enough not to have any illusion that his deft fingers were unsnarling the tangle of recollection.

If he hadn't passed that motel. No, it wasn't the fact of the motel. If there had been no motel, just the place, nothing changed—just the cedar-plumed bluff, the big sycamore in proper position, bluegrass untrodden in the little enclave where it had happened, the water purling on stone— then things might have been worse. Yes, the motel made it better, if anything. Yes, the motel was splendid. He might, in fact, try the experiment of taking some girl to the motel. Some real tarty character, the tartier the better for the purpose. To lay the ghost, you might say.

To lay what?

Language was sure as hell a trap, and this time it just happened to be a funny trap. Well, moderately funny, he decided. No, not even that.

He began in his head:

There was a young man from the Coast—

He thought then how he wasn't very young any more. But you couldn't put *middle-aged* in there. The meter wouldn't permit. He had learned that much about poetry at Darthurst. Besides he didn't feel middle-aged. He wasn't, in fact.

Hell, he thought, *maybe I am. Or nearly.*

Maybe I am, he thought, *and to hell with it.*

So he revised it to fit the meter:

A middle-aged man from the Coast
Came home to lay him a ghost—

It frazzled out. He had never made a limerick in his life and there was no law that said he had to begin now. It was not very funny, anyhow. Nothing was very funny, anyhow. The sun, westering, was hitting him in the eyes. He reached up and pulled down the sun visor.

He thought, with a grim flicker of pride, how he had been back in Fiddlersburg for more than three weeks, and nothing had seemed to touch him. Not even being with his sister so much. Not even being in the house where, long ago, before it happened, he and Lettice had been. Not even going into the very room.

When he walked a street and remembered something, it was like reading it in a book. This was fine for the job, he had thought. You opened your mind and it all flowed in. It would fall into place for the movie. Things were beginning to take shape already: the Tolliver Touch.

After all, a man stood to learn something about his craft after twenty-five years, one book and half of another one (and damned good, if he had ever finished it), five lead reviews, one screen writers' award, two Oscars, seventeen picture credits, and two marriages.

The road was swinging left, southward. Suddenly, the sun visor afforded no protection, for the blaze, striking over the ridges, was direct in his eyes. He fumbled on his lap to find his sunglasses, the expensive Beverly Hills articles, twenty-one fifty, guaranteed to take the glory out of any sunset exploding at you over the Pacific.

Squinting at the road, he put them on.

Over Tennessee, the light, on the stroke, changed. The last gold of April leaf was gone from the hills. The cedars had gone totally black. Objects were clear in this light, but they were not the same. It was not the darkening before a storm, for there were no clouds. It was not a twilight, for the sun was yet high. The sun burned red, well above the ridges. It looked like the death of the sun. The sun was dying.

No—the wave of light that brought this news had left the point of origin light years ago. The news was, therefore, outdated. It was like last week's *Time* magazine. The sun was already, in fact, dead.

It was dead, and yonder, far off, there was an ash heap suspended in nothingness with, now and then, gas coldly, obscenely blobbing through the surface, exploding the ash, and the ash would fall back upon itself, and right now waves of darkness were racing those light years to bring the disturbing information. Meanwhile, people didn't know. They did know the nature of that information that was dutifully, and icily, racing toward them.

Then—how stupid!—he remembered. The sun wasn't that far away. The sun was only ninety-odd million miles away. It was youth that was light-years away. And it was dead.

He took off the glasses. Light poured again over the land. The sun was not dead.

For a moment he had forgotten that he was not alone. Alone in Tennessee. But he did not look at the silent passenger at his side. He carefully did not.

The road again veered left, southward. There it was: the place. The thought boomed up in his head like a partridge busting from a blackberry thicket.

She turned. She is turning her face toward me.

She had leaned her head down a little and turned her face toward him so that the auburn hair of the page-boy bob hung down evenly and glossily from the right side of her head. One strand lay across her left cheek. The large fox-brown eyes were bright. The head was inclined enough to make her look up at him to give the smile. The smile was shy, innocent, wistful, as unpremeditated as a dream.

She said: "I still like you, Brad."

He gripped the wheel of the three-year-old Dodge coupe, and stared up the road. The car beat along over the broken blacktop. This was part of the politics-crooked blacktop laid down back yonder before the Depression, and hell, the Depression hadn't done it any good. But he guessed they'd make Nashville and Union Station on time.

"You don't mind, do you?" she asked, in a small voice.

"Mind my still liking you?"

"I thought we had everything settled. I thought it was all nailed down," he said, flatly and distantly.

He was proud of that tone. He didn't, in fact, feel a thing. Not any more. Except sort of corked up. After he got her on the train to Memphis and Points West he would have the whole afternoon. What would he do to uncork?

He realized that he had not thought of the afternoon. He thought now of the afternoon dwindling to long shadow over the flats of West Tennessee as the train trundled on toward Memphis to meet the shadows. He thought of her sitting alone in the dreary, factitious glitter of the diner, studiously scrutinizing the menu, her face rather close to the card, a little V between her eyes against the child-smoothness of her brow. She was, he said to himself, getting near-sighted. She ought to start using glasses.

He was, suddenly, aware of her voice, coming as from a distance.

"Yes," she was saying, in that small voice, "everything is settled."

The hell it was. For there was the afternoon. He wondered what he, alone, would do in the afternoon. There would be the afternoon lengthening to shadow. There would be the night.

After he put her on the train he might ring up somebody in Nashville. He could have dinner with somebody. Get drunk with somebody. But there was nobody to call up. Those boys he had known in prep school ten or twelve years ago—he couldn't even remember the names of half of them.

A face came into his head, some blank boyish face, and he could not attach a name. But suppose he could remember the name. It would be a different face now.

And he thought, with a sudden shiver, as when you put your bare foot to the floor the first cold morning in September, of some time to come, years from now, when he might remember her face. Oh, yes, he would remember the attached name—oh, who could forget the preposterousness of *Lettice*? And he would never forget the face. But the face he would remember, it would have become a lie. If he should meet the real thing on the street, with all the work the years had done, he would not recognize it.

She was saying something.

"I want to remember liking you," she was saying.

"Thanks," he said.

"Wouldn't you like to remember liking me?" she said.

He said nothing, and looked up the black road.

"Nice, I mean," she said. "Not the way things got."

"I told you everything is settled."

"Yes," she said, "and now because everything is settled we could just relax. We could just relax and forget everything that has happened and shut our eyes and just be ourselves, just one more time."

She waited.

Then: "Wouldn't you like to remember us really ourselves?"

"God damn it," he cried out, with a burst of bitterness like an abscess breaking in the heart, "I don't want to remember a God-damned thing!"

He stared up the beat-up blacktop. He was sure that her shoulders were bowed submissively forward and her head leaning so that the swatch of auburn hair hung down, and she was looking up sidewise at him, but he did not look at her.

Her left hand reached over to lie, palm down, in his lap, cupping his genitals.

"Poor Little John Henry," she murmured. "Hasn't Little Hims even waked up this morning?"

There, ahead, was the bold limestone bluff that had just hove into view.

And now, in this instant, as in that instant so many years ago, he was staring at the heave of that limestone bluff above the road.

Chapter

4

YASHA JONES WISHED that the car would not go so fast. He did not look at the speedometer, for long ago, he had disciplined himself out of that. Discipline, it could do a lot. He had learned that much, anyway, in the war. It could take the place of any natural virtue. It could take the place of joy or sorrow. It could do anything except take the place of sleep.

He looked at the face of the man beside him. The face was somewhat round, but not too fat, strength yet showing beneath the fat. It was a good face, he decided. The skull was rather round and heavy, with thinning short blond hair which the wind of their passage made waver in little wisps, like grass uncertain in the current of a stream. The face was a healthy tan—but then, Yasha Jones reminded himself, the

sickliest faces in Beverly Hills and Malibu wear a healthy tan.
Yes, he thought, and amused himself with the conceit that
the mortician, at the end, puts Golden Glow on the client's
face. He even puts it on the face of the old bank clerk who
hasn't been in the sun in twenty years.

Health in death, he thought.

But the healthy tan of this face beside him now was
streaked white around the mouth. Yasha Jones realized that
the jaws of that face were clamping hard together. The eyes
were staring straight up the road. The eyes wore a blank
gaze, and with a flash of terror Yasha Jones thought that the
man was in a catatonic state.

Yasha Jones was aware of the cold sweat gathering in
the palms of his hands, which lay casually, palms down, on
his thighs. Secretly, he let the third and little fingers of each
hand curl back to verify that wetness in the palm. It was not,
he knew, the sudden thought that the man might be in a
trance that had brought the sweat to his palms. The sweat
had been there for a full half-hour.

Oh, yes, that was another thing no discipline could do.
When the time came, that sweat would ooze in the palm of
the hand. The sweat knew its own time. You could no more
predict than prevent it.

Again he stole a glance at the man's face, at the eyes,
then looked up to find what they stared at. They were staring
at a curve that rushed at them around the jutting nub of a
ridge. Again with that flash of terror, Yasha Jones thought
how the strong, brown hands on the wheel might not respond, might keep that same stiff grip as though there were
no curve. The car would plunge on.

But the hands, he saw now, were making the first slight
adjustment.

The terror—if it had been terror—was gone. Idly, Yasha
Jones asked himself if it had been terror. He had asked himself before, and had never got the answer. Terror was so near
to joy, anguish to ecstasy. If they should crash, what would
he really feel?

They made the curve.

He looked at the hills around and saw the white bursts of
dogwood, the crimson of the Judas tree. He thought: *The
hills are beautiful.* He thought how beautiful the world is,
but he still held the third and little fingers of each hand bent
secretly under the palm to verify the dampness there. He

made himself straighten out the fingers. He looked down at them lying on his thighs. He felt the slight preliminary swerve of the car, and looked up. Another curve was rushing at them.

At the curve there was a tree.

He thought: *There is always a tree.*

Then he remembered himself that this thought was crazy. Many times it was not a tree. He would read the papers, and very rarely was it a tree. For ten years now he hadn't been able to break himself of the habit of racing through the paper to find the story; and usually the paper said it was not a tree, but a pylon, an abutment, a bridge, a stone wall, a parked truck, the pier of a trestle. But the paper lied, for the image that always leaped at him, even as he read, would be a tree, a eucalyptus, the trunk blazing white out of darkness, sudden in the glare of the headlights.

But just last January, in that story in the paper, it had really been a tree. And there, on the front page, was the photograph of the man he himself had sat with in the little room, long back, in 1944, not a large man, not even a well man, but with a peculiar completeness and compactness of face, a calmness of strength, a certitude beyond the obvious illness, obvious youth, obvious fatigue.

There were three of them at the table—the man whose face, after all the years to come, would suddenly look out at Yasha Jones from the front page of a newspaper in Los Angeles; another Frenchman, with an injured right arm, a clipped mustache, a strained, aging face, curly yellow hair incongruously boyish, and a brusque military manner, who was called only *Mimile-le-frisé;* and Yasha Jones himself. In the middle of the bare boards of the table there sat the little radio, at which the two Frenchmen, smoking their cigarettes in slow, fastidious, parsimonious inhalations, fixed their eyes as though they expected it to move, to perform some significant action. Out of that little box on the table, from far off, from London, a voice was singing.

Yasha Jones was not smoking. Nor was he staring at the radio. He was staring at the damp-stained plaster of the wall to the left of, and above, the bulky figure seated on a bench against the wall—the figure of a man dressed in the faded blue smock of a mechanic, hunching forward, saturnine, brooding, with a glass of untouched wine in a big fist. Yasha Jones

was trying not to listen to the radio. He was trying not to wonder, not to think, not to expect anything.

In a crisp, tinny gaiety, that voice from far off in London
was now singing:

You're the cream in my coffee,
You're the sa—

The music stopped in the middle of a note, the middle of
a syllable, and another voice, in a tone of automatic, professional authority, interrupted: "We interrupt for an important
announcement. The sky is blue in the east. The sky is blue in
the east. That is all."

The left arm, the uninjured arm, of the man with the
clipped mustache and the brusque military manner thrust forward and, with a small, decisive gesture, switched off the radio. "Bien," the man said. "Voilà le code."

He rose and gravely thrust the good hand out toward
Yasha Jones. Yasha Jones took the hand. "Sans cette confirma-
tion," the man said, in a dry, detached tone, "ça n'aurait été
drôle pour personne."

The other man, whose face was later to look out from the
newspaper in Los Angeles, smiled slowly, and said: "Bon, eh
bien, maintenant, on peut desserrer les fesses."

"Moi—" Yasha Jones said, and laughed, "c'est moi qui
peut desserrer les fesses!"

"Et vous êtes de l'OSS," the other one said, with a brisk
air of business, "affecté au MI-six?"

"L'OSS—je ne comprend point," Yasha Jones said, feeling light-headed and gay and foolish at his own little joke.
"Moi—je suis Monsieur Duval."

"Monsieur Duval," the youngish man mused, and smiled
slightly, inspecting him. "Pas mal."

And Yasha Jones, in that little room, looked down at his
own dark, decorous shabbiness that, in its scrupulous detail,
was part of his triumph—the painful respectability of the
petit fonctionnaire, the petit avocat, the pharmacien du village. He touched the sad perfection of his coat. He really felt
now that it was his coat. "Depuis toujours, j'ai eu la plus
grande admiration pour Monsieur Duval. Toujours—c'est à
dire depuis la première fois que j'ai fait sa connaissance—à
l'école, dans mon livre de lecture. C'était à Chicago."

"Vous étiez un bon élève," the man said. "A Chicago."

"Et à Paris," Yasha Jones said, and laughed. "Au lycée. Trois ans."

The dark-browed man sitting on the bench by the wall, in the dirty smock of a mechanic—the man who had been the conductor of Monsieur Duval to this room—suddenly sat up straight and took his first drink of wine from the glass he had been clutching in his fist. He spat it on the floor.

The man whose face, so many years later, was to be that of the deceased in the newspaper in Los Angeles, turned to the man who had rejected the wine. "Mais non, mon ami," he said quietly, and grinned. "Buvez. Il n'est pas fameux, mais que voulez-vous y faire?"

Sixteen years later—last January—in Los Angeles, the words under the photograph had been:

Nobel Prize Winner Dead in Crash

There had been a tree.

By God, the paper was right that time, anyway. For there was always a tree. There was always the burst of flame. There was always the one cry. You never knew what it said.

You never knew whether the cry had come before or after the flame.

There was another curve coming. The man beside him said: "Look to the left when we get around this curve."

Yasha Jones prepared to look.

They rounded it and there was Happy Dell.

"It is the new Tennessee," the man beside him said. "I know it may not strike you as much, you being fresh from the space-age vulgarities and Disneyland fantasia of L.A., but this is the best a backward state can do, and as such, is not to be scorned. You have to begin somewhere. And you will admit that this is a step in the right direction. America, I love you. Nigh twenty years ago it was, I hied me to the nearest Marine recruiting station and practically sent the Japs an engraved invitation to shoot my ass off just because I wanted to defend the Four Freedoms and the right of Tennessee to have a Seven Dwarfs Motel in Happy Dell, just like everybody else. And now I know I have not lived in vain."

Yasha Jones looked up the road and wished that the man could be a little more natural. He had looked forward to the work here, the project was really his project and he had high hopes for it, at least as high as he ever allowed himself to have about anything, and he wished that Tolliver would relax.

He let the wish die. He did not want to prejudge anything. He did not want to prejudge anybody. You could not
read a man's mind. You could not always know what necessity was underneath something. Or behind a face.

He shut his eyes and toyed with the vision of a shadowy
whirl and dance of infinitesimal flecks and numberless parti-
cles. Yes, you could look at a human face and if you chose,
you could see nothing behind it but that system of—

He was aware, suddenly, by a sixth sense, that Bradwell
Tolliver was stealing a look at him.

"You—" Bradwell Tolliver was saying, "you were in the
war, weren't you?"

"Yes," Yasha Jones said.

"What arm?"

"I could speak French," he said, "so I got myself made a
spy. OSS."

"French—was that what you were a near-miss professor
in?"

"No," Yasha Jones said, and thought how long ago something had been.

"What?"

"Physics," Yasha Jones said.

"Whew! The Queen of the Sciences."

Yasha Jones did not think it worth while to correct him.
Then the man corrected himself. "Theology," he said. "That's
what the old Queen was, wasn't it?"

"Yes."

"Well, I reckon it still is," Brad said, "only it is a different theology we got now." After a moment he turned to
Yasha Jones, demanding: "If you were a physicist, how did
you get to be a spy? I thought they locked you physicists up,
you were so precious."

"I wasn't all that precious," Yasha Jones said, and
laughed. "Besides, I got away before they had a chance to
lock me up. I was on leave for private research, so I just
joined, and when they found out, I was off in France, having
cold feet."

"Oh," Brad said, and sank into himself. Yasha Jones
stared up the road. The first symptoms of dusk were coming
on. Now and then a ridge would swell up and blot the sun;
then, as the car made a shift of direction, sink away and let
the sun come back. Now a ridge was rising to snatch the

sun. It was black in the midst of the green. It had been burned over, apparently not long ago. The hog back of the ridge humped slowly against the sun, over the sun, and the spikes of burned tree trunks on the crest bristled blackly against the pink sky of that artificial, premonitory evening.

"That motel back yonder," Brad said.

"Yes?"

"I didn't show it to you just to shoot that line of crap. I just sort of let the crap come. I guess what I really had in mind was transferring it to Fiddlersburg. The motel, I mean. In the mind's eye, you might say. For our beautiful moving picture."

Yasha Jones said nothing. He shut his eyes and summoned up the motel.

"Yes," his companion was saying, "whenever they put in one of these big river projects the whole new lake for seventy-five miles gets cluttered with docks for spun-glass speedboats and Chris-Craft cruisers and guys with Hawaiian batik shirts hanging outside the belt and occasionally parting in the slight breeze of a Tennessee summer, temperature 98°, humidity absolute, to permit the fat character to toy with the manly hair on his belly and drain the sweat out of the navel. They put up motels, with kitchen facilities for the family vacation and with more cozy accommodations for adultery among nature-lovers.

"I can see it now. As Fiddlersburg, with its wealth of Southern tradition, unassuming charm, homely virtue, and pellagra, sinks forevermore beneath the wave, the Seven Dwarfs Motel will rise in spray, glimmering like a dream. It will rise like the vision of the palace of Fata Morgana, and there will be a mulatto in a fairyland brown jerkin with little brass bells on it, and trick pants, one leg red, one yellow, leaning on the high-test pump.

"But in a more serious vein, to tell you something about Fiddlersburg, you ought to see River Street. It got froze long before the last steamboat lifted plank. It got—"

"Excuse me," Yasha Jones said.

"Yeah?"

"I hope you'll understand," he said. "Do you mind not telling me anything now about Fiddlersburg?"

The other was staring at him in blank amazement.

"Please understand," Yasha Jones said. "We are going to work together, and we have to learn something about each other's way of working. You see"—he reached out and touched the other man's arm, felt the tensing of muscle under that light contact—"you see, I like to keep my eye innocent as long as possible. I want to see the thing as naked as I can. I have deliberately refrained from reading anything that might bear on our business. I want to see it."

He lifted his hand from the man's arm. The muscle, he could tell, was still tensed.

"No, not see," Yasha Jones said. "Feel. I want the feel to come in through my eyes. For me that's the way it has to come. Forgive me."

Bradwell Tolliver said nothing. His face was aloof, inward, heavy.

After a while, Yasha Jones said: "I should tell you how much I have looked forward to working with you. Back during the war, I read your beautiful little book, *I'm Telling You Now.* I remembered it. I read it again this winter. It had stayed with me. When I read it again, I knew you were the man for me. I would have known it, even if I had not known you were from Fiddlersburg."

Brad swung toward him, and the car lurched a little before he returned his attention to the road. Then he blurted out: "Mort—Mort Seebaum—I thought he—"

He did not finish.

"No," Yasha Jones finally said, very quietly. "It was my choice. I wanted you for the job."

"Thanks, Mac," Brad said, grinning.

It was a boy's grin, full of warmth and pleasure.

Yasha Jones looked at that grin, and thought that this, yes, was the man he had hoped to find. Everything was going to be fine.

The car was rolling downgrade now. Yasha Jones caught the flick of a sign beside the road.

"Lions Club," the other said. "All that Fiddlersburg can offer. Sorry, you'll have to miss your weekly tizzy with Kiwanis."

The road was rising again, very slightly around the shoulder of a ridge. They made the shoulder, and veered left. The land dropped away sharply. There, in a great bend, was the river, sliding northward under the evening light. The river looked cold and gray as steel, except where it picked up the red of the now legitimate sunset.

Directly across the river, the low fields, some of them plow-land, stretched miles away, cut here and there by the brush of fence lines or the dim-glinting meander of ditch or creek, lifting far away to a darkness that must be woods on the western horizon. The sun was sinking beyond that rim of darkness. Downstream, to the north, the land across was even lower, and wooded. Here and there were openings in the trees, and you could catch the glint of water. Some kind of creek or big bayou seemed, a mile or so downstream, to debouch into the river. A shantyboat—something like that, indistinct in shadowy distance—was moored there.

Without a word, Brad had stopped the car, drawing it off to the side with scrupulous care, with the air of a man anxious to make no noise in a sickroom. Yasha Jones, aware of the care in the action, preferred to accept the fact without acknowledgment, without, in fact, even looking at the man's face. He stared down-river, beyond the distant shantyboat that seemed so lonely there on the stretch of waters backed by the darkness of woods and swamp.

Farther down, beyond the swamp, there was more woodland, dim in the failing light, tangled with shadow. There the ground was higher, a kind of low rim, he surmised, through which, long, long ago, the river had cut. There he could barely make out the newly tumbled earth, the white glint of what he took to be new cement, a small, mathematical rawness in the shadowy land. That would be the dam.

He was again aware of the same careful motion beside him; then felt the car inch forward, very slowly, moving by gravity. The driver had released the brake. The car stopped again, ten yards farther, beyond a clump of growth beside the road. Yasha Jones looked beyond the clump down into the valley. Down there was Fiddlersburg.

It looked very small.

Even that structure which hung above Fiddlersburg and dominated it, looked small. It looked small, even though you knew that, in the human perspective, it would be great and hulking, set on a big isolated hump of rock that had stood, over the ages, against the probings of the water, and now overhung the bed into which the river had, at last, settled. The structure, as he could now make out, must be brick, with sheer outer walls, and had square, squat, crennelated towers, one at each corner, like a fortress. Around its base, wooden houses clustered, scrabbling up the slope, hanging on like barnacles—no, like fungus—like colorless fungoid growths, clutching and shelving about a big rotten stump.

Yasha Jones stared at it. Finally he said: "And that—what is it?"

"The pen," the other said. "The penitentiary."

Yasha Jones continued to stare. Beyond the big structure humped on its hill and the houses scrabbling there in the dimness, he could get some impression of the rest of the town, a string of buildings along the river, an isolated grove beyond this, above the massive-sliding river. So this was Fiddlersburg.

Yasha Jones tried to think of nothing. He tried to surrender himself to the mere vision of what was there by the river in the middle of the dimming land. Southward, far away, a crow beat up from the land, attained height, and moved across the sky. In a slow, fatalistic assiduity it sculled across the enormous emptiness. Westward, a pink glow yet touched one tatter of cloud.

Yasha Jones watched the flight of the crow until the black dot had disappeared northward. He let the loneliness move into him, like shadows rising.

He saw a light come on, far off there, in one of the houses clutching at the shadowy base of the hill. He thought of the human moment in the midst of the land. His heart stirred. He thought of the preciousness of that moment. That, he thought, was all he had ever tried to get: that moment of preciousness.

But he had never managed to do it. At least, not the way he dreamed it. Perhaps he would, this time.

Chapter

5

THE MOONLIGHT—the moon was full—fell on her head as she leaned to lift the big silver coffee pot from the tray. The moonlight gave a velvety gloss to her dark, straight hair, hair drawn back and secured very tight, almost painfully tight one felt, into an old-fashioned knot, or bun. She did well, Yasha Jones thought, studying her, to wear the hair that way. The skull was a fine one, high in the arch, cleanly molded.

He wondered how much gray was in her hair. He knew there was some. He had seen that by the candlelight at dinner.

"You take two, don't you, Mr. Jones?" she was asking him, lifting her face, the sugar tongs in her hand.

The moonlight fell on the face, defining the clarity of

the oval, making the face seem paler than he knew it to be,
and smoother. The candlelight at dinner had not been so
kind. The lines, even in candlelight, had been quite clearly
discernible in the brow, and the lines at the mouth indicated
the firmness with which the jaw closed, even in repose. He
had seen that much, even in candlelight, in those moments
when she seemed to withdraw into a life that had nothing to
do with him or with Bradwell Tolliver.

"Maggie," Bradwell Tolliver had said to the woman who,
in the big, bare hall where night encroached to compete with
the parsimonious light from the crystal-dangling, askew wall
brackets, awaited them, "this is Mr. Jones, Yasha Jones."

And turning to Yasha Jones he had said: "My sister,
Mrs. Fiddler."

Then had added: "Mrs. Fiddler of Fiddlersburg."

"Oh, dear," the woman mourned, "must we—ah, must
we—have that old joke?" Then offering her hand to the guest,
smiling at him, she said: "And I imagine, Mr. Jones, you
thought Fiddlersburg just a place where old fiddle players go
when they die. A kind of what-do-you-call-it?"

"Fiddler's Creen," he had said, "but I prefer this."

Now in the garden he watched her turn, with a clean
motion of the waist, to hand a cup to her brother. There was
something definitely girlish in the motion, he decided, but
added to himself that, although the waist was trim enough,
and the legs too, for that matter, the figure was not, exactly,
girlish. He assumed that the breasts were somewhat—and
he used the technical word to himself—prolapsed.

He thought of the technical flavor of the word, then
thought, with a shade of amusement, of himself sitting here
undressing his hostess in the Tennessee moonlight, here in a
doomed, God-forgotten little town, by a deep-bellied, silt-
laden river, in a poorly maintained garden where, even in
moonlight, it was plain to be seen that the rose trellises,
those not already beyond repair, badly needed attention.

The dyer's hand, he thought—it was a mark of his trade,
this undressing business. In any métier a man works up little
tricks for doing things, and he remembered when he had first
hit on this one, the trick of seeing his actors, as they moved
into a scene, in merciless, common nakedness, totally defenseless, moving in their poor human nakedness into some
moment of significance. It had come to him all at once one

day, a miserable day when nothing went right with a scene that had seemed so simple—the goodbye of an old slum woman to her grown son. It had come in a flash, the vision of the woman's poor old flesh naked, the son naked too; and in that vision he had perfectly known how to make move the flesh of Millicent Murdoch, $2500 a week and an old bitch if there ever was one, so that any spectator would know how that old female flesh yearned to repossess itself of that flesh which had once been its own and which now, without protection, in the person of that brawny, surly, brutal, bored son was to move out into the blankness of the world.

Yes, if you could see the bodies move in their nakedness, you could then envision the inner necessity of the motion that would reveal the pathos or comedy of their fate.

He admitted that there was a little prurience in his trick, and God-ism to boot. He was old enough, he told himself now, sitting in the moonlight, to know that nothing is ever simple: the surgeon bending in his task of devoted mercy is the twin brother of Jack the Ripper. No doubt, in that peculiar mixture of sex and sexlessness which, too, was associated with his trade, he had done some hypothetical undressing dictated not entirely by the demands of art; had, now and then, received some infra-artistic stimulation. He would have to admit that. Well, what of it?

He looked at Mrs. Fiddler. He decorously drew the brown dress back over her bosom. He replaced the pale yellow shawl on her shoulders, shoulders which, he had observed, she carried well. The shawl did not show pale yellow now in the moonlight. It looked white, or pale gray. But he knew, from the candlelight at dinner, that it was a pale yellow, and knew, too, that it had been carefully mended in more than one spot.

"—such a pleasure if you will, Mr. Jones," she was saying. "There's just us, and Mother Fiddler. Mother Fiddler and I, we'd love to have you. We're just two lonely females, and nobody ever comes to Fiddlersburg. Mother Fiddler, she's a sweet old thing, but you wouldn't, I guess, see much of her, she's so old. She takes a little supper and goes up long before we have our dinner. She says she'll wait up with us tomorrow, in your honor."

"I look forward," he murmured, thinking, yes, that big table of battered rosewood in the cavernously dim room with the red paper, or was it cloth, scaling and blotching from the walls—what that table needed was an old face, white hair, multitudinous wrinkles, eyes staring into the candle flame. He tried to imagine what the face would, in actuality, be.

"Tomorrow," she was saying, "you just scout around the house. See if you can't find a room to do for your study. There must be one, somewhere in such an old barn of a place, and if you—"

"It's a charming place," he murmured, meaning it, turning to look up the slope to the bulk which, with all windows dark, was washed bone-white by the moonlight. A big TV aerial, he observed, rose anachronistically above it. Below the house, shelving down toward them, he could make out two levels of the terracing, retained by old brick, overgrown and crumbling, and the brick walk that led down, between the disreputable rose trellises, to the ruinous gazebo that hung over the river.

Just then there was a halloo—the kind of hail one expects from a hillside or across a draw—from the darkness of the house. Brad called back.

"That must be Blanding," Maggie said. "I forgot to tell you he said he might drop by." She turned to the guest. "To help welcome you," she said, "he being kin, on Mother's side."

A figure had emerged from the shadow of the house into moonlight, a short stocky figure that moved with brisk ease down the walk toward them.

"Blanding," Maggie said, "here's Mr. Jones. And this is Blanding Cottshill, our kinsman and dear friend."

The men shook hands. Cottshill, Yasha Jones observed to himself, was short—short in the legs rather than in the body—but with a large, handsome rough-hewn head, too big for the body but not for the shoulders, the head thatched with thorny white hair around a spot of baldness. The bald spot gleamed in the moonlight. Cottshill, Yasha Jones also observed, wore cowhide boots, carelessly laced up. But he had on some kind of dark coat.

They sat before the gazebo. A low brick wall separated them from the drop to the river. Underfoot, Yasha Jones felt the softness of crumbling brick.

"I was just telling Mrs. Fiddler what a charming spot this is," he said.

"Oh, it's charming by moonlight," she said in a tone which Yasha Jones could not quite interpret.

From the slope came a burst of bird song.

"Yes," she said, "the first mocker! Coming just in time to help the moonlight maintain your kind illusions. But—" she paused.

"But," she resumed, "you will see us by daylight."

She laughed, and he supposed there was some real gaiety in it. At least, a little flash of abandon.

"I'll tell you one thing you can see by daylight," she went on. "Stick your head over the wall and look down at the river and you'll see all the trash and broken bottles and old shoes and rusted tea kettles and empty tin cans and sprung corset stays that ever came out of this house in a hundred and fifty years. It is all there, tangled up in black-berry bushes and honeysuckle vines and poke salad plants. Oh, I forgot to mention the garbage. I do try to prevent that. But I don't always succeed. Promise to look over the wall, the first thing in the morning. Just for a touch of reality. Will you solemnly promise?"

"Yes," he said, "I promise."

"By daylight," she said, "you'll see, too, that we're fall-ing to pieces here. All Fiddlersburg has always been falling to pieces. All my life, anyway." And she turned to Blanding Cottshill: "Isn't that right, Squire?"

"That's right," Cottshill said. "Mighty little happens here except things gradually falling apart. Not much excitement here since U.S. Grant and his ironclads puffed up-river. Then later on, the last steamboat tooted the whistle to lift plank, and things really got drowsy. And, I may add, money got scarce."

"Fiddlersburg," Brad said, "it is as far as you can get out-side of history and still feel that history exists. If," he said, "it does."

"When things fall down in Fiddlersburg," Maggie said, "nobody ever leans over to pick them up. I used to think that was normal, when I was a child. Then I went to school in Nashville and—"

"She went to Ward Belmont," Brad said. He had poured himself another brandy.

"Brad thinks it is funny to have a sister who went to Ward Belmont," she said by way of explanation. "Ward Bel-mont was a girls' school in Nashville. A very nice little finish-ing school. I'm sure you never heard of it."

"As a matter of fact, I have," Yasha Jones said.

"He heard of it in the first scene of a play called *Cat in the Hot Tin Pants*," Brad said.

"No," Yasha Jones said, laughing, turning the brandy glass in his fingers, "it wasn't in the opening scene of *Cat on a Hot Tin Roof* that I heard of Ward Belmont. Back in Chicago, when I was young, I used to know a girl who went there."

"Oh, bother Ward Belmont," she said, and laughed again. "What I meant to say was that when I went to Nashville I found out when things fell down somebody picked them up. Sometimes, anyway. At least often enough to make me think that those folks in Nashville must be Yankees or something."

"No," Brad said, "not Yankees. It is merely that Nashville has always aspired to be nothing more or less than a shining middle-bracket example of the Great American Middle Class. It aspires to be the Kansas City of the upper Buttermilk Belt."

"Oh, leave poor Nashville alone," she said.

He ignored her, and drank the brandy.

"The slogan," he said, "of the Junior Chamber of Commerce of Nashville, Tennessee, is 'When Better Bourgeois Are Built Nashville Will Build Them.'"

"Brad just loves to use that word," Maggie Fiddler said. "*Bourgeois*, I mean. At least, he used to love to use it. I reckon he still does."

"I got it from my first wife," Bradwell Tolliver said. "The Commie one. I now use the word to commemorate the good times we had together. Some of those good times would certainly have *épaté*-ed the bourgeois."

"Give Cousin Blanding and Mr. Jones some more of that old sweet French whiskey you are drinking," she said, "then there won't be quite as much left for you, and that, my poor old Brad, might be a good thing."

She laughed again; and again Yasha Jones, as he held out his glass for the cognac, tried to assay just what was the deep inner meaning of that quick, easy ripple of sound.

"All I was ever trying to say, Mr. Jones," she said, turning toward him, "was that all my life things fell down in Fiddlersburg and never got picked up. Maybe that was some kind of wiseness, after all. Suppose all those years everybody in Fiddlersburg had gone around all day picking up things and trying to put them back together again. Think of all that wasted energy now, when they're just going to flood us anyway."

"It's funny," Cottshill said, "why things do fall down here. You think of things falling down, decaying, as something that happens in Time—the category of Time. But why do things fall down in a place where there isn't any Time? For, Mr. Jones, Fiddlersburg is the place where the courthouse clock, opposite my office—"

Brad broke in: "The Squire is a lawyer."

"No," Cottshill said, "I'm a farmer, but I practice a little law. And that clock opposite my office has stood at eight thirty-five for a hell of a long time—A.M. or P.M., nobody knows.

"Yes, sir, Fiddlersburg is the place where God just forgot to wind His watch." He paused, then, in sudden gaiety, resumed. "Let 'em flood us," he said. "Never was a place—or a society, for that matter—didn't deserve drowning out." He paused again, resumed. "But you know, that moment when some place is just overpassed but still extant and waiting for the flood, that's the time you can see its virtues and vices most clearly. Like that queer light before a storm in summer. You get a queer feeling then.

"Yeah," he said, "and I'll tell you all something queer." He turned to Maggie. "Unless you've been down town today and heard it."

"I haven't budged out of the house," she said.

"Well," he said, "you remember Miss Pettifew? Used to live in what is now the Bascom place?"

She nodded.

"You remember she moved away, of a sudden—maybe fifteen years ago. Nobody knew why nor where. Well, she came back last night."

"She did?" Maggie asked politely.

"Yes," Cottshill said, "such is the deep shudder of soul set up by the impending death of Fiddlersburg. She came in the middle of the night. By stealth. With a common garden spade. And"—he paused for his little drama—"got arrested."

"Arrested!" Maggie exclaimed, not in politeness.

"For what?" Brad demanded.

"Don't rush me," Cottshill said. "I'll tell it in my own way. Last night about two A.M. old man Bascom heard a racket from his dog. That German shepherd chained up in the yard. So in the traditional way, he appears on his back porch in a nightshirt, shanks bare to the breeze, flashlight in one hand, twelve gauge in the other and the safety off. The first thing that flashlight beam picks out is a female form, white in the face, clutching something to the bosom.

"Old Bascom yells, 'Hands up,' and the female form puts up hands, letting fall whatever had been clutched to the bosom. Then old Bascom yells for his wife to call the constable. After a decent interval, during which old Bascom holds the intruder at gun-point, Constable Small drives up in his Chevy.

"So this morning, bright and early, I get called to the jail to take over. Not that the prisoner, who had been yelling for a lawyer, would, at first, even tell me her name. But it was old Miss Pettifew. I say 'old' advisedly. She can't be sixty but she looks a million. Anyway, she finally cracked and started talking. She told me all."

He stopped, and considered.

"No, not quite all," he resumed. "She didn't tell me the name of her lover."

"Her what!" Brad demanded.

"Her lover," Cottshill answered calmly. "For in a world where mystery is the order of nature, we can accept even the mystery that this old fence post of a female, as Miss Pettifew was even in her prime, once found a lover. The real thing, mind you. For can you figger out what she was digging up? In the middle of the night? Under an old rosebush? In the back yard of a house she hadn't seen in over fifteen years?"

"No," Maggie said.

"A Mason jar," he said. "Yeah, an old-fashioned fruit jar, sealed with a rubber sealer, top still screwed on tight after all this time. And in it there was—well, the thing she could not bear to leave lying in the ground, under the weight of water, when Fiddlersburg goes under."

"You mean—" Brad began.

"Yes," Cottshill said. "That old Mason jar contained the pore little thing that would have been Miss Pettifew's baby. If it had ever got that far along. Not that she'd done anything to herself. I believe her. It just happened. It was her luck. Well, to wind up, she is gone. She has taken it with her. In an old Mason jar. Off in an over-age Ford. Destination unknown."

Blanding Cottshill peered slowly from face to face, his

eyes pale and bright in the moonlight. "That, ladies and gentlemen of the jury," he said, "is Fiddlersburg."

Yasha Jones looked up the ruined terracing toward the dark house. He looked down at the dark river, where, southward, an eddy broke into silver. He looked up at the moon riding infinitely high, and with disdainful ease, across the milk-pale emptiness of the sky. In this pale light you experienced an unassuageable emptiness. You felt the infinite flight of emptiness beyond the moon.

The mockingbird burst out again, then hushed.

It was all a perfect cliché, he said to himself. He wondered, wryly, what they would say if he—Yasha Jones—put this in his picture, absolutely as it was. But Yasha Jones, he reflected, was cunning enough not to put this in a picture just as it was. He would, very cunningly, do something to it so that it would no longer be what it actually was, what it really was, but because it was unreal would be taken for real.

Yes, reality was the uncapturable. That was why we need illusion. *Truth through lie,* he thought. *Only in the mirror, over your shoulder,* he thought, *does the ghost appear.* He wondered, fleetingly, what was the difference between what he was doing now, or was about to do—to make a picture based presumably on the death of a town like Fiddlersburg but really based on some mysterious process in the viscera and synapses of Yasha Jones—and what he had been doing, more than twenty years ago, alone in that laboratory, far off in England, in Cambridge, or in that room in the University of Chicago with a blackboard covered with figures and those portentous hen scratches of symbol.

Yasha Jones again looked about him: dark house, garden, moon, ruined terrace. The mockingbird obligingly gave a long cadenza. Over the edge of his brandy glass he looked at the woman. She sat there in the moonlight, quite erect in her chair, the pale shawl laid with mathematical exactitude over her shoulders, the hair parted with exactitude on the good skull, and she looked westward over the great bend of the river and the dim land as though she were alone.

He looked at her, and knew that she was accustomed to sit here alone.

He said: "Mrs. Fiddler."

She turned toward him. He noticed how calmly she came out of her trance, her distance, and turned. There was no start, no jerk of surprise. She made the transition from one dimension to the other, he thought, with the ease of one long accustomed to slip, by some secret trick, over that frontier.

"Yes?" she said.

"I am glad to have seen this spot," he said. He made a little gesture to indicate his surroundings. "I shall be saddened when it is gone."

She turned to glance up at the terraces, at the dark bulk of the house, then cast her gaze about her, as though discovering and assessing it all for the first time.

"I'm not sure that I'll be," she said.

She sat thoughtfully.

"What I mean is," she resumed, "it's not as though there were a life here. As though the town weren't dying anyway. As though you could feel the place belonged anywhere. Oh, I don't mean there ought to be a lot of pickaninnies rolling at the little cabin door. I don't know what I mean, I reckon."

She paused, then added: "Maybe the place never did belong here. Maybe it never belonged anywhere. Maybe it was just some notion in the head of the first Fiddler who came here."

Brad stirred in his shadow. "Colonel Octavius Fiddler," he said, in the tone of official announcement, "Virginia, Revolutionary commission—militia, I regret—here by way of Kentucky, land-grabber, made last grab here, built house and became a Tennessee aristocrat. Portrait, genuine oil painting, on left as you enter."

"My brother," the woman explained, "prides himself on not being an aristocrat. He is afraid somebody may mistake him for one."

"I am a descendant," he affirmed, "of a long line of Choctaw-screwing, jug-walloping, muskrat-skinners from the deep swamps. And"—he turned to the woman—"so are you, Ole Sis."

"I reckon so," she said, "but you might put it a little bit prettier."

"I want Mr. Jones to know the truth," he said. "I don't want him to think that I am here under false pretenses. Rather"—and he took a sip of his brandy—"I do not want him to think that I am in this house under anything except false pretenses."

The woman looked up at the house.

"No," she said, "I won't mind it being gone. The house.

Except," she said, "for Mother Fiddler. It would kill her to have to leave. I'd rather she just died here."

She turned to Yasha Jones.

"You see," she said, "it's sort of a race."

"Yes?"

"Between the flood coming and that killing her," she said, "and her just dying here. Maybe she'll die soon, just naturally. It is a race between two kinds of dying."

Yasha Jones, out of the tail of his eye, had seen a light come on in the house, in an upper room. He turned his head, and the woman caught his motion.

"Yes," she said, rising, "it's her room. She gets up at night, poor old thing, and goes to see if—"

She paused.

"She wanders around," she finished, lamely. "Excuse me," she said, and was hurrying up the walk, toward the house.

Yasha Jones watched her.

"She breaks her back over the old girl," the other was saying. "Has to watch her pretty close."

Yasha Jones watched her disappear into the dark doorway of the house.

"Mr. Jones," Cottshill said, "make Brad bring you out to my place. I'd like to show it off once more before it's flooded out. I've got one interesting feature, even if it is a small thing. I got two artificial lakes nigh big as a small farm, pumps to fill 'em from the river and drain 'em, and I raise buffalo fish. Every year I drain one pond and ship the buffalo to Chicago to make *gefilte* fish. You ought to see a million darkies in hip boots out harvesting buffalo like watermelon, and refrigerator trucks backed up a mile for loading. It's a sight. But here's what I'm getting at. Come fall, and those ponds give me the best duck shooting this side of Arkansas rice. I have big shooting parties out there.

"I give one every fall for folks I know from all over. We take an eye-opener and a light breakfast before sun; then out to the blinds. After we get rowed back from the blinds, we have a big shindig, sixty or sixty-five at long tables and my colored boys moving in the food and drinks. But, man, the ducks. You ought to see 'em coming over the woods high, then dip for the long coast to the pond. Dawn light and they come sailing in."

He paused. Then in a quieter tone: "Next fall is the last

shoot. Before we're flooded. Wish you'd come, Mr. Jones. Do you do any duck shooting, Mr. Jones?"

After a moment Yasha Jones spoke, very slowly: "I used to. Long back, before the war. But it seems that I've given it up. But"—and he smiled—"thank you. I appreciate the invitation."

Cottshill got up. "I'm gassing too long," he said. He put out his hand.

His good nights were almost abrupt.

When he had gone, Brad turned to his guest. "Want to go to bed?" he said.

But Yasha Jones was looking toward the dark house.

"I suppose I should explain to your sister," he said, "before accepting her kind invitation to stay here, that I am the world's most talented insomniac. I can usually manage to stay in my room with literature as therapy, but not always. I hope the stairs don't creak."

"They do," Brad said, "every God-damned one. When I was first getting the sap up, I got a few flailings from my old man because the stairs creaked. He would waylay me sneaking out. You see," he added, catching some look of puzzlement on the face of Yasha Jones, "this is my boyhood home. Though no Fiddler be I."

He waited, apparently relishing the moment.

Then: "I reported fact when I said what I did about my lineage. My old man was a true-born muskrat-skinner, but when the muskrats thinned out, he came out of the swamp to dry land, bar' foot and one gallus, and started skinning the local townsfolk. By the time he begot me he damned near owned Fiddlersburg. If he had been born to wider horizons he might very well have owned Nashville, too, and Chicago to boot. But Fiddlersburg was all he knew about. By the time I came along he owned half of River Street, most of the bank stock, six farms, four hundred head of cattle, and fourteen mortgages, including one on the Methodist Church. By the time I was six or seven, just after World War I, a nice little depression hit, and he foreclosed on old Doc Fiddler, and we moved in. He even got most of the furniture and fixings, including the library. He wanted the rugs so he could track in swamp mud or cow dung or whatever he happened to have on his boots, and the furniture so he could take out his frog-sticker and whittle on Chippendale—when he fell into a reflective mood. My father—"

Brad Tolliver paused, took a sip of his brandy, set the glass down.

"My father," he resumed, "had deep, complicated and unresolved needs. He was, in short"—he picked up the glass, drained it, set it down—"a son-of-a-bitch."

He stood up. "So you got insomnia?" he demanded.

"I invented it," Yasha Jones said, and smiled up at him.

Brad stared down at the thin long-nosed face, the deep-set eyes, the high-domed, hairless head over which pale moonlight poured. His stare was insolent and angry.

"I do not have insomnia," he said. "I am not so favored. I am not the sensitive aesthetic type. When the time comes, as it does now and then, when I, if I were the sensitive aesthetic type, would have insomnia, I, being what I am, go on a high lonesome. Do you, Mr. Jones, know what a high lonesome is?"

"No."

"Do you think that I now am drunk?"

"No."

"Though by your smiling, you seem to say so," Brad said, peering down into the face of Yasha Jones. Then he added: "I had feared that you, by reason of the excessive complication of my syntax, had begun to think that I might be drunk. But I assure you that I am not. I am merely dusting off the launching pad for a high lonesome. Do you know what a high lonesome is?"

"No."

"Have you ever been South before?"

"No."

"Well, in the Deep South, in certain circles, upper-class circles—upper class, that is, by old-fashioned standards and not those of Dun and Bradstreet—the locution *high lonesome* means a strictly private booze-soak, alcoholic concentration of point five percent or better, undertaken for strictly philosophical reasons. It is the nearest the State of Mississippi comes to Zen. It is the nearest even the State of Tennessee comes to Zen. It is the nearest Bradwell Tolliver comes to Zen, and he is coming there now because, in this flood of moonlight and memory, he is about to retire to the chamber where he, as a boy, lay and, while moonlight strayed across his couch and the mockingbird sang, indulged what the bard has so aptly termed the long, long thoughts of youth."

He leaned, quite competently, and picked up the bottle
of cognac.

"Sure you don't want a slug before I go?" he asked.
"There's plenty. I picked up a case in Memphis. I drink sour
mash on the Coast and now I drink cognac in Tennessee. Do
you know why?"

"No."

"Well, I'll tell you," Bradwell Tolliver said, and leaned
confidentially. "Planning my return to Tennessee, after an
unbroken exile of many years, I surveyed my experience to
decide what likker had given me the worst hangovers.
Clearly what my provincial sister calls that old sweet French
whiskey. So I determined to get a case of that to provide a
combination of Keeley Cure and penitential exercise. I am
now making preparation to undergo both."

He held out the bottle.

"But don't you want one snort before I go?" he asked.

"No, thanks," Yasha Jones said, pleasantly.

"Good night," the other said, "and happy dreams."

"Good night. And thank you," Yasha Jones said.

He watched the sturdy figure take three steps up the
walk. The figure stopped, seemed to reflect, then returned.
Bradwell Tolliver was again staring down at him.

"I want to assure you," Bradwell Tolliver was saying,
"that if you have any fears that I drink on a job, you may dis-
abuse yourself. This," he said, "is strictly Zen."

Again he moved up the walk. The huaraches made a
dry, crumbly, dragging sound on the old brick. He got to the
first terrace, again stopped and seemed to reflect. He came
back.

"You know what room you're in?" he demanded.

"Oh, I won't get lost," Yasha Jones said.

The other shook his head in a gesture of impatience.

"Hell, I don't mean that," he said. "What I mean is what
room it is."

He leaned a little, staring into the face of the seated
man.

"That room—" he said, "that is the one my wife and I
had when we lived here. Back before the war. My first wife.
You know, the one I mentioned?"

"Yes," Yasha Jones said.

"She was a Commie," Bradwell Tolliver said, "and she
was nine feet tall, had a twenty-two-inch waist, was double-

jointed as a garter snake and was juicy as a busted pome-
granate when all the bees of the San Fernando Valley start
for it in the hot sunshine. I leave you with that thought."

This time he did not stop. He moved up the walk; up
the steps of the first terrace; up those of the second. His
movements were sober and methodical. He reached the
house.

Yasha Jones watched the figure disappear into the house,
then sat there and thought that he was glad he was not a
writer. He had been spared that. He had been spared the
yearning for immortality.

He had never known, he reflected, a writer, not even
the meanest, most time-serving, and most convicted of failure, who did not, in some recess of his being, cherish the
yearning, even the hope. The disease was in the very medium.
He thought of those things that seemed to promise the crafts-
man a survival beyond himself: paint, stone, wood, the chain
of notes, the word. He reflected on the difference between the
disease of those who work in this promise of immortality and
the disease of those who do not.

The actor, the singer, the dancer—each knows that the
best of himself, all that is really of value, is snatched from
him in the very moment when it comes into existence. He
knows he cannot hope for immortality. His disease is, therefore, more desperate, more frenetic, more destructive, more
suicidal. His struggle with Time is different. In his very art
he lives in an immediate and frantic awareness of the death
of the ego. He knows that any promise of fame is fraudulent,
for the only fame that can come to him is always in the past
tense. Language puts it that way. You say: "Garrick *was* a
great actor." You say: "Milton *is* a great poet." There is a
fame in Time, and a fame out of Time.

Yes, he thought, the disease of those who can struggle
only for fame in Time might, for that reason, seem more
desperate. He thought of the damned ones he had known.
But the disease of those who struggle for the fame out
of Time—that is a deeper kind of damnation. It is deeper
because the medium promises more. And the word promises
most of all. Yes, the disease is in the very medium. There
is no escaping the dream. Each one, despite all the lies he
tells himself to the comforting and finger-crossing contrary,
dreams that someday, somewhere, somebody will find the

message in his bottle. He will be great. He will enter upon his immortality.

Well, Yasha Jones said to himself, as he had said it many times before, he had been spared that. He knew that he worked in evanescence. When had he learned that? He thought of those years at Cambridge, and at Chicago. Now he had for an instant the vision of a great screen, like a blank screen in an empty theater, a screen flickering and pulsing with subdued waves of silvery light, then the shadow of a human figure drifting across it, dim and without feature. Evanescence—if you knew you worked in that you could have joy. You could have joy because you knew that in evanescence there was no immortality.

He sat there in the moonlight, in his greatness, and was not aware that his awareness of evanescence was what had made him great.

He sat there and was filled with pity for the man who had gone into the dark house. Yasha Jones was not aware that, long back, he himself had mistaken the warmth of pity for the warmth of joy. He was not aware that the pity in a little book written by a boy from Fiddlersburg, some twenty-five years earlier, was what now put him in this ruined garden, in the moonlight, waiting for sleep. He was not aware that the pity in that little book had come before him as an image of the pity in his own heart which he thought was joy.

He sat there and knew he was not yet ready to try to sleep. He sat there and wondered if the other man was asleep yet.

The other man was not asleep. He was staring out the window, where moonlight washed over all the land westward, remembering how Yasha Jones, that afternoon, had said that he had chosen him. Because he had once written a little book. And now Bradwell Tolliver was remembering his own burst of warmth and gratitude that afternoon, like the relief of forgiveness, when Yasha Jones had told him that.

But staring into the moonlight, he could feel no warm relief, like forgiveness.

Chapter

6

In the moment of waking, on the same bed in Fiddlersburg, Tennessee, where he had lain as a boy, Brad Tolliver
became aware, first, of the throbbing head and uneasy stomach which he had predicted from the brandy. Then, even before memory could sort out the facts of the recent past, even
before he was quite certain in what bed he lay, he was aware
of a sudden swooping descent into despair, like lying in a
dory, at sea, eyes closed, and the dory sliding side-on, down
the trough of a wave.

He had, actually, shut his eyes.

Now he opened them again, recognizing the ceiling, the
gray plaster, the familiar cracks—would that plaster never
fall?—and knew that it was late, knew that it was Sunday,

knew that he had certain obligations to a guest, to an employer, Yasha Jones, and knew the source of his despair. Long
ago he had written a little book. Now, because of that book—
not because of *The Dream of Jacob*, which last night had been
on a million marquees, not because of two Oscars or one
award from the Screen Writers Guild, not because of seventeen credits, not because of any of these things that had filled
all the years between—he was here and Yasha Jones was
here, and they would make a beautiful moving picture. Had
all the years between gone, therefore, for nothing?

He shut his eyes and knew that that was the way it had
begun last night: with that question. He had lain on this bed,
and moonlight had fallen across it, and he had remembered
writing that book. If he had not written that book he would
not, late one sunny afternoon in June, 1937, have been walking in Central Park, along a narrow, winding path bordered by
high hedges, chewing a grass stem, while Lettice Poindexter
leaned down at him a little (she was wearing high heels), or
rather, had let her head bend a little forward and sidewise so
that she could scrutinize his face while, to the accompani-
ment of small, weaving gestures, merely from the wrist, on
the left wrist two heavy gold bracelets, East Indian or something, with barbaric jangling things hanging from them, she
explained to him the deeper meaning of his work.

He had great talent, she said. She would hate to see it
wasted, she said. Besides, she said, there was only one way,
in the modern world, to find happiness. She had found it. She
was explaining to him how he could find it and, at the same
time, bring forth the deeper meaning of his work.

If there had been no work there would have been nothing to talk about the deeper meaning of.

Work, he thought now. *Deeper meaning of.*

The editor who was responsible for the collection of
stories called *I'm Telling You Now* was a graduate of Yale,
magna cum laude, class of '15, had taught briefly at that institution, in the Department of English, had been rejected
for military service in 1917 because of a slight curvature of
the spine, and shortly afterwards had gone into publishing
because, suddenly, he found the academic environment stul-
tifying. After being in publishing a few years he himself had
written a novel, a thing vaguely resembling the work of
Ronald Firbank, and had very competently translated sev-

eral German classics. In 1924 he had married a socially appropriate girl of some beauty and no imagination whatsoever,
by whom he had one child, a son. For the first two years of
the child's life, he was a fanatically devoted father, but when
he began to live apart from his wife, who would not give him
a divorce, he lost all interest in the child.

During the late 1920's he took all his vacations in Berlin
and wrote political articles accurately predicting the rise of
Nazism. On his last vacation in Berlin, in 1931, he had, to his
profound astonishment, a homosexual adventure, his only
one, this with a middle-aged political organizer, a militant
who had been maimed by Nazi toughs in Munich and whose
courage the young publisher greatly admired; but thereafter
he returned to his satisfactions among the young women of
the literary and political circles he frequented, including
several young women whose work had been published by the
house to which he was attached. He now wore a beard, red-
dish, cut square.

Previously his dress had been rather elegant, an in-
souciant combination of British and campus, but now the in-
souciance deteriorated into a somewhat dramatic unkempt-
ness, though the tweed, even when in need of mending, was
always good. His name, in this period, appeared more and
more frequently among the signers of manifestoes and letters of protest in the magazines.

The name of the editor was Telford Lott. He was a good
man, singularly free from ambition and rancor, conscien-
tious in his work, anxious to do something for the better-
ment of mankind, but worried because his way of life gave
such small scope for significant action. His grandfather had
been an eminent Unitarian clergyman, in Massachusetts,
and Telford Lott resembled the grandfather far more than he
realized. He was sometimes moved to tears by fiction pre-
senting images of generosity or of human suffering patiently
borne. In the spring of 1934 a certain story in a small magazine affected him profoundly, a story called "I'm Telling You
Now," a simple tale about an old Jewish tailor whose natural
decency and dignity had touched the life of a woebegone,
bigoted little Tennessee town by a muddy river. Telford Lott
wrote the author, and when he discovered his proximity in
the unlikely milieu of Darthurst College, invited him to come
to see him at the office. The story became the title piece of the
little collection which Telford Lott shortly assembled.

The book had a *succès d'estime* of some proportion. It was praised in the usual organs of reviewing, but even more highly in the liberal and radical magazines. The author had, it was said, great compassion. He had reported, without flinching, extenuation, or romanticism, the degradation of life in his native region. He exhibited an instinctive awareness of social problems, and with maturity and doctrine he might be counted upon to make an important contribution.

In those days a peculiar elation suffused the life of Telford Lott. It did not come from the little gleams of reflected glory which he enjoyed at cocktail parties before the conversation moved on from the discovery of Bradwell Tolliver, to politics, adultery, or money. Telford Lott was happy now because, in the person of Bradwell Tolliver—that heavy-skulled young man, with pale blue eyes, slightly off-set ears, raw frame, big hands, untidy dress, and strange, appealing combination of brashness and timidity—he had found a way, however modest, to touch the future. He would give Brad— he already called him Brad—that quiet confidence and sense of mission he would need to sustain him, and that doctrine needed to supplement his compassion.

A man could do that much, at least, to touch the reality of his time, Telford Lott decided. He began to think of returning to his wife. He was, after all, past forty. He was losing interest in parties. He began to think of his son, how he might train him to bear the burden of the human future. His back, which lately had been causing him pain at night, got much better. He became aware one day that not for a long time had he had the old exasperating fantasy of facing a firing squad to die for some belief which, just at the moment of execution, he could not remember the nature of. He dreamed several times of the death of his mother, and his grief was delicious. He returned to an early passion for the poetry of Wordsworth and even began an essay on the relation of the social conscience and the love of nature.

Telford Lott did go back to his wife and resumed his old devotion to his son. The son fulfilled the father's highest hopes, making a brilliant record in classics at his father's university, taking a doctorate at Oxford, and then fighting bravely in Korea. But he was captured by the Chinese. A year later the news was published that the son had defected. Telford Lott shot himself.

When Bradford Tolliver, in Beverly Hills, read the news

of the tragic death of the distinguished editor he felt, at first, nothing. For the moment, he did not, in fact, really identify the name. It was familiar, yes—but in that split second he couldn't quite place it. Then he saw his own name among the writers who had been discovered by the deceased.

What he felt then, looking at the announcement of death, was a secret relief. Mixed with the relief was a sense of slyness, of adroitness, as though he had executed some coup— just what, he could not say. That satisfaction in his unspecified cunning sustained him all day. Little bursts of wellbeing would jet up in him.

But by night he was in a black mood. He was so quarrelsome at a party that his host asked him to leave. His wife— he was married then to Suzie Martine—refused to sleep in the same room with him, and went to a guest room. The occasion was, indeed, the beginning of the end of the marriage to Suzie Martine, who loved him.

For several months Bradwell Tolliver made an impression at parties by recounting how Telford Lott, whose own son had defected in Korea, by God, had tried to make a Commie out of him, how he had given him Commie books to read, how he had even provided him with Commie tail. Hell, he would say, he was just an innocent boy from the Buttermilk Belt and he got dialectical materialism so mixed up with something else he might have been a Commie himself if he hadn't escaped back to the healthy degradation of the muskrat skinners. He even developed a comic parody of the most anthologized story from *I'm Telling You Now*—a combination of muskrat-skinner accent and Marxist patois—to illustrate what Telford Lott really wanted him to do.

One night—after the loyalty purge in Hollywood—he had special success at a party at Malibu. He held seven people completely enraptured in a pantry for forty-five minutes. That night when he got back to his own house, still having a house then though Suzie had gone off for the divorce, he was very drunk. He could not bear to enter the dark house. He lay down on the lawn by a Japanese quince and looked up at the beauty of the starlit sky.

When he had finished weeping, he kept on staring up at the sky while his eyelids prickled astringently with the drying tears. He lay there by the quince, and thought that now, after the tears, he had some notion of the sweetness of being born again in the spirit. He went to sleep lying there by the shrub. Just after dawn he woke up, entered the house, and went properly to bed. He never again mentioned the name of Telford Lott.

In fact, as time passed and his professional success grew, he almost forgot the name, and even forgot the intimation of peace he had felt that night lying by the flowering quince and staring up at the stars. But when, some four years later, in the fall of 1959, Mort Seebaum, having summoned him through a descending hierarchy ending with Brad's agent, asked him how he'd like to go to Fiddlersburg—a name Mort Seebaum had to verify by glancing at his pad—he felt, for a split second, the tears well up in him as they had that night as he lay under the stars. And suddenly he remembered, too, how he had felt, years ago in a lonely dormitory at Darthurst, sitting up late at night while the radiators got cold, trying to put on paper the words about Fiddlersburg that made tears mysteriously come to his eyes.

Telford Lott had introduced him to Lettice Poindexter, who was, he said, extremely interesting—a painter of promise and a person who had struggled to transcend the limitations of her class and education.

Telford Lott not only introduced him to Lettice Poindexter, he presided over the early stages of their acquaintance. For example, when the girl confessed to him that she found the young man not very attractive (she having an inclination to older men and Bradwell Tolliver being, in fact, two years younger than she), Telford Lott reminded her of her duty. Her duty, he said, was clearly to use her influence to canalize his talent in the proper direction and not let it be dispersed in the sands of bourgeois sentimentality.

What Bradwell Tolliver felt for her was, at that period, awe. To begin with, she was, in her high heels, taller than he, not much, just a shade, but enough to do something strange to him, to make him feel incompetent, gauche, angry.

She came from a bracket of society which Telford Lott had not quite accurately described as a world where yachts and polo ponies were as common as Kiddie Kars in the nursery; and though often she might wear old sneakers, a frayed flannel skirt that seemed to be held precariously in place by a safety pin, and a Normandy fisherman's jacket, she always wore a sizable square emerald which, when she let her cheek rest against her hand, brought out stunningly the range of color in her hair, rust to deep auburn, and brought out, too, certain auburn glints in her large dark brown eyes. At calculated intervals she would lay aside the sneakers and old flannel and appear in clothes which, in their severity or flamboyance, it did not matter, indicated some deep self-confidence—or at least, and more impressively, some class confidence—and even to the untutored nose of Bradwell Tolliver, smelled of money, a great deal of money.

He had felt rich in Fiddlersburg. He had not felt poor in prep school in Nashville, or even at Darthurst. Now she made him feel poor, and worse, made him feel ashamed of feeling poor, and then ashamed of being ashamed, for she herself seemed to have no respect for money. She seemed, even, contemptuous of the rich world of her origin, and seemed proud only that she could now move in a world of people of talent, moral devotion, and distinguished reputation. This fact compounded his awe of her in another way, for as she, with Telford Lott, initiated him into that world, he soon began to feel that if the name of any person mentioned was a name he had never heard of, that fact merely emphasized the poverty of his past experience and the hopelessness of his present condition.

Significant as were these objective reasons for his awe of her, they were overshadowed by something not at all objective: by a sense of inner freedom that the girl seemed to possess. She was, for instance, the first woman he had ever heard use as an expletive the vulgar word for excrement, and the word came so naturally, so innocently, that his first shock was quickly absorbed into shame for having reacted with shock. And she referred to her own mother as a bitch— the first person, male or female, he had ever heard who did not bother to make at least some side obeisance, however false and *pro forma,* to the conventional expectation of reverence toward that quarter. Her mother was a bitch, she said simply, and added that she would have to take him to have cocktails with the old girl just so he could see what a bitch she was—"a bitch in heat, forty-six years old, and you sit there and hear her pant. It's enough to make you want to be a nun."

Then she added wryly, as though in recognition of some secret joke: "If you've got it in you."

The remarks about her mother were made in connection with an easy reference to her own psychoanalysis, a refer-

ence which came to Bradwell Tolliver with as much shock as
had her use of the vulgar word for excrement. He knew, he
thought, what psychoanalysis was, but what he knew was
something totally abstract. It was something that happened
to people in Austria or London, usually to Jews. Everybody
knew that Jews like to suffer, anyway. But when that thought
came into his mind he remembered Old Izzie Goldfarb, in
Fiddlersburg, sitting in a split-bottom chair, on an evening in
April, looking out over the swollen, clay-red river toward the
west, and with that image came the thought that Old Izzie
had, somehow, seemed equally beyond suffering and the giving of suffering. For Israel Goldfarb had, in Fiddlersburg,
been himself.

Anyway, if psychoanalysis happened to anybody you
knew, you wouldn't know it anyway, for it was too shameful,
they would never tell. And here this girl was saying it out
loud in a restaurant, where somebody might hear you. He
found himself guiltily stealing a glance over his shoulder to
the nearest table. When he returned his gaze he found her
smiling at him in some amusement.

No, not smiling—grinning; for at times, usually very unexpected times, that was what she had, a grin. It was a grin
not at all to be expected, too, in a girl of such height and
challenge of bearing, mixed with the supple femaleness. It
was anachronistic, the grin of the little girl Lettice Poindexter must have once been long ago at the stage of one front
tooth missing, socks that slid down into grimy saddle shoes
that just wouldn't stay tied, long little shanks that bumped
each other, a covey of inordinate freckles on a round nose
not too well wiped, and hair that, holding no promise of
depth and auburn shimmer, was pure carrot. That was, for
an instant, the kind of grin she now offered, with no malice
or condescension in it, merely the recognition of something
pretty funny.

But he found himself flushing, feeling guilty and caught
out, even before she said, still with amusement and no malice: "Afraid somebody will spot you out with a leper, huh?"

He mumbled something that, even to him, made no
sense.

"Oh, Bradwell," she said, for during a short period she
called him Bradwell, "I swear it wasn't leprosy!"

She laughed, and in the instant of that laughter, when
she tossed her head, and he looked at her across the red-

checked tablecloth of a one-time four-bit basement speak-
easy on Perry Street where the red ink was now legal and im-
ported and inferior to that of the old days, and saw the hair
catch a deep shine from the candle stuck there in a straw-
covered chianti fiasco, he felt himself flushing again. Then
all at once, he saw the laugh stop and the brown eyes, with
pupils suddenly distending a little, as though belladonna had
been applied, stare beyond him at what he knew to be exactly
nothing; and in that moment he had the shadowy flicker of a
vision of her lying on some kind of couch, something white
and surgical about the couch it seemed, with her head moving slightly from side to side as though in pain and the eyes
distended, as now, and staring at exactly nothing.

The vision was, instantly, gone. There was only the tall
girl sitting there across the red-checked tablecloth, staring
beyond him, the slight pucker of the V between her eyes, the
usual fox-brown glint of her eyes dimmed, the candlelight
accentuating the golden glowing tan of her skin (a glow
which, for a redhead, must have required endless care and
expensive leisure), and a small scale of lipstick sticking up
minutely from the now somewhat lax lower lip, like the beginning of a fever blister, a little to the left side, sharply visible, as though under a microscope, in the candlelight. He saw
her, still staring beyond him, tighten the lower lip across the
teeth. He saw her lift the upper lip slightly and draw it back;
bring the even row of upper teeth out to cover the lower lip,
exposing the canines, one of which, he noticed for the first
time, was a little discolored as though from a dead nerve;
and draw the lower lip slowly out, against what seemed to be
the painful pressure of the upper teeth. When the lower lip
was released, he saw that the little flake, or scab, was gone.
The lip had been raked smooth by the sharp even pressure of
those upper teeth, and now, in its provocative laxness,
gleamed bright with saliva.

He looked at her, and felt that, suddenly, he knew her. In
a peculiar way it seemed that she was the only person he had
ever known. In that nakedness of knowing her, as though he
were the one caught naked, he experienced shame, embarrassment, and a somewhat frightening involvement. He felt
involved in whatever dark, warm, deep, coiling, shifting,
viscous thing was implied by the psychoanalysis which she
had avowed. He felt involved by the scale of dried lipstick or
bit of scabrous lip tissue, by the faintly discolored canine, by

the vision of her head on that white couch, rolling slightly from side to side, in that mute and unspecified distress. He felt like getting up and getting out of the ex-speak-easy, quick. Then he felt a strange deliquescence of spirit, frightening but insidiously sweet, then out of that, an abrupt shudder of will, like a great dog leaping from water and shaking off the drops like spray, then an awareness of strength, new and peculiarly calm. The future seemed like a great fruit hanging in darkness, the skin already burst with the pressure of a ripe inward potential.

It had all happened in an instant, the whole thing.

Then she was grinning again, she was saying: "Buck up, Bradwell. It was not leprosy. It was just old-fashioned Q-trouble."

He looked at her, befuddled.

"Q for *quimm*," she said, still grinning in that innocence. Then inspecting his befuddlement, continued. "It is British," she said. "It is British for what little girls have and little boys don't. It is what Lord Rawthorneboop had his hand on," she said, shifting to a fluting, gulping burlesque of English upper-class speech, "at the banquet at Buckingham Palace when he was sitting beside Lady Fidget and she said, 'Oh, do take your hand off it and put it on the table,' and he said, 'Oh, rahly, my dear, I cawn't think that either decent or pratt-icahble.' "

She waited again for an instant, watching him, grinning at him with a more muted amusement.

"That," she said, "is a British joke."

Then she dropped the grin, looked seriously at him, and said, "I don't want to talk about that, about my analysis. What I want to talk about is—"

She did not want to talk about it then. That was to come later, considerably later, in his grubby basement room on MacDougal Street, when, late at night, she would lie by his side in the dark and, in some kind of belated backwash from the analysis, which had been abandoned several years before, tell him what her life had been.

In the dark there, she would offer him her life, all of it, all she knew of it, in a slow, humble way, in a ritual of love and redemption. It was as though she knew that the slightly overlong body which was Lettice Poindexter had no value beyond dreary animal warmth and nervous spasm unless it could be put in a perspective of the past events which had brought it here, to MacDougal Street, and that Bradwell Tolliver, whose breath she could hear in the dark and who would soon embrace that body, must, in the same moment, be led to embrace, and redeem, all the past and in that process create the true, the real, Lettice Poindexter. He had to be led to understand all the confusion and unhappiness of the past as a necessary part of the certitude and happiness which, she told herself, she was about, at last, to discover.

As for Bradwell Tolliver, this progressive unveiling was an aphrodisiac which, more and more, he came to crave. It was, as it were, the most subtle of the several arts of love in which he recognized, secretly, her skill, a skill that put him, with his limited and blundering experience, in further awe.

But there was an awe that compounded this awe: awe at her ability to speak without shame of her life, to move around in her life as though it were a house she inhabited so familiarly she could find anything in the dark. He would lie by her side in the dark, hearing the story unwind, and feel cramped and bound in some dark mystery which was himself, like a box.

Or perhaps, he sometimes thought, it was merely that he, himself, had no story worth telling. Perhaps, even, no story at all. He did not surmise that this fear was what had led him to try to recognize the stories of those who seemed to have no story. He did not realize that as soon as he began to try to create, to enact, a story for Bradwell Tolliver, he would lose that gift, the only one he had, of recognizing the story of someone who had no story.

When, a little later—later, that is, than a certain episode in Central Park, in June, 1937—he went to Spain to fight, he did not recognize that his fear of having no story was one of the motives that impelled him. Or rather, mistily recognizing it, he quickly denied the fact, out of shame.

He did not know that every man yearns for his story.

He did not yet know that the true shame is in yearning for the false, not the true, story.

That afternoon in Central Park came in the rather early stages of Bradwell Tolliver's acquaintance with Lettice Poindexter, shortly after her remark to Telford Lott that she did not find the boy attractive. As for him, it was the period when worry about his inability to work was his dominant emotion. He had been in New York for more than a year, and he had written nothing that he himself liked or that Telford Lott

liked. Telford Lott did not seem disturbed; all the shocks of
present experience and new ideas would be absorbed later,
he said. But Bradwell Tolliver felt like a man bleeding to
death from some inner wound.

All the people around him seemed so confident. Their
pronouncements, on the page of a magazine or coming
through the cigarette smoke over the half-empty glass,
seemed so final. They all, like Lettice Poindexter, had some
inner freedom which he felt could never be his. As she
seemed to move around inside her self, inside her own life,
with that remarkable familiarity, so they all seemed to move
through the darkness of History with the expertness of a blind
man in his own house.

For him History was merely what happened, no matter
how blank the happening. In a kind of grim humor he
thought of himself as one of those muskrat-skinners of long
back, of his great-grandpa's time, who had peered out of the
willows to watch the squat, improbable-looking ironclad gunboats of General Grant puffing and clawing their way southward, up-river, out of nowhere, toward nowhere. Yes, for
him—out of nowhere, toward nowhere—that was History.
But for the people around him now History was a train that
arrived on time, or only a little late. He was in awe of them.

Christ, he would think, *Fiddlersburg.*

But what, that afternoon, Lettice Poindexter was talking
of was not History. It was happiness. At one time, she had
been miserable, she said. She had been leading a life of no
meaning. When she had moved out on her mother and gone
to the Village and begun to work seriously at her painting,
that had done something, she said. But she had still been the
way she was inside. She had still been trapped in the same
way.

"You know," she said, inclining her head to inspect him
better, letting the glossy swatch of auburn hair fall evenly
away from her cheek, in the sunshine, "you can't be happy
if you feel trapped. Now can you?"

Quite soberly she asked him the question. She had to
make him say, no, you couldn't. She had to make him understand. He was so ignorant. His ignorance, she suddenly and
surprisingly felt, was touching.

No, he was saying, he reckoned you couldn't be happy if
you felt trapped.

He was, at that moment, feeling trapped. He was thinking of the old Oliver typewriter on the table in his basement room on MacDougal Street, the table that doubled for eating and for work, with the old cracked plate full of cigarette butts and the glass jug of red wine and *Roget's Thesaurus* beside the typewriter, and on the floor, the wadded-up, discarded sheets of paper. He wanted to be a writer. He wanted it so bad at that moment, his head swam in the sunshine. Being a writer, that was the only way he could see how he could live. He would never be one, he thought, in misery.

But she was talking of happiness.

The painting hadn't been enough, she said. Then she had gone into analysis. You get so miserable you have to do something. Oh, yes, it had helped, some anyway, she got to know why she had been living the way she had. But knowing hadn't made her happy. It hadn't made her act differently, at least not much.

"But psychoanalysis," she said, "it is merely a fancy kind of bourgeois self-indulgence. It is what the bourgeois buys with his money when he discovers there's nothing else he wants that his money can buy. It is a private pleasure of the liberal individualist intellectual, like masturbation. It is—"

She was repeating, with only the most shadowy awareness of echo, the language Telford Lott had used two years before when, during the course of their affair, he had tried to help her out of her unhappiness by showing her how she could attune herself to the fate of mankind and work for human justice. He had succeeded beyond any expectations. He had talked her out of her analysis and, to his astonishment, out of his bed.

He had talked her out of his bed and into happiness. She had found some meaning in her life. She had found, strangely, that she did not need men as before. She had felt herself, sometimes, in a state of tiptoe expectation of something to come. What that was to be, she had not tried to say to herself, but had felt, somehow, that a man's hand upon her would defile that thing to come: that happiness beyond happiness.

"It is like a conversion," she was saying to Bradwell Tolliver, telling him what had happened to her, but making the elipses and deletions that left the whole story teasingly abstract, like the feeling left over from a dream whose details you can't remember.

"Yes, exactly like a conversion," she was saying, as they

moved down the narrow winding path between the high
hedges, at the slow pace of her seriousness.

The seriousness was, if anything, emphasized by the fact
that this was one of the occasions when the sneakers and old
flannel skirt were discarded. She was taking him, this very
afternoon, to see her mother. To see the bitch, who lived over
there on the east side of the Park, in the upper Sixties, and so
she was not wearing the old flannel skirt. She was wearing a
rust-colored linen dress, with a bold skirt and a yellow
leather belt drawn so tight it made the bold skirt even bolder.
She made her serious, small gestures from the wrists, and
the barbaric bangles of the heavy bracelets clinked. She inclined her head to regard him, saying: "Yes, exactly like a
conversion. It happens, and then you—"

At the turn, the path gave, unexpectedly, upon a graveled
enclosure, some forty feet across, into which, on the other
side, a wider track entered. There was fairly heavy growth
around the enclosure. To the right were a couple of benches.
Beyond the benches, there was, predictably, the metal trash
container with the letters NYC-SD. A pigeon was drearily
skirmishing the gravel in front of the benches. The sun was
getting fairly low. Light, falling from the west across the top
of the enclosing growth, glinted on the radiator cap of a car
over there on the left, all that was visible of a car backed
into the bushes.

In a flash, Bradwell Tolliver became aware of every item.

In a flash, too, he became aware that over yonder where
the car was backed into the bushes, the bushes, in one spot,
were not quite high enough, and on each side of that spot, the
taller growth, rising to the overhanging boughs, made a kind
of oval frame in which appeared the head and upper torso of
a woman, a woman with dark bobbed hair, wearing a blue
dress, with short sleeves. Her face was tense, her eyes were
closed, her arms reached out before her as though the un-
seen hands held reins, and her body rose and fell, in a
decorous rhythm, as though posting to an easy trot. The body
was leaning forward a little, as at the first instant of approaching a jump. Over there across the gravel, in the oval
frame of the greenery, the dark bobbed hair tossed gently
with the motion.

Bradwell Tolliver stood absolutely motionless. He heard,
suddenly, what he had not been aware of before, the pervasive, insistent undertone of the traffic swelling from the city,

and now and then above that pervasive context, muted in distance, the irascible and anguished sound of the horns. He
was, suddenly, aware of the light as the light of evening. It
fell across the high roofs and towers. The sunlight falling
across the graveled area seemed smoky.

He was holding his breath. He did not look at Lettice
Poindexter, and he knew that she was not looking at him. He
knew that she was holding her breath. He knew it, for he
knew that he was holding his own breath so that, if she did
breathe, he could hear her breath—and he could not hear it.
He wondered what her face looked like. He thought he would
die if he did not see what her face looked like. But he did not
turn his head.

He heard, then, the slight movement of her foot on the
gravel. He knew she had turned, was moving away. He
waited an instant, and then turned. What he looked at was the
heels of her alligator-skin pumps being set on, and lifted
from, the gravel. Then he overtook her. He walked by her
side, but not close, and as they moved eastward across the
park, did not look at her.

He was sure, however, that now he could hear her
breathe.

Now he lay on a bed in Fiddlersburg and thought that it
was a long way, and a long time, from Fiddlersburg to Central
Park.

He thought: *I am in Fiddlersburg.*

He was lying there staring up at the gray plaster where
the old cracks were, when he heard the knock on the door.

"Come in," he said.

It was Maggie. She was wearing a blue-checked gingham
dress and was bare-legged, in old loafers. "Survived?" she
asked, closed the door, and, smiling, came toward the bed.

He grunted, and as she approached, observed to himself
that she still had nice legs. Not a mark on them either, as far
as he could tell. He wondered how she kept herself in such
good shape.

And what for.

She was by the bed, smiling distantly down at him.

"Get it off your face, Ole Mag, Ole Sis," he said.

"Get what off?"

"That look of loathsome superiority," he said. "That look

that females always get when they see a good man down."

She leaned, picked up the empty cognac bottle from the floor, inspected it judiciously, and set it on a chair on which lay one of the huaraches, a battered pack of cigarettes, and a half dozen butts crushed out against the wood seat. She looked down at him again, still smiling but differently.

"Was it rough?" she asked.

He meditated.

"No," he finally said, "not rough."

He thought again, then added: "Just interesting."

She looked out the window, into the sunshine, out over the river, where, he knew, the land would be stretching away westward as though the land itself were flowing, floating westward with the morning light.

Then he emended: "No, not even interesting."

Studying her as she looked out the window, he said: "Do you find things interesting?"

After a moment, still looking out the window, she said: "I don't really know, dear old Brad."

"Things don't have to be exactly the way they are," he said.

"How do you know?" she demanded. Then without heat, added: "You're just a writer."

"Whatever the hell I am," he said, "things didn't have to get the way they are."

She was looking down at him now with, it almost seemed, compassion.

"Is that something anybody can ever know?" she demanded.

"Well, there is one thing you can know," he said. "They are going to flood this place out and you can be damned sure things are going to be different then."

She looked out the window again. "Maybe some things can't ever be different," she said.

"You aren't so damned old," he said, with added vehemence. "Why do you want it so rough? You weren't built for it this way. Hell, just because I'm your brother doesn't mean I never figured out how you were built. In fact, if you hadn't been built in a certain way, then—"

He stopped. He had expected her to turn from the window. But she did not.

Very evenly, not looking at him, she was saying: "Why don't you go on?"

"I didn't even mean to begin," he said.

And he hadn't. He lay there, with the brandy suddenly tearing his guts out as though he had swallowed a couple of live tomcats, and didn't know how he had ever let that bust out. He didn't even know it had been there to bust out.

His head was swimming, a little.

She was looking down at him, with a kind of gentleness. The expression was so different from anything he might have expected that he knew he was gawking up at her.

"Don't worry, Brother," she said. "I am glad to find I have a brother, after all the years. I had almost forgotten."

She smiled down at him, a very dim smile that seemed to grow out of that expression, then sink again into it.

"You better get up," she said, in a sudden tone of female practicality, and moved toward the door.

She stopped at the door, with her hand on the knob, then turned back to face him, the hand still on the knob, leaning back against the door. "You know," she said, "I guess I never told you how much I appreciated what you did. I mean when you left, what you did then."

"What I didn't do, you mean," he said, and could not fathom his own tone.

"I never thought of it that way," she said. "I thought of it as something not negative. Something positive."

"A negative-positive," he said. "It is like something I read in the newspaper—something new in physics they call anti-matter." He hesitated. "You know," he said, "my hotshot pal Yasha, he started life as a physicist."

She seemed not to have heard. "Do you still have it?" she asked.

"What?" he asked. Then, knowing perfectly well that he did have it, seeing it in his mind in an old coming-apart typing-paper box, in a trunk off in California, now telling his lie and not knowing why he was telling it, he said: "Hell, I don't know whether I've got it or not. I reckon I lost it. Moving around so much."

She looked across at him for a moment. Then she said: "It might be a shame."

"It wouldn't be any use now," he said. "If I saw the thing now I might vomit."

He was surprised at the word he had used. Sure, he halfway felt like vomiting. But not about that.

"What I mean is," he said, "I'd do it so differently now."

"Would it be as—" she began, then stopped.

"Would it be as good?" he demanded. "Is that what you mean? Well, I'll answer for you. It would be a hell of a lot better."

She leaned back against the door, both hands on the knob behind her, and turned her face again toward the window. Then she asked, in a distant voice: "Did you hate me? For having made you do that? Do you hate me now?"

"Maybe I ought to thank you," he said, glumly. Then he smoothed the sheet carefully up to his chin and stared at the ceiling. "Hell, I've done all right," he said. "If I had kept fooling with that I might never have gone to the Coast."

He wished she would get out of the room.

"I'm glad you are here," he heard her say, over there by the door. Then he heard the door close.

The door had scarcely closed when, with no preliminary knock, it opened again and her head popped in. "Get up quick," she ordered. "You said last night you were going to take Mr. Jones to church, and you'll have to hurry."

She closed the door.

Church, Bradwell Tolliver thought.

Yes, he had said he would take Yasha Jones to church in Fiddlersburg. That, he had added to Yasha Jones, would be as good a way as any to begin.

Church, he thought and lay there and did not move. He had not been to church, that church, the only church he thought of as church, since his father died:

It had been night, the night before the funeral, when he got to Fiddlersburg. The light was dim in the hall when he came in, and nobody was there. Standing in the hall, beside the suitcase he had set down, he could smell the flowers in the library. He walked in there. His sister, all alone, was standing in the middle of the floor crying. She had grown a lot, he noticed. She was shaping up.

She was alone in the dim room.

She came to him, took his hand, and led him to the coffin.

"Look," she said, "he's not big any more."

No, Lank Tolliver was not big any more. He was not standing in the middle of the floor with that black hair sprouting out of his head so thick and tough you needed a curry comb, pulling one end of the long black mustaches, glowering. He was not tramping around with cow dung on his boots and with $2,000 in cash in his hip pocket, apt as not to kick the leg off a table or spit on the rug.

"Oh, why did you hate him so?" she asked.

How could he tell her when, now, all of a sudden, he knew that he did not know?

"How can you hate him," she cried again, in pain, "when he's so little now? Oh, look how shrunk he is!"

She flung herself into his arms. He could never remember her doing that before. But, then, he really didn't know her very well, he had been away so much.

But he stood there, in the dim room, with the smell of flowers that, suddenly, reminded him of the smell of baby vomit, and patted her shoulder, and tried to comfort her as best he could.

Yes, she had grown a lot.

He lay on his back, determined to get up in just one more minute to go to church, and remembered that event, long back. Then he thought of how his sister had come in this morning, and he decided that it was just right for a horny old boy with a hangover to notice his sister still had good legs, particularly since he hadn't seen her in near sixteen years. He wondered how much incest it took to make you admire your sister's legs.

Most poetical of subjects, he thought. *That's what Shelley called incest.*

Yep, he thought, and grinned as much as his head would let him, *what's good enough for Shelley is good enough for Bradwell Tolliver and Fiddlersburg.*

Yep, he thought, now he had it, the beautiful moving picture. Middle-aged writer—no, writer approaching middle age—comes back to Fiddlersburg, sees sister, becomes aware that he admires her legs, discovers she is really his mother in disguise, which explains everything. End: view of healing waters rising over Fiddlersburg in the dawn.

No, he thought, in comic sadness, he was afraid Yasha Jones would never buy that one.

He decided he had better make another try to get up and take Yasha to church, and then write the beautiful moving picture.

But before he got up he decided something else, too. He decided that he had better watch that self-pity. It could be worse than booze. He had licked the booze, long back. He had not, he confessed in his famous honesty, licked the other. Well, here was the test case. If he could come back here, to Fiddlersburg, to this house, and lick it, it was licked.

He lay there and thought: *If I don't make this picture right, I am a failure. I am a failure, and good.*

This thought was new. He had never had it before. But he felt, suddenly, that the thought had been there a long time, solid and objective like a rock or a post, and his face had been averted from it. But now he was looking at it. The thing he was looking at was cold and glittering like ice.

He shook, thinking: *I don't want to be a failure. Or do I?*

So he got up.

Chapter

7

THEY HAD BEEN SITTING at the outer end of a pew, and so, when the sermon was over, Brad could easily draw Yasha Jones to one side to wait. Light fell through the colors of the stained glass beyond the altar. Through the windows ajar on the side aisle came the sweetness of blossom, of bruised grass, of river mud.

Waiting, watching the congregation drift out the door, Yasha Jones murmured:

"And I will plant them upon their land, and they shall no more be pulled up out of their land which I have given them, saith the Lord thy God."

He stood there wearing that rumpled gray suit, and watched the people. He himself might have been the preacher, Bradwell Tolliver thought. No, there was the soft collar. But something more. It was the way Yasha Jones could stand there as though he weren't there. He had that trick of quietness, of letting the world flow beneath his eye.

"Didn't he say it was Chapter Nine?" Yasha Jones suddenly asked. "*Amos* Nine?"

"I reckon," Brad Tolliver said.

The congregation was thinning out, passing through the door one by one, each shaking hands with the preacher.

"Well, you've seen it," Brad Tolliver said. "You have seen Fiddlersburg at prayer. At least you have seen all the Baptists, which is all there is. White Baptists, that is. Used to be Presbyterians, Campbellites, and Methodists to boot, but they couldn't stay the course in Fiddlersburg. The Methodists hung on longest. But my old man, he helped 'em on their way. Had a mortgage on the Methodist Church, and when it got rough in the Depression they just walked out and joined the Baptists or took up serious drinking and let my old man have the real estate. I suppose Fiddlersburg piously opined that God-a-Mighty struck down my old man with an oversize blood clot as vengeance for having foreclosed on a church.

"No, on second thought, I don't reckon any Baptists ever took that view. No, the Baptists would hold that my old man was an instrument in the hand of the Most High to strike down Methodism to the dust. Yep, that is more—"

The preacher was waiting now. He was a tall, thin, dried-out man, in worn blue serge and a stiff collar, going sandily bald, his face distorted by chronic pain or preoccupation, and pale blue eyes blinking rapidly at you as though your brightness were a little to much to behold. His left sleeve was empty, pinned to the coat.

"Brother Potts," Bradwell Tolliver said, and put out his hand, "I'm—"

"Yes, sir," Brother Potts interrupted, "we all know who you are. Everybody in Fiddlersburg is glad a Fiddlersburg boy has been heard from. And"—he turned toward Yasha Jones—"this gentleman, the big moving-picture director. I'm proud, Mr. Jones, to greet you here in the House of the Lord."

"You are kind," Yasha Jones said. Then added: "I enjoyed your sermon. Amos is a rather neglected prophet. He gave you a very poignant text today."

As Yasha Jones spoke, the head of the preacher twitched ever so little, in the rhythm of the words. In that painful absorption, with his sharp nose coming forward at each little jerk, he was like a scrawny chicken pecking at grain, every precious grain as it fell before him.

"This must be a very poignant time," Yasha Jones was saying.

"Oh yes, yes sir," Brother Potts said, and a gleam of gratitude came into his blue eyes. "Oh yes it is, Mr. Jones. It's a time when people are stirred up inside and don't know why. Most of them have been here all their lives. Now they got to move, and they are stirred up. Even if they're going to be relocated, better maybe, at government expense. That text from Amos now—"

"Yes," Yasha Jones said, "about relocation, too."

"Yes, relocation. It is their life these folks are being jerked out of, but if I can only make 'em see how the Gospel of Christ is about relocation. It is jerking a man out of one life and relocating him in the life of the spirit. I mean if I can get their stirred-up feelings sort of tied up with the Promise—"

He was looking into the face of Yasha Jones with a humble pleading in his eyes.

"It is a very precise and moving comparison," Yasha Jones said.

"You know when a place dies, even just an old house gets torn down, it is like a lot of living goes with it. Some folks are hopeless now, some feel happy and sort of crazy with an excitement they got hidden in themselves like they could be young again, or get rich. But you know the hardest to deal with though? It is the ones bitter in the heart. They feel all their living was somehow for nothing. But we have got to remember, the life we had was the life God wanted us to have. Now take me. If when I was twenty-five you'd told me I'd spend my life in Fiddlersburg—"

They drifted out into the sunshine, and the pained, blue eyes of Brother Potts blinked. Somewhere, far off in some house, a baby was crying. Brother Potts stood close to Yasha Jones. He seemed to have to stand close to him.

"I never even heard of Fiddlersburg," Brother Potts said softly, as though confiding a shameful secret. Then he began

again: "I was a city man. Memphis. My father had a good insurance business. I started with him. I could sell. I could sell
insurance. I could make a man feel how something might
happen and I wanted to help him."

He paused, thinking.

"Maybe I did want to help him," he said, "and didn't
know it myself. Maybe that was why I could sell. Then—"

He paused again.

"—then it was the Depression. My father—he got mixed
up with money. You know, that wasn't his. So he went
away. I mean, they put him away. He had insured a lot of
people against a lot of things, but I laid awake nights thinking how a man can't insure himself against himself. Then,
one night, another thought came into my head. How you
can't insure against God. He is looking at you in the dark.
The next thing I knew I was on my knees.

"Next thing I knew," he said, "I was a preacher.

"Next thing," he said, "I was in Fiddlersburg."

He waited a moment, rummaging into himself. "Next
thing," he said, "there won't be any Fiddlersburg."

An automobile went by. Its sound died away into the
hush of Sunday noon in Fiddlersburg, in spring. Then the
baby, far off, wailed again.

"More'n twenty-five years here," Brother Potts said, "and
it is gone in a twinkling."

He fell into silence.

Then he turned toward Yasha Jones: "You know what I
look forward to?"

Yasha Jones shook his head.

"Well, I'll tell you. A last big service, when we all get
together. When we can all pray to know that the lives we
lived are blessèd."

"That," Bradwell Tolliver said, "is a big order."

But Brother Potts was exploring, inventorially, his pockets. Finally, he produced a piece of paper, worn and crumpled. He studied it as though he did not recognize it. Then he
said: "I am not a poetry-writing man. But I thought if I could
just get down what a man can feel. And Miss Prattfield might
do the music. A hymn for Fiddlersburg. For the last service."

He stood there on the square patch of concrete, held the
paper between thumb and forefinger, and blinked off into the
distance.

"Will you read it?" Yasha Jones asked.

The eyes found the paper, the washed-out blue of the eyes darkening with a sudden intensity. The voice began:

> "When I see the town I love
>   Sinking down beneath the wave
> I pray I'll remember then
>   All the blessings that God gave.

> "When I see the life I led
>   Whelmed and drowned beneath the flood—"

He lifted his eyes. "That's as far as I've made it," he said. He frowned dismally at the paper. "I'm stuck," he said. "I know how I feel, but the words, they won't come."

"I'm sure they will come," Yasha Jones said.

"I been struggling and praying," Brother Potts said, and sank into himself.

Then he looked up, his face twisted more than before in the chronic pain or preoccupation. "You know," he said, "maybe the words won't come till you got the right feeling."

He leaned, or seemed to lean, a little closer to Yasha Jones.

"Mr. Jones," he said, "what do you think?"

"You have touched one of the deepest questions," Yasha Jones said, "so I don't know the answer." He paused, then looked directly into the man's twisted face. "But I know one thing," he said.

"What's that, Mr. Jones?"

"I know that you have the feeling," Yasha Jones said. "And I am glad you read us the poem."

"You know," Brad said, "I'm afraid we're keeping Brother Potts from his dinner."

"Oh, no," Brother Potts hastily declared. "I'm—"

"I know we are," Brad said, and put out his hand.

Brother Potts shook it, then turned to find himself confronted by the hand of Yasha Jones. "It has been a pleasure," Yasha Jones said.

Brother Potts shook the hand. He seemed unable to let it go. "Do you mind—" he finally managed, then stopped.

"If when it's done," he tried again, "I mean the poem—you know, not many folks around here go in for poetry, and if you'd spare a minute—"

"Dr. Potts," Yasha Jones began.

"Oh, it's plain Brother Potts—" Brother Potts said.

"Brother Potts," Yasha Jones said, "I happily expect to see the final version."

Moving across the road toward the higher ground where the cemetery was, Brad looked back once. Brother Potts was still standing on the little patch of concrete in front of the red brick structure.

"No place to go," Brad said. "Nobody invited him to the big Sunday dinner today. And his wife, she is dead. Dead a long time. He is standing there trying to decide whether to go down to the You'll Never Regret It Café and blow himself to the Sunday Special or to go home and open himself a can of pork and beans."

Yasha Jones turned to look back.

"I give odds on the beans," Brad said. "The shades will be drawn in the kitchen. He won't take the trouble to raise them. He will be afraid something will happen if he raises them. He doesn't know what, but something. He will get the can out of the safe."

He paused.

"Say," he said, "do you know what a kitchen safe is? In Fiddlersburg?"

"No," Yasha Jones said.

"It is a kind of tall, shallow cabinet with doors of tin panels perforated in some design, geometrical or floral. Brother Potts will get the can of beans from the safe. He will get a saucepan off a nail and a can opener out of a drawer. He will open the can. It is very difficult for a one-armed man to open a can of beans, but he has worked out a system. Shall I pause to explore it?"

"No," Yasha Jones said. "Continue."

"He will stand in those shadowy precincts and hold the open can in his right hand—his only hand. Then something will come over him. He sees the saucepan. He sees the coal-oil stove. He sees the tin matchholder on the wall. But all at once he will drop a stitch. He will, suddenly, fail to understand why it is the fate of a man to stand alone in a nigh-dark kitchen at one-thirty on a Sunday afternoon in passionate April and pour out cold beans from a can and heat them and put them into his mouth and swallow them. Standing there, he will find, all at once, that he has lost touch with God's Great Plan."

After a moment, Yasha Jones asked: "And then?"

"He eats the beans. But he eats them cold, directly from the can, using two fingers to scoop them out. How does he hold the can? Under the nub of his left arm, naturally. Thus he finishes the can. Then he licks his fingers. He wipes the juice off his chin with his fingers, then licks them all again. His jaw hangs a little slack now. He peers all around in the dusk of the kitchen, with a kind of heavy, bestial cunning. His eyes gleam in the shadow. He gives a great, slow, rumbling, deliberately uncontrolled fart. No, correct to *belch*. Do you see him standing there?"

"Yes," Yasha Jones said.

"He stands there and takes a grim delight in what he has done. Nobody sees him. Nobody hears him. Nobody cares. He is alone. In his aloneness he feels, suddenly, mysteriously, strong. He feels heavy, dangerous, merciless, like a beast. He feels, all at once, free. 'I am alone,' he says out loud, relishing the utterance, rolling his tongue on it, grinding his jaws on it like a great bone the beast still worries after the glut. He wipes his tongue on his lips to get the last of the coagulated bean juice."

They were now drifting through the cemetery, very slowly, toward the old part.

"Yes," Yasha Jones said, after a moment. "He is standing there in the dark kitchen, in his glut." And after a moment he asked, softly: "And then?"

"Don't you know?"

"Thus far," Yasha Jones said, "I know that the story is, *mutatis mutandis*, the story of us all."

"I bet you never ate cold pork and beans, out of a can, in a dark kitchen."

"I said *mutatis mutandis*," Yasha Jones said. "I am an insomniac."

"Well, *mutatis mutandis*," Brad demanded, "what do you do in such a moment of vision?"

"Something very conventional, I fear. I turn on the light and read poetry. But what does Brother Potts do, in the dark kitchen?"

Brad Tolliver looked at his watch. "He hasn't quite had time to make it home and into the kitchen, much less to the crisis. But let us assume that he has reached the stage of glut, belch, and grim, leonine freedom."

"Then?"

"He bursts into tears. He falls to his knees in the middle of the dark kitchen and prays. He presses his forehead against the edge of the seat of a split-bottom chair and works at the business of prayer. He does not know what will happen if he doesn't manage to swing it. So he works hard to rouse God from His lethargy."

Brad interrupted himself to look again at his watch.

"About two-forty, shall we say, he will make it. Word comes through from On High. Brother Potts rises, and goes to wash his face in cold water. In the bathroom mirror he notices red welts, now turning a little blue, where he had pressed his forehead down against the hickory splits in the chair bottom. He is worried that the marks will not go away by seven P.M., when he has to go to the meeting of the BYPU and—"

"Please?"

"Baptists' Young People's Union," Brad said. "He can't turn up with his forehead black and blue. He thinks he will tape a bandage on it. He will say that he had run into a door. But now he worries about the lie. But he has to tell a lie. If he said he got that punishment praying, they will think he is lying. Or if they believe him, they'll think he is putting on airs. They will convict him of the sin of spiritual pride for trying to beat his brains out praying. Oh, hell—"

Brad Tolliver stopped.

"Hell," he repeated, "let's leave the pore ole booger alone."

They had now reached the edge of the older part of the cemetery, weedy, abandoned. Brad kicked at a fallen tombstone, then looked over the river.

"You rather like Brother Potts," Yasha Jones said, inspecting him. Then: "Don't you?"

"I don't know whether I like him or not," the other said. "He exists. He is Fiddlersburg. That is enough for me."

He leaned to inspect another tombstone, kicking the weeds. He shook his head. Then he looked at another.

He caught the gaze his companion had turned upon him.

"Yes," he said, "I'm hunting something. I am hunting the stone of Old Izzie Goldfarb. He was the little Jewish tailor—the only Jew in Fiddlersburg, live one I mean, when I was a boy. He taught me to play chess and never let me win. He would look at a sunset or a man or a dog in the same way, a way that made the thing seem real. He was not of Fiddlersburg, but he made Fiddlersburg real. It was his being in Fiddlersburg made me know what Fiddlersburg is."

"What is it?" Yasha Jones asked.

"Damned if I know. But if I had the wings of an angel and were flying higher than flying saucers and space ships, I could look down and smell it and come coasting home straight as a buzzard heading down to dine on a dead horse."

He investigated another stone.

"He left me his chessmen," he said irrelevantly. "There was a letter pinned on the wall in the hole where he slept, must have been pinned there a long time, saying give Master Bradwell Tolliver the chessmen. That *Master*—that dated it back a long time. For by the time he died I was in college, up in Darthurst. No wonder the ink had faded."

The stone he was inspecting did not have the name of Goldfarb on it.

"When I was a kid," Brad said, "he gave me all-day suckers."

"Yes, I know the story," Yasha Jones said, "the title story."

"Hell," Brad said, "I forgot that was in the story."

Then he was looking backward toward the road, some fifty yards off, peering into the sunlight.

"There she goes," he said, "just as though all were bright as day." He turned to Yasha Jones. "Did you see her in church?" he asked.

"Who?"

"Leontine Purtle. Blind from birth. Her pregnant ma got sick, and they rushed her to Memphis and the car hit a truck, and the papoose bounced out ahead of time and got put in an incubator, and in an excess of humanitarian enthusiasm, some nurse gave the papoose too much oxygen. Result, can't see. They call it *retrolental fibroplasia*. Blind as a bat, but you don't know it at first. You can't even tell looking at her straight in the eyes. It is just as though she were not blind but staring right into you. It is as though she

is the one has got your number. It is as though she is the
only one that ever looked straight into you. Me now—I went
to the Purtle house last week—hunting one of the dam engineers that boards there—and I saw her for the first time
since she was a kid. I didn't recognize her she'd changed so
much. Man, I'm telling you she is built. You know how blind
women sort of hang dry goods on themselves, not knowing
or caring. Well, even through the blind-folks dry goods you
can tell about Leontine Purtle. She is evermore stacked up."

He watched the woman moving up the road, through
sunlight.

"Got a face on her, too," he said. "Pale, pure and noble.
Slightly touched by the refinement of suffering. Lady of
Shalott sleepwalking and in need of a decent hair-do. Got
lots of pale blond hair—corn color you'd say in a lyric mood.
Sort of heaped on her head like a hay rick, but with some of
it slipping down wistfully over one cheek. There is, I fear, a
faint intimation that a man might like to let down the whole
pile and run his fingers through it."

The woman was farther off, moving steadily. She was a
complex spot of light and shade moving through the glare.
Some sort of white blouse, some sort of dark skirt, the pale
hair, a black umbrella held like a parasol—all was reduced,
in glare and distance, to the stippling of light and shade.

"She can walk all over Fiddlersburg," Brad said.

For a moment he stared after the withdrawing figure.

"You know," he said, "there is no way to relocate Leontine Purtle. Unless for her relocation you totally reconstruct
Fiddlersburg—every hump in the road, every sagged gate-
post, every cocklebur patch and pig wallow, every flake of
rust on the iron posts that hold up that corrugated metal
awning in front of Perkins Dry Goods and the P.O."

He morosely leaned over to scrape back a tangle of
weeds and love vine from a stone. It was not the right stone.
He straightened up.

"Yeah," he said, "as one who knows. I bemoan the fate
of Leontine Purtle. Her hand, in darkness, shall seek what
is not to be found. Her foot shall be set on a stone that
speaks not. The air shall be a heaviness unto her lungs and
the dawn bird in the rose arbor utter a note of no comfort."

He turned suddenly on Yasha Jones, glaring at him.

"You know how I know?" he demanded.

"No."

"Well, I'll tell you, Yasha my boy," he said. "I know because I, too, have been relocated."

Yasha Jones regarded him for a moment. "I didn't know you loved Fiddlersburg so much as all that," he said.

"I don't," Brad said. "It is not that I love it. It may be that I do not even like it. But, you know one thing?"

"What?"

"The only thing more traumatic than being removed from that which you love is to be removed from that which you hate."

He burst into whoops of laughter.

Yasha Jones, in underwear shorts, boxer style, and a russet and black Japanese robe of coarse silk, with the belt loosely knotted at the waist, his shoulders and tall bald head well propped on bolsters and pillows, lay in the middle of a big tester bed, and stared down the length of his body, over a well-stuffed manila filing folder which lay closed across his lap, over his naked upward-pointing toes, over the end of the bed and across the big, bare room and out the window, westward. He stared into the light, across the river, over the far fields. The sun was striking into the room now, between the loops of somewhat bedraggled and, no doubt, heavily mended lace curtains that had been drawn back on both sides. It must, he thought, be getting on to five o'clock.

He shut his eyes and thought of Fiddlersburg. He thought of River Street, the length of which, and back, he and Brad had walked after leaving the cemetery. He saw, in the inner clarity of his head, the street where, in the Sunday hush, nothing moved. He saw the three blocks of buildings, the corrugated iron awning over the sidewalk in front of Perkins Dry Goods and the P.O. He saw the objects in the windows of stores, where objects were minimally displayed, and thought that now, when an object was removed, it would never be replaced. He saw the store windows in which no objects were displayed, where dust gathered on disintegrating cards that announced, in big uncareful letters, a sale, a liquidation, a church social, a picnic, a high school basketball game.

"Hell," Brad Tolliver had said to him, "some of these stores haven't been occupied since 1930. Look, half those signs are flaking to pieces, not just the paint flaking off but the damned cardboard itself. They date back, some of 'em,

before Pearl Harbor." He stared at a big card announcing
a basketball game. "Yeah," he said, "one of the local boys
got killed at Pearl Harbor. He was one pretty basketball
player."

Brad had paused again.

"Went up to Kentucky State," he had resumed. "Made
national headlines. Got into some kind of trouble and joined
the Navy. One raw-headed son-of-a-bitch, his own mother
would confess, but when the Japs got him, they got one
sweet ball-handler."

Yasha Jones shut his eyes and again saw the sign from
which the paint fell away. You could barely make out the
big scrawled lettering:

BASKETBALL!

Tuesday Night

GAME CALLED 8

SHARP!

RAH! TEAM!

GO IT BUTCH—OUR BOY IS BUTCH!

Now in the strange light in the head of Yasha Jones,
the sign hung there and the paint flaked from it, and the
very process of flaking was visible in that timeless light in
his head, and Yasha Jones had the faint apprehension that
tears might come into his eyes.

He got up and walked around the room, his feet bare.
Then he came back, propped himself again, and again, very
deliberately, closed his eyes, and stared down the length of
River Street. He saw it, in that light in his head, in the
blankness of Sunday afternoon. He saw a black and white,
hairy dog cross the sunlight toward shade. He saw the big
sign identifying the You'll Never Regret It Café and the spot
where an interpolation had obviously, and without total success, been painted out—the Halloween addition: *But Once.*
He saw the ruin of the old steamboat landing, the stone ramp
now nothing but weed-possessed rubble, sinking into alluvial
deposit. He saw the river sliding gravidly past, heavy-bellied
with silt. He saw the sunlight golden on the new willows
across the river. He saw, on a block of granite, on a little

rise of ground in front of the P.O., overhanging the river, the Confederate soldier, in bronze, staring northward, downstream, the way the gunboats, long ago, had come.

That was the image of River Street in the head of Yasha Jones. On his lap lay the folder in which were the people who, day in and day out, walked down River Street, or had once walked there. He opened the folder. He fingered the sheets, reading at random what, lying there, he had already read.

. . . when he closes store in the afternoon, always gets wife and goes to cemetery. Only child, boating accident 25 years ago. Pray and leave flowers. Not known to miss since week after funeral. Wife raises flowers in kitchen to have something to carry in winter. Once in snowstorm. Sends ½ profit of store to orphanage. Tried once to give home to orphan, but boy probably delinquent to begin with and spoiled by them, robbed till and ran away. Afraid to try again. "Not God's will."

PS: Have to keep store open late on Saturdays. He and wife cemetery near midnight. Used to be oil lantern, now flashlight.

SYLVESTER PURTLE:

Sheriff 20 years. Noted for fairness. Once tried to save Negro from mob, and got beat up. Soon as on feet again went and arrested the one man he had identified. Man acquitted, but Purtle got re-elected on published statement in Fiddlersburg *Clarion* that Sylvester Purtle would arrest any man without fear or favor or die trying. Ways of electorate of Fiddlersburg inscrutable. Later, time of big prison break, two cons holed up in Lorton's Hardware, plenty of ammunition and guns there, bad hombres, lifers, going to shoot it out. Prison guards timid on $30 a month. Purtle went in by himself. Got a slug in shoulder but stayed on feet, killed one, took one. Arthritis now. Wheel chair on porch, weather permitting. Boys come by to make him talk (but less and less). Old Mr. Darling plays checkers with him. He can see down road to the false front on Lorton's Hardware. He can remind himself. Relocation?

(Note: Wife dead, daughter blind, son killed in Korea,

takes in boarders. One engineer from dam, one school-teacher. Old woman, cousin or something, runs joint.)

CYRUS HIGHBRIDGE, MATILDA HIGHBRIDGE

In their fifties, married 30 years or more. Perennial lovers of Fiddlersburg. No kids. Great for picnics together, nutting and pawpaw expeditions, fishing, walks after supper, holding hands, along river, or up Ben's Bluff for view. Once in gloaming detected in porch swing behind screen of moon vine, she curled on his lap. But climax some five years back. Fiftyish, old for Fiddlersburg, except for the extra curricular, which is not readily available except in assorted colors, and that not what it used to be. Climax when two kids squirrel hunting surprised Cyrus and Matilda, 4:30 of an October afternoon, in a golden dell, *in flagrante* on the golden leaves of autumn. Strange effects of news on Fiddlersburg. Emotional repercussions. Moral reprehension, envy, emulation. One divorce, one separation, one adultery, and two high school elopements directly traceable. One couple, old enough for hanging up the sword and shield, produced twins. Cyrus and Matilda still walk hand-in-hand. Fiddlersburg is watching. But Fiddlersburg doesn't quite know whether or not it wants to catch them. For Fiddlersburg, like all of us, finds true love an unsettling spectacle. Kids stalk Cyrus and Matilda in the gloaming.

Cyrus runs garage and filling station. Very careful about getting grease and grime off hands. Washes up and changes clothes before going home. Has habit of . . .

MORRIS TATUM

Son of local drunkard and no-good, killed by falling off wagon, loaded with lumber, and being slowly run over, too drunk presumably to crawl out of way. Son bright, studied at school, supported self, tried to be genteel, eschewed fun and rough company, got job as clerk in Perkins Dry Goods, now owns share, poor bastard. Married old maid, Jane Fiddler, older than he, as a mark of respectability: "my wife—you know, Jane Fiddler—etc." Poor bastard. What happens if relocated where nobody knows or cares if the horror he is tied to is last

surviving female blood-Fiddler? Secret dream to change
his own name to Fiddler.

MRS. SIBYL PARRIS

Wife of druggist. Once a looker. Now a burning, bug-
eyed, anguish-eyed wreck, but eyes can be beautiful
even with hot anguish. Twenty-year affair with local
dentist, Dr. Tucker, because he would give her dope
after hubby had cut off the supply. Tucker got hooked
by her because he had nothing at home except moral
rectitude, bad cookery, and four ugly daughters with
buck teeth like a lemming, poor advertisement for a
dentist. But Doc Tucker wants out from Sibyl from long
time back. She wears him down. But she can black-
mail him on dope. Would too. Medea type in Fiddlersburg. Has Doc Tucker started on dope too? Not many
patients any more. Long afternoons in office. Sibyl has
to have a lot of dental work. Big bills for hubby. What
does hubby think of relocating? Tucker wants to relocate far, far away, but maybe the druggist says to
Tucker that he's gonna relocate wherever Tucker does
—"you bought in and you're gonna stay in." Druggist
doesn't want Sibyl around his neck, and dental bills are
cheaper than dope. And less risky.

Fiddlersburg is laying bets. Or perhaps . . .

ABBOTT SPRIGG

Made small start on stage in New York, off-Broadway.
Suddenly back home, 5 years ago. Now counterman in
You'll Never Regret It Café which his father owns.
Dyes hair. Getting belly; beer and starchy foods. Takes
NY *Times*, Sunday, for the theater news. He is . . .

BLANDING COTTSHILL

Kin on my mother's (i.e., Confederate-commission) side.
Well-off, maybe rich, 1,000 acres bottom land plus
sound investment sense. Lawyer, Washington and Lee
University, Yale. Great hunter and murderer of ducks
and quail. Best wing-shot in section. Likes company of
swamp rats and the colored as well as senators and retired colonels. Also likes dark meat—or, to be more ac-
curate, the high-yellow meat. Keeps one out on his
1,000 acres, a looker by all accounts. Law practice a

sort of joke now—scrabble farmers and colored folks.
CF. *TRIAL.*

LEON PINCKNEY

Negro preacher. Only person now in Fiddlersburg who
has ever finished college—except a couple of guys in
the pen. (Me never having finished, and Blanding Cottshill not properly of town.) Howard University and Harvard—very intelligent, tactful with white folks, devoted
to good of flock—sick, hungry, bereaved, jailed, condemned. Gives goods to poor—Jesus what goods he's
got to give! Held up by the mealy-mouthed as example
of what "a nigger can do if he really tries to take religion serious and do like a white man," etc. But Fiddlersburg now in confusion about Leon Pinckney. Report that Potts went to see him about a big general
outdoor prayer session for the last day before evacua-
tion, after the blacks and whites had held services in
their own churches, etc. Reported that Pinckney said:
"Yes, if you think we all pray to the same God and for
the same thing." To which Potts said: "Brother Pinckney, let's us now fall on our knees and pray together
that God teach us wisdom and mercy." To which Pinckney replied: "Let us fall on our knees and pray together
that God teach us wisdom and mercy and justice." Report that Potts didn't say a word, just fell to his knees
and lifted up his hand. (Does left nub twitch to go up
too to clasp in prayer?) Leon Pinckney sank down, and
said the words. Then Potts said them too. Witnessed by
several. For scene on front porch of LP's shack, Potts in
for some criticism.

Then, scribbled freshly on the edge of the sheet, Yasha
Jones saw:

QUERY: reason nobody invited Potts to dinner today?
QUERY: how did Potts lose his left arm? When? Had it
twenty years back when I used to see him on the
street.

At the bottom of the sheet, neatly typed:

NB: See GENERAL: NEGRO—queries.

Then, again freshly scribbled:

Any merit in bringing guy in trick pants from Seven
Dwarfs Motel to Fiddlersburg? Could be new motel
under construction for sporting and tourist trade, etc.
Drop him into strange world of Fiddlersburg.

Yasha Jones turned another sheet. It was almost blank.
It read:

LANCASTER TOLLIVER—"LANK"
My father.

Nothing more.

He closed the folder and let it lie on his lap. He stared
out the window, over the river and the land stretching away.
"Fiddlersburg," he said out loud.

Then he closed his eyes.

What he saw now, however, was not the street of Fiddlersburg. It was a rich, dim, enormous room full of tapestry,
gilt, and mirrors. His own father was coming into that rich
room, tall, thin, black-bearded, clad in black and gleaming
linen, saying, "I am dining with you tonight. I have instructed François to order dinner sent up."

And that room faded into another room, and another,
and another, and always a window gave grandly on something—on the sun-glitter of blue sea, the gleam of snow on a
noble massif, the sweep of a Scotch moor, the roofs of Chicago. The rooms were all different, but they were all the
same, and his father was saying: "I shall dine with you
tonight."

Or saying: "Mr. Jarvis reports you inattentive to Latin."

Or saying: "We leave tomorrow."

Yasha Jones opened his eyes.

"Fiddlersburg," he again said, out loud.

He lay there and wondered what it would be like to have
walked down River Street every day of your life, watching
the seasons swing over, noting the changes on each face, in
time. Feeling your own face change, day by day, in Fiddlersburg.

There was a knock on the door.

.   .   .

"Come in," he said.

Before he could sit up, the door opened. For an instant, most disconcertingly, no one appeared, then there was Maggie Tolliver Fiddler, one foot pushing the door farther open, hands holding a tray on which was a glass pitcher and a plate of something.

"Hello," she said. "Hope I'm not disturbing work."

"Not at all, not at all," he said, smiling. "Merely, I'm not very decent."

He had managed to sit up, get the robe around him, slip off the bed. He stood there in bare feet, feeling rather defenseless.

"It's a very pretty robe," she said, eyeing him with unabashed candor.

"Rather," he said. Then to his astonishment heard himself saying: "But not exactly what I'd pick out. A gift."

He felt even more defenseless, for the lame, irrelevant, mysteriously extorted explanation.

Somewhere, deep in his being, he knew that something was saying: *I don't want to explain anything. I don't want to explain myself. If I do not try to explain I can at least endure to the end.*

He had heard that secret voice before.

But the voice of Maggie Tolliver Fiddler, as she looked at him, at the robe, over the tray and pitcher, and smiled, with the slightest trace of female slyness and impertinence, was saying: "Oh!"

He was aware of how naked his feet felt on the floor. He wondered if he was flushing. Anyway, he thought, he was too tanned for it to matter much.

She was saying, with that smile still on her oval, rather olive-colored face: "Well, somebody had good judgment. It's becoming."

She studied him critically. "I don't know where it came from," she said, "but it makes you look like pictures in the Old Testament. Egyptian, you know—like Pharaoh, or something."

"Just dug up," he said.

"No, just waked up," she said.

"Cruel libel," he said. "I was working."

She looked at the folder on the bed.

"Oh, yes," she said. "Brad's little job on Fiddlersburg."

She paused, then suddenly thrust out the tray.

"Lemonade," she said, "and some sugar cookies. To hold you till supper. Dinner, I guess. Seven o'clock. But if you want a drink—"

She had made her way to the door, leaving the tray on the foot of the bed.

"By the way," she said, "Mother Fiddler promises to come down with us tonight."

"I am delighted," he said, and then was about to thank her, but the door had closed.

He drank a glass of lemonade and ate two cookies, tasting nothing, wandering on his bare feet about the room, then standing at the window, looking over the river. He came back and lay on the bed.

He shut his eyes, and saw River Street. The river slid heavily, glossily past. That strange light inside his head fell bright across River Street, and nothing moved there.

He thought: *This may be it.*

Because he knew nothing of it, it could float before his eyes in its ultimate meaning. He suddenly hated all the things he had done, the things that had made him great.

Yes, this may be it.

He thought how waters would rise and people come to know that the life that they had lived was blessèd.

After a while he got off the bed, went to the basin in the corner of the room, an arrangement which reminded him of a provincial hotel in France, ran hot water, and shaved his head. He then rubbed the lotion into the skin.

Chapter

8

IN THE GARDEN ABOVE THE RIVER, Maggie Fiddler, as the evening before, leaned to hand him coffee, this time not asking, he noticed, how many lumps of sugar. He took the first sip, then said: "I'm sorry Mrs. Fiddler couldn't come down tonight."

He noticed that, before answering, Maggie Fiddler's glance turned, for the fraction of a second, toward the house. There was no light in any upper part.

"I'm sorry, too," she said. Then by way of explanation: "She needs something to interest her."

"She *has* something to interest her," Brad Tolliver said, to no one in particular, into his coffee.

The woman, Yasha Jones noticed, turned her eyes on her

brother, giving him a straight, full look, which Yasha Jones could not interpret and which her brother ignored.

Then, very calmly, she said: "Yes, Brad, she has an interest. I mean, she needs some additional interest."

"I'm sorry," Brad said. "Sorry I brought it up."

But she had turned back to Yasha Jones and in the even tone resumed: "She does watch TV. But that isn't enough. I don't even know how much she gets out of it. She never says a thing. Only that some actor or actress reminds her of somebody—always somebody long dead. Somebody I never heard of."

She took a sip of coffee.

"You see," she said, "Mother Fiddler only came here when she married Dr. Fiddler. From New Orleans. Well-off people. I've seen the old photographs—a young lady in Saint Mark's Square—that's Venice, isn't it?"

"Yes," Yasha Jones said, "Venice."

"Anyway, there were pigeons. And Egypt. On a camel. A young lady done up in veils, on a camel, and a pyramid behind. Now and then she looks at the pictures herself. She stares in a quiet puzzled way. Oh, once—just once she—"

She stopped.

"Yes?" after a moment Yasha Jones asked.

"It was a picture of some park in Berlin. Nobody in it, just the park. But she brightened up, and for a second she looked almost like a girl. Then she said that she had seen the Kaiser there, on his horse, and he had bowed. For just that split second, you had the crazy feeling that time had got all mixed up, she looked so young, blushing and her eyes bright."

She looked out over the river. Where the moonlight did not strike, the water looked blacker than ever. She turned her face back toward him.

"Poor old thing," she said. "It's sort of pitiful. After all the things that happen to people, the good things and the bad things, it makes you feel like crying, doesn't it, to think how that is what can make a person brighten up for a second, just because that old idiotic murdering Kaiser, with his funny mustache and crippled arm, bowed to you in the park when you were young?"

"If he did," Brad Tolliver said.

"I hope he did," she said.

"But I have observed," Brad said, "that all Southern ladies of a certain station, aspiration, or economic status have a similar anecdote. Sometimes they distinctly remember being kissed in the cradle by Robert E. Lee. Sometimes they remember being goosed on the stairs after dinner by the aging Jefferson Davis. Time has no meaning in the realm of vision. But Mother Fiddler's anecdote, let us grant, does not violate chronological possibility. She is old enough. We have the picture. We have seen the hole where the Devil came out. Ergo—"

"Oh, let her have it!" Maggie Tolliver cried out. "Let her have the old fool Kaiser bowing to her. Oh, Brad, hush, or I swear I'll cry."

She tossed her head. Her eyes did, in the moonlight, seem too bright.

"Tell him," she commanded, turning on her brother, "tell Mr. Jones I never cry."

She made a funny, sharp laugh.

"I'll tell you," Brad said to him, "Ole Sis is a pretty tough gal. She never cries."

"Oh," she said, "I don't know what's wrong with me to-night. It's just I can't bear for that fool story to be taken away from Mother Fiddler too. Everybody ought to have some-thing."

She reached out with a sudden gesture and laid her hand on her brother's knee.

Yasha Jones looked across at the hand on the brother's knee. He could see it quite clearly in the moonlight, a good, medium-sized hand, thin-fingered, graceful enough, looking strong enough for the work of the world, and soft enough to do the things a woman's hand does. He tried to remember its feel when they had shaken hands the evening before.

He could not remember.

"OK, OK," the brother was saying, "let the old girl have her whopper. And you know why?"

"No," she said.

"Because I like you, Ole Sis," he said, patted her hand, then rose to get the brandy glasses off the brick wall, where they had been set, unfilled, forgotten. "Forgot it," he said. "How about a touch of this sweet old French whiskey?"

As the brandy was being poured, Yasha Jones turned to look at the woman. She had her eyes fixed across the river, to the land stretching whitely off there in the moonlight.

What had she said?

She had said: *Everybody ought to have something.*

He wondered what she had.

Watching her as she stared across the land that seemed to slide whitely westward with the moonlight, he found himself, all at once, asking another question: *What have I had?*

So he told himself, that he had had most things. He had tasted the good things and found their exact worth. He had seen men do worthy things and had found that he had the gift to recognize their worth. He had worked hard and had earned a vision of the structure of the world. He had known danger, and had admitted fear, and had survived both danger and fear. He had had, he thought wryly, fame, or what passed for fame in the world of time. He had had—and here he was aware of having to push himself to the admission, as though it were shameful or incriminating—love.

Then, as the three sat there in communal silence—he became aware that he had asked the question, and had answered it, in the past tense. Very slowly now, he asked himself the other question. He asked himself what he now had.

After a moment, he gave himself the answer: *joy.*

And now looking out westward over the moon-washed land, he felt his joy in the thought that now, even this late, he had stumbled upon this place, and its doom, and the place and doom would give him—in spite of, no, because of, his very abstraction from place and event—the perfect image of his pure and difficult joy.

He wished that the palms of his hands would stop sweating.

He thought: *Fiddlersburg.*

"Fiddlersburg," her voice said, "I suppose you—"

"Yes?" he said, turning, with a start, toward her.

"Fiddlersburg," she repeated, "I suppose you got a good dousing in Fiddlersburg today. The Baptist Church and River Street, and then—"

"Yes?" he asked.

"—then that old typed-up stuff of Brad's." She turned to her brother. "You know," she said, "I most indecently stumbled into Mr. Jones' room this afternoon, just trying to ply him with lemonade, and there he was propped up in an Egyptian robe, like a Pharaoh in the pictures in the Old Testament part of the Bible, and there—"

"Japanese," Yasha Jones interrupted, "the robe, I mean."

She ignored him: "—and there stacked on his stomach, so the poor man couldn't even breathe, was all your illiterate typing. Yes, all Fiddlersburg in a big folder, weighing on Mr. Jones' stomach like too much fried food. Yes, there it all was —the evidence."

"Evidence?" Yasha Jones echoed.

"Yes," Brad said, "that's a good enough word. By this evidence, you might say, Fiddlersburg will be convicted of the crime of having existed. When soon oblivion's deepening veil hides Baptist Church, poolroom, and the You'll Never Regret It Café, my little dossiers will insure conviction. There Cyrus and Matilda Highbridge will forever clasp connubially on the golden leaves of autumn, much to the scandal of Fiddlersburg, there Miss Prattfield's silver reflecting globe will glitter forever in her ghastly rock garden among sprigs of sedum, there Leontine Purtle will forever, in her midnight brighter than day, walk confidently an immortal River Street, there—"

"Hush," Maggie commanded. "This whole family talks too much. If we'd be quiet Mr. Jones could say what I see getting ready in Mr. Jones' head for him to say."

"Maybe I did have a thought struggling to shape up," Yasha Jones said, laughing. "But I'm sure it's not ready to be plucked."

"All right," she said. "I'll ask you a question. How did you ever pick out Fiddlersburg?"

"Luck," he said.

"Luck?"

"You have to trust your luck," he said, and thought of the morning, months ago, at breakfast in Beverly Hills, the egg in the egg cup just broken to expose the pale gold, the faint trace of vapor rising in sunlight from that hot, gold inwardness, the faintly sweet organic scent of that hot inwardness, like a bruised flower, the morning sun of California falling over the starchy brightness of napery and the glint of silver—the instant when he had seen the paragraph in a newspaper saying that a little town in Tennessee, dating from pioneer times, would be inundated for a great new dam. He remembered the moment, the excitement, the little skip of the heart, the fleeting sense of disorientation, all so seemingly unrelated to the drab little paragraph that he had thought, in that moment, that perhaps he had indigestion.

No, he had thought, perhaps an occlusion, he ought to see a doctor, thinking *occlusion* with a strange, sly sense of pleasure, of relief, of promise.

Then he had realized that it all came from the little paragraph, after all.

Something from that paragraph had spoken to him in his secret language. It was a language he had heard so infrequently that he was only a bumbling scholar in it, but he knew that it was the only language in which truth came to him. He had not been sure, in that moment, what it was saying. But he had known that something was being said.

Now she was looking at him, in question. The moonlight showed that on her face. She was waiting, he realized, for the spoken answer to the unspoken question.

"I saw a paragraph in the newspaper," he said.

She was still looking at him.

"About Fiddlersburg," he said.

He waited. Then: "So, you see, I'm here." He gave a deprecatory laugh. And added: "In Fiddlersburg."

She was still looking at him.

"It's a long way," he said, "from a paragraph in a paper in California—at breakfast, it was—to Fiddlersburg, to this charming garden, in the moonlight. You want to know why, is that it?"

"Yes," she said.

"I had a vision," he said. "I won't apologize for the word," he said. "It's the only word for what happened. A feeling rose from that paragraph. An image seemed to hang there in the air, but the sunlight struck through it. California sunlight, you know, is so very bright. So—"

He relaxed back into his chair. He spread his long-fingered sinewy hands before him, dismissing something.

"Yes?"

"Just that," he said. "I suppose I am here to recapture the vision. No, I haven't really lost it. But it comes and goes. Like that mist over the river, across those flats, in the moonlight. Yes, I am here hoping to document the vision. Yes, that's it!"

He looked down at his hands. He clenched them slowly, in the moonlight, then unclenched them. He felt defenseless, as he had that afternoon when he had stood before her with his feet naked on the floor, aware of the unevenness of the old planking.

"I sound rather pretentious," he said, "don't I?"

She did not answer immediately, turning something over in her mind. He found a flicker of anxiety as he waited for her to say something.

"No," she said, "you don't sound pretentious."

"You have to document things," he said, leaning at her. "But if you depend on the documentation, then the real thing—all right, I'll say it—the vision, it may be—"

He hesitated. Then resumed. "—be gone," he said.

He stood up abruptly. "Listen," he said, "a long time ago I read a book about Fiddlersburg."

"Are you referring to my little book?" Brad demanded.

"Yes."

"It was documented to the hilt," Brad affirmed. His hand moved out toward the bottle of cognac. Then the hand stopped in the air. It returned to lie on his knee, restively, like an animal drawn back on a leash.

"Yes," Yasha Jones said, leaning toward him. "But the vision was there. It shone through all the documentation. And now, Brad—"

Bradwell Tolliver thought: *That's the first time he's called me that.*

He conquered the resentment which had sprung up in him. He was aware that it had sprung up because pleasure had sprung up first. It was resentment at his own pleasure. No, it was just that he wished Yasha Jones would lay off that book.

"—that's what we'll hang onto," the man was saying, turning back to the woman. "Whatever it was in Brad's stories that, long ago, hit as improbable a creature as an ex-student of physics and a déraciné Georgian who had never heard of Fiddlersburg, and made him—"

"Georgian!" Maggie exclaimed.

"Not that kind, I regret," Yasha said, and laughed. "Georgia in Russia. Like Joseph Stalin. You see, my father got out in 1917—with my mother and me. Though I was too little to remember much. For a while my father sold sweetmeats on the streets of Beirut. Then, not awfully much later, he was selling oil leases in London. And he had changed his name, legally, to Jones, because he admired the English. And I had three tutors. I hated them!"

"I thought you were a Jew," Brad said.

"I sometimes think I am," Yasha said. "But we Georgians have a noble history, too."

"I thought you were an Egyptian," Maggie said. "In your robe of state I thought you were an Egyptian Pharaoh."

"No," he laughed, "not even the mummy of one."

She laughed too, but a very peculiar thing, even before she laughed, had happened to Yasha Jones. Even as he made his own little joke, even as he stood there before them, he had suddenly thought of himself—no, actually felt himself —lying on the big tester bed, the bed where, he remembered, that strongly made, thick-skulled man there had once grappled, in darkness, with a tall, slim, yearning girl who happened to have had a CP card. He thought of himself not, however, in darkness, but lying there in late afternoon light, as this afternoon, wrapped in that russet and black robe, looking out over the river and far fields, with, somehow, the head of Maggie Tolliver quietly on his arm, her body, clad in the blue-checked gingham, at a slight angle to his own, her legs drawn up childishly as she lay on her side, the bent knees just showing, the legs and feet bare, out of his range of vision but known to be bare, the loafers somewhere at random on the floor. In his imagination he knew that one old loafer would be lying on its side. That fact seemed terribly, touchingly important.

Even in that instant of imagination, and in the habit which made him, even in the act of imagining, examine the self which projected the imagination, he asked himself why this image, with its special vividness, should have seized him.

He quietly sat down.

Yes, it had been nearly eight months, he told himself. And he wasn't much over forty, he told himself. After one of those periods of celibacy it was only natural, he told himself. It was simply the signal that such a period was drawing to an end—the phase of flight, if it was flight, from all those pleasures which came so easily to Yasha Jones because he was Yasha Jones: the expectant innocence, the expertise, the autobiography whispered in twilight, the moist lip, the lifted thigh, the thigh slightly shifted, the well-aimed prevarication and, even, the gesture of sincerity.

He thought, well, he would not be here long, three weeks, not much more anyway. He thought, with a faint stirring of relief, of getting on a plane, of getting off at Los

Angeles, of seeing his chauffeur waiting there, of wondering what next, of feeling, for a moment, the thrill of youth in the face of the unexpected and unpredictable. But oh, something cried out in him, wasn't everything in life predictable?

His palms, he found, were sweating.

He looked covertly at the woman there. She was what she was. She was nearly as old as he was. She was totally unremarkable. She sat there, in the moonlight, in the slow, infinitesimally sagging, scheduled failure of her body, the body covered decently by the undistinguished brown dress, the pale yellow shawl, with the careful mending, on her straight shoulders. Yes, she was what she was. Fiddlersburg was what it was.

He sat there and wondered when he would die.

He sat there and remembered that night when Monsieur Duval—who was Yasha Jones of the OSS—had heard the keel grind on the shingle of the coast of Les Landes, south of Bordeaux. Even as the grinding stopped, Yasha Jones had said to himself that he, Henri Duval, was already a dead man. He had hoped that the process of this death's fulfilling itself would not be too hard.

So now, in moonlight in Fiddlersburg, he sat in the garden and remembered that some years later in California, he had forgotten all about Monsieur Duval and that night when the keel ground the shingle of the beach. He had forgotten it in a dream of happiness. Then in a crashing instant and a burst of flame, the happiness had gone.

All he now had left was joy: or that difficult and austere thing that, because it was all he had salvaged, he called joy.

He heard Brad stir in his chair.

"You know, Sis," Brad was saying, "I don't seem to remember way back yonder that Brother Potter—"

"Potts," she corrected.

"—that Brother Potts was one-armed."

"He wasn't," she said. "Cancer of the bone. It began in a finger and they cut that off. The third time they went way up. I hear he hasn't too much time now. But he is determined to hold on, they say, till he can have that last farewell service."

"Do you know why he is going to have it?" Brad asked.

"No," she said.

"Well," he said, "it is so everybody can know that the lives they have lived were, in his lingo, blessèd."

She did not respond, for a moment. Then she turned back to them. "Oh, I hope he makes it," she said. "Till the service."

She paused. "Yes," she said then, "it's another race—like Mother Fiddler's race—somebody, something, in a race with the flooding."

"Speaking of Mother Fiddler," Brad said, "you better turn around."

A light had come on in an upper room. She rose. "Excuse me," she said, and moved hurriedly up the walk.

Brad Tolliver stirred, too. "Here we go again, boys," he said. Then he turned toward the other. "Twenty-four hours a day of watching the old gal," he said. "No time-and-a-half for overtime, either."

Yasha Jones said nothing. He was staring toward the house.

"The old gal is sort of gaga," Brad was saying.

"Yes," Yasha Jones said politely, but not turning toward Brad.

"She has lost her marbles. She has not got all her buttons. The trouble though," he said, "is that Sis doesn't know exactly how many there are left. She doesn't know exactly how much the old gal knows about anything. The dam, for instance. She doesn't read any more, but she does look at TV, and the colored folks talk, whatever she makes of it. She just goes spooking around and—"

He paused, looking up the walk.

"—and," he resumed, "here she comes spooking."

Yasha Jones turned.

She was almost upon them, a thin figure, not very tall, in some sort of old-fashioned wrapper, or kimono, white cap with lace edging somewhat askew upon white hair, a strand or two of white hair escaping over the left cheek, and the face white as chalk in the moonlight.

The eyes were very bright. They caught some glint from the moonlight.

Yasha Jones decorously rose and faced her as she moved upon them in whatever soundless footgear she had on, and as she moved he had the impression of a soundless creaking. She stopped unsteadily in front of him and peered up into his face.

"Mrs. Fid—Mother Fiddler—" Bradwell Tolliver began, rising, "I present Mr. Jones."

She was putting her hand out, not saying anything, her eyes still peering up into his face. The hand was uncertain in the air; Yasha Jones had to capture it, and as he held it he was aware of the feeble, twitching, bird-claw movement it made.

"I am delighted to know you, Mrs. Fiddler," Yasha Jones said.

Peering at him, speaking in a thin, reedy voice, she said: "You—you're the man who's going to make the moving picture."

"Yes," he said.

"I see moving pictures," she said. "I see them on the TV screen."

"I am glad," he said, ashamed for the fatuity of his words, or ashamed of something else, of her age, her infirmity, the squamous bird-claw that kept twitching in his grasp. He could think of no way to get rid of the hand.

Her other hand, which, at breast height, had been clutching together the kimono, reached out and took him by the right sleeve. He stared foolishly down. On the third finger was a very big diamond in a very old-fashioned setting.

In the midst of a revulsion, really a disorientation, which he could not fathom, which seemed excessive to the occasion, Yasha Jones was thinking that the other woman, the young woman, the woman whose name was Maggie Tolliver Fiddler, daily suffered this touch, daily did services to maintain the life in this creature. He did not know what to make of his feeling.

"Listen," the old woman was saying, and he felt the little bird-claw move in his palm.

He knew that the sweat had begun in his palm.

"Listen," she was saying, thrusting her face closer, peering upward. "Don't you put it in the picture. Don't you put it in."

"What—put what?" he heard himself saying.

"What people say," she said, clutching his hand with the little bird-claw that was her hand. "They say terrible things about Calvin—they lie about him. But don't believe them," she was whispering, closer. "It wasn't like that. It is lies—lies—promise you won't believe and put lies in your moving picture. Promise!"

He said: "I promise, Mrs. Fiddler," and then he saw the arm of Maggie Tolliver Fiddler come about the shoulders of the old woman, and looked up to see her standing there, to catch the quick shake of her head directed to him, to catch, in that instant, the expression on her face, not apologizing, not even explaining, simply assuming that he would share the human concern of the moment.

Then she leaned over the old woman, murmuring at her ear: "Yes, Mother Fiddler—yes, he'll do what you want—come along before you catch cold—come along, Mother—"

His eyes still on them as they moved toward the house, where lights now burned in several quarters, Yasha Jones sat slowly down.

Brad held the brandy bottle out at him. "Want some?" he demanded. "For your nerves?"

"No, thank you," Yasha Jones said, and returned his gaze toward the house.

"You still want to stay here?" the other demanded.

Looking at the house, Yasha Jones did not reply.

"Of course, you won't have to see much of her," the other continued. "Unless, of course, you develop professional reasons for investigating the psychology of a decayed Southern gentlewoman."

Brad picked up the cognac bottle and inspected it. "My nerves," he said, "are, after three weeks, inured. You observe that I am not taking a drink to steady them. Besides, I do not drink on a job. But are you sure you don't want one?" He proffered the bottle.

"No, thanks," Yasha Jones said. "I'll make it."

Maggie returned down the walk, toward them.

"She must have got out the side door," she said.

She looked back at the house. The lights were out now.

"It is not one of her good nights," she said.

"I am sorry," Yasha Jones said.

"You were sweet to her," she said.

He stood there thoughtfully. Then he said: "I don't want to—" He seemed to be groping for what he meant to say.

"Oh, it doesn't matter," she said, and her right arm started up in a gesture that promised to be wide, jagged, repudiative, but was suppressed. "Don't feel you have made any promise to the poor old thing. Do what you want, you and Brad. I mean—" she hesitated.

She had crossed to Brad and laid a hand on his shoulder. "I mean that, Brad," she said.

Then all at once she was crying, crying with the tears bright on her face in the moonlight. She did not seem ashamed. But she said: "Excuse me. It's just that she is having a bad night, and sometimes when she—"

She managed to compose herself, then turned to Yasha Jones.

"The penitentiary," she said, as though changing the subject. "Has Brad promised to show you the pen?"

Before he, staring at her in some astonishment, could answer, she had plunged on, saying: "Oh, yes, the pen, that's what we call it—oh, it's the real heart of Fiddlersburg—it's all that keeps Fiddlersburg going—and it's—"

Yasha Jones stood there before her. "Mrs. Fiddler," he said.

But she ignored him.

"—and it's all that keeps us all going."

She laughed apologetically.

"Mrs. Fiddler," he said in a tone that, all at once, was edged with authority.

"Yes," she said, her voice tired and, it seemed, humble.

"Mrs. Fiddler, will you be candid with me?"

Staring at him, she stood there very erect in the moonlight.

"Wouldn't you prefer," he said, "that I stayed elsewhere?"

She stared at him.

"Oh, no," she said. "Oh, no. And please forgive me. Really, it almost never happens. Once a year. Now—" she said, making a little gesture toward him, "—now it's April, and it won't happen again till April next year, and that's a long time off and you won't be here and by then we'll all probably be flooded anyway and it won't matter. So—"

She paused, apparently waiting.

"I'll stay," he said.

"I should have felt a—a mess," she said, "if you hadn't. You don't think I'm a mess, do you, Mr. Jones?" she demanded, and laughed.

He stared at her for a shaded instant longer, then said, "No."

"Thanks," she said, and put out her hand.

He took her hand, released it.

She had gone a couple of paces up the walk before she turned.

"Make Brad tell you," she said. "Brad knows all about it and he'll—"

"Damn it," Brad said, not unpleasantly, "stop picking on me."

She stood there for an instant. "I'm sorry, Brad," she said. "I guess I am a mess. I better get on to bed and try to sleep it off."

They watched her enter the house.

"Her husband," Brad said, "he is in the pen."

The other turned slowly toward him.

"He has been there going on twenty years," Brad said.

Yasha Jones, sitting there in his quietness, said nothing.

"He is in for as good as keeps," Brad said. "He tried a crazy one-man break, and got caught."

He waited.

"Well, why don't you ask me why?" he demanded. "Why he is in."

Yasha Jones thought a moment. Then he said: "Why do you want me to ask you?"

"So I can say that I will not tell you," Brad said. "Right now my sister is lying up there in the dark and she thinks she hears my voice telling you how everything happened a thousand years ago. She will not be able to bear for you to know, but at the same time she wants you to know. That is her pride. She will find out that I have not told you, and then her pride will make her be the one to tell you."

Yasha Jones sat there in his stillness. Finally, he stirred. "I am going to be impertinent," he said.

"Shoot."

"Do you hate her?" Yasha Jones asked.

"I don't," Brad said. "I like her. I even admire her."

"Yes," Yasha Jones said softly. "Yes—but—"

"I even admire her legs," Brad said.

After a moment, more softly than before, Yasha Jones said: "But the question stands."

Brad moved, and the old wicker chair creaked with his weight. He got up and walked to the low wall and peered over it down toward the water. "You know why I am not taking you to see the pen until the day after tomorrow?" He turned. "It is because tomorrow is a visiting day. It might be

slightly embarrassing to encounter my sister on the premises. My sister, you see, takes Mother Fiddler to see her
son, in whose innocence she, in her foggy way, believes. My
sister will sit in a room smelling of formaldehyde, on a varnished bench, looking at her knuckles. She will not enter to
see Calvin Fiddler, who is her husband. She has not seen
him in all the years he has been there. No doubt, when
she tells you the story, she will explain why."

He turned away, leaned, and spat deliberately over the
wall.

"Oh, Fiddlersburg," he breathed, "I love you."

Chapter

9

IT WAS, as the young engineer had told them, a natural place for a dam. Here the valley of the river narrowed. On the east was a limestone bluff to tie to, on the west a remnant of the spur that water, a million years back, had cut through like a loaf of bread. Both the bluff and the spur were wooded, except where the naked rock had been slashed into, and showed white as bone. The engineer had a round freckled face, nose red and peeling, hair sandy, crew-cut. He grinned a lot, out of some reservoir of good nature. Now and then he'd clasp his hands and crack knuckles. The dam was going to be a whopper, he said, and God knows they needed something here. Good hunting and fishing around here, he admitted, but Jesus, he said, the way people lived back in the swamp

ground and what they called coves. And the towns, they
ought to been drowned out long back. He was from Wiscon-
sin, he said.

The dam was going to be great, the young engineer said.
Going to be near a hundred square miles under water, going
to back up the water for twenty-five miles, he had said, gesturing south, up-river. Most of the land not much but
swamp or second growth. And what good land there was—
hell, they didn't know how to farm it anyway. But with power
and cheap transportation it would all be different. A real sky-
line on the river, plant after plant. Getting shoes on the
swamp rats too, teaching 'em to read and write and punch
a time clock, and pull a switch. It was going to be a big industrial complex, he said. He liked the phrase, industrial
complex.

He had said it again.

Now, as the outboard pushed upstream, Brad and Yasha
could look back and see the enormous mounds of earth
and stone, and the great white structure, the scaffoldings,
the cranes, small in distance, swinging against the sky, the
tiny trucks in unbroken procession moving on the ramps of
earth and rubble. The raw ends of the bluff glared bone-
white and the land to the west looked mute and subdued as
though, somehow, only the gray undersides of the oak leaves
were showing now. On the bluff side, on the east, high up
among the trees, a big white sign glittered, the black letters
dwindling slowly in distance:

UNITED STATES ARMY ENGINEERING CORPS

They were opposite the swamp land now. There was the
shantyboat, tied to the stub of a dead tree, swaying gently in
the current. Brad swung the outboard slowly in toward the
shantyboat, and throttled down some twenty feet off. A
woman was squatting on the back deck, cleaning a fish. She
flicked entrails overside, then looked up.

"Ain't heah," she said.

"Where is he?" Brad asked.

"Meat," she said, and jerked a thumb toward the
drowned woods. "Gone to take some meat."

"Tell him it ain't legal," Brad said, and gave a little gas
to put the outboard back in position.

"I'll be shore and tell 'um," she said, soberly. Then she

wiped back a lock of hair, and grinned across at them. Some
of her teeth were missing.

"That meat he brings back in that jug, you tell him, it
ain't legal either," he said.

"I'll be shore and tell 'um," she said, soberly, as before.
Then she grinned again.

A head, the towhead of a child, showed over the rim of
a rusty washtub beyond the woman. The small fingers
showed, clutching the rim of the tub.

"How many more you got in the tub?" Brad called.

The woman stirred, leaned over, looked into the tub,
and lifted her head to report. "Ain't nary other," she said.
"Least as I kin find. And this un"—she reached over to give
a pat to the tangle of cotton-colored hair and to wipe a finger
across the damp nose—"this un ain't much of a ketch. But
reckin I'll keep 'um for bait."

The outboard was slewing off with the current.

"Tell Frog-Eye I came by," Brad called.

"I'll be shore and tell 'um," she called back.

Brad gave throttle, and they swept off in a wide arc. He
waved once, and the woman waved back.

"Ole Frog-Eye," Brad said.

"Is that—" Yasha Jones began his question.

"Yeah," Brad said. "He is in—"

" 'Wings of an Angel,' " Yasha Jones finished for him.
"One of your best stories."

"Frog-Eye is no longer the kid he was in the story,"
Brad said. "He has matured. Along, you might say, predictable lines."

He looked back at the woods.

"The mature Frog-Eye is no ornament to society," he said.
"He does not shave. He scratches when and where he itches.
Which is almost constantly and almost all over. He has
no marriage license. He has no divorce papers. When the
time comes, he simply pushes 'em overside, so gossip has it.
He drinks illegal likker. He does not give to the Community
Chest. He has swamp-syphilis and does not hesitate to in-
crease the incidence thereof. He does not pay taxes. He
would cut your throat in your sleep. Unless, of course you
were his friend and he sober enough to remember that fact.
He is not constructive in attitude. He does not have a Social
Security number. In short," he said, "Frog-Eye does not believe in society. He is, to be blunt, free."

"I should like to see him," Yasha Jones said.

"Oh, I'll bring you back to see him. Perhaps we should put him in our beautiful moving picture. Freedom is what our country is founded on, and Frog-Eye is the only free man left. Now I want no carping objection that Frog-Eye is the slave of his freedom. He undoubtedly is, but in this slavery to his freedom, he, in a spirit of self-sacrifice, serves as a symbol for that freedom for which every red-blooded mollycoddle in America, in his deepest dreams, yearns. Put the head of Frog-Eye unshorn on the body of the bald eagle and we have the true national symbol. But if we intend to get him into our beautiful moving picture we had better act fast."

"Why?" Yasha Jones asked.

"If we don't, paresis will get him first," Brad said. "It looks like everything in Fiddlersburg has turned into a race, at least my sister says so. So this is a race between us and paresis. With Frog-Eye for purse."

He looked back at the woods.

"Ole Frog-Eye," he said, musing, "he taught me all I know. He was a couple of years older and light years wiser than yours truly. We hunted every foot and fished every creek and backwater in three counties. That was the main curriculum. But there were the extras.

"One extra was smelling snakes. I mean cotton-mouth moccasins. They are not always lethal, but they are always unhealthy, and Frog-Eye could point 'em like a bird dog. Me, I could never get the hang of it.

"But the chief extra was swamp twat. Now do not be deceived by the spurious and cynical folk-wisdom in the old saying that all cats are gray in the dark. Swamp twat is, I affirm, a different breed of cats. It seems, at first blush, a simple, robust wine of the country, but no, there is a depth and range, and the subtle tang of sunlight falling on the green scum of backwater.

"It was Frog-Eye who got me my first piece of swamp twat. In fact, it was my first piece, period. All that I am and all that I hope to be I owe to Frog-Eye. Had it not been for Frog-Eye, and my fear of his derision, I—a simple lad lulled in my fastidious and romantic dream derived from pin-up girls, brassiere ads, and the more moving passages of Shakespeare's *Venus and Adonis*—might have funked it. But the prospect of Frog-Eye's baleful mirth steeled my soul, and I entered the dark wood of manhood in which I yet wander and weeping go. With, of course, sporadic bursts of bliss and philosophic certitude.

"Yeah, when Fiddlersburg got too thick, I was off to the woods and the tutelage of Frog-Eye. In my blood, I reckon. I told you my old man came boiling out of the swamp, didn't I?"

"Yes," Yasha Jones said. He, too, was looking back at the woods, downstream. The westering sun threw the shadow of the woods over the river. But the outboard now moved in sunlight.

"The woods," Brad said. "The woods and those durn books. Yeah, if it hadn't been for the woods and those books, and the fact of my old man being such a son-of-a-bitch, I would, no doubt, have settled down happily in Fiddlersburg and become a prominent filling-station operator, waiting for doom."

He turned toward his companion. "You see," he said, "when my old man foreclosed on Doc Fiddler, the books— yeah, they even had a room they called the library—they were part of the fixings my old man took. Not that he was a book lover. Took 'em for meanness, I reckon. But it got so I'd go in there and read. I read everything from Gibbon to *Little Women.*"

He was staring at the woods but he was not seeing them now. He was seeing his father sitting by the fire—the smoldering fire against the chill of early spring—in that room the Fiddlers had called the library. Sitting with a book open on his knee, but not reading. He would carefully tear out a page and roll it into a spill, add the spill to a pile on the floor, and then repeat the process.

Brad saw, in his mind, the man sitting there. He saw himself come in the door, a boy of thirteen, and walk to the man and, wordlessly, take the book off the man's lap. He saw the man—a big, booted man with black mustaches and coarse black hair—rise slowly. He saw the man snatch the book from the boy, toss it into the fire, and, all in one motion, swing and flip out a snapping, controlled blow—a blow not too hard, just hard enough—to the side of the boy's head. The boy broke the blow, slipped to one knee, and jerked the book from the fire. He rose, put the book on a table behind him, and looked wordlessly at the man.

Very deliberately the man reached into the book shelf. He took out another book. The boy snatched at the book.

The man snapped a blow at the boy's head. Then he tossed the book into the fire. All was as before. As before, no word was uttered. Then the whole business began again.

The fourth time, the blow broke the boy's guard, and he stumbled back against the wall, slipped to his knees there, propping himself against the wall. The man had tossed the next book into the fire. The boy made a motion to rise, to move to the fireplace. Not that he was hurt. He was merely dazed. The man stared at the boy, and saw that he would not make it.

The man leaned over and thrust his own hand into the fire and jerked out the book. He stared at the book very curiously. It was as though such an object were preposterously strange to him. Then he flung the book to the floor, in front of the crouching boy, and with no word, was gone.

After a while a little girl came in. She was crying. She stared at the crouching boy and said: "You made him do it."

The boy said nothing.

"You made him do it," the little girl said, weeping, "and now he's gone. You know where he's gone."

Yes, the boy had known where he had gone. But he had not known what he had gone to do.

Now Bradwell Tolliver, sitting there in the outboard, twitched his shoulders like an animal annoyed by a fly. "Yeah," he said, and did not continue.

"Yes?" Yasha Jones asked, after a moment.

"My old man came boiling out of the swamp and took Fiddlersburg," Brad said. "Then he couldn't stand Fiddlersburg. He would disappear into the swamp. *Nostalgie de—de* what? How the hell do you say it in French?"

"*Nostalgie de la boue,*" Yasha Jones said.

"That's what he had. About once every four or five months, he would collect a black henchman he had had forever—Ole Zack, some older than he was—his only friend, I reckon—and they would get in the boat and be gone. Two, three, four days. Then he'd come back, sort of quieted down. For a whole week he wouldn't kick a leg off Chippendale.

"Back then I didn't know what quieted him down. I didn't know what he went for—hunting or fishing or visiting kinfolks or just having a hanker for swamp twat. Like that lovely snag-toothed piece we just saw on the Frog-eye's shantyboat. Then I found out."

Brad fell silent. He gave himself seriously to the duty of the outboard. He did not even look back at the woods that now fell away, down-river, behind them.

After a while Yasha Jones said: "And what was it?"

"What I said."

"What was that?"

"Literally what I said," Brad said irritably. "*Nostalgie de la* however-the-hell-you-pronounce-it."

"*De la boue,*" Yasha Jones murmured.

"Frog-Eye," Brad said. "It was Frog-Eye found out. He showed me. I was about fourteen then and I was out with him and he asked me if I knew what my old man did. I said no, and he said he had been trailing and watching for two years and didn't I want to see. He was grinning. He wouldn't tell me what. He took me to it.'

Brad fell silent.

Then after a time, he turned to Yasha Jones, saying: "Look, we could put him in our moving picture. My old man, I mean."

He fell silent again. Up ahead sunlight was slanting across the river to strike Fiddlersburg. One ray struck a glitter, high up, from a searchlight on a corner tower of the pen.

"Don't feel that you must tell me," Yasha Jones said, at last.

The man gave no sign of having heard.

"You might say," Yasha Jones said, "that science is the right telling. And that art is the right not-telling."

"He was lying in the mud," Brad said. "I peeked through the brush, and there he was, out cold, on the creek bank. The jug was by him, of course. Ole Zack had a willow branch and was waving off the flies. Sitting there, like he had been sitting there forever, waving off the flies. You know how an old colored man can sit, like Time had dwindled into the irrelevance of Eternity and to hell with it.

" 'Look,' Frog-Eye whispered to me. 'Look at his face.'

" 'It is streaked,' I said.

"The dirt and mud was sort of streaked on his face.

" 'You know why it is streaked?' he whispered at me.

" 'No,' I said.

" 'He has been crying,' Frog-Eye said.

" 'It's a God-damned lie,' I said.

" 'I seen 'um,' Frog-Eye said. 'I seen 'um lay and cry lak a baby.'

" 'It's a God-damned lie!' I yelled, and jumped through the brush toward my old man. 'Say it's a lie!' I yelled at Ole Zack, who was, all of a sudden, one bug-eyed old black man.

" 'Say he has not been crying!' I yelled at him.

"Ole Zack's mouth was working like it was trying to say something. Then I figured out what it was trying to say. It was trying to say my name, but the sound wouldn't come.

" 'Say he has not been crying!' I yelled at him.

" 'He been cryen,' Ole Zack managed to get out. 'He lays and cries. When he comes to it.'

" 'It's a God-damned lie,' I said to Ole Zack and lifted up my arm like I was going to belt him one.

" 'But he can't he'p it,' Ole Zack wailed. It was a wail, that was what it was.

"I guess I let my arm down.

" 'He can't he'p it,' he said then. 'The time come, he jes lays and cries. Then he goes to sleep.'

"I heard a snigger behind me. I swung to look and I saw the snigger on Frog-Eye's face. Now, Frog-Eye was older and bigger and meaner than I was, but there must have been something on my face that made him think that right then was not a good time to have to try to prove it. The snigger went off his face like when a BB shot goes through the bulb of a lighted street light on a dark night, the way we used to shoot 'em out in Fiddlersburg. That snigger just wasn't there any more.

"I turned back to Zack. That willow branch keeping the flies off hadn't missed a beat, but Zack looked pretty gone.

" 'Mr. Brad,' he kept saying, 'Mr. Brad—' Then he managed to say it. 'Doan tell yore pappy,' he was saying, 'doan tell yore pappy I tole you—you tell yore pappy, he kill me daid!' "

Brad fell silent. Before they pulled into the dock, he turned to Yasha Jones and said: "I never told anybody. Not a God-damned soul."

He cut the engine down and swung in.

"Not even my wife," he said, "even when she was living in Fiddlersburg and we would be lying up in that house. Hell, she even knew Frog-Eye. She was dead game, Lettice was, she'd put on an old pair of jodhpurs, pick up a bottle of citronella and a little sixteen-gauge, and go swamping with Frog-Eye and me. Those jodhpurs were sure tight across that fancy beam she had, and Frog-Eye couldn't take his eyes off. Sometimes I worried that if I turned my back on my pal there might be a hunting accident. Oh, she got along swell with Frog-Eye. But what I mean is, I never told her about that time. About my old man. It looked like going swamping and lying up there in bed in the dark, in that house, spilling my guts to her, I would have got around to telling her. But I never did."

The engine was off. They were nosing in.

"I never even told my sister, either," Brad said, just before he cast the line over the stub. "Not even her."

Yasha Jones, at the head of the ramp, leaned against the side of the Jaguar, waiting for Brad to come back with the cigarettes, and stared at River Street. He held his hat in his hand and felt the warmth of the sun on his head. Nobody, nothing, moved on River Street, in the afternoon light.

Yasha Jones thought that if you established your camera here, at this very point at the head of the ramp, you would have a base to work from. Then if you—

He did not complete the thought. He sank into the expectation of fulfillment which was Fiddlersburg.

He was standing there, thus, when he heard the music. He turned to look southward, down the street. He saw a big truck coming very slowly, behind it three cars festooned in crepe paper, red and white. People were coming out of the stores.

The body of the truck was a big platform, on which stood a man in a frock coat, string tie, and panama hat. His face was extremely red. He clutched a microphone in one hand. At a piano, an upright, sat a large too-blond woman, wearing hoop skirt and crinoline, much awry because of the piano stool. As she labored at the piano, two other young women, not so large and not blond, began to sing. They were singing "Jeanie with the Light Brown Hair." Above all, painted on a canvas on a great frame moored to the truck cab at one end and to uprights bolted to the truck bed at the other, rode a face smiling with inhuman zeal. Over it were the words: TOM ZELTEN. Beneath it was the one word: GOVERNOR.

The singing stopped. But the piano, in another tune, was going steadily on, and now, as the truck moved past, two little girls wearing mauve fairy costumes, with filmy

wings, gauze on wire, and patent-leather shoes, tap-danced
to the new tune, as expertly as the sway of the platform permitted.

The people who had come out of the stores stood with
eyes rigidly fixed after the truck and its escort of cars. They
stood there until the truck had made the turn, three blocks
up, that led through the streets at the base of the penitentiary. Then they went back into the stores, seeming, Yasha
Jones decided, to melt soundlessly back into shadow.

There was nobody on the street now.

Brad Tolliver came out of the drugstore, letting the
screen door slam with a dry, flat sound. He was opening
a pack of cigarettes.

"Politics," he said. "They will now go up the hill and
serenade the cons, then they will go back to the cemetery and
serenade the corpses. Corpses and cons—in Fiddlersburg they
have cast many a decisive vote."

He climbed into the driver's seat. Yasha Jones got in.

"Politics," he said, "is hot here. Half Republicans, half
Democrats. The great-grandpappies of the Democrats held
the bottom land and a few slaves, and the great-grandpappies
of the Republicans lived off in the swamps or on those
ridges where you can't even raise chickpeas and certainly
couldn't raise black folks. The boys from the bottoms, they
went off with Gin'l Forrest, and the boys off the ridges signed
on with Grant and fought for freedom, one of the freedoms
they fought for being the right of Tennessee Republicans to
lynch niggers without let, bar, or hindrance. Now me—"

He paused to flip his butt overside.

"—me, I'm mixed. Confederate as hell on my mother's
side—the Cottshill side. The grandfather of Blanding Cottshill was even a gallant brigadier. You remember, Blanding
was here the other night. But I bet it was Blue-Belly all the way
with the Tollivers. I say I bet, because the Tollivers were
clearly not the kind of folks to keep written records. Sufficient unto the day is the history thereof."

He sank into thought for a moment.

"No," he finally said, "my old man, like his grandpa before him, would not have been a Blue-Belly. No more than he
would have been a Confed. He would have been like Frog-
Eye."

"And what's that?" Yasha Jones asked.

"Bushwhacker," Brad said. "In other words, outside of society. In other words, no victim of rhetoric he, no lackey of ideology."

The Jaguar lounged down the street—the road, rather, for houses were thinning out now—while Brad lighted a cigarette.

"In other words," he resumed, "like Frog-Eye." He exhaled the first puff: "Free."

The Jaguar held its minimal pace.

"Yeah," he said, "I am bulging with the genes of bushwhackers. I am a son of free men."

They drifted on.

"Free," Brad said, as though to himself, staring down the road.

He was staring at the form that, not more than thirty feet ahead, was moving on the right shoulder of the road. It was the form of a woman, swathed in some indiscriminate dress, blue, with an indiscriminate heap of pale hair on the head, a paper shopping bag, with handles, in the right hand.

The Jaguar drifted even, then stopped.

"Leontine," Brad called, not loud. "Leontine, this is Brad Tolliver."

The woman turned.

"How-de-do," she said.

"How about a little lift?" he said. "Since you've bought out Mr. Parham's grocery."

"Oh, it's not far," she said. "It really ain't. Isn't, I mean."

Yasha Jones had got out of the car.

"I want you to know my friend," Brad said. "This is Yasha Jones. Miss Purtle, Mr. Jones. Call him Yasha."

She switched the market bag to her left hand and put out the right. She put it out, Yasha Jones noticed, directly at him. He took her hand, wondering, with a little sense of guilt, if she would have found his own.

She was staring into his face with a gaze that seemed to spring from some deep, devoted clarity of being. He said something appropriate, in that moment studying her face, feeling again guilty, as though he were spying on a defenseless nakedness, thinking, too, that it was a beautiful face, pale except for the patch of color, faintly hectic, on each cheekbone, the short chin rounded but with a slight cleft, the lower lip full, delicately pink, the teeth rather small and very even, very white. The color on the cheek, it had to be natural, he decided. No blind woman—no woman, in fact, without the benefit of an expert make-up technician—could get anything like that effect. The lips, too, he decided.

He had leaned to take the shopping bag. He touched her left arm, holding it lightly to guide her into the car. She turned a smile upon him, a smile of the utmost simplicity. He was glad, somehow, that she didn't say anything, not even "Thank you."

She sat in the middle of the big bucket seat, sitting straight, her feet side by side on the floor, her knees together, her hands lying on her lap. Yasha Jones had slipped into the back and let the market bag down between his feet.

"Oh, it's so deep," she said, "the seat. They say it's a Jaguar. I've never been in a Jaguar before."

"You're in one now," Brad said.

"Oh," she breathed.

"Well," he laughed, "you might lean back and enjoy it."

"Oh," she breathed again, and timidly let herself lean back. Then, after a moment, she let her head down against the cushion, her face upward now, the eyes open, apparently staring into the depth of the sky, where the first color of evening had begun to grow.

Yasha Jones thought: *She cannot see the color of the sky.*

Then he saw the other man take a quick sidewise glance at her, and in seeing that, felt a little abortive flush of anger. Then, with some humor, he said to himself that that was exactly what he himself had been doing: spying.

Propped on the cushion, the girl's head rolled, ever so gently, with the creeping motion of the car. Her hands lay on her lap. The faintest smile, the smile of a person alone, or dreaming, touched her face, over which the light washed. She had shut her eyes. For an instant Yasha Jones thought that she had shut her eyes against the light. Then he remembered that there was no reason for her to shut her eyes against the light.

"Listen, Leontine," Brad was asking, "is it all right if we stop by a second? I wanted to introduce my friend to the Sheriff. He wants to meet him."

"Of course, Mr. Tolliver," she said, in a quiet, dreamy voice. "Poppa—he would like to see your friend."

She had not lifted her head from its luxurious motion on the seat back, and all the while her body seemed to flow into, flow with, the motion of the car.

Then the car stopped.

It was a small, squarish white clapboard house, a story and a half, set rather high on spindly brick piers, between which some latticing, here and there, yet remained. On the porch, under the gingerbread scrollwork that sparely decorated the eaves, was the bright metal of the wheel chair. In the chair was the Sheriff.

At the gate, Yasha Jones gave a quick glance back toward town. Yes, from here you could see the upper part of Lorton's Hardware Store. For an instant, he had the fleeting sense of an enclosed space, shadows, the boom of a .44, the smell of burnt cordite.

Sitting there on the porch with the Sheriff, Yasha, and Leontine, he had that overmastering impulse. He had to see the inside of the house. He looked at Leontine and knew that he had to see the upstairs. Sitting there on the porch, he shut his eyes and thought of her, walking at night, down a hot, stuffy little pine-box hall upstairs. He opened his eyes, and the world swam dizzy with brightness. So he told her that he had to leave a note for Mr. Digby, he had forgotten to tell him something today at the dam, would she please show him his room. She led him into the house.

The interior was precisely what he would have predicted, the varnished pine floor, the patches of floral carpet, the beaded portieres, the chromo of a woman, flimsily clad, holding on to a great stone cross in the midst of a dark and stormy sea, the smell of something cooking. She had led him up the narrow stairs, to the room rented by Digby. He had leaned over Digby's table, aware of how close the woman stood beside him, just out of range of his vision, wondering what the hell he would write to Digby now that he was here in this little house that smelled of varnish and pine resin. He heard a sparrow in the gutter. He heard the breathing of the woman. He wondered what the hell she was thinking. He wished she wouldn't stand so damned close, it was spooky. Suddenly, he wrote something. He invited Digby to come the next night for a drink.

You had to write something.

Now, in the Jaguar, driving home with Yasha, both silent, he was thinking of that impulse that had forced him upstairs, to stand in that little pine-box room, to hear, in the silence, the breath of Leontine Purtle. Suddenly, he turned to Yasha Jones. "Christ," he exclaimed, "I just got it! Oh, Christ," he breathed, "it would be great."

"What?"

"Listen," Brad said. "Juicy blind girl. Young engineer rooming in house. Sympathy. Wonders what it is like to be blind. Light is dark, dark is light. To be in velvety darkness which is your light, to be free of something, to fall deeper into something—Jesus!"

He turned again to Yasha Jones, letting the car drift.

"Listen," he said, "did you notice how she was? How she could sort of let go and sink into something?"

"Yes."

"OK," he said. "Work up all that jazz. Young engineer thinks how they say a blind person feels more, gets to wondering if it would rub off on you with a blind person. Young engineer, out of sympathy, gets her to talk about how it is to be blind. He practices shutting his own eyes. Gets strange excitement shutting his own eyes. But listen—"

He paused.

Then: "Here is the gimmick. The guy is a perfectly decent-looking guy. But for one thing. He has a—"

He stopped.

He found that his glance had fallen upon Yasha Jones. Yasha Jones was not wearing his hat. His left side was toward Brad Tolliver, who, in that instant, with a sickening swoop of his guts, saw the scar on the skull and thought: *Christ, that's where I got it! Christ, he'll know I got it there.*

"Yes," Yasha Jones was asking, courteously, "a what?"

"A birthmark—" Brad said.

And thought: *Did I come in fast enough?*

Saying: "—a hell of a thing, purple, on one side of his face. It comes up under the eye, too high for a beard to help, yeah, you've seen 'em, yeah, a hell of a thing—"

He wished to God he could quit laying it on. But if you laid it on thick enough then, somehow, you were innocent, you were bound to be innocent.

"—one hell of a thing. And you know, he has always felt ugly. He feels nobody can love him. He had never had a piece of tail. I mean true love. I mean not a quid-pro-quo tart. So—"

He waited.

"No," he said, "let's change that. Make him married. After the quid-pro-quo's, to a real cold-blooded battle-axe, older than he is, who took him because she couldn't get anything else, and he has to live with that fact and the fact that he took her because he thought nobody else would have him. A ghastly brat thrown in. Well, now it grows on him that in that world of light-is-dark and dark-is-light he could be all right. It would be like being in bed forever, and the lights out, really out black. You could really let go, for she couldn't see you. Well—"

He stopped again. He could not help stealing a look at Yasha Jones' face. The face told him nothing. He could not help stealing a look at the scar. The scar told him nothing.

"Well," he said, "let the battle-axe be going to come down to join Scar-Face. He has found a place to live for her and the ghastly brat. Say in a trailer camp. They come. Well, the time comes for the waters to rise. Battle-axe finds out about Blind Girl. Well—"

He stopped. He felt lost, a trifle sick in his middle.

"Naturally, I haven't worked out details," he said. "It just came to me."

"Naturally," Yasha Jones said.

"Listen," Brad said, "did you notice how she could really let go? Just give up to every whisper in the motor? Let go and flow with you like she and you were sort of flowing downstream together, sort of nudging each other with the tide?"

Yasha Jones laughed.

"Well," he said, "I hadn't thought of it quite so poetically."

They were in front of the Fiddler house. Yasha Jones unlatched the door, let it come ajar, but did not push it open, waiting courteously for the other man, who, with both hands still on the wheel, seemed about to say something.

"Yeah," Brad said, "a man can't help but wonder."

"Wonder what?"

"Wonder about the difference. Wonder if you are different. Blind, I mean. Because you don't exist in a certain way. Because you exist a hell of a lot more completely in another way. Wonder if it could be different, doing it, with a— Hell, you're bound to wonder about things. Wonder if it is like falling into midnight and black velvet and, oh, mother, not a star in the sky!"

Suddenly he got out of the car. Yasha Jones got out, too. Brad came around to the little patch of brick in front of the gate, where the other stood, apparently deep in thought.

"What's the matter?" Brad asked.

"You know," Yasha said, "we have to feel our way into this. The picture, I mean. But one thing comes to mind. We don't want it to get plotty, do we? We want a flow of feeling, don't we?"

Bradwell Tolliver stood there and wished to Christ he had not said a word about the whole damned business.

The other was laughing in the friendliest fashion, but with something rueful in the laugh.

"Yes," he was saying, "it is life that is so plotty. Life is so logical—superficially, that is—therefore so plotty. Even the accidents seem contrived for effect. But we, Brad, don't we have to violate life? To stylize life?"

"I reckon so," Brad said.

"To give the impression of the mysterious inwardness of life," Yasha Jones said, "not the obvious plottiness. Isn't that it?" He stood there a moment, very still, as though alone, then said: "To be overwhelmed with the outward, moving multiplicity of the world—that means we can never see, really see, or love the single leaf falling. And, therefore, can never love life, the inwardness of life. Yes—"

He paused, then resumed: "That is the last sin, for people in our business—no, in any business—the sin of the corruption of consciousness."

All at once, as he stared at Brad, a clear, simple smile was on his face. "But what am I yammering at you for, old man?" he demanded. "You're the guy who wrote that beautiful book."

Brad went to his room. There was plenty of time to get ready before drink time. He lay on the bed, on his back, and stared up at the gray, cracked plaster of the ceiling.

He thought of his father lying on the muddy ground.

He wondered if he himself had had to come back to Fid-dlersburg, as his father had had to go back to the swamp, to lie in the mud and weep.

Book
TWO

Chapter

10

THE OTHER SIDE of the three-quarter studio couch was still warm. But nobody was there. He let his face sink into the other pillow and breathed the characteristic odor of her person and that of the very expensive perfume which subtilized and accentuated that odor of her person. He lay there, eyes still shut, and breathed the odor and scrutinized the degree of his desire.

He remembered last night—sitting up too late, too much whiskey, too much talk, too much politics, too many voices, too much certitude. Then a young woman, good-looking in a sallow way, with glossy black hair—or was it oily? he had asked himself—pulled back in a knot with a comb stuck in it, and wearing what was presumably the authentic costume of a Spanish peasant, read, in a Chicago voice, some poems translated from Spanish. When the reading was over, she passed among them selling copies of the yellow pamphlet from which she had been reading. When she got to Brad, he gave her a dollar but did not take the pamphlet.

"Don't you want it?" the young woman asked.

"No," he said, "I heard it."

"Oh, I'll take one, too," Lettice broke in, a little too quickly, and held out a bill.

Later, in the apartment, she said he had been rude.

"Maybe," he admitted, "but I wasn't rude more than seventy-five-cents' worth." He picked up her copy from the table where she had laid it beside his typewriter. "Look," he said, "it says on the cover, twenty-five cents. I gave her a buck. Maybe I just took my change in being rude."

"You're drunk," she said.

He ignored her, cleared his throat like an orator, opened the pamphlet, and announced: "Our title is 'A Spectre Is Haunting Europe.'" He read:

> "Where are you?
> Where?
> We are pursued by shots.
> Oh!
> The peasants pass, trampling our blood.
> What is happening?"

"You're reading the worst part," she broke in. "Besides Rafael Alberti is a great poet."

"In that case," Brad said, "his translator is not." He inspected the back cover of the pamphlet. "I learn here," he announced, "that the Critics Group will sell you the Marxist low-down on the Bard of Avon for thirty-five cents."

She said nothing. She was wearing the green robe and was sitting in a chair combing her hair. She was, it now appeared, counting the strokes. He stood there, the yellow pamphlet in his hand. Finally she laid the brush down on the table, by the typewriter and the cracked plate full of cigarette butts, rose, and came to stand directly in front of him, close. "I wasn't listening to a word you said," she said.

She began to smile a slow, innocent smile.

Now, with the light of morning on the worktable and

his arm flung across the empty half of the couch, he remembered the long evening, and that slow, innocent smile, but how, in the end, love had been a ferocious flash into blackness. Now he lay there, behind the saggy burlap curtains that served to cut off the alcove from the rest of the room, and wished to God she'd come on back from the bathroom.

She did not come back.

He sat up, saw that the front shades of the room were up, saw a pair of feet passing at eye level on MacDougal Street, saw the table where his typewriter was, with a sheet of paper in it, saw there a bottle of milk, half empty, saw the cracked plate of cigarette butts on a stool near the head of the bed, saw her elegant green silk robe on a chair and the gold mules askew on the floor.

He knew she was gone.

On the table he found the scrawled note:

> Dear Old Mess—
>   gone to work—got sudden notion—see
> you at 4:30—
>   I loved last night
> I am going to love tonight
>   I love YOU
>   L
>
> P.S. write me something BEAUTIFUL

He looked, then, at the typewriter. He read what was on the sheet, what he had written yesterday. He drank the rest of the milk and ate a doughnut. He got the morning *Times* from the hall. He read that the Loyalist government had fled to Barcelona. He again read the note; then what was in the typewriter. He took the sheet out of the typewriter. He did not even bother to crumple it up. He let it drift, waveringly, to the floor.

So she had a notion. She had got out of bed and had gone to her studio and was putting paint on canvas. He looked down at the sheet of paper he had drawn from the typewriter and let fall to the floor; then he closed his eyes and saw her, how now, this minute, she would be standing in the middle of her loft studio, the little V-shaped pucker of concentration bisecting the child-smoothness of her brow, and saw how she would be putting paint on canvas on the last picture for her show at the Forecast Gallery.

He stared down at the sheet of paper on the floor, and was in despair. He remembered what was written on it, and out loud said: "Shit."

Then he thought: *If I can't do better than that, I better quit.*

With that thought a terror struck him, for, suddenly, he was thinking, too, that if he was not a writer then he was nothing, he was not real, he did not exist. He stood there in the cold terror of nonexistence.

Then the terror gave way to rage. He flung his gaze about the room. He felt trapped in this room, with that sheet of accusatory paper on the floor.

He remembered then, how five days back, when, in answer to her usual solicitous question on her return in the late afternoon, he had said that things hadn't gone at all, he was stuck. And how she had said: "Bradwell, my boy, you need a change. I tell you, let's up and go to Mexico!" And how he had said he couldn't afford it. And how, just as she, suddenly smiling, had been about to answer him, he cut in, saying: "Look here, I can read your mind, and the answer is no. For I'm not going to screw you, my pet, in any place I don't pay the rent on. Or the railroad fare to get there."

He wished to God she were here now. If she hadn't left so damned early to paint that picture, they could knock off a piece. Then he could forget things.

For at least as long as it took.

He dressed, went out, stood heavily for a moment blinking in the sunshine. It was autumn now. He walked up and over to Fifth. Then he began to walk uptown. He looked into many show windows and inspected many kinds of merchandise. He went into Brentano's, bought a copy of *The Nation,* surreptitiously looked for a copy of *I'm Telling You Now,* eventually located one, very poorly displayed, but even so, felt a little better, then felt a lot worse; and so he went out, and kept walking until he came to Central Park.

He walked in Central Park, in the bright autumn sunshine of noon—as he suddenly realized, it had been foreordained he would do. He returned to Fifth Avenue and stood and looked up at the tall gray stone building. A doorman in blue uniform with red braid looked incuriously at him.

He thought: *Buddy, I know one thing about yore ole house you don't know.*

He stood there and knew that, with Lettice Poindexter, he had, one afternoon last June, passed by this very doorman and entered an elevator and been swept soundlessly to the top floor. That he had followed her through rooms of luxurious dimness and discreet glitter. That she had led him up a flight of steps, to a small conservatory. That she had, wordlessly, left him there, the door closed. That he had stood there smoking a cigarette, staring out into distance, over the green trees of the park and the towers of the city. That he had heard a faint click. That he had turned and seen her adjusting the latch of the door.

That she had said: "What time is it?"

That he had said: "Four-twenty."

That she had said: "My mother—they say my mother will not be in until five."

That he had stood there and seen her gaze move slowly away from him, then come to focus upon a straight chair beyond the row of philodendrons.

Now, in the middle of this October afternoon, knowing what he knew, he stood on the pavement and out of his knowledge stared insolently at the gorgeous doorman who would, he told himself, have given an arm for what he, Bradwell Tolliver, had had for nothing. He knew what he knew. But he did not know why neither he nor Lettice Poindexter had ever referred to that event.

That night he waited until, with her head on his right shoulder, he felt the breath against the side of his neck sink to the regularity which presaged sleep. Staring up into the dark of the alcove, behind the burlap, he said: "Lettice."

She made a little friendly grunt, not relinquishing her drowse, snuggling her head a little deeper into his shoulder.

"I am going to Spain," he said.

The body did not, at once, respond. It lay there in its relaxed softness, the breath as easy and steady as a child's; and in that instant he had some sense of how warmly, how softly, with what pathos, that flesh, in its own inward darkness, caressed the bones, the bones that held it up and made it, in fact, what it was: Lettice Poindexter. In that instant of

awareness he felt a sudden tenderness like the possibility of
tears.

Then the body had gone tense, had uttered a cry, the
simple cry of "Oh, oh!" like a throaty exhalation, had heaved
up, making the springs of the old couch creak. In that movement he was aware of the heaviness, the awkwardness,
which, like the throaty exhalation, certified that deepest sincerity, the animal sincerity of pain.

The voice, like a wail in the dark, was saying: "But you
didn't tell me—you never told me!"

He could not tell her that there had been nothing to tell.
He could not tell her that he had stood in front of a radio
store and heard the 2 P.M. broadcast, how Arriondas in the
Asturias had fallen, how the Loyalists had regrouped on the
ridges toward Infiesto, that that was all. He could not tell her
how in that moment, thinking of men grimly falling back,
regrouping, settling among the rocks to receive the next as-
sault, he had a vision of the beauty and spaciousness of life—
the beauty and spaciousness that would come if you suddenly
saw reality and embraced it. He could not tell her how he had
stood on Fifth Avenue, shaken as with desire. He could not
tell her because he did not know the name of what had shaken
him.

He could not even tell her how troughed the old marble
stairs had been that led up to the third floor of the decrepit
office building; how people—that was all you knew of them
—had left their spittle on the stairs; how drearily matter-of-
fact the hole of an office had been—like a fly-by-night rental
office, in the West Thirties—with the scarred desk and cranky
green metal filing cabinet stinking of failure; how unfriendly
with fatigue and bad teeth the middle-aged, black-bearded
man in the black turtleneck sweater had been; how the tall
girl at the typewriter—brown tweed suit, a quick glossy social smile, good legs in expensive stockings, legs slightly too
long and therefore stuck out sidewise, close together, from
under the typing table—had reminded him of Lettice Poindexter herself; how, with a shade of the superciliousness
which now he felt entitled to, he had thought: *Park Avenue
volunteer*.

He could not tell Lettice Poindexter how it had been, for
he himself did not, at the deepest, know. To tell about it would
be like trying to tell a dream. You know you are lying. You
know you are only making up a new dream.

"Oh!" Lettice Poindexter again cried out in the dark. "You never told me!"

"Hell," he said gruffly, "a man can't tell everything—" telling, in the same breath, the truth that it is impossible to know and therefore to tell what happens, and telling the lie that he had been engaged in a deep struggle for a decision.

"But you didn't tell me," she said.

She was weeping now. Even in the dark he knew that it was a kind of weeping he had not known before. He could sense how the tears were swelling up with inexhaustible ease, as from a secret inner wound, how there was for the weeper of these tears almost a paradoxical joy in the discovery of such an unsuspected depth of life.

He groped for her hand in the dark, took it firmly.

"Hell," he said, "I didn't want to mention it till I was sure. Can't you understand that?"

She had, all at once, collapsed to the bed beside him, her head, he could tell, somewhat higher than his. She was fumbling out for him, drawing his head against her bosom, cradling his head, murmuring through her tears now, calling him Baby, saying she was proud of him, saying he was right, saying she was a silly fool, calling him Baby, her Baby.

He lay there and felt very cold and austere and manly. He felt that he had conquered fate.

When he had gone, she lived for his letters. When there were no letters she lived for the newspapers. She worked less and less at her painting. She cancelled her show at the Forecast. She even tore up the letter in which she had written him about the cancellation: if she wrote the fact to him something would be tarnished. She gave a great deal of her time to work for the Loyalist cause. Half of the quarterly income from the trust fund she donated, anonymously, to the cause.

She became, deliberately, more careless in her dress. She rarely went to any gathering except those having to do with Spain or the Party. If, as was not unusual on such occasions, a man made advances to her, she would gently repulse him, telling him that her fiancé was in Spain.

Unknown to Brad she kept his old basement room on MacDougal Street. Day or night, whenever the impulse struck her, she would leave her own place and go there. She would go there to clean it up, even when it did not need cleaning. She would go there to read his letters, even when the letters had already been read a hundred times. She would go there to lie on the three-quarter couch and stare at the ceiling. Once she went there in the early evening, carrying a little valise, and got properly to bed, even with a nightgown. But it was too painful. About three in the morning she got up and took three Seconals—for more than six months now she hadn't taken a single one, but she always carried them, ritualistically, with her.

When she woke early the next afternoon, she felt, in a daze of despair, that she had betrayed him, Brad, and was doomed to that life of compulsive meaninglessness with which the little red capsules were associated.

Waking there in the empty room, with the recriminatory noise of the afternoon street, she knew, very coldly, why she had always felt compelled to carry the little bottle: if things got too thick she would have it. She had never really said this to herself before.

Now, having said it, she immediately got out of bed and, barefoot, went to the bathroom and dumped the contents of the bottle into the john and flushed it.

As in the period before Brad's departure, she had felt, lying beside him in the dark, the need to relive her life, she now had the need to resume the process. No, it was not a need in any ordinary sense of the word. It was, rather, a doom, something that happened to you, like being run down in the street by a bus, something massive that plunged at you, surprised you, crushed you.

There was no telling how it would happen. She would be sweeping the floor, keeping the room tidy for Brad, and suddenly her hand would freeze on the broom, and there her life would be, plunging mercilessly at her. She would look up from whatever letter of his she was reading, and there it would be. She would lie on the bed, and there it would be. Some old event would be there, being re-enacted in her head, sharp, jerky, colorless, slashed and spotted with blurs of silver, soundless, like an old movie being run off without music, without that music which had been the flesh of feeling.

She would think: *This is my life.*

She thought that this reliving was a penance she would have to go through. Alone, she would have to relive it all— the touch of a knee under the table at a dinner party long

ago; the blackness under a lifeboat on a liner on a starless
night; the tickle of a forefinger on her palm; dance music
from an orchestra far below on some hotel terrace; the arrogant, bloodshot glare, over the cocktail glass, of the successful
German painter who knew he had your number and you, with
sudden shame, knew it too; the shallow-breathed excitement
at the first touch of a stranger who might, really might, be
different, who might come like unexpected good news; the
uneven British teeth in the British smile of the archaeologist
from Leeds or Manchester, or some such provincial university, who had taken her to the inner room of the museum in
Naples, and then, just at the right moment, when she was
staring at what she was staring at, had reached out to seize
her by the nape of her neck, driving the nails into the flesh;
the ghastly *kitsch* of Telford Lott in putting that God-damned
paint-thick reproduction of Picasso's Woman in White on the
wall of his bedroom, right where you had to look at it, and
telling you it was Picasso's masterpiece; the laugh of the
pansy actor who used to hurt her so and to whom she would
go because he did; the strange momentary glut of satisfaction in finding the single gray hair on a man's chest and
twisting it in your fingers—was it the chest of Telford Lott?
—yes, it was his; the heading of the news story in the clip-
ping she had hired a researcher to dig up and ever since had
kept in her jewel case: *Financier Steps from Window.*

The room on MacDougal Street—that was the place
where her past was re-enacted. The re-living happened only
when she came there. Coming into the dark vestibule she
would stand before the door, the key in her hand, afraid to
enter. But she always did. And there it would be, the old,
silver-jagged movie reel, something you had to endure without music, hearing only the pitiless whirring grind of the
projector in your head.

You could endure it if you clung to the thought that,
somehow, sometime, at the end would be the blessedness.
This was the price of blessedness, she thought, and remembered what Dr. Sutton had once said: "You are, my dear Miss
Poindexter, a Puritan. If I were more mystical I should say
that you do not have your heredity for nothing. You are a
Puritan idealist. Unfortunately your Puritan idealism does
not square with your compulsive sexual rivalry with your
mother. If you can only realize that she is to be pitied, that
she herself is—"

But lying on the bed, in the room on MacDougal Street, she would cry out, "Oh, oh!" in pain and deprivation, hating Dr. Sutton, who had never heard of Bradwell Tolliver and to whom Lettice Poindexter was now scarcely more than a name under P in the filing cabinet, because from the expensive gloom of his Park Avenue office he would not reach out and restore Bradwell Tolliver to her arms, in place of that pillow which she clutched and wept into.

Then the letters ceased coming. Lerida had fallen, Spain was cut in two—and she was sure he was dead. When a letter did come, with the address in a strange hand, a clearly feminine hand, addressed to Mlle. Poindexter, she could not bring herself to open it. Holding it numbly in her hand, her feet feeling wooden as she walked, she went to the room on MacDougal Street. Once there, she held it a long time before she dared to open it.

He had not been wounded. He had had typhus and had been evacuated to France. He had, miraculously, survived the disease, but the convalescence would be long. The nurse —who had written the letter—offered her sympathy and most distinguished sentiments.

That night Lettice Poindexter was on a plane to Europe.

That afternoon, before she left the room, Lettice Poindexter had a strange experience. She had gone into the bathroom to wash her eyes after the tears of relief. Lifting her face from the basin, she had, in a characteristic motion, pushed the swatch of her hair back with her right hand, and in that motion had caught the rich accent that the emerald ring gave the auburn. She had detected, in that instant, her characteristic flicker of pleasure in the sight.

Staring at herself in the mirror, the hand frozen against the hair, the ring doing its beautiful work, she had the idea. Very slowly, she lowered her hand, removed the ring, and dropped it into the pocket of her flannel skirt. Then lifting her eyes, she saw, with surprise and shocking clarity, the old razor blade lying on the glass shelf. She picked it up.

Again staring at herself in the mirror, she reached her left hand across her body and seized the swatch of auburn hair on the right side of her head, pulling it brutally taut, pulling it so hard, in fact, that her head inclined a little in that direction. The right hand held the razor blade poised for the slash. But the blade did not make the slash that would cut off that swatch of hair which gave her such pleasure.

It did not slash across the hair because, in that instant of poise, Lettice Poindexter saw in her imagination, as clearly as would have been possible in fact, the razor blade doing something quite different. As though staring into the mirror, she saw it slash, not the hair she held so brutally ready for the sacrifice, but the cheek. She saw the blade slash across the right cheek, not once but twice, splitting that smooth, subtly gleaming surface, defaming it.

Shaking as with a chill, she quietly laid the blade on the shelf and left the place.

That night, on the plane, she kept remembering what had happened. She felt again the strange mixture of fear and sick excitement that had come with the moment. She did not try to understand what had happened to her. She said to herself that it was because she loved him so much. It had all been like a prayer saying how much she loved him.

Looking out the window of the plane at the moonlight gleaming on cloud and sea, she thought, absurdly, that she would, in fact, pray. She shut her eyes and moved her lips. All she could say was, "Now I lay me down to sleep—" She said that several times, but she could not go on with it.

She had, in accordance with the original impulse, left the emerald to be sold, the proceeds to go to the Committee.

Chapter

11

BACK IN NEW YORK, Bradwell Tolliver was soon strong enough to appear at a rally. His pallor and his halting manner on the platform gave an impression of deep conviction. He was interviewed by reporters. A slick-paper magazine asked for an article on his experiences, an article which, despite the fact that he was nearly broke, he declined to write. He did not know why.

He would wake up at night and think about what had happened. He had been in battle. He had seen death. He had been afraid, but he had behaved as well as the next man. He had believed in the justice of his cause. So he did not know why he now woke in the night and felt that all his experience came to nothing.

His experience, he insisted, was perfectly valid and worthy. What, then, was the source of this spiritual lassitude? Then, lying in the dark, he gave himself the answer.

He told himself that, somehow, he was outside of his own experience.

He tried to fathom the meaning of those words that came into his head. He knew that they meant something, but he could not paraphrase them. He felt that if he could go back to Spain everything would be all right. If he could relive what he had lived he could find its inner meaning. He haunted the office of the doctor, to persuade him that he was all right, that he had to go back to Spain.

"You have a heart murmur," the doctor told him one day, for the tenth time. "You will be all right, but meanwhile you don't have to be a hero."

"It's not that," Brad retorted, "it's—"

But he did not know what it was.

"Yes?" the doctor demanded.

"To hell with it," Brad said.

After that day, he never went back to the doctor's office. But he had to tell himself something, and so he gave himself a new answer: he said that it was the typhus. Everybody knew how depressed typhus left you.

That was what he told himself. And Telford Lott was telling him that everybody knew that after a fundamental experience, time was required to digest and evaluate. Telford Lott also said that the only way for a writer to digest and evaluate was to write. He said that he should write a novel on Spain. He could provide an advance of two thousand dollars.

In six months he wrote eighty-three pages. Rather, he had kept eighty-three pages of what he had written. He woke up more and more often in the night. He began to pick small quarrels with Lettice. He told her she ought to reduce, knowing even as he said it, that this was a code for something else, just what he did not know. When, one night, he woke and found her silently crying, he was very angry.

Another night, at a party, he made a scene when he announced that if anybody else in that room who had never seen what a man was like with his head blown off made another remark about Spain such as a certain bloodthirsty son-of-a-bitch had just made, he would probably vomit.

He was mysteriously shaken by his own violence. He left the party. In bed, Lettice held his head on her breast and smoothed his hair. He had been, she whispered, perfectly right.

The next day Telford Lott, coming back to work after lunch, philosophical from his accustomed brace of martinis, yearning for a half-hour of peace in the big shadowy office before turning on the light, found a figure looming there in the dimness, in the middle of the floor, in ambush.

Telford Lott was just inside the door, and so all he had to do was to touch a switch and the place was flooded with light from the ceiling fixture, a powerful light which he never permitted when he was in the room and which now poured down to define the flushed young man in the costume of khaki pants, sneakers, old cheviot coat. Suddenly frozen, diminished in that flood of light, the figure stood there, now without menace. Telford Lott noted the red-rimmed eyes, the cruelly bitten nails of the hand stretched at him in the gesture of accusation.

"That God-damned book," Brad blurted out immediately, even as Telford Lott entered.

Before Telford Lott could sort out his perceptions, the young man had taken a step toward him, still pointing a finger at him.

"That God-damned book," he said, "there is not a word of truth in it. There is nothing but a pack of lies in that God-damned book you persuaded yours truly to write."

Telford Lott had been an editor, a very successful editor, for a long time. Now he did not even have to decide what tone to take. He slipped into the appropriate stance as instinctively as a boxer coming out of his corner at the bell. A shade of mournful, paternal patience fell across his features, which were handsome in a rugged way.

"Brad," he said, and his mellow voice trailed off.

Brad was glaring at him.

"Brad," he said, "no man could have greater confidence in another than I have in you. I want you to know that."

Brad said nothing, still glaring.

"Listen," Telford Lott was saying, with just the right tinge of discovery and dawning enthusiasm in his voice, "I have an idea. You bring it all in. Tomorrow. We'll get out of this sty here, and go to my place and slosh out some Scotch and soda, and work it over."

"It won't take long," Brad said.

"Well, that's all right, it's not length that matters. I can envisage a very short, very taut, very—"

"It will not take any time at all," Brad said.

"What?"

"What I mean is, it won't take any time to discuss something that doesn't exist. I tore it up."

At the door, he turned.

"Screw the doctors," he said, "I'm going back to Spain."

He went out the door. Down in the street he stopped, stood solidly on the pavement, and thought, for a moment, that he really would try again to get back over, maybe he was well enough. He thought, with a flash of elation, of killing a faceless enemy. Then, in that split second, the faceless enemy wore the face of Telford Lott.

That afternoon when Brad got back to MacDougal Street, Lettice, to his surprise, was waiting for him. She hadn't been able to work, she said, because she had a little headache. She did not add she had the headache because she could not forget the episode of the night before. Now she found him numb, malleable. She made him take her for a long walk along the Hudson. She made him take her to a good dinner at the Lafayette. She made him take her to a bar in the Village where there was dancing in a back room. She made him dance with her, keeping the drinks discreetly spaced, letting her head droop a little so that her cheek now and then brushed his and now and then a strand of her hair, gently tossing in some turn or reverse, would drift across his face. She whispered to him that she was so happy.

Suddenly he stopped dancing, stock-still in the middle of the floor. He disengaged himself from the embrace of the dance, seized her by a wrist and led her to their table, thrust her into a chair, sat down opposite her. "Listen," he began.

She inclined her head a little, humbly, the brown eyes wide, bright, and sad, upon him.

"I'm going to Fiddlersburg," he said.

For a moment she said nothing. Then she reached out and took his hands. She held them very tight and said that she was going to Fiddlersburg, too.

"Hell," he said, "you don't know Fiddlersburg. Maybe you can't take Fiddlersburg."

"I can take you, my darling," she said.

"Well, you don't know Fiddlersburg if you think you can just stroll in and—"

He stopped the sentence in mid-air, and scrutinized her. She was smiling timidly at him. "Christ," he said, "there's only one way you can go to Fiddlersburg." He began to laugh. He laughed uproariously.

"What are you laughing at?" she asked.

"At you," he said, "dumb dame. You make me take you out to dinner and to dance. Going to cheer me up, eh? Oh, I can read you like a book. Well, that joke is on you."

"The joke?" she echoed.

"Yep," he said, and laughed again, and energy filled him. "Your little therapeutic project has turned into something else."

"What?" she demanded. "What?"

"This is your engagement party," he said, and rose from the table, jerked her up, seized her and whirled her away in a dance that had little to do with the music but made her laugh in her dizziness until, dizzier than ever, she let her head fall, unashamed, on his shoulder while she felt the tears of joy brim innocently to her eyes.

While Brad was in Fiddlersburg, where he had gone to arrange for repairs on the house, now unoccupied since the death of his father, there came to New York, on a mission of propaganda, a hero of the Loyalists, just recovered from wounds. After one of the occasions on which Dr. Ramon Echegaray was to speak, a certain Mrs. Filspan, a wealthy and socially prominent woman, was to entertain him at a reception designed to attract the sympathies of a carefully selected group of persons of influence, distinction, or wealth. Mrs. Filspan, a friend of the mother of Lettice Poindexter, invited her to dine at the Filspan house, with Dr. Echegaray and a few others, before going to the hall where he would speak.

Dr. Echegaray had abundant, very black hair that curled and writhed uncontrollably in all directions as though it had some angry, secret life of its own. A black patch was over the right eye. His eyebrows were very bushy and from under the left eyebrow the eye, black, peered mercilessly out. The nose was big and jutted from a head that seemed too big for the body. For the body of Dr. Echegaray was not big. He was small and fierce—fierce and unforgiving in his smallness.

But at dinner, there was no hint of the fierceness—only

the awkwardness, the diffident smallness. Later, at the hall, when he appeared on the platform, he seemed even smaller, little more than a boy, a boy with a preternaturally large chest, as he hunched in his chair, stared at by all eyes, encased in an ill-fitting dark suit, wearing an old-fashioned stiff collar clearly too big for his neck, flanked by adults of normal size. When, finally, he stood up, it seemed as though some hoax of very poor taste were being perpetrated, as though he had been trapped into a public embarrassment. He stood glaring out from under the bushy eyebrow that casemated the good eye, and waited for the polite applause to subside. His English was imperfect.

He should begin, he said, by telling a little about himself. He was of Basque blood, he said. He was a Catholic, and believed, as deeply as the infirmity of his nature would permit, in the doctrine of love, mercy, and justice taught by the Mother Church. He was not a medical doctor, he said, almost apologetically, but a professor, lately—and he pronounced the word *lately* with a sardonic grimace—a professor of medieval history at Madrid. He, as a Catholic, believed that God's hand moved in history, and as a historian, believed that man's obligation was to enter history, not to flinch from history. For to be a man, he said, a man must—

By this time the fierceness had emerged. Under the too-bright lights, sweat ran down from the angry hair. The face, which had been sallow, was flushed as though with drink. The black bow tie in the old-fashioned high collar had come untied, and between gestures that quivered with rage, the hands —unusually big hands for such a small man—made futile efforts to retie the tie. The man would stretch his neck up above the collar, glaring, thrusting his nose at the world out there below him, and utter his spate of guttural words, and all the while he looked like a small, badly damaged gamecock that staggers up and even in its daze fiercely casts about for the adversary.

Later, Lettice Poindexter tried to tell Brad how pitiful he had looked. He had looked, she said, like one of the hurt birds that she had seen taken from the ring and dropped into the drag-pit to wait the end, at the fights in Havana.

Later, she tried, too, to tell him about the reception. How at first the guests had asked Dr. Echegaray the polite questions, and had waited politely. How he had stood there, surrounded by the glittering shirt fronts of men of normal

size and by the sheen of the bare arms of women of normal
size. How he, now and then, had set his glass down to struggle spasmodically with his tie. How gradually the adults of
normal size had ignored him, uttering to one another their
own opinions. She even told Brad how, seeing the small
man's face when some such opinion was being uttered, she
had felt sorry for him and had stood by his side.

But she did not tell him what she had said.

She had said: "I know what you are thinking."

He had said: "What?"

She had said: "You were thinking that if you hear another man who has not seen what you have seen say a
thing like that, you may vomit."

He had stopped messing with his tie. From under the
thorny black-gray eyebrow he had swiveled that black eye
at her, black as the hole in the muzzle of a gun, and held
her fixed there.

In his guttural way, as though in anger, he had demanded: "You can know that? You?"

Unable to find a word, suddenly hearing in her head
the voice of Brad at that party threatening, in the midst of
the argument about Spain, that he would vomit, she had
slowly nodded.

Still holding her fixed there, as at gun-point, speaking
in his harsh voice that seemed to belong to a man twice his
size, the small, fierce, pitiful man had said: "Tell me your
name. I did not hear your name. What is your name?"

This was the only part she never came to tell Bradwell
Tolliver. This was the only part she could not tell him.

By seven forty-five, as early as she dared the next
morning, already exhausted by her anguish, she was calling
Dr. Sutton from a telephone booth in Grand Central, the
nearest place to his office she could think of to wait in. She
had been waiting for two hours. Dr. Sutton was, at first,
sleepy or irascible, apparently not able to remember who she
was, but he did agree to see her at eight-thirty, for a stolen
few minutes before his first regular appointment. She had
been pacing the hall for a full half-hour when, at eight-
thirty, the secretary arrived to open the office.

When Dr. Sutton did arrive, he did not smile, or smiled
so tepidly that it was worse than no smile, worse than no
recognition, and she felt, in that instant, condemned ir-

revocably. She noticed, too, a little smudge of drying tooth-
paste in a corner of his mouth. Her pain exploded into rage.
Oh, how could you tell anything to a man like that—who
stopped to wash his fool teeth when your heart was dying?

But she plunged on, summarizing in three minutes what
had been the life of three years. She finished, and breathing
heavily, as though she had just run upstairs, waited. Clench-
ing her fists, she hunched forward and stared imploringly
at the face of Dr. Sutton; but as he sat there deep inside
the thick folds and gray bulges of his aging flesh, hidden
behind very large, very thick, aqueous bifocals, she could
determine nothing.

He smoked half of a cigarette before he spoke.

Many factors, he said then, had entered into the situation. The very milieu had been significant, the fact of a rich
house such as the house of her girlhood, such as her mother's house, where she had witnessed certain things, surmised certain things, and had had certain experiences; the
fact that Mrs. Filspan was a friend of her mother; the fact
that Mrs. Filspan was, as it were, the possessor of Dr.—
Dr.—what was his name?

"Echegaray," Lettice said.

The fact, Dr. Sutton continued, that Mrs. Filspan had
been the possessor, as it were, of the distinguished visitor,
as her mother had been the possessor—yes, *possessor* was
the word—of certain men. But he wanted to emphasize, he
said, certain other factors, factors that in themselves were
valuable and constructive but had been absorbed into the
old pattern of vengeful compulsion. For instance, the fact
of her passionate and idealistic identification with the Loyalist cause. Even her devotion to the man she was in love with
—what was his name?

"Tolliver," Lettice said.

Even that fact, Dr. Sutton said, entered here in a
strange double sense, he would hazard. For one thing, her
lover had fought in Spain, and she had spent months of anguish yearning to protect him; if Dr. Echegaray had not
been Spanish and had not seemed to need her pity, nothing
would have happened. For another thing, she was now on
the verge of marriage, and in her desperate desire to prove
her worthiness, her capacity for fidelity after her past history of confused and compulsive adventures, she had, as it
were, submitted herself to a test.

"And, oh," she wailed, "I flunked it!"

"My dear Miss Poindexter," he said, "no."

"Goddammit," she said, "you know what I did!"

"My dear Miss Poindexter," he said, "you acted out what it was necessary for you to act out to know what you now know. Your present anguish tells you what intellectually you knew but needed to know in your very viscera. You cannot live except in devotion to the young man you have chosen. You are Puritan—you remember our talks about that? And now, to misapply a quotation from Shakespeare, you and your honesty begin to square."

He studied the burning tip of his cigarette.

"My dear Miss Poindexter," he said, "I am now convinced, for the first time, that you have every chance for the kind of happiness you yearn for. Ideally, of course, now would be the time to resume your analysis and push it quickly through. I do not mean with me. I mean with—"

"No!" she cried. "No, I am going to Fiddlersburg!"

He again studied the burning tip of his cigarette, then laid it by and turned the aqueous blankness of the bifocals back at her.

"Fiddlersburg let it be," he said.

His big leather swivel chair creaked. Then he rose, as abruptly as possible for a man of bulk. His shoes creaked as he came around the desk. He thrust out his hand. Rising numbly, she took it.

"I congratulate the young man," he said.

She mumbled something.

"My dear," he said, "my dear, I really do."

In her confusion she hung on to his large, soft hand and thanked him several times.

As she was about to go out the door, he said: "Miss Poindexter."

She turned. He was standing there in the middle of the floor. There was just one thing, he said. She must not indulge herself with a confession.

"I won't lie," she affirmed. "Not to him, not ever!"

Dr. Sutton stood there in his deliquescent heaviness. He repeated the word *lie*. Then he said: "What is a lie? Can you call by the word *lie* certain words you utter, or refrain from uttering, in order to give fullest scope for the deepest truth that is in you?"

"Well, I know what that is!" she cried, in a burst of bliss, and almost ran from the room, with that truth that was in her bubbling up into delicious laughter that she could scarcely contain until she was out in the street, in the sunshine.

She stood in the street and thought how the plane from Nashville should be in at five-forty P.M.

Dr. Sutton looked at the door that had closed behind her. Slowly he turned and moved toward the mirror on the wall. He knew he was the sort of man whose shoes tend to creak, and now he heard the creak under his soft ponderousness. He stared into the mirror. His face was large, colorless, round, grayly lunar as though seen through mist, the features recessive and ill-defined. The eyes seemed lost behind the big, thick bifocals. As he stared into the mirror he had the fancy that his whole face was floating remotely behind the thickness of some such single enormous aqueous lens. He stood there and wondered what people thought when they looked at him. He remembered that, years ago, a hulking, wheezy boy on a farm in Indiana had wondered that.

Suddenly he had in his mind the image of Lettice Poindexter. She had run from this room as though nothing in it were real, as though he were not real. With that, he thought of the impending burden of the day. He was not sure he could go through with it. There, in that moment, he was confirmed in a decision with which he had been toying: to shut his office for a few months, go to Boston, and again undergo analysis. That, he decided, would restore perspective. He might regain the hope that he could do good.

He stood and stared at his own face in the glass and mournfully wondered what good he had ever done anybody.

Then the thought was in his head: *Have I ever done any good for myself?*

Then he was shaking, as in a cold blast, saying to himself, over and over, that that wasn't what he had meant—oh, no, it wasn't.

He found himself staring into the mirror and trying to remember the strange name of that town where Lettice Poindexter, with that laughter of truth on her lips, would go, and he would never see her again.

Suddenly he remembered: *Fiddlersburg.*

Chapter

12

THE WARDEN—glittering black, hundred-and-fifty-dollar, cus-
tom-made boots, gray pants with black stitching on the
seams hanging too short over the boots, black frock coat long
enough to exaggerate the literal height of his strung-out bone,
a bony sepulchral face with a gray goatee like a whiskey ad,
curled and pomaded hair on which was set, as carefully as on
a show-window dummy, a panama hat of enormous brim and
delicately pinched-in sides—had received them. The Warden,
leaning on his ebony cane with the gold head, and stroking
his goatee, said he was sure glad, yes sir, to have the letter
from the Commissioner about Mr. Jones. He only wished he
could hang around now, he sure did, and do it all personal.
But, he said, there was going to be a primary, he had to work

for the right man, he said, and he gave a thin, conniving smile, the smile appropriate to an obscene, man-to-man confidence, twitched one eye in the high sepulchral face into a wink that gave the abrupt impression of bone winking, and uttered one word: "Politics."

He turned them over to Mr. Budd—"Boots" Budd, who was one foot shorter and two feet wider than the Warden. Mr. Budd's square face, rust-red from weathering, was noncommittal in the introduction, but his enormous hand was not: it was, quite casually, bone-crushing. Mr. Budd said that he was the Deputy Warden; that he was the officer of discipline and welfare, the word *discipline* being pronounced with a strong accent on the second syllable; that he had been a guard, then Yard Lieutenant before the war; that he had got to be Deputy Warden after he came out of the First Airborne; that long back, ever since he figured out his legs were too short to ever make world champion heavyweight, he had wanted to be Deputy Warden and now, by God, he was; that he ran the pen clean, hard, and fair, which he said is the only way to run a pen if you didn't want steel in you, like the Deputy before him got it; and that the First Airborne and the pen was all he knew and he was satisfied and maybe he had rather be Deputy Warden than world champion heavyweight anyway. His voice moved in a dry, rasping monotone, not loud, and when the words were over, one felt, looking at that rust-red noncommittal face, that Mr. Budd was a taciturn man, that he had made only a minimal utterance, and that the information you had was nothing he had said but something you had heard long back, from other sources.

They had long since passed the great steel doors. They stood in the cold light of the cell block; on one side the bare brick wall lifting twenty feet before it reached the level of the barred windows, on the other side the cages stacked three high, steel catwalks hung along the front of each level. The cages were empty now. In some there were pictures gummed to the cement of the back wall, the photograph of a relative or a magazine beauty, the water color of a bulldog done without talent. In one a bit of scrim curtain cozily hung at each side of the open-barred cell-front.

"Some," Mr. Budd said, pointing with his walking stick, "they try to make it homey."

"Homey," Yasha Jones murmured, studying the scene.

"It is the nearest thing some of 'em ever had to a home,"

Mr. Budd said. Then, after a moment, added: "It is the only one some will ever have."

He stood there scrutinizing the block.

"But some," he said, "they don't want nothing. They want it bare. You could fix it up like the Hermitage Hotel in Nashville, and they would throw it out. Having it bare is the kind of homey they want. Bare is their kind of homey. They are built like that."

He continued to scrutinize the block.

"It ought to be tore down," he said, glumly. "This block."

"Why?" Yasha Jones said.

"Ain't enough money in half Tennessee to fix a pen like it ought to be, so there ain't much use in asking why. But I'll tell you. An-tee-quated. It is an-tee-quated. This part was the part old Colonel Fiddler built—when he was Governor and made 'em do something for Fiddlersburg. Built their second pen here long back. After the Civil War, I reckin. Got a oil painting of Governor Fiddler downstairs. You can see it."

Speaking to Yasha, he jerked a thumb toward Brad.

"Git him to tell you," he said. "Knows more about them Fiddlers than I do." He meditated a moment. " 'Cept fer one," he said.

"Yes," Brad said. "Except for one."

Mr. Budd moved on, his thick rubber soles making no noise on the cement.

"Are you armed?" Yasha Jones asked.

"Don't allow any guns in," Mr. Budd said. "Guns give somebody the notion of tryen to take a gun off somebody. But heft this," he said, holding out his innocent-looking, dandyish stick, head foremost.

Yasha took it.

"Hold it by the little end," Mr. Budd continued. "Heft it."

Yasha Jones obeyed. The stem was slightly flexible. The head was a heavy brass knob. The balance was inviting.

"Bamboo on steel rod," Mr. Budd said, and reached out and retrieved the stick. "If you can use this here you don't need no gun." He hefted it gently. "They know what it can do," he said. "They stand back. They don't come crowding. I never had to use it but once. Long back."

They moved to the end of the block. "See that pillow?" he demanded, pointing to the lower of the two shelf bunks in the last cage.

They nodded.

"Was a head on it one morning," he said. "Setten on the pillow. The eyes was open, and the tongue was hanging out." He paused a moment. "The body was under the bed," he said.

He moved on.

"Gal-boys," he said. "It is hard to keep down trouble in a pen. If I could get shet of these old double cages, then—"

He did not finish. A guard, a harmless-looking middle-aged man, clearly not in good trim, passed them into another section. There three convicts were scrubbing floor. "Good mornen, Mr. Budd—Good mornen, Mr. Budd—Good mornen, Mr. Budd," they said in voices of identical respect.

"Good morning, Bumpus, Mr. Budd said. "Burrus. Coffey."

His voice was easy, the raspiness thinning almost to a whisper. They moved on. Mr. Budd did not turn his head.

"Do you know all their names?" Yasha Jones asked.

"I know every God-damned name," Mr. Budd said.

Yasha Jones studied the rust-colored stiff neck ahead of him.

"Do you never turn your head?" he asked. "To look back?"

Mr. Budd did not turn his head.

"You git the habit of turnen your head," he said, "and you will soon get the habit of gitten dead. They will know something is gone rotten in you. If you can't tell all you need to know without turnen yore head, you better git into another line of work. Like shoe-clerken," he said.

He stopped suddenly, and swung on them.

"You know the loudest noise in a pen?" he demanded, leaning at them.

"No," Yasha Jones said.

"Silence," Mr. Budd said.

He turned, and moved on.

They went to the shops ("Good mornen, Mr. Budd"— "Good mornen, Mr. Budd"). They went to the store, where the souvenirs, made by the convicts on their own time, were for sale ("Yeah, they can save up money, for comen-out time"). They went to the gymnasium, grim and underequipped, but a gymnasium ("Yeah, when I come in as Deppity, I come to trouble. So I got up a-fore 'em and told 'em. I am runnen this joint. Any man thinks he can, and I will take him for ten rounds, pro referee. If he takes me he will git ice cream for a month. If I take him, it is solitary for a week. Nobody said a word. The Commissioner—he got sore. Made me stop it. Hell, maybe just as well. A man gits older and softens up. But hell, them days I was hard-bellied. You could bark yore knucks on my belly"). They went to the kitchen ("Clean—yeah, clean, hard, and fair is my motto, and I start with clean"). They watched the long lines file into the hall. They saw the two guards quietly pick a man from line ("Look at his face. It is dope. Got it on him now. A stool pigeon tipped us this mornen. You can't run a pen without no stools"). They sat at a table on a platform, visible to all, where they were served by trusties ("They kin see me eat what they got to eat, no different. One time a day").

They came out of the mess hall.

"We will go to the hospital," Mr. Budd said. "We runs it. Some of our boys have learned right well. We got a real pharmacist. Gonna have him a long time. Had him a nice drug store in Brownsville and killed his wife. She caught him with the soda-fountain gal. We are waiten for a real good doctor somewhere in Tennessee to kill his wife for ketchen him with the nurse."

Mr. Budd paused to laugh.

"A guy gets real sick we got to call in a outside doc," he said. "Not we ain't got a good inside doc. Went to Johns Hopkins. But he has lost confidence. He says he is afraid of doctoren now. He just sort of piddles around the place. Hell, he'll even empty bedpans, do stuff the nigger orderlies is supposed to do. He helps out, but he has lost confidence."

Mr. Budd turned to Brad.

"Hell," he said, "bet you know who that is."

"Yep," Brad said. "It is my brother-in-law. And that is why I am going to sit this one out."

The other two men went into the hospital, one of the wings of a new stone building set in the shadow of the great brick wall. Brad stared after them, standing there by a canna bed not yet in bloom. He took off his old panama and let the sun warm his scalp under the thinning blond hair.

They came back.

"Did you see him?" Brad demanded of Yasha Jones.

"Yes," Yasha Jones said. "He came and shook hands with me."

"I haven't seen him since the trial," Brad said.

"You would know him all right," Mr. Budd said. "Funny,

he ain't got old like some." He turned to Brad. "How old do
you reckin he is?"

"Forty-five, about."

"He don't look no age," Mr. Budd said. "He looks like he
was not much more'n a boy. A boy what has got gray, and is
thinken about somethen, he don't know exactly what." He
turned to Yasha Jones. "Ain't that the way he is?"

"It is a good description," he replied.

Yasha Jones had turned suddenly thoughtful, his head
lifting toward one of the big squat towers that squared the
wall. Up there a man was leaning on the parapet. Sunlight,
far off, gleamed off what he had in his hand, lying across the
parapet.

"Durn fool," Mr. Budd said. "That Doc Fiddler, he'd a
been outa here long back. If he hadn' tried that break." Then:
"Hell, a man like him ain't built to make no break."

Yasha Jones was still staring up at the tower where sunlight gleamed on metal. Mr. Budd followed his gaze. "That is
Lem," Mr. Budd said, "and I'll show you what Lem can do."

They climbed to the tower and he showed them.

"Show 'em, Lem," he said, when the introductions had
been completed, and each had, in turn, grasped, then relin-
quished, the hand that was offered, hanging off a thin wrist,
the hand itself long and thin and dry, giving the impression,
when touched, of a dried herring hung up by the tail.

Lem stood there, waiting.

"Yonder," Mr. Budd said, "see that sparrow, must be a
sparrow, setten on that flagpole?"

The flagpole jutted high, at an angle, above the entrance
of the prison. The sparrow sat on the knob. It was a full thirty
yards.

"You bust that knob," Mr. Budd said to Lem, "and I'll
dock yore pay."

Lem said nothing. The rifle started up slow. Then, suddenly, it was at the shoulder, and the sparrow was not on the
knob. A blue wisp of smoke drifted from the muzzle of the
rifle. It thinned to nothing in the sunlight.

Lem turned away.

"The feller up here a-fore Lem," Mr. Budd said, "he was
nigh handy as Lem. But he lost me a guard. One day a gar-
dener, a trusty, started choppen on that guard with a sickle.
Just got grudge-happy and started choppen, and you know,
would you believe it?"

He stopped and stared at them, overwhelmed by the old incredulity.

"Yeah," he said, "and thet feller up here, he never fired a round. Hell, I marched him to look at that-air sickle-work. 'You think you kin shoot,' I said to him. 'All right, why didn't you shoot?' And you know what the son-of-a-bitch said?"

He stopped, again overwhelmed.

"Well, I'll tell you. He said he was afraid of hitten a innocent man. You know what I said to him?"

"No," Yasha Jones finally said.

" 'Jesus Christ,' I said, 'a innocent man! There ain't no innocent man! You are fired.' "

The old rage, the old incredulity, still smoldering, Mr. Budd stared down at the yard where the sickle-work had taken place, where now four gardeners squatted, weeding a pansy border.

"You know," he said, brooding, not looking at them, "if you turned out every guy in the pen tomorrow mornen—yeah, with a thousand dollars apiece—most of 'em would be back in six months. Hell, even them as plans breaks, they don't really want out. They want something but it ain't out. They want in."

He swung suddenly at them.

"You know why they got in in the first place?" he demanded. Then drove on: "It is because they are lonesome. Some folks are born lonesome and they can't stand the lonesomeness out there. It is lonesome in here maybe, but it ain't as lonesome when you are with folks that knows they are as lonesome as you are."

"Mr. Budd," Yasha Jones said, "you are a philosopher."

"I am a Deppity Warden," Mr. Budd said.

His gaze roved slowly over the yards, over the reach of brick wall, back over the yards. He seemed to have forgotten them.

"You ever seen a man come out of solitary?" Mr. Budd asked, not even turning to them.

"No," Brad said.

"Sometimes," Mr. Budd said, "it is like they wanted to lay their head in your lap and cry. They are so grateful to see you. Solitary," he continued, "you can't run a pen without it. It is the last lonesomeness. It is the kind of lonesomeness a man can't stand, for he can't stand just being himself."

Mr. Budd stopped. His gaze had never turned on them. It roved the yard, the walls, the roofs.

"Mr. Budd," Yasha Jones said.

"Yeah."

"Mr. Budd, what will happen when the waters start to rise?"

"Maybe trouble, maybe not," Mr. Budd said. He paused. "But hell, if it's trouble you roll with the punch, then you come in swinging. That's the way you stay in business, in this business."

"But, Mr. Budd," Yasha Jones said, "if being in is what they want, and the rising of the waters makes them more cut off from the outside lonesomeness, more in, then why—"

"Hell," Mr. Budd said, "I never said the sons-of-bitches knows what they wants."

"Yes," Yasha Jones said, quietly, "yes."

"Let's go see Sukie," Mr. Budd said, rousing himself, it seemed, from meditation.

"What is Sukie?" Brad asked.

"You'll see," Mr. Budd said.

"Four dollars and ninety-three cents," Mr. Budd said, standing there just inside the steel door. "That was what he beat her head in fer. A old woman runnen a store out in the sticks, late at night. She came in and caught him at the cash register. A new claw hammer was a-layen there fer sale, and he picks it up. Looked like once he started he couldn't stop beaten her head in. Didn't more'n half try to hide, neither. Stuck his bloody shirt down a privy hole and went to bed. Now all he does is set. Set and maybe pick some music on his box. Won't pray or nuthen. The nigger preacher, he comes every day, but he won't pray. You know, folks down town they done got so they stop the nigger preacher on the street and ask him, 'Has yore boy prayed yet? Has he done cracked yet?' It looks like folks is worked up and got to know."

Mr. Budd paused. "Well," he said then, "he has got eight-nine weeks to go. A-fore he sees Sukie. You can do a lot of prayen in eight weeks."

His rubber soles moved down the corridor, then stopped in front of the cell. The Negro, a young man, sat on the cot, wearing gray denim pants, no belt, khaki shirt, tennis shoes with no strings. His face was very dark, very smooth. His hands were curled on his lap, like pets curled up to sleep. He stared fixedly at an invisible spot on the wall opposite him.

Mr. Budd tapped gently on the steel with his cane.

"Pretty-Boy," he said, in his raspy, whispery tone.

The man looked up.

"How you feelen, Pretty-Boy?" Mr. Budd asked.

"All right," the man said.

"Want to make some music?" Mr. Budd said.

The hands on the man's lap stirred. One reached out and lifted the guitar that lay on the cot beside him. He began to sing to the music, low and throaty.

> "Where did you come from?
> Where do you go?
> Where do you come from,
> Cotton-eye Joe?
>
> Come fer to see you,
> Come fer to sing,
> Come fer to show you
> My di-mint ring."

All the while he played, his eyes remained fixed on the invisible spot on the wall. When he had stopped singing, the eyes never moved.

"Thank you, Pretty-Boy," Mr. Budd said. "These gentlemin here—I am sure they 'preciate it."

"I appreciate it," Yasha Jones said.

The man lifted his face toward Yasha Jones, and peered studiously at him. "Thank ye," he said, then.

The eyes returned to the spot on the wall.

Mr. Budd peered assessingly into the cell. After a moment, he said: "Listen, Pretty."

The man turned his head.

"You gonna make it, Pretty," Mr. Budd said, in the raspy whisper, and moved up the corridor, the rubber soles making their silence on the cement.

"You mean he is going to make what?" Brad asked him. "You mean he is going to pray?"

"I mean he is goen to rise up and walk," Mr. Budd said. "When the time comes. He is goen to rise up and walk right down this here corridor. Like a man."

They stood before the door.

"Do most of them make it?" Yasha Jones asked.

"You'd be surprised," Mr. Budd said, "at 'em as can make it. Once a man gits the notion it is his one and last chance to be a man. I say to 'em, 'It is yore last chance. It is yore job and nobody can do it fer you.' I say, 'Maybe you never done a decent day's work in yore life, but here is a job you can't pass.' I say, 'I am pullen fer you.' You'd be surprised."

He paused.

"Mr. Budd," Yasha Jones said.

"Yeah?"

"Why did you call him Pretty-Boy? The one back there, I mean."

"It is his name," Mr. Budd said. "It is the name his mother give him. It is the name he was tried by. It is the name the doctor will write on the papers when they take out the fried meat. Pretty-Boy Rountree."

Mr. Budd looked back down the corridor.

"Look," he said. "Yonder comes the preacher. Brother Pinckney. The nigger preacher. Maybe he will crack him today."

And then, as the guard arrived to open the door, he said, "Here is Sukie."

He stepped into the room.

Mr. Budd stooped to pat the back of the chair.

"She is waiten here with her arms wide open," he said. "She is waiten and she will take you when you come. She is ever-man's sweetheart. She will give any man a ride. She is the gal with the juice. She will give a man a jerk like he ain't never had. One round with Sukie, and you ain't never gonna want no other kind of a jerk."

Mr. Budd, with his rubber-soled ease, had swung around, and dropped himself into the chair. "You come in yonder," he said, nodding back toward the door, now closed. "You take a seat. You lean back restful."

He leaned back.

"You lays yore arms on the arms of the chair."

He performed the action, laying his arms on the straps.

"You sets yore legs straight."

He set his feet straight on the floor. The electrodes were there.

"You holds yore head steady and they drops a black cap

on. I always get 'em run up in the sewing shop, special for the business."

He adjusted an imaginary cap.

"Now they pulls the big leather cap down, the one with the juice, and you are ready to ride. Sukie is achen to go. She is groanen with juice."

He sat there a moment as though the other men were not there, in that moment looking down, it seemed, at his own body in the chair. He lifted his head at them with a glint of cold challenge sudden in the pale gray eyes. "You know what I am?" he demanded.

No one answered.

He said: "I am the executioner for this here state. I am the guy that throws the switch."

He picked up his right arm from the arm of the chair where it had been lying on the straps. He scrutinized the hand as though discovering a new interest in the object. He lifted it that others might see better.

"That is what throws the switch," he said. "It has lost count."

He lost interest in the hand, and again looked at them.

"Twenty-five bucks a throw," he said. "Same price it was before the war, inflation and all. Yeah," he said, "you used to buy somethen with twenty-five bucks. You could buy a purty, and soften up a gal. Hell," he said, and laughed, "fer twenty-five bucks you could soften up a half a dozen. 'Afore the inflation."

For an instant longer he sat there, then suddenly rose from the chair. He leaned at Brad. "You set there," he commanded.

Brad looked at him, at the sudden, cold gray challenge of the glance in that rust-colored face. Then he looked down at the matter-of-factness of old oily sweat-soaked wood and leather and metal, set in the dreary cleanliness of the little room. He thought of how you would come through the little door and would not be able to believe that this was all, that this matter-of-factness, the dreary matter-of-factness of an antiquated dental chair discarded in a junk shop, was all. He thought how, in that instant, a wave of deprivation, of irremediable diminishment, would sweep over you. Was this all? Was everything—all life and death—as inconsequential as this?

He sat in the chair.

He thought, quite suddenly then, of that dreary inconsequential office, like the office of a fly-by-night, failing real
estate man, where he had once signed up for Spain.

Mr. Budd was leaning at him from one side, over him,
speaking in his raspy voice. "Listen," Mr. Budd said, not very
loud.

"What?" Brad said.

"Think of the worst thing you ever done," Mr. Budd said,
whispering, and suddenly peered into Brad's face; then broke
into roars of throaty laughter.

When he had conquered his mirth, Mr. Budd slapped
Brad on the shoulder, then turned to Yasha Jones. "It is my
joke," he said. "It's a joke I pull on folks. Hell, you oughta see
some of the faces on some of 'em. Hell, one time a man just
pee-ed in the chair."

He turned to Brad, who now stood there, looking down at
the chair, and again gave him the brotherly slap on the
shoulder. "Hell," he said, "you didn' pee."

"Mr. Budd," Yasha Jones said, "I should like to sit in the
chair."

"Sure," Mr. Budd said, "she is ever-man's sweetheart.
Sukie—she is waiten for you."

Yasha Jones took his place, adjusted himself. "I suppose
I would spare you the usual haircut," he said, and smiled, a
simple smile with no wryness in it.

"Yep," Mr. Budd said, looking at the baldness.

Yasha Jones was still smiling up at Mr. Budd. "Aren't
you going to ask me the question?" he said.

Brad stared down at the brown, aquiline face that was
smiling there, under the shadow of the heavy leather-and-
metal cap, and wondered what was the worst thing that this
man had ever done. He was wondering this, he knew, because when he himself had sat there under that question, he
had been able to think of nothing, nothing at all. He had not
pee-ed. But he had been able to think of nothing.

Chapter

13

"Not it," Brad said, rising from his inspection of a tombstone which, long back, had fallen into the tangle of weeds and briar.

Yasha Jones said nothing. He was looking far off, upward, back at the towers of the penitentiary, from which they had just come. His gaze fixed on the southwest tower.

"Hope you don't mind stopping," Brad said, "poking around here."

"I am here to see Fiddlersburg," Yasha Jones said.

"Old Izzie Goldfarb," he said. "He is Fiddlersburg. I have been ten thousand miles away and I have shut my eyes and I have said the word *Fiddlersburg,* and what I saw was Old Goldfarb. I would see him in my inner eye, sitting propped back in his split-bottom chair, outside his shop, looking out over the river toward the sun going down. I don't know why he is Fiddlersburg, but he is." He paused. "Yes, I do know why. He made me see Fiddlersburg."

He took off his hat, took out a handkerchief and wiped his forehead. It was unseasonably hot. An insect was chirring somewhere in the green brush, then stopped. He looked out over the river.

"You know," he said, "you know what—"

He stopped.

"What?" Yasha Jones demanded.

"Old Goldfarb was alone," Brad said. "Nobody knew anything about him. Where he had come from, nothing, and—"

Yasha Jones was murmuring softly:

> "Where did you come from?
> Where did you go?
> Where do you—"

"Yeah," Brad broke in, "yeah. He was Fiddlersburg and at the same time he was not Fiddlersburg. He was non-Fiddlersburg and he was anti-Fiddlersburg. What I mean is this," Brad went on. "He was alone. He would sit there absolutely alone and watch the sun go down. But he was not lonesome. He was complete. Alone but not lonesome."

Yasha Jones looked up at the tower. Brad saw the lift of his glance, followed it.

"Hell," Brad said, "your philosopher friend Mr. Budd is right. It is the lonesomeness. The only reason everybody in Fiddlersburg does not get himself in the pen out of lonesomeness is because Fiddlersburg is a kind of pen already, and everybody knows already he is with folks who are as lonesome as he is. Hell, the whole South is lonesome. It is as lonesome as coon hunting, which has always been a favorite sport, and that is lonesomer than anything except frog-gigging on a dark night in a deep swamp and your skiff leaking, and some folks prefer it that way.

"Hell, the South is the country where a man gets drunk just so he can feel even lonesomer and then comes to town and picks a fight for companionship. The Confederate States were founded on lonesomeness. They were all so lonesome they built a pen around themselves so they could be lonesome together. The only reason the Confederate army held together

as long as it did against overwhelming odds was that everybody felt that it would just be too damned lonesome to go
home and be lonesome by yourself.

"The South," Brad went on. "Folks say 'the South,' but the
word doesn't mean a damned thing. It is a term without a
referent. No—it means something, but it does not mean what
folks think it means. It means a profound experience, com-
munally shared—yeah. But you know what that shared experience is that makes the word *South?*"

"No."

"It is lonesomeness," Brad said. "It is angry lonesomeness. Angry lonesomeness makes Southerners say the word
South like an idiot Tibetan monk turning a broke-down
prayer wheel on which he has forgot to hang any prayers.

"Hell, no Southerner believes that there is any South. He
just believes that if he keeps on saying the word he will lose
some of the angry lonesomeness. The only folks in the South
who are not lonesome are the colored folks. They may be
angry but they are not lonesome. You know what?"

"What?" Yasha Jones obligingly asked.

"That," Brad said, "is the heart of the race problem. It is
not guilt. That is crap. It is simply that your Southerner is
deeply and ambiguously disturbed to have folks around him
who are not as lonesome as he is. Especially if they are black
folks. Take that poor bastard up in the death cell this afternoon—the reason everybody in Fiddlersburg wants him to
crack and pray is because if a man prays you know he is took
lonesome. That's why they want that black boy to pray.
Fiddlersburg is a praying town, just like the South is a praying country. But it is not because they believe in God. They
do not believe in God. What they believe in is the black hole
in the sky God left when He went away. Look!"

He pointed up to the sky, where the sun was still blazing
high and bright enough to make you blink.

"Look, Yasha Jones!" he commanded, "see it."

Yasha Jones blinked obediently upward. "No," he said,
after a histrionic interval, "I don't see it. I do not see the hole.
Perhaps because I believe in God."

"I don't believe in God," Brad said. "And I don't believe
in the black hole in the sky either." He paused. "What I believe in," he said, "is Fiddlersburg."

"Fiddlersburg," Yasha Jones murmured. Then asked,
softly: "So that is why you are back here?"

"Yes," Brad said. "I am here because I am full of angry lonesomeness. But"—and he suddenly stared at the other man—"maybe you are, too. Anyway, you came to Fiddlersburg."

He turned away. In the new growth and old briars he found a tombstone. It was not what he sought. He found another, examined it, rose from it. He looked up at the sky.

"My God," he said, in a tone like despair.

Yasha Jones looked questioningly at him.

"My God," he repeated, slowly turning to look at Yasha Jones. "Maggie—my sister Maggie Tolliver Fiddler—can you imagine how lonesome she must be?"

"No," Yasha Jones said, "I cannot."

The afternoon was absolutely still. The sun beat down. The only sound was the sound of that insect in the growth. Then it stopped. Yasha Jones stood there in the silence and thought how hot and still it had been one afternoon long ago, far off, in France, lying in the undergrowth. After the single dry crack of the rifle down toward the village there had been only the silence. Then in the hot silence, as he lay there on the ground, hiding in the growth, he had become aware of a sound. It was a tiny sound, a single dry crack. The crack would come. Then, in the heat, in the silence, another would come. It was a tiny sound like the dry crack of a minuscule rifle, far off in the minuscule world of dried grass stems and broken weeds in which his head lay, a sound that echoed, on that tiny scale, the real rifle.

Then he had realized what it was. It was the little black pod of the *genêt* cracking open in the August sun. He had been staring at a pod, and under his very eyes, it had cracked open, with that small sound.

Lying there, face down in the thin shadow of the *genêt*, he—he, Henri Duval from the old schoolbook in Chicago—had known what the fact of the shot's being single meant. The first shot had found its mark. There had been no need for a second. So Jean Perrot, his friend, was dead. The Germans had got him. And Yasha Jones, lying there, thought how Yasha Jones was dead, even though he yet lived a kind of shadowy life in the person of Henri Duval, the village schoolmaster, the village pharmacist, the unsuccessful notary. He hoped that, when his turn came, it would be one shot.

Now Yasha Jones, standing in the hot sunshine of afternoon in Fiddlersburg, thought back with envy on that Yasha Jones who had lain in the gorse and known himself as good as dead, peaceful, beyond fear and desire. But now he stood in Fiddlersburg, knowing that he was not dead and would have to endure, with joy, his life.

He felt the sweat come in the palms of his hands and looked at Bradwell Tolliver, who, suddenly, seemed very strange to him, who, standing there among the unkempt graves, had just asked him if he, Yasha Jones, could imagine how lonely Maggie Tolliver Fiddler must be.

"No," Yasha Jones repeated, "I cannot imagine how lonely she must be."

Then, slowly, he added: "But I have tried."

Brad, standing there, eyes blinking, seemed to have drawn into himself. After a moment, he said: "The South—it is full of women like that. Or used to be. Women stuck with something—the paralyzed old father, the batty mother, the sister's orphan kid, the uncle with paresis, the booze-bit brother. Stuck with that—and lonesomeness. Hell, I've seen 'em, lots of 'em built for something very, very different. Sitting it out. Lonesome in the long hot summer afternoons or fall nights, sort of storing up lonesomeness like honey, storing it up for someday, somebody. You know what I mean. That devotion, that absoluteness, just stored up for somebody. But," he said, "nobody comes."

He stood there, blinking in the light.

"You know," he said, then. "You know, there've been times back on the Coast—even when I was sober—when I figured I might just come back here and find me one of those lonesome women with all that honey just stored up. All that devotion, that absoluteness. You know what I mean?"

"Yes," Yasha Jones said.

"Well, damned if I do," the other said, "exactly. But the sort of woman you could just lie down by the side of and take her hand and know that everything in the world was all right."

He moved a couple of paces, found and examined a stone, rose and faced Yasha Jones. "You know what I mean?"

"Yes," Yasha Jones said.

"Well, suddenly I do too," Brad said and spat. "It is incipient middle age. It is the symptom of creeping idealism, and that is the nastiest star in the syndrome. It is something you got to watch. You better get a damned good surgeon and cut it out just in case it is malignant. It is, in fact, always malignant."

He laughed, spat again, and found another stone. He rose from the stone.

"Christ," he said, "Maggie."

Yasha Jones stood at his distance, waiting.

"You know," Brad said, "when I came back here after the war, to write me a novel—hell, I never finished it—it got so I couldn't bear it about Maggie. She is not made for this non-life. Hell, I knew what she was like, and I couldn't bear it. I would tell her to get a divorce and get out. Something would just come over me, I'd be in a rage. I never could figure why it burned me up so. We had awful rows about it, finally. Then—" his voice petered out.

"Then what?"

"Then I got a good offer on the Coast." He shrugged. "I've been out there ever since, and she's been here," he said. He looked up into the hot sky. "And she is as lonesome as God."

Yasha Jones studied him.

"There is one possibility," Yasha Jones said.

"What?"

"That perhaps she is not lonesome at all," he said. "That we merely think she is lonesome."

"Christ," Brad burst out, in anger. "You can look at how she is—how she is built, how she walks across the floor, the look in her eye—"

"Listen," Yasha Jones said. "You know what Mr. Budd said about being put in solitary? How you can't stand it, for no man can stand being himself. You remember what he said?"

"Yes, but—"

"But perhaps she can stand it," Yasha Jones said, "and therefore is not lonesome. Perhaps she is the kind of person who can stand being herself and can therefore stand being with herself."

Mr. Budd had gone back up on the southwest tower. His gaze swept the land westward across the river. He looked, then, down at River Street. Down in front of the pen gate, he saw the car of that nigger preacher. The preacher was just sitting there, not moving, in the car. He wondered why.

He looked farther down River Street. Way off, over yonder, he saw the white Jaguar parked by the road, down at the old graveyard. He saw the two figures, very small off there, in the graveyard. He wondered what the hell they were doing there.

Then he thought how that baldheaded fellow with the scars had asked him what would happen when the water rose, only the baldheaded fellow had said "waters." He abandoned the figures in the graveyard and turned to look along the east wall of the prison. Under the wall there, the houses, some vacant now, some decrepit, some paintless, clung to the slope under the wall. He saw the house where he had been born.

He saw the house, and thought of himself a boy there. He thought of his father, a guard in the pen, thirty dollars a month, smelling of whiskey on his day off. He thought how, long ago, when he was a boy, at the time of the big break at the pen, when the cons had holed up in Lorton's Hardware, his father had been too yellow to go in. He thought how it was Sheriff Purtle who went in. He thought how at school he had fights because kids said his old man was yellow.

He looked down and thought of water rising, and a grim joy filled his heart. He thought how the water would rise all around, and only the pen would stick up out of the water, and how he would be here alone where he had always wanted to be.

Leon Pinckney, Howard University, B.A., M.A., Harvard University, M.S.T., sat in the 1949 black two-door Studebaker Champion sedan, with the broken glass of the right front door held together by adhesive tape. He was in anguish because he had not been able to bring Pretty-Boy Rountree to prayer. But he was in anguish, too, because he was afraid that Pretty-Boy Rountree would, in the end, pray.

There was a third reason he was in anguish. He was in anguish because he himself, at this moment, could not pray.

Bradwell Tolliver stood among the weed-choked, briar-embraced stones, in the sunshine which now failed of heat, and suffered an obscure distress, like chalk in the throat, be-

cause he had suddenly remembered that the engineer Digby
was probably going to turn up tonight for that drink he had
invited him for. But Christ, he thought, it wasn't his fault.
You had to write something when that Leontine Purtle was
standing right there behind you.

Chapter

14

BOTH MEN NOW SILENT, the Jaguar drew from the cemetery
gate, lounging with its fluid ease over the breaks and heaves
of the road that now, with the waters coming so soon, nobody
bothered to fix any more. In the lingering light the car eased
on past the vacant lots where black stalks of old ironweed
appeared above the new green, past the fences nobody
propped up any more, past the houses nobody bothered to
paint any more, past the Tomwit place, already abandoned,
with windowpanes broken, past the house where Sylvester
Purtle sat in his wheel chair and where Brad saw that Digby's
car was not yet parked and thought, with a flicker of hope,
that maybe the son-of-a-bitch would not turn up tonight after
all. Staring at the house, Brad thought of the little varnished

pine box of a room occupied by Digby, and the studio couch with the patched white counterpane, and wondered if Digby had made the grade with Leontine.

No, he decided, it would not be Digby's dish. You could not imagine Digby, with his round face, freckles, peeling red nose, sandy crew cut, grin exposing square teeth with spaces too wide between them, and the habit of cracking his knuckles, as the man to enter that mystic dark of Leontine.

No, Digby would never do for the engineer of the story he had made up. He had no purple birthmark.

As they mounted the wide stairway in the hall, Brad suddenly stopped, just before they reached the level of the second floor, and turned to Yasha. "Listen," he said, "it has got to be. It's mandatory."

"What is mandatory?"

"The pen, the penitentiary," he said, "for our beautiful moving picture. Inside-outside. Someone waiting inside. Someone waiting outside. Lonesomeness. Waiting for the waters. You see—"

"Just walk off and leave him, Mr. Jones," the voice said, and they turned to see Maggie standing above them, leaning on the railing on the second floor, laughing.

"Brad would talk under those waters he's talking about," she said. "Once he got started. He will talk on the stairs. He will keep you on the stairs all night, Mr. Jones. Go away and leave him."

"Ole Sis, you are ignorant of the ways of literary inspiration," Brad said. "I am working."

"Who is Digby?" she demanded.

"What?" Brad said, with a little twinge of alarm.

"Somebody named Digby," she said. "He just telephoned and said he'd be a little late, said you had asked him for a drink. I covered up. I cooed and said, oh, yes, we were expecting him. Who is he?"

Brad burst into a gay chant:

"Oh, who is Digby, tell me who?
Oh, what would a guy like Digby do?"

Chanting, he hated the crinkled attempt at a carefree smile he felt on his face. He saw that she was looking at his face.

"Well, what *does* he do?" she asked dutifully.

"He digs," he said, maintaining gaiety.

"Oh, Jesus!" she breathed, and suddenly looked like herself, not studying his face any more, turning toward Yasha. "Oh, Mr. Jones," she cried in a burst of sympathy, "how can you bear it? Do you have to hear it all day long?"

"And," Brad broke in, mounting the last few stairs, "when he gets through digging, they will call him Dugby."

He felt that crinkled attempt at a carefree smile fade from his face. So he said, brusquely: "He is an engineer on the dam." Then, turning to Yasha, "I know you want to wash up," he said.

"Guess you're right," Yasha Jones was saying, smiling, moving away, turning once to wave back at them, moving off, with shoulders erect and stride easy, down the shadowy hall.

Brad turned to face his sister, trying to make out what her expression meant.

"Damn it," he said, "I didn't mean to ask that Digby over tonight, it was an accident the way it—"

He stopped. There was no way to explain to her how it was not his fault, how he hadn't meant to put that in the note, the invitation to have a drink, but you had to write something when that Leontine Purtle was standing there, so close you were afraid you would bump into her, would touch her, with some sort of aversion in you which you were ashamed of because it was an aversion to her infirmity, and all the while as you stood there trying to think of something to write and get it over, you knew she was standing there behind you, so close you were afraid you'd feel her breath, with that pile of pale yellow hair slipping askew on her head, and that mystic, annunciatory, damp-lipped smile on her face that wasn't quite a smile, and her eyes looking off at something you couldn't ever see, and that little varnished pine box of a room so quiet you could hear her breathe. You couldn't explain how you had stood there and heard that damned sparrow in the gutter.

"Brad," she said.

He tried to read what was in the face, in the word.

She was saying: "You don't have to worry. Just because he's a young engineer. It was all so long ago."

"Damn it," he said, "the guy won't get here till long

after dinner. You could be in the house. You don't have to see him."

"Oh, yes I do!" she exclaimed, her voice with a bright edge in it which might have been mistaken for gaiety.

"I don't see why," he said defensively.

"Then you don't have so much imagination," she said, and now he could see—or thought he could see—that the knuckles of her hand still on the railing had gone white. "Try to imagine me," she was saying, "sitting up here in the house, in this house, in the dark, and not seeing his face. It would be not seeing his face that would not be all right."

Bradwell stood there and wished he had never come back here. He wanted to get out of here.

He would never have got out of Fiddlersburg in the first place, or at least not half so easy, if it had not been for Frog-Eye. His father would have seen him dead on the floor and cold as a pile of drawn chicken guts before he would have let him go off to Nashville to prep school, and then up North to Darthurst. Even if he himself did have the money. His mother had seen to that, having left what little money she had to the children, in trust, specifically marked for education "at some institution of standing, not situated in Fiddlersburg."

She had left it to be administered by a cousin of hers, a banker in Memphis, who was not the type to be bullied by Old Tolliver and who would, rather, enjoy bullying Tolliver as a kind of vengeance for Tolliver's having had the impudence to mix his muskrat-skinning genes with the High Confederate blood of the Cottshills, even at the distance of a second cousin in Fiddlersburg. In this vengeful attitude the Memphis Cottshill was, no doubt, executing the deep intent of the dead woman. For Calistha Cottshill had, in the end, come to hate herself for the black gust of passion that had swept her shivering and overage virginity into the horn-handed, hairy mercy of Lancaster Tolliver; and had come to hate Lancaster Tolliver for the numberless things he, out of the deep need of his nature, had done to humiliate her, the thing highest on the list being the very thing that, haunting her dreams, had, in the beginning, delivered her to his mercy. So she had died, even as she ejected from her body the child that was the fruit of the last indignity Lank Tolliver had visited upon her, upon her self-contempt and her self-incredulity.

It was not, however, the banker Cottshill from Memphis who forced Tolliver to let the son go. At that time, when Brad was fourteen, Lank Tolliver was in his prime, his natural arrogance still bolstered by whatever wealth and prestige Fiddlersburg could afford. Under such circumstances there would probably have been little that even a Memphis banker could do to break down the cussedness. It was Brad himself who managed it. But he had Frog-Eye to thank. For Frog-Eye had led him to the spot where Lancaster Tolliver lay in the mud of the deep swamp, unconscious, with the marks of tears yet on his cheeks.

From this fact two things had followed.

First, the boy, who had been able to bear the brutal cussedness of the father, and had, in fact, been held to the father by that very brutality, and had learned to play upon that brutality as on an instrument, could not bear the knowledge that that father, in his brutality, could lie in the mud and weep. That knowledge tore at some fundament of his own being. He would wake in the night, and feel, actually, sick. He could not bear to be in the house with that fact.

Second, the boy had known that now he held the weapon he needed to work his will on the father. And so, one morning in July, 1929, the boy calmly announced, at breakfast, that he was going to go, in the fall, to the school where Cal Fiddler went—to the Maury Academy in Nashville.

"You are, in a pig's ass," the father said.

"I wrote Mr. Cottshill, Momma's cousin in Memphis," the boy said, "and he made the arrangements."

He was watching the purple rush of blood to the father's face, thinking it was like a thunderhead piling up in the hot summer sky, and the first lightning was about to come. Suddenly exhilarated with the image, he said, as innocently as possible: "You know—that cousin of Momma's who handles that money she left me and Maggie."

"God damn it!" the father exclaimed and heaved up like a stung bull crashing the brush. The chair clattered behind him. He started around the end of the table.

The boy did not rise from his chair. He simply said: "Listen—I know something on you."

The man stopped. It was not the words that stopped him, for he had not really understood them. It was the absolute

calmness on the face of the boy. The face was completely
smooth, unpuddled, unruffled by any emotion. The blond hair
was still darkened by water from the morning toilet and was
plastered smoothly down, every hair in place. That smoothness of face and hair, that was what stopped the man dead
in his tracks, his right hand lifted as for a blow.

"I have seen you crying," the boy said.

The man stared at him. The purple of the face was, all
at once, streaked with white. But the hand was still raised.

"Yes," the boy said. "I've seen you lying in the mud, in
the swamp where you go to cry. You had been crying."

The man's hand was quivering in the air.

"Listen," the boy said, almost whispering now, "you
won't stop me from going anywhere. You want me to go
now. You don't want me around the house looking at you
and you knowing what I am knowing every time I look at
you."

The streaks of white on the man's face were more pronounced now. He looked sick.

"Anyway," the boy said, "you'll still have Maggie. You
can hold her on your knee and ruffle up her hair and I
won't be there looking at you."

That was all. The man's hand came down, slowly. The
man looked at his own hand, then held it against his thigh as
though it were wounded and he were ashamed of the wound.
He went out of the dining room, without a word. The boy sat
there while the Negro woman, soft-footed and wordless,
came in and began clearing the table. The morning sunlight
of summer fell across the ruins of the meal. He was in a
trance of joyous power.

Chapter

15

THE MOON WAS BEGINNING TO SHOW above the bulk of the unlighted house. Digby had not come yet. Nobody had spoken for some minutes when Maggie said to Yasha Jones: "You said the other day that when you can't sleep you read. What do you read?"

"Poetry," he said. "Do you read it?"

"Yep," Brad answered for her. "Ole Sis reads it."

"I guess I read anything," she said. "Sitting here in this house. The old Fiddlers had a lot of books."

"Ole Sis reads poetry," Brad said, "the way a mountain climber climbs a mountain. She reads it merely because it is there. What do you read it for?"

Yasha Jones laughed.

"Because I'm a physicist," he said. "Or rather, an ex-would-be or would-have-been physicist."

He paused.

"You see," he resumed, "lots of physicists play the violin or listen to chamber music. I assume they do it because music gives them an emotional dimension—a sort of emotional paradigm—of what they are doing anyway. It is an image of law and flow, of depth and shimmer. But me"—he laughed again, a hint of rueful comedy in the sound—"I have a tin ear and I'm not a real physicist. So I am stuck with poetry."

"Depth," Maggie Fiddler said, "depth and shimmer."

"Yes," Yasha Jones said, "all good poetry has it. But I guess I'm thinking of a special kind, the kind that belongs to our time. To our physics. That, rather, predicted our physics. Some Baudelaire, some Pound, some Eliot, some Perse. A few others. Coleridge in his craziness, Wordsworth in his peculiar way, they had it, that early.

"Not Yeats. As great as any of them, but he's an anachronism, an old Newtonian mind, just a passionate old Newtonian mind, like a cromlech in moonlight. All his nonsense about cones and gyres and ouija boards and Celtic twilight—all of it is just an attempt to generate something corresponding to the mysterious shudder of Einstein or Freud or Perse. Even Marx, perhaps. But Yeats had it backwards—he thought that the shudder comes from a flight out of nature. It comes from a flight into nature."

"It would put me to sleep, all right," Brad said. "Poetry would."

"It isn't that poetry puts me to sleep," Yasha Jones said. "In the beginning, quite the contrary. Oh, quite. It wakes me up. I sit propped up in bed, in the middle of the night, and then if I hit the right thing, I suddenly get the sense that the world is silently exploding around me. In all directions, in absolute silence, in a kind of continual and flowing explosion, into absolute darkness that flees out in all directions. It is as though the walls of the room just flee infinitely away, just leaving that little spot of light; or rather, if I shut my eyes, or turn off the bed lamp, just leaving the words glowing inside my head like infinitely tiny little bulbs glowing and winking inside a big computer. Not that the big computer is me. It is the place where I might have been if I were there.

"Then suddenly I relax and go to sleep."

"It sounds like the way Rube Goldberg goes to sleep," Brad said. "It is the kind of cartoon he would draw of an insomniac getting to sleep."

"I am the guy he's hunting for for his cartoon," Yasha Jones said, and laughed. Then added: "You know, to stop what Brad would call my horsing around, it is a sort of depersonalization, and if you can accept it, it lets you sleep. This is an age of depersonalization. You can think of a person as definable only at the point—no, only *as* the point—where an infinite number of lines intersect in flight inward and outward. Person equals point-from-which. And point-toward-which. Which is nothing. This is the issue of our age, but people are afraid of the fact. That is why people try to grab something, doctrine or dope. Anything to hold on to.

"You take a person as keenly aware of the process as Eliot, whose very genius stems from that awareness—he is afraid of it, he has to count bishops the way old Samuel Johnson used to count fence posts because he was afraid he would explode into space. But you know, once you accept that process, you can sleep. It is very restful at that point where all the lines intersect. The traffic has all gone away."

And, in his own head, Yasha Jones added: *You can have joy. That is all that is left at the point from which the lines, intersecting, flee away.*

"I bet you were one hell of a professor," Brad said.

"Mr. Jones," Maggie said, "that remark may sound like a compliment, but coming from my brother, it is not intended as such."

"I feel myself exploding silently," Brad said. "I feel the *Me* exploding silently into the *non-Me*."

"Hush," Maggie said, "and listen to the mockingbird. He is starting up."

The bird made an experimental sally, then stopped.

"He has exploded silently," Brad said.

"Mr. Jones," Maggie said.

"Yes?"

"There is one sort of unusual and agreeable thing about you," she said. "You talk exactly the same way to anybody and everybody. You don't talk down. You don't talk sideways."

"You mean I don't have much imagination," he said. "I don't take that as much of a compliment."

"I have to mean it as a compliment," she said. "I have to

mean it that way, because that makes it, you see, a compliment to me. Yasha Jones is talking to somebody in Fiddlersburg—to me—the way Yasha Jones would to somebody in California or New York."

"Maybe Yasha Jones is just talking to himself," he said. "Maybe that is all Yasha Jones knows how to do." There was, all at once, a hint of dourness in his voice. He heard the inflection himself, and for that flicker of an instant, was shaken in a gust of darkness. He felt absolutely alone.

"I don't want you to talk differently," she was saying, "whatever way it is. And what I'm going to say is a compliment. At least I mean it that way. I was really trying to understand what you said."

"Thank you," he said evenly. Then added: "But I don't know that I did."

They fell into silence. The moon was well over the house now. The TV aerial stood on the roof and caught a faint gleam. The mockingbird had begun again. Again it stopped.

"Brad," Yasha Jones said.

"Yes?"

"If we can just catch that."

"Catch what?"

"What we were talking about. The depth and shimmer. Just catch a little bit of it. Like light striking across water, when the sun is low, just rising or setting. As though the waters were rising very calmly over the flats yonder, and we caught the glimmer of light."

"Hi, there!" a voice called cheerily from the shadows at the upper end of the garden. "Where is everybody?"

It was Maggie who answered first.

"Oh, Mr. Digby!" she called back in a voice light and clear, as though with happiness. "We're down here. Come down here!"

Brad rose, went to greet him, escorted him back; and Digby stood in front of Maggie's chair, as she offered him her hand and smiled up, and said: "It's awful nice of you to come. I could just kick Brad he didn't do it sooner, invite you sooner."

He stood there, solid, round-faced, round-headed, in the moonlight. He rocked slightly from one just-whited saddle shoe to the other, in a motion suggesting a boxer treading the resin box; and finally managed to say, thanks, he was sure glad to come, and maybe she had a sweet tooth; and thrust out a box of candy, a two-pound box, two pounds being what, standing for a full minute before the candy counter of the Rexall store, he had decided was just about right, not chinchy like one pound or sort of overdoing it like five pounds.

She said that it was just darling of him, he shouldn't have, she'd be eating chocolates all night, and she certainly did wish that Brad had asked him sooner for she hadn't had a real chocolate debauch since she could remember—all with that vivid, clear voice in which she had answered his hail from the shadows, sitting up straight in her chair as though to show her good waist to advantage, looking up with a smile, her eyes never leaving his face.

And his face grinned back. He looked happy, standing there, with the fingers of his right hand adjusting the striped bow tie. It was an attention the tie obviously didn't need, for it already sat with mathematical exactitude on the collar of the fresh white shirt. The moon was so bright now the stripes of the tie came very clear.

Then he sat in a chair and leaned forward to hear her speak. Now and then he took a drink of the whiskey. He drank with small, systematic appraising sips, the way of a man in an advertisement who cannot be fooled about his whiskey. Now and then, almost always at the right moment, he laughed at something she said. For, while her brother looked at her with faint surprise and unease, she was telling tales of Fiddlersburg, gaily, innocently, with gestures, with mimicry, with the clear sense that she could please, that her mission was to laugh in the moonlight, and please.

". . . and poor Miss Euphemia, she'd steal anything. Fiddlersburg didn't have a very clear idea of kleptomania, but it had a very clear idea of Miss Euphemia. Of her kind of stealing which wasn't like other folks' stealing. For instance, she was the only person—I swear it—who ever stole the stained-glass windows of the Methodist Church. That was back yonder when we had a Methodist Church and—"

"Before our old man put the Methodists out of business," Brad interrupted.

"Hush," Maggie said, "you interrupt."

"He foreclosed on 'em," Brad said.

"The windows," she said, ignoring him, "had been taken

down for cleaning. Propped against the wall. Along came Miss Euphemia in the hot noontide, with a blue-and-white parasol with one broken rib. Nobody was there and it was a challenge, you might say. Down the road right then came Ole Zack, an old colored man, in a wagon, with a team of mules. 'Uncle!' says Miss Euphemia. 'You load my windows and take them home!'

"He did. People did what Miss Euphemia said. He loaded them up, and she climbed on the wagon board with him, black knit gloves and pince-nez and broke-rib parasol and all, and drove right to her own barn, broad daylight at high noon on a hot summer day in Fiddlersburg being about the most private, secret and unpopulated time there is anywhere.

"Now the Methodists couldn't figure out who had stolen their windows. But Ole Zack—he worked for our father—he told our father and—"

"—and if you think," Brad put in, "our old man was the kind to let a mortgagor milk a piece of property of its stained-glass windows you are wrong. He wrote a letter to the Methodist minister, demanding that the windows be recovered and put back in place. Instanter. Now the poor Methodists didn't know where the windows were, but they knew our old man. Our old man knew where the windows were, but he wasn't going to tell 'em. He really had it cooking in the way our old man liked best. So he—"

"Hush," Maggie said, "we're talking about the windows, not poor old Poppa." She turned to Digby. "Anyway, the Methodists had to sleuth around and try to find out. All the Methodists turned hawkshaw. Finally one little Methodist boy happened to chase a cat into Miss Euphemia's barn, little Methodist boys being hard on cats.

"But that didn't solve anything. You can't let on that a nice old Episcopal maiden lady like Miss Euphemia steals. The Methodists tried to pass the burden to the Sheriff. The Sheriff—Old Mr. Purtle it was then—he wouldn't touch it. He had an out. He just said, 'Hell, I'm a Baptist,' and took another chaw."

"What—" Digby said, after a moment, "what did they do?"

"Now, Mr. Digby," she inquired earnestly, and leaned at him, "suppose you were a Fiddlersburg Methodist. What would you do?"

"My folks," Mr. Digby said, "my mother anyway, she's Lutheran."

"Well, just suppose," she said. "Suppose you weren't Lutheran and it was Fiddlersburg, what would you do?"

Digby thought, took another judicious sip of whiskey, set the glass down on the bricks, cracked his knuckles, grinned, and admitted that he didn't know what he would do.

She accused him of not putting his mind on the problem. He just didn't know.

"You're just too honest," she said. "The answer is simple. Go steal them back. And that was what they did, the preacher and the elders and all. Got a wagon and team and waited for a dark night. But Miss Euphemia was not a heavy sleeper. She gave two barrels of an antiquated fowling piece out of a second-story window. Just too late, however. They were pulling out of range. No, not quite out of range. One mule got stung with bird-shot and started rearing and kicking, and since preacher was not exactly a Ben Hur this created difficulties that, for a moment, it seemed faith would not solve.

"Things get rather confused at this point," Maggie continued. "Just trust me to do the best I can. The shots woke people up. Somebody rang the fire bell. People thought there was a break in the penitentiary. Those searchlights on the penitentiary began to sweep around. People began to pop out on their porches, those who hadn't popped under their beds to avoid gunfire. The searchlights finally picked out the mule team, the load of stained-glass windows and the preacher— him with his hands on the reins and sweat running down his poor face.

"By this time he had an escort of half-naked little boys who had come pouring out of windows and doors, for a holiday in the middle of the night, whooping and hollering. Some Godless—or at least non-Methodist—adults began to join the procession. The preacher kept on driving. Driving and sweating, sweating like high noon in dog-days, they said. He never looked to one side or the other. His lips, they reported, were moving in prayer. It was, everybody said later, a great testimony to the power of prayer." She turned to her brother. "Brad," she said, "give me a freshener, before I get your habit of talking too much. I'll just switch to your habit of drinking too much."

He gave her the freshener.

She took a sip, then turned back to Digby. "That's all,"
she said. "Except one thing," she said, after another sip.
"Miss Euphemia."

"What about her?"

"She was mad as a wet hen. She went to poor Sheriff
Purtle—before breakfast, it was—and said Fiddlersburg was
not safe. She had been robbed. He better get on the job and
recover her stolen property, she said. He said for her to
make a written complaint and description. She sat right
down on his porch, before breakfast, and wrote it out. Now
what do you think she described as reft from her, Mr.
Digby?"

Mr. Digby's mouth made a movement, but no sound
came out. His eyes brightened, as with an idea, then glazed
over. His mouth again made that spasmodic motion, quivering on the verge of speech. But, apparently, he lacked the
courage of his inspiration.

"I'll tell you, Mr. Digby," she announced in gay triumph.
"Miss Euphemia made formal complaint that a person, or
persons, unknown, had stolen from her barn six stained-glass
windows."

"Gee," Mr. Digby said. He grinned slowly. "Gee whiz,"
he said.

"And you," she cried, in grief and despair, "you, Mr.
Digby, are going to flood Fiddlersburg. You are going to flood
the only town in the entire world where poor Miss Euphemia could be Miss Euphemia. Oh, what shall we do, Mr.
Digby?"

He said he was sorry, he bet she hated to lose her nice
house too. She said, oh, bother the old rattrap of a house,
she was worried about the Miss Euphemias of the future,
wherever would they come from?

Brad said for her to tell how Miss Euphemia stole herself a coffin to try on, when Mr. Lorton had just got in a new
shipment, uncrated and lined up in his alley.

She said she would try to remember it.

Brad shut his eyes and listened to the bright voice. It was
going to be all right.

Digby, at a decent hour, after three mild, well-spaced
highballs, took his leave. Brad saw him out to the front,
then returning, stood a moment in the moonlight to give a
very histrionic yawn, and announce that he was, by God,

bushed and was going to bed. He moved rapidly up the brick walk and into the house.

Looking after him, Maggie said: "Poor Brad."

Yasha Jones said nothing.

And she: "He worries so."

He said nothing.

"He is worrying about me," she said. "Now."

She waited as though for some response, for a question. But he, again, said nothing.

"Don't you ever ask questions?" she said.

"Yes," he said, "sometimes. When I forget a great principle I once arrived at."

"What's that?"

"The Yasha Jones Law of Information and Evidence."

"That's a big help," she said.

"Here is my law," he said. "A straight question gets a crooked answer. So I won't ask a question. I'll make a statement. Brad is not worrying about you. He is worrying about himself."

She looked at the dark house.

"That is a way of putting it," she said, at length. Then, after a silence in which each seemed, somehow, to be sinking deeper and deeper, neither aware of the other, she said: "He is worried because he is afraid that we—he and I, just the two of us—might be left alone together tonight."

When she had said those words, it was as though she had released some cord, some hold, that had kept her from sinking entirely into that dark medium of silence. Once the words were said, she seemed to slip from sight, and the moonlight striking across the face which, as Yasha Jones knew, was not naturally pale, made him fancy her as vanishing with that last glimmer of white into the depth of water. But, Yasha Jones thought, there was no last backward appeal on that sinking glimmer of a face. It was as though at the moment when the woman sank, you saw the first glitter, as in a fairy story, of the magic transformation, saw the first luxurious sweep of her easy force in the transforming depth of darkling water, and knew that she was withdrawing triumphantly into the medium that was more truly her own than that upper air of bright confusion.

Yasha Jones thought, then, that he, too, was sinking into a silence, into the deep medium of himself, which, he suddenly felt, was shadowy and shifting, suffocating. His mind made some unspecific gesture of reaching out, of grasping, as though to establish connection with something. There was, for that split instant, a swirl of undefined images, as unsubstantial as the slosh of a wave in the dark, and his hand could close on nothing.

He sat there and wondered how he had come all the years, and miles, to sit here in this undistinguished garden in Tennessee, in the middle of the night, and fall perilously into the shadowy depth of himself. In that moment he felt, suddenly, an angry envy of the woman who had sunk away, triumphantly, contemptuously from his reach, into her dark inner ease. In that moment of desolation he lifted his eyes to stare at her. She was looking at him.

She was, in that instant, saying: "My husband—did you see him today?"

He had to bring himself from some depth to answer. He even had to rephrase the question to himself, to reconstruct the time and the place, before he could say, yes, he had seen him.

"Yes," he said, "in the hospital—the infirmary—he was there. I was looking around, and all at once I saw this man staring at me. He came over, and introduced himself. He did it very calmly, with the air that he knew I would know all about him. He put out his hand and said, 'Mr. Jones, I've enjoyed some of your pictures. We get them here, if a little late. I'm Dr. Fiddler.' "

She withdrew again, meditating. Then she said: "What did he look like?"

"You know who Mr. Budd is—the Deputy Warden?" he asked. Then continued: "Well, he gave—gave to Brad—what I consider a perfect description. He said—"

"To Brad—" she cut in. "Brad—didn't he go into the infirmary?"

"No," he said.

She waited a moment, absorbed in that fact. "So he didn't go in," she said soberly. Then added: "They were best friends, once." Then she lifted her eyes again toward Yasha Jones. "What did Mr. Budd say?" she demanded.

"He said that Dr. Fiddler looks like a boy gone gray."

She drew those words into herself, sat there pondering them. Then she said: "I could have guessed that about him." Then, more directly to him: "Do you know how I could have guessed it?"

"No."

"Because that's the way I feel," she said. "Yes," she said, "like a girl gone gray. Like something got frozen. But the hair kept changing."

"Yes," Yasha Jones said, after a slight hesitation. "Yes, you have some gray."

She flung him a quick glance.

"Yes," she said. "But I'm sort of surprised. To hear you agree so—so ungallantly."

"I'm sort of surprised, too," he said. "But I couldn't say no. And I couldn't just say nothing. That would be doing you some kind of a wrong. I don't know exactly what kind, but some kind of a wrong. So"—he spread his hands, palms up, in the moonlight, in that gesture of fatalism—"I had to say yes."

"So you had to tell the truth?" she said, and laughed.

"I don't make a vicious habit of it," he said. "But sometimes you have to."

She was silent.

Then, with an air of rousing herself, she said: "Why do you have to?"

"I'll violate the Yasha Jones Law of Information and Evidence," he said. "I ask you the question."

After a little bit she said: "You have to tell the truth—I mean the time comes when you have to, if—"

She waited, then finished her sentence.

"—if you want to exist," she said.

She got up from the chair. There was, he noticed, a certain heaviness, an awkwardness, about her motion, almost a hint of age, as she turned from him. She went and stood by the low brick wall, staring over the river.

He felt curiously detached from the scene. He remembered how before breakfast, the first morning here—thinking now with sudden surprise that that was only four days back—he had come down to walk in the garden and had looked over the wall. In bright sunlight he had seen, he remembered, the tangle of honeysuckle and briars over the bank below, and the ruin of the old poke-berry plants. He had seen the rusty lard tins and rusty coffee cans not yet drawn down into the matrix of clutching tendrils, an old shoe, old bottles, a broken glass jug. He had seen the spot of ranker green where a pipe must drain down.

Now he watched her stand there staring over the moon-

lit river and the land westward, and wondered what that
bank looked like in moonlight. He wondered how you might
photograph this present scene. You would, of course, photograph it from the river side. You could find footing below the
bluff for your camera crane. It would be difficult, but possible. You should pan slightly from below to find the figure
there above the wall, in moonlight, the female figure with
some slight droop to the shoulders under the pale shawl, the
moonlight on the face. You would have to find, too, the glint
of that broken glass jug, find it but not linger on it. Panning
up, you should find it as casually as you would find the ferny
spray of the locust leaf whitened by moonlight. For everything must seem a part of everything else.

Yes, he observed again, the shoulders were drooping a
little now. He observed this without any feeling. He thought
how, for some years, his concern with his craft had been
a way, his only way, of feeling himself into the world. But
now, this moment, he thought how this concern with the
ways of his craft—had it become, rather, a flight from the
world? This observation about himself—he made this, too,
without feeling.

She had turned from the wall toward him. The shoulders, he now decided, had straightened. She was standing
a full fifteen feet from him, but she spoke with her voice un-
raised. She said: "Digby—that boy Digby."

"What?"

"A boy like that," she repeated, "who goes home from
work and shaves and washes and smells of eau de Cologne
and puts on a white shirt—while you and Brad get more
disreputable every day—"

"Yes."

"—and whites his saddle shoes and gets his good tweed
jacket and ties his striped bow tie three times to get it absolutely balanced, just like an engineer, and when he leans
forward in a chair, even in the dark, keeps the small of his
back straight, and does fifty push-ups every morning, and
strikes a match for your cigarette on his thumb nail, gets it
the first time too, and when he leans over to light your cigarette you see his face come sudden out of the dark and he is
grinning and you see all those white square teeth, with the
little spaces between, like a little boy's teeth, and—"

She stopped.

"And what?" demanded Yasha Jones, aware of the harshness of his voice, aware too of some small grain of elation glittering cruelly in the dark of himself. Or was it, he asked himself in that tiny instant before she could speak again, that he knew that she had to say whatever it was, and he had to make her say it?

All right, he thought, *let it be both, both the cruelty and the non-cruelty!*

"And what?" he repeated.

"And brings you this," she said.

She was holding out toward him, in the moonlight, the box of chocolates that had been left on the wall.

"He brings me this!" she cried out, and began to laugh.

Suddenly she stopped laughing.

"If I'm not careful," she said, "he will ask me to the senior prom—and oh—"

"Oh, what?"

"Can you imagine him dead?" she asked, very quietly.

"Not very well," Yasha Jones said.

"Well, I can," she said. "All too well. And do you know why?"

"If you want me to know, you should tell me."

"Why did Brad bring him!" she cried. "I hate him for that."

For a moment, he meditated the moon-washed distance. He said: "No, I don't think there is much hate in you."

She was standing there with the box of chocolates in her hand, looking down at it. All at once, as though something had given way, she sat on the low brick wall. "No, I don't hate Brad," she said, drained bleakly of passion. "It is just that I hate myself for being weaker than I thought."

She had seemed to be speaking to herself, not to him. Now quite deliberately, thinly as though sustained by will alone, she lifted her gaze toward him, across the distance.

"It was a long time ago," she said, in a voice that, too, seemed bleached by time. "That other young engineer off the river. His name was Al Tuttle—Alfred O. Tuttle—they called him Tut—and my husband shot him."

Book
THREE

Chapter

16

IN LATE JANUARY, 1939, immediately after he and Lettice had decided on marriage, Brad flew to Nashville, where he picked up a U-Drive-It Chevrolet, and within an hour was on the road to Fiddlersburg, a road which, in that period, quickly deteriorated into a gnawed-out blacktop. When he hit the ridge east of Fiddlersburg, the sun was low, and red with winter redness.

He drove through town. No one was on the streets. A light burned dimly in Parham's Grocery, and as he drove past he could see, through the glass of the door, a gray-bearded man with a large paper sack in his arms, on his way out, on his way home. A light was on, too, in the Rexall store. He could see the chrome and marble glint of the soda fountain, but nobody was visible.

He drove on out River Street. The front windows of all the houses were dark, but in some you could see light in the back. From the darkening land, from the streets, from the hollowness of a house itself, life had withdrawn back there, around the stove, around the table where food steamed.

As he drove slowly out River Street, past the last lighted window, past the vacant lots, where darkness seemed tangled in the tumbled fences, past the last street light, a peculiar calmness filled him. When he reached the house, he drew up and cut off the motor. He sat there a moment, staring at the lightless bulk of the house. It was the first time he had seen it since his father's funeral, four years before.

Inside, the house was pitch dark. The electricity was, of course, cut off. He set the suitcase in the middle of the hall and, by flashlight, carried back to the kitchen the box of supplies he had bought in Nashville. In the drawer where, as he remembered from boyhood, candles had always been kept in anticipation of the storm that would blow down the power lines, he found them. He set three on saucers, and lighted them.

He wandered across the kitchen to a west window. The last red light was still in the sky, low to the horizon. Far across the river, across the flat land west where, here and there, a flooded ditch caught the last red gleam, beyond the bare black trees, small in distance, that occasionally sprigged that shadowy flatness, he stared at the red sky.

After a little, he caught the reflection of a candle flame in the window glass to his left. When he turned his gaze back to the sky, the light there was gone.

He left the kitchen. He began to wander the cold dark house, now by flashlight, now by old instinct. He would stop in a hall, on the stairs, in a room, the flashlight dark in his hand, and stand perfectly still, perhaps holding his breath. He had the sense that he himself was, somehow, the dark house. He was the dark house in which he stood and, at the same time, the person standing there, holding his breath, in that enclosed darkness. He had no memories. He relived nothing. He simply lived into the silence and darkness. The rectangle of a window would hang dimly gray in the black air. It would be merely a shape, giving no light.

Some piece of furniture would begin to assume identity—
not a form, merely a special density of shadow. It was as
though the very silence and darkness of the house were a rising flood, a medium that rose deeper and deeper around him,
and in him, absorbing him. In his own calmness, he had a
sense that the house was, in the darkness and silence, slowly
forgiving itself.

In a north bedroom, upstairs, he stood at a window and
looked out over the town. He saw the lights in the distant
houses. He strained to make out a human form in some
lighted room. But all the houses were too far away. He
thought of the nameless gray-bearded man he had caught
a glimpse of through the glass of Parham's Grocery. He
thought of the man taking the sack of food home down the
street, passing under a street light, going into a white house,
where the boards of the front steps needed fixing, giving the
sack to a woman who would cook the food, dish it up, set it
before him on the old oilcloth table cover. In his mind Bradwell Tolliver tried to see the woman's face, to see her push
the gray hair back off her forehead and adjust her glasses,
which would be somewhat bleared with steam. Would she
smile at the man over the steaming platter?

The calmness in him had, he discovered, become the
very substance of his flesh and bone. It was as though he,
Bradwell Tolliver, were discovering a buried self. It was the
true self that would live forever.

From the high window he looked down over the dark
roofs, then up to the dark mass of the penitentiary, up to the
sky where the stars now shone in their winter clarity. He
found himself lifting up his arms. And in that instant—
summoned up by the gesture, or summoning up the gesture,
he did not know which—he saw the face of Lettice Poindexter in the air before him, as though that image floating there
in shadowy translucence were fused with that dark land and
sky on which it was superimposed.

She was looking at him with love, with a smile of sad
sweetness, with longing, and she inclined her head toward
him in a motion that her height sometimes made necessary,
a motion that now was tenderness and submission. He felt
time flowing over him, through him, in a deep process which
was infinitely sweet.

He went back to the kitchen, opened his bag, took out a
pad of paper and a bottle, poured himself a drink but did

not touch it, and by the candlelight, still wearing his overcoat, feeling no hunger, began to write.

My Darling:

*I have just arrived. I am sitting in the kitchen, with
three candles in saucers, and I am writing to you. I have
walked the dark house, where there is no sound, and in
that darkness and silence I know that your goodness
and beauty and love are what I live by and shall always
live by. I have seen your face in the darkness, and I
held my arms to it, and I felt Time simply flowing
through me and over me in a deep process which was infinitely sweet. From you, in that moment, I learn how
humanly sweet it is to live in Time, to have the past and
the future in a present vision. I now have the vision of
what our life will be; and when, soon, you come into
the dark house, all will be . . .*

He awoke in the middle of the night, in the dark, in the
room of his boyhood, where tonight he had merely wrapped
himself in blankets and plunged his head into the coarse
ticking of the pillow. The thought was, even in waking, fully
formed in his head: *There was one room I did not go in.*

He crawled out of the blankets, fumbled his feet into
shoes, put on his overcoat like a robe, and, with the flashlight, went out into the hall, down the stairs, across the big
hall, into the library. He had not been in that room since the
day his father's coffin had been carried from it.

He swung the beam of the flashlight around the room,
sweeping it over the shelves of books, over the empty
hearth, over the floor, settling it finally on the spot where
the coffin had rested on its trestles. Had he, finding his way
toward this room, expected something that now did not happen?

He remembered what his sister had said. He had come
into the room, fresh from his journey down from Darthurst,
and she, a young girl, with small new breasts and wide
dark eyes, standing in the middle of the floor, weeping, had
cried out: "Look, he is not big any more. He is so little now!"

Now, hunched, shivering, in that room, in his overcoat,
the beam of the flashlight on that spot, the same spot over
there where the coffin had been, he began to weep. The weeping began suddenly, surprising him. It was as though some-

body else were weeping. Then he tried to appropriate the process. He tried to profit from it. He even felt, momentarily, a pride that he, Bradwell Tolliver, could stand here in the dark house and weep. He waited for the reward, the sweetness, the relief that should come. Nothing came. The sobs wracked him dryly. The tears ran sparsely down his cheeks. He wondered why the wracking sobs produced so few tears.

All at once, he felt that it was some stranger who stood and wept in a grief that had not been divulged to Bradwell Tolliver. He had been tricked.

"Shit," he said, out loud.

The memory of this episode was something that, in subsequent years, he tried to keep out of his mind. He could not bear to think of it. He did not know what it meant. But he did know that when he thought of it he also thought of his father lying in the swamp mud, weeping; and he knew that that thought was something he had never been able to bear.

On his way back to New York he stopped overnight in Nashville to see his sister.

She was then a student at Ward Belmont, where her presence had been made possible—though for her happiness it was just as well that she did not know the fact—only by the death of her father.

In the spring of 1935 Banker Cottshill from Memphis, the cousin who managed the trust Mrs. Tolliver had left for the education of the children, had made a visit to Fiddlersburg. He had told old Lank Tolliver that the time had come to fulfill the terms of the bequest—to put the girl in "some institution of standing, not situated in Fiddlersburg." Old Lank Tolliver had said that, Goddammit, he would keep the girl where she belonged, with him, in his house, in Fiddlersburg.

At this point Banker Cottshill really began to enjoy himself. He said that he knew that Mr. Tolliver's affairs had suffered with the times, that Fiddlersburg was a dying town where normal economic recovery could not be expected, that Mr. Tolliver ought to be glad that the girl was taken care of. He added that he knew that Mr. Tolliver held most of the stock in the People's Bank of Fiddlersburg and that he knew the bank was rickety. He said that he, as a banker, could not understand how a man who was showing such poor judgment as Mr. Tolliver now exhibited could expect assistance from the "outside."

Lank Tolliver, with purpling face and bulging eyes, told Mr. Cottshill to get the hell out before he broke his neck. Mr. Cottshill, feeling splendidly masterful, bade the old muskrat-skinner good day, and walked briskly out to the big black car where his uniformed Negro chauffeur sat smoking a cigarette, greatly admired by three small boys. The car had not cleared the city limits of Fiddlersburg before Lank Tolliver was in his outboard, heading for the swamps. He was alone. The body was found two days later, sprawled face down in the damp black earth. But the bottle was almost full.

Now, after four years in summer camps, Ward Belmont, and the rich shadowy house of the childless Cottshills, Maggie Tolliver was eighteen. She was a dark, slender, well-built girl, with a warmth and humor that made it easy for her to get on with her classmates, but the giggles and confidences had never been enough to make her feel that this life was hers. She sometimes dreamed of Fiddlersburg, which she had not seen since the death of her father, dreams full of a mysterious fear and excitement, like looking into a mirror with the sense that a face has just disappeared over your shoulder. She kept a scrapbook about her brother—the little collection of clippings and reviews, his rare letters to her. She had no very clear image of him from the early years, and, in fact, any attempt to summon up such memories made her feel uncomfortable; but when she received his letter saying that he would see her in Nashville, she almost wept for happiness.

He found her in the reception hall of her school, standing with her roommate and two other girls, who looked at him with a mixture of awe and sly feminine assessment, and said they were glad to meet him. The roommate produced a hitherto concealed copy of *I'm Telling You Now* and asked him to autograph it, and the others, after a slight flurry which seemed to indicate that they had been foxed, found some scraps of paper and asked him to sign those, too. They said they had read one of his stories in English class. One of them said it was awfully romantic to think he was getting married and would bring his bride to Fiddlersburg. Another one said that his story in English class made her think Fid-

dlersburg must be awfully romantic. The roommate said that
it certainly was romantic and brave of him to go fight in
Spain against those Fascists. He stood there among them, and
thought how young they looked, and laughed throatily and
felt old, wise, strong, indulgent, and possessive. Then he
caught the dark gaze of his sister upon him.

He felt himself flushing.

In that instant he knew, too, how different she was from
her friends, from those girls with their soft cashmere sweat-
ers, and soft little stomachs on which the elastic of the panties would leave a pink line all around when the panties were
pulled off, and sharp elbows, and charm bracelets on wrists
where little blue veins were sweetly threading the whiteness.
Maggie had nothing of that warm, provocative Memphis innocence or kitteny, sleepy, cream-dish Chattanooga compla-
cency. She stood there in her aloneness, in her waiting, her
dark hair drawn straight back from the olive oval of her face,
standing firm and erect, rather small, but without that girlish
air of something about to take flight. She looked a thousand
years older than the others, and fixed him, from some distance, with that dark, steady gaze.

Even as he felt himself flushing, he flung her a broad,
brotherly grin which was supposed to set right whatever
might be wrong. It succeeded. Her eyes brightened, her lip
lifted in a smile to show how white her teeth were against
the olive skin; and he recognized, with a small start of the
heart, the child face he had known long back. He straightened his shoulders.

"Come on, Sis," he said, in burly good humor, "we can't
keep these gals standing here all night."

He put her into the U-Drive-It and took her out to a
farmhouse that had been converted into a restaurant, a joint
he had got a line on at the hotel, where booze was on hand
and they'd serve you wine. He dropped his right arm over her
shoulder, saying he didn't often get to hug Ole Sis, and drove
with speed and casual competence. He tried to make her tell
about herself, to catch up on lost time, he said, but she kept
saying that there was nothing to tell. There really wasn't, and
besides, she was too happy to talk.

". . . and I remember it even now, after all these years,
how happy I was. It was as though I had been waiting for
something all that time, and it was about to happen. I didn't

know what it was, but something. It was as though there had
been some life back before Fiddlersburg that I couldn't quite
remember and there was a life promised to me for someday,
some place, exactly what, I didn't know. But all the time in
between, at Ward Belmont and in Memphis, had been nothing but the aloneness.

"It was not lonesomeness. It was a waiting. All the time I
was living like the other girls, going to classes, talking about
clothes and dates, arguing that some boy was cute or was
pesky, going to dances, dreaming in a vague girly way of having a home and a cute husband and babies. But nothing
seemed really real to me, just a way of waiting.

"Maybe now and then I thought, or tried to think, that I
was in love with some boy. But deep down I always knew it
wasn't true. I had dates, sure, but nothing ever very heavy,
not like some of the other girls, what they'd tell me, even
how you could just slip over the line before you knew it. I
would just fool around some. It was all just a way of waiting,
like the waiting in a fairy story for some spell to be broken.
Well, Brad was going to break the spell.

"Not that I really knew Brad. We hadn't been close as
children. For one thing he was a lot older, he was away from
the house a lot, off gallivanting with other boys, or in the
woods with some swamp rat like Frog-Eye, or down playing
chess with that sweet old Mr. Goldfarb. For another thing, he
and our father got along so bad—that was awful. But now
the fact that I hadn't seen him in years, that made us closer
in a way than if we'd been close as children. Here he came
out of nothing, nowhere, suddenly. He had written a book.
He had fought in Spain. He was sort of good-looking in a
strong, tweed-jacket-out-at-the-elbows, good-humored way—
when he wasn't frowning. He was getting married to some
New York girl, and if you knew how a girl like me—or some
of the other girls at Ward Belmont too, if they'd have admitted
it—felt about a really-truly New York girl.

"Well, that was Brad, out of the blue. He was going to
bring some sort of magic, all right. Even the restaurant was
part of the magic, a strange kind of place for me, not the
kind of place girls—girls as young as I was anyway—got
taken by nice boys. Brad got drinks and made me have one. I
had had a drink a few times before. Some of the girls sitting
out in a car at intermission would take two or three out of
paper cups with Coke or Seven-Up and then eat Sen-Sen to

kill the smell, and the drinks I had had were just to keep from feeling too different from them. I didn't really like it. But I drank it for Brad. Then I had a glass of wine at dinner. And he talked about his girl. More and more it seemed that she was part of the magic too.

"He would talk about her in spurts. He would tell me something, then he would fall silent, as though he were thinking of a lot of things but had to pick which one he could tell me. He would say now and then how much I'd like her and how she'd like me, and how they wanted me to spend the summer with them at Fiddlersburg. That kept weaving in and out of the conversation, and every time it got mentioned I felt happier. That was the promise of the real magic.

"Brad really was sweet to me that night. There was a juke box there and he danced with me and said I was great. Which I wasn't. He said I had really turned into a looker. Which I hadn't. He asked my advice about some painting and repairing on the house in Fiddlersburg. I had the feeling—or maybe I had the feeling later—that he was trying hard to reach out to me, that he needed to establish something, to find something. It was that need I decided later that made him do what he did.

"He had been dancing with me, whirling me around and around till I was dizzy, and he hadn't said a word, just seemed to be a million miles off, and as I whirled I shut my eyes and could almost feel him thinking of that girl. I wanted to think of him whirling her around and around, with her eyes shut, and how happy they would be. Somehow, in a magic way, I could understand and go into that happiness. It was, you might say, a promise to me. It was that sense of his wanting to be with her, to be dancing with her that made me say what I did. I wanted him to know that I understood him. I said in some silly way that I didn't see how he could get time to see me, why he hadn't dashed right back to marry her.

"We had just sat down at the table. My head was whirling with the waltz and the wine. He was looking at me in a funny way, his eyes glittery. I can see them now, just a little red from the drink, and glittery. 'Christ,' he said, and gave a laugh, 'you don't think we have been hanging around waiting for Mayor La Guardia's blessing, do you?'

"I guess I didn't connect, and my face showed it.

" 'Christ,' he said again, 'Lettice is a grown woman.'

"I sat there. My head was still whirling. I felt small and

lost. Things seemed to be changing shapes, and distances. He was grinning at me, I suddenly discovered, but that grin was from a long distance. Then he reached over and patted my hand. 'Little Ole Sweet Ward Belmont Sis,' he said, 'come on, and I'll fling you around some more.'

"So we danced again, and he whirled me around and around. It was awfully exciting. It is strange how vividly I remember every . . ."

Late that night, in his hotel room, he remembered how the need to tell his sister what he had told her—how Lettice was a grown woman—had been building up in him for an hour beforehand. Even at the time, he had been aware of an incorrigible compulsion. Now thinking back on the episode, humped on the bed's edge with a shoe held meditatively in his hand, he felt a grinding discomfort. The episode, something in him decided, was definitely an item to be shelved away and forgotten.

After he had got into bed and turned off the light, he remembered another impulse he had had during the evening. He had felt the impulse to tell his sister how, in Fiddlersburg, he had risen in the night and gone down to the library and focused the flashlight on the spot where the coffin had rested, and how he had wept. For an instant now, lying in the dark, he wished he had told her.

It was as though that telling might have wiped out the other telling.

Then he remembered that that episode in the dark library was, too, something to be stowed away. It was to be put in the back of the dark closet. A man just couldn't go around remembering everything.

In the vestibule on MacDougal Street, he stamped the fresh snow off his feet, unlocked the door, and entered into surprising darkness. But almost immediately he heard her. "I'm here," she said, in a voice that seemed very small and far away, in the denser darkness at the other end of the room.

"Oh, darling," he said, and let his suitcase drop, and took a step toward her in the dark, and in that instant felt as he had felt that night in the house in Fiddlersburg when her face had leaned at him from the dark sky.

But her voice was saying: "Turn the light on."

In astonishment he took a step back, and fumbled for the switch at the door. The ceiling light broke harshly over the room. He saw her sitting in a straight chair by the end of the table, her elbow on the table as though for support. "Darling—what—" he began, and took a couple of strides toward her.

But she made a gesture of protest. "Stop!" she said.

Neither the gesture nor the word was actually stopped him. It was the gray, drawn face that she raised toward him, the face of a stranger. The shaded table lamp, unlit, was in easy reach of her hand, but it was as though she had refused it, had made him turn on the wall switch so that in the brutal light from the ceiling that gray face might be offered without extenuation.

"Your letter—" she said, and her hand reached out as slowly as a sick woman's to touch the unfolded sheet that lay there on the table.

He looked toward it, recognized the sheet.

"I only got it this afternoon," she said.

"I mailed it Saturday," he said, faintly defensive, "in Fiddlersburg. But I was running around about the house business. I guess I missed the Saturday pick-up. I guess there isn't any Sunday pick-up, and—"

"Oh, Brad," she said, lightly moving her forefinger back and forth on the sheet, "that isn't it. Your letter was here yesterday, I'm sure. It's just that when I got your wire here yesterday I didn't expect a letter, I didn't come back here, I was in my studio working, I stayed there to dress, my fancy clothes are there, you know, to go to the reception, you know about the reception at Mrs. Filspan's, and I didn't come back here, I—I stayed at the studio, I didn't get here until—"

"What the hell—" he began again.

"If only I'd got the letter yesterday," she said dully. "Or if I'd never got it. Jesus, I've had to sit here with it all afternoon and I thought I would die."

He took a step toward her, his hand lifted.

"Don't touch me!" she cried, drawing back.

He stopped. He stood there in his overcoat, his hat on his head, snow yet clinging to the hat, one hand still lifted. He stared at the face lifted toward him in that brutal light.

She told him.

"Listen," she was saying, "listen, I'll tell you."

Bradwell Tolliver stood there and heard the words and felt like a man being tumbled and torn in surf too heavy for him. One feeling after another struck him and whirled him. There was the pure animal rage. There was the hurt vanity. There was the savage mirth that even as he stood there he should see on the table the letter telling of his new awareness of love and of human life in Time. There was the black desolation. There was the savage mirth that said that fucking is only fucking, rip off a piece right here and now and to hell with it. There was the anguished sense of some secret justice in the world, or at least a punishing logic, that said that this was all that could ever happen if you began with that leaf-hung peep show in Central Park. There was the impulse to knock her teeth out, anything to make her stop talking. There was the anger at her for being honest. There was the savage mirth that Brad Tolliver—bright old Brad—had been getting him a pair of round heels for a wife. There was the self-contempt in the fear that even now she held some power over him, even now in the gray unbeauty of that lifted face. There was the panic fear at the beauty of her suffering. There was the impulse to run out into the snow.

There was so much. And at the same time, there was so little, only a dreary diminishment, like age, like flannel-gray water draining slowly, with no sound, down the clogged drain of a bathtub. There was, finally, nothing.

For in one dimension of his being he was merely an observer of a charade. He saw the two figures fixed in that harsh light, the man standing in his overcoat with snow melting on his hat, the woman in the chair lifting that gray face. Nothing seemed real. He was not sure what might be the inner reality. Was there ever an inner reality?

The voice was saying: ". . . and I didn't know whether Dr. Sutton was right or not—I mean about me—but I knew he was wrong to say I shouldn't tell you. I had to tell you. Feeling the way I do about you, I know now I can't be with you a minute unless you know all I am. For if you want me at all, Brad, I want you to have all of me. Whatever I am. All day I have been wanting to die, but maybe even the awfulness of what happened is worth something if I can feel this way. I mean about wanting to be all yours if I am anything at all. I didn't know anybody could feel exactly, totally, this way and now I . . ."

He was staring at the gray face. He saw how the flesh seemed pinched back at the corners of the eyes. He saw a vein throbbing in the left temple, the side toward the light.

The voice was saying: ". . . but more than anything I want you to do exactly what you want. I mean want in your deepest way. I wouldn't blame you if you just walked out that door. I wouldn't blame you if you just came here and hit me across the face. So the blood came. I wish you would. I'd just hold my face up for you. I wouldn't blame you for anything except—if you did want me—not being sure that you really want me. All of me. For that's what you'd have."

She looked at him, a moment, across the distance. Then her body sagged slowly forward. She stretched her hands forward, the wrists flat over her tight-together knees. For a moment she stared at the hands as though examining the nails. The nails were a deep blood-red, and he thought how strangely that bright red went with that gray face.

Then the wrists collapsed, and the hands dropped slackly forward beyond the knees. Her head sank forward, a little to the right side. The red-brown hair fell forward, the heavier swatch on the right side. In that glaring light from above, he could see the exposed, unfended, merciless whiteness of the back of her neck. He was aware of the tension of the tendons there, drawn by the slack weight of the head.

"Listen," his voice said.

Her head did not lift.

"Listen, gal," his voice said, trying to be something it wasn't, for there was some possibility that it might not hold steady, "you got that paper?"

"What?" she said.

"That paper," his voice said, "the one from the City Hall?"

"Yes," she said, almost whispering, lifting her face.

"Well, hang on to it, gal," his voice said, very burly now, "for by tomorrow morning you're going to need that paper awful bad."

He watched the smile start slowly on her face. Then he took a step toward her. But she shrank back in the chair.

"Don't touch me," she said.

"What the hell?"

"I've got to cry," she said. "I've just got to lay my head down and cry before you touch me."

She laid her head down on the edge of the table and cried, almost without sound. He could see the tears running out of her open eyes.

In this manner Bradwell Tolliver entered the House of Forgiveness. He did not know that this is a house in which there are many mansions, some of which are lightless.

Chapter

17

ON THE WAY BACK in the cab from the City Hall, Lettice took Brad's hand and said that she couldn't wait, she wanted to get to Fiddlersburg right away and work on the house, for it was the house they were going to live in, they could get a car and just start out.

"It's me who will get the car," he corrected her, squeezing her hand. "And it will probably be a jalopy, for that is what I can afford."

"I'd love a jalopy," she said, "and just the two of us in it and we can be ourselves. We will be just us—everywhere we go. And forever. Say, 'Forever,' Bradwell Tolliver."

So Bradwell Tolliver said: "Forever."

"I've never been anywhere except New York, and Maine

and Havana and Florida," she said, "and of course that horrid
Europe, and I can't even bear to read the papers about that
any more. I want to be just us in some place like Pittsburgh,
whatever that's like, and in some tourist camp with pink silk
bed lamps in Wheeling, or in some God-awful tourist home
in some God-awful little town in Ohio, or—"

"Take it easy," he said. "When you say God-awful you
are talking about Fiddlersburg. You are talking about the
town I love."

"I love Fiddlersburg," she said.

She loved it while, dressed in faded blue jeans and a
shirt of Brad's, she helped Ole Zack clean years of trash out
of the basement, or worked with him to lime and reseed the
lawn, or dig flower beds. She loved it while she wrangled
with the painters on their scaffolds outside, or with the car-
penters and plumbers who were rebuilding the kitchen. She
loved it, quite literally, for her every activity, with smudged
face, broken fingernails, and sweat-matted hair, seemed to
carry some secret symbolic value; to be a profound ritual of
preparation. And she loved Fiddlersburg when, the first crisis
of renovation being passed, she set up her easel in a north
room on the top floor, and looked out over the river sliding
away, and over the roofs of the town.

She had chosen the room for the light, but after Brad
had helped her get installed, he said that this room was
where, that night back in January, he had seen her face rising out of the dark, smiling at him. After he had said this
and shut the door and left her with her paraphernalia, she
stared out the window. She wished it were night, and she
could look out over the darkened town, as he had. Then she
went and lay on the bed—an iron bed with only a mattress
on it—and shut her eyes. She lay there and thought how,
after all the blind scrambles and compulsions of her life, a
shape like happiness seemed to be rising before her. She felt
floating and sweet, as she had felt—the recollection came with
sudden vividness—when recovering, as a child, from a long
fever.

She lay there, with eyes shut, and lived that forgotten
happiness. She could remember that far-off morning, when,
after the fever, the terrible dryness of the throat, the itching
skin; she had awakened to the simplicity of sunlight falling

across her counterpane. That was what her life, she thought now, would become.

So she carried her market basket through Parham's Grocery; or received the ladies of Fiddlersburg who came to call and sat in the parlor with a slight tendency to huddle together for comfort; or stood looking out the window in the north room upstairs and tried to catch the way the light of evening hit the roofs and the river; or went to the swamp with Brad and Frog-Eye; or cooked Brad's supper on the cook's night off while he sat at the kitchen table with a glass in his hand and, night by night, harangued her on the history of Fiddlersburg. After dinner, they would sit on a bench by the tumbled-down old garden house, and watch the last light dim over the flat lands westward.

With incredulity now, she would remember the nights in the room on MacDougal Street when she had needed to tell him, night by night, the life of Lettice Poindexter. There was no need now to tell him anything. He knew and possessed everything, the past and the future. She could shut her eyes, as the light faded out of the sky, and feel that she was being borne away effortlessly on a great stream; that she herself was not the thing moved but was part of that movement, was herself flowing away, but without diminishment, under the slow-blooming starlight.

As for Bradwell Tolliver, he was always to regard that spring of 1939 as the period when the parts of his life had seemed to belong to each other. And this was the time, too, when he seemed to rediscover, in Fiddlersburg, some inwardness of the scenes he had known in the years before. In the long nights at Darthurst he had dreamed of them; now he saw them in the full light of day. He often remembered Old Israel Goldfarb.

Once or twice during that spring, he remembered, too, that night back in January when, standing in the cold library and fixing the beam of the flashlight on the spot where his father's coffin had been, he had felt, in the fact of his unexpected tears, the intuition of some new possibility in himself. Perhaps this, he now fleetingly thought, was the fulfillment of that intuition.

His life, in that period, seemed to be self-contained and self-fulfilling. The world seemed to fall away from his life, leaving it in its balance and perfection, with no need now for many things that had once been needed. The copies of the *New York Times,* their wrappers unripped, were left, more and more often, to accumulate on the table in the hall. Copies of *Time* and *Newsweek* and the *Nation* and the *New Republic* and the *Partisan,* in their wrappers, accumulated like cordwood under the table. One night in May, when a newscast followed the hillbilly band on the Nashville station, and they heard that Germany and Italy had signed a ten-year military pact, Brad laid aside *Our Mutual Friend*—he had worked half across the shelf of Dickens in the library—and got up and turned off the radio. "All crooks," he said.

Lettice looked up from her knitting. "There's going to be a war," she said, in a voice that seemed to come from behind glass.

"All right," he said, "and if Franklin D. gets us into it, he will be the Sap of the Century."

"There's going to be one," she said.

"Damn it," he said, "don't look at me like you blamed me. I didn't make that continent of crooks over there. Look what they all did about Spain. Look what they did about Czechoslovakia. Hell, I don't mean Hitler and Musso. I mean the lovely French and English. And that lovely Joe of Moscow, what he did in Spain. I didn't make the world, and I didn't make history. I am going to make myself a drink and dismiss the matter until the hour for the shooting off of asses catches up with me."

He took a step toward the hall door.

"There's going to be an awful war," she said, even more mutedly, and let her body sink sideways on the couch, then rolled onto her stomach, hung her toes over the end of the couch, and began to cry.

"For Christ's sake," he said.

"It's just the God-damned cramps," she said. "You know I cry at anything when I'm like this."

"You want a drink and an aspirin?"

"I wish I were pregnant," she said, her face muffled in the couch.

"Someday you are going to be as pregnant as a tub full of catfish," he said.

"When?" she said, her face still down.

"Let's don't rush it," he said. "We've got all next month. In fact, we've got all next year. You want a drink?"

"Yes," she said, "and an aspirin."

He looked back at her, lying there with her face still pressed into the couch. He stepped back, leaned over, and whacked her on the behind. "For you," he said in a thick, highly improbable East Side accent, "und I vill do anything." Then added: "That's what Old Goldfarb used to say to me."

"I want an aspirin," she said.

"That is what Old Izzie used to say to me," he said, ignoring what she had said, "when we played chess and he'd take my queen. He didn't talk that way except when he made that joke. It is not a very funny joke, but I used to always laugh when he made it. He didn't think it was funny either, but he always laughed too."

When he came back from the kitchen she was sitting up, again knitting. She took the aspirin and a good pull of the bourbon. He lay down on the couch, put his head in her lap, set the drink on the floor within reach. That day he had finished a long story, and he knew that it was good.

It was very good. His agent sold it for $2500. It was widely praised. It became, in 1946, a fine if rather arty movie —his second one—and it was in all the anthologies for years to come.

"... and when I got to Fiddlersburg in June—that was in June, 1939—she was wonderful to me. I was awful timid in the beginning, she was so New York and grand and tall, and now and then she'd shuck off blue jeans or old khaki shorts and appear with some wonderful dress and a great bangle or something that cost a million dollars, and she made sweeping gestures and sometimes talked in a bold, flashy way, like nothing I'd ever heard. There wasn't anything she wouldn't say, but it never seemed vulgar, just sort of gay and funny, sometimes even, you might say, delicate. She had such a gay innocent smile—it seemed to come right out of her, just because she loved you and everything around her. At least, it was that way that first summer. But smile or no smile, in the beginning, she overpowered me, in a way.

"She must have sensed it, for one night, after I had gone to bed and had the bedside light on, trying to read but not making much of a go of it, I felt so lost, she knocked, and came in. She was wearing a green robe, very bright, of light silk, I guess, with what looked like real metallic gold braiding and belt. That color was wonderful with her red-auburn hair and those big brown eyes with gold lights in them. Of course I'd have to tell you about the clothes before anything else. Oh, yes, I forgot—she had on some kind of high-heeled gold sandals, too. She was tall, but she didn't mind being even taller. She carried herself like being proud of it.

"Well, after all these years I remember those high-heeled gold sandals and that stunning robe, and I guess I remember, too, being painfully aware of my little Nashville department-store nightie, and of the little robe with discreet blue ribbons lying across the foot of my bed.

"As for Lettice, it was quite clear that she didn't have any nightie on. She had that gold belt tight as could be about that incredible waist, and the green silk flared very free above and below, and I was quite sure there wasn't a stitch under it. I don't know that I even remarked to myself on this fact—at the time I mean—but it is very clear to me now. It has stayed in my head all the years, for whatever the fact is worth.

"She came and stood by the bed and looked down at me. Then she said, 'Little Maggie, it just came into my mind to tell you something before I went to bed. I was combing my hair and it just came over me how happy I am. I love Brad and that makes me happy. I love this house, and I love Fiddlersburg, and that makes me happy. And having you here makes me very happy. And if you'll let me, I'd love to love you too. May I?'

"I felt the tears swimming in my eyes. It was as though right now all the aloneness of the years in Memphis and Ward Belmont would be over. She was looking down at me. She must have seen the condition I was in, about to get blubbery. All at once she gave a smile—I reckon I never saw a sweeter one, or so it seemed to me then—and said: 'I'm not even going to ask you if I may love you. For I do, Little Maggie, and you can't help it!'

"With that she leaned down at me with a strong swooping motion that made a little flutter of the green silk, and set the gentlest, softest, timidest, ghostliest little kiss right on my forehead. It was strange to have that kiss come out of that strong fluttering swoop, and that timidness of it—that made my timidness all right too. Then, all at once, without another word, with a sweep and flutter of the green silk, with a flash of the gold, she was gone, and the door was shut. From that moment on I followed her around like a puppy.

"Brad would be working a lot, leaving Lettice alone, or sometimes when he went prowling around the country Lettice stayed home. She knew it was his way of doing things— one of his ways of working, I reckon you'd say. Off mooning around, or talking to people, maybe fishing. So I would tag around with her, except the times she was in her studio. Then I would read—then and at night when they sat around reading. That's how I got the habit, I guess, and it stood me in good stead all the thousand years after, alone in this house. There were stacks of books in this house, and I guess I've read them all. Including Bishop Paley's *Evidences of Christianity*.

"But Lettice, as the summer went on, was in her studio less and less. She even said to me once that she wasn't a real painter, not the way Brad was a writer, that or nothing. She said she was crazy about painting, but not her own painting, that as soon as she discovered how much she loved Brad, really loved him, she understood that painting had just been, for her, a way of filling up her life. So I tried to tell her how, until I had come to Fiddlersburg that summer, everything had just been a way of filling up life. Then suddenly she stared off into space, and said, yes, everything had just been a way of filling up life before she found Brad.

"I was sure she was telling the truth, for if anybody ever seemed crazy about somebody, she was about Brad. When she did any little thing for him, like getting an ash tray or cooking Sunday-night supper, it stuck out all over her. And he was crazy about her. When they were together you felt that some soft glow of happiness came out of them, something so pale you couldn't see it in the daylight, but you had the feeling that if they were in the dark there would be a shine on them, like fish leaping in the moonlight.

"No, not a leaping and flickering—a steady faint glow. Sometimes at night when we were sitting out on the screened porch at the north end, with no lights turned on, and he'd take her hand—there in the porch swing, that's where they always sat—I would have sworn I could see that faint glow around their hands clasped in the dark. But all this didn't make me feel left out and lonesome. They were living in their happiness, but their happiness was a promise to me. It was part of the magic.

"I must have bored Lettice stiff with my stupidity, after all the life she had had in New York and Europe and those

places, but she never showed it. She had a trick when she
told me something about that life—showed me clothes or
jewelry, for instance, the way girls do—of making this a way
to involve me, not to make me feel different or inferior. I
suppose of all the relics of that life the thing that fascinated
me most was her dressing table. My God, it was ten feet long
—Brad had made it for her in that big bathroom on the
northwest corner—and it had a million jars and bottles and
atomizers and boxes on it. There was a case with, I promise
you, not less than forty lipsticks. Everything was gold and
glittery. Perfumes I had never even heard about. Creams and
powders and astringents specially prepared for her in Paris,
with her initials on the cases.

"She would spend hours, too, at that table, doing things
to herself. To give Brad a treat, she would say. And I would
sit there and watch her till she was ready to appear with purple eye shadow, and mascara on her eyelashes, and lips some
shade I had never seen, ghost pale perhaps—or crimson. Then
she'd appear before him, and Brad would make some fool
joke, in a fake French accent, like, 'For one night with you,
Mam'selle, I give my inheritance, I shoot myself in the morning.' And once he didn't say a word but just got off the porch
swing and walked straight to her and bit her on the shoulder,
hard.

"She yelled, and slapped him. He didn't even jerk his
face from the slap. He just stood there grinning in his heavy,
sure way, and watched her then as she rubbed the place on
her shoulder where he'd bitten—there was a real mark there,
the two little half-circles going blue, for she bruised easily—
and while she rubbed the spot she was staring at him in a
slow, dreamy way.

"It was all over fast. They had just forgot I was there.
But Lettice came to. She looked at me and laughed and said
that was what you got for marrying a muskrat-skinner from
Tennessee. She implored me never to marry a muskrat-
skinner, for their bite was deadly. Marry a Gila monster, she
advised.

"Even back at that time, there was one thing that struck
me as strange—and wonderful, too, I reckon. Lettice would
do all that primping and getting herself up fancy, and at the
same time she could do the dirtiest work and not give a
damn. She would break every fingernail. She would go to the
woods and swamp with Brad and that Frog-Eye, and come

back sweaty and muddy and grinning. It was a kind of split, a doubleness, right down her middle. She had to grab, it seemed, all kinds of life. She was boiling with energy. She was a terrific swimmer, the best I ever saw, then when Brad got the speedboat, she was great on the aquaplane, she knew a dozen tricks, which she'd learned, I guess, down in Florida or off yonder on the Riviera, in France. Here in Fiddlersburg, she'd be out in the river all afternoon, with Brad or giving swimming lessons to the Girl Scouts. Yes, would you believe it, she had taken up with the Girl Scouts, even gave them lessons that winter in sewing and dress designing, and taught them how to put on lipstick and hold their stomachs in. She even went to church that winter, and helped at a bazaar.

"But what I'm saying is, other times that summer she'd go totally lazy. She had rigged up a sheet in the back garden toward the river, so nobody could see from the house, and she'd lie out there on a towel, not a stitch on. She said that being a redhead she had to work to keep from being boiled lobster, and she'd be damned if she wanted to be striped either, like the Cathedral of Siena—whatever that is like. She wanted, she said, to be just done to a nice even juicy turn all over, and that was what she got too, a juicy goldie-brown, with some freckles on her quite wonderful shoulders, like a ripe pear. I didn't have to worry about sun, being so dark-skinned, but lying out there was a way of being with her, so I'd oil up too. I can smell that fresh fragrant oil right now, whatever kind it was she had in her collection of stuff.

"We'd lie out there, with not a stitch on, breaking the drowse now and then to put a little oil on the other's back, or to turn over. She could be so completely natural about all that, being naked and lying there. Innocent is a better word, I reckon. She'd stretch like a cat, flex her ankles, wriggle her toes, maybe do hip-rolls then lie totally still, maybe with eyes closed just seeming to flow away, she could be so relaxed, maybe talking to me now and then in a slow wispy way, with the sentences sometimes not even ending, just dying off into her snooze. Sometimes she'd do some waist exercises. 'When you're as big as I am,' she said, 'you've got to watch it. Save the waist and save all.' So she'd do her bends and twists even if it seemed she'd never have anything to worry about in that department.

"One day we were lying out beyond the sheet, our bodies in the sun but each of us with a light towel over the face,

cooking. Neither had said anything for a long time. I thought
she was drowsing off. But all at once in a distant, muffled
voice, like talking in her sleep, she said: 'Your body—it's
funny—you don't know whether it is you—or whether it is
just something the *you* has to live in—to use to get around
in.'

"The words sort of drifted out, in little clusters, with
long pauses between them, without any emphasis, just a
drift. I didn't say anything. I didn't really know what she was
talking about. I just lay there, feeling the sun on my naked
skin, with the cloth laid over my eyes.

"But suddenly I was aware of my own body in a way I
had never known before, and in that instant I squinched my
eyes shut to make it even darker inside myself under the
cloth on my eyes, my face to the sky, and I lay there shivering in my nakedness while the sun burned down on me all
over and seemed to outline my body down to the smallest
detail. It was like a million tiny, terribly sharp hot-cold nee-
dles outlining my body. To make it real for the first time.
That was what it seemed like.

"Then, as I lay there shivering with the sun's heat on me,
I heard her voice, in a distant, muffled way. She was saying:
'I used to hate my body.'

"Then, after a pause: 'Oh, I took good care of the nasty
old thing. It seemed I had to. That was one of the reasons I
hated it.'

"Then: 'I don't hate it now.'

"Then: 'Do you know why?'

"After a minute, I said, no, I didn't.

"And after a minute, she said: 'Brad.' Just that.

"I don't know how long we lay there before she spoke
again. Then she said: 'You feel you can live when one thing
finally comes to you.'

"Then: 'When you can feel that your body is not the *you*
—and at the same time is you—there's no way to say it—it has
to come true for you.'

"But that dressing table. Sometimes even now I close my
eyes and get a sense of that old bathroom, the sunlight coming through Venetian blinds, a robin making a drowsy afternoon stir in a tree, the glitter of all those bottles and atomizers, the sweet complicated smell that seemed to enter into
your body, the sense that your body was, somehow, infinitely

valuable, and at the same time a sense of disembodiment. That was what that dressing table came to feel like to me— after that talk lying out in the sun that afternoon, behind the strung-up sheet. I have sometimes wondered what would have happened to me if I had never even gone into that bathroom. In recollection sometimes I see it, all the glitter of the dressing table, and I smell the smells.

"Late one afternoon I was in there and she gave me a sudden studious look and said: 'Let's give Brad a treat, a new kind. That brute doesn't know what kind of a sister he's got. You sit here.'

"She got to work on me. She plucked my eyebrows, and, gosh, did that hurt. Then she got my hair gathered in a crazy clump on one side of my head with a big gold barrette with red stones in it, and purple eye shadow on my eyes, and mascara, so my eyelashes looked a yard long, and made my mouth purply red, with a very sullen expression. I sat there in a halter and faded blue denim shorts and grinned into the mirror.

" 'For Christ's sake,' she commanded, 'stop grinning. I want a slow, sullen, unforgiving glow, like the spark on a fuse creeping toward the bombshell. Hey, look sullen. Puff out your lower lip and bite it, girlie.'

"I did, and we both burst out laughing. But you know, suddenly I did feel sullen and dangerous. I even scared myself. I felt suddenly tragic. I was going to die young. I was sad for all the men who would love me hopelessly. Sad for myself too.

"She said then she'd have to dress me. And she did. She stripped me to the skin. Then she rummaged around and found some sort of big white shawl—wool but so light and fine it was like silk—and rigged me up a dress, one shoulder bare, held together with concealed safety pins, gathered at my left hip in another big gold thing-a-ma-jig with red stones. 'Sandals,' she cried, 'sandals.' She stopped. 'Oh, what a fool I am,' she wailed then. 'You can't wear mine—not with your little old Fiddlersburg feet.' She thought a half-second. 'Go barefoot,' she cried. 'That will fix 'em. Bare feet get 'em every time.' She looked down at my feet.

" 'Oh, those toenails,' she cried in anguish. But she squatted down and got to work. My toenails, fingernails too, wound up that same purply red as my mouth. Then she put perfume behind my ears and touched some in my hair. 'Now,' she said, surveying me, 'all we need is a caste mark and you will be the prize floozy of the maharajah.' She paused. 'But of course we haven't got a maharajah, either,' she said.

"There wasn't any maharajah. But there was an unexpected guest for dinner. An old Fiddlersburg friend and classmate of Brad's at Darthurst. He had just come to town that day and Brad had run into him on the street and brought him home. When I came downstairs in that fool rig, barefoot, and found him in the hall I thought I would die.

"I thought he might die too. He went pale as a sheet. It was Calvin Fiddler. I hadn't seen him since I was seven years old. When he left to go to prep school."

Calvin Fiddler had, that very June, got his M.D. from Johns Hopkins. After an internship in Nashville he planned to come back to Fiddlersburg to practice. It was, he said, the only place in the world a Fiddler could live. Anywhere else they thought your name was funny. He was, probably, uttering about himself a deeper truth than he knew. He suffered greatly if he thought somebody thought he was funny.

Calvin Fiddler was, in fact, quite prepossessing. His shoulders were good, and his face was handsome, though in a thin way. The face habitually wore a serious expression, relieved by a boyish tousle of dark hair and a smile that came shyly but infectiously, like the smile of a young boy trying to make friends.

That smile evoked something deep and protective in the nature of Maggie Tolliver. And she thought that it was very fine and romantic of Calvin Fiddler to come back to Fiddlersburg and be a doctor where they needed one, when he could practice in Nashville or Memphis and be a big specialist. She was in love with Fiddlersburg, or with something that Fiddlersburg, that summer, seemed to be; and in love with something that Fiddlersburg that summer in that house seemed to promise, like a first blossom unfolding in warm darkness. Besides, that smile touched something deep in her heart.

They were married in August, at a church wedding. Everybody in town came to the reception in the garden. The young couple went to the Gulf Coast for a brief honeymoon before the groom had to report in Nashville for the duties of the internship.

.   .   .

One morning, shortly after Maggie and Calvin had left, Lettice came into Brad's workroom, a copy of the *Nashville Banner* held out. "Look at that," she said.

He looked at it. The headlines announced the Berlin-Moscow pact. He handed the paper back to her, with an air of returning it to its proper place.

"I told you they were all crooks," he said.

"Yes," she said, "but I can't help but feel that I've lost something. It is like losing something over again that you knew you had lost already."

"All crooks," he said. He sat down at his table and whistled almost soundlessly through his teeth.

"Oh, it's just I wish things were different," she said.

"They aren't," he said.

He resumed the near-soundless spooky whistling through his teeth. The fingers on his right hand made a near-soundless tattoo on the table near the typewriter.

"You needn't be rude," she said, grinning thinly. "I know you want this gal out of here so you can work."

She took a step toward the door.

"No," he said. He got up. "I want this gal in here so I can work. On her. You got that thing on?"

She shook her head.

"Well, go hang it on. And report for duty. I have a notion of an entirely new approach to my work. It may revolutionize the industry."

The *Nashville Banner* lay on the floor, face up, the black headline showing.

Far off, the whistle of the steam plant at the pen blew for noon. The top leaves of the catalpa tree beyond the window glittered furrily in the August light. By the chair at the work table the jean pants were on the floor, the stained sneakers beside them. The green-striped seersucker dress was flung over a chair with some wispy odds and ends. On the iron bed to one side of the room, the mattress covered by a sheet, Bradwell Tolliver lay on his back, naked, holding a cigarette in his right hand, staring at the ceiling. The girl's head—the auburn hair tousled and damply dark, the eyes closed—lay on his left arm.

"Christ," he said, softly, staring at the ceiling.

"Huh?" she said, and opened her eyes.

"Just I was thinking," he said, "how if I'd got my ass shot off in Spain I would never have screwed you in Fiddlersburg."

She said nothing.

"Think of all the guys," he said, "who got their asses shot off in Spain thinking they were doing something for that continent of crooks."

She began to weep, quite soundlessly.

"What are you crying about," he demanded angrily.

"Because I love you," she said, "and oh, whatever the world is, my heart would just die if ever you threw away the wonderful thing you really are."

Chapter

18

BRAD EASED THE JAGUAR out of the side street that led from the old high school tennis court where they had been playing, and drifted down River Street. There she was.

"The Lady of Shalott," Brad said.

Yasha Jones looked at the figure nearly two blocks away, vibrating in the sun-dazzle, swathed in some kind of light blue dress with short sleeves, poised on the curb in front of the Post Office. "Yes," he said, and began:

> "The Lady hath a lovely face,
> God in His Mercy lend her grace . . ."

He stopped quoting. "Your conceit is very apt," he said. "The Lady was in her tower and could not look out at the real world. Leontine is blind. The Lady could only look into her mirror to know the world. Blind Leontine looks into something—her illuminated darkness, shall we say? What does that make you? Lancelot?"

"It was the Queen he was getting it off of," Brad said.

"But," Yasha Jones said, "Lancelot came riding by, through fields of barley and of rye, and the Lady saw him in her mirror and she leaped up and broke her loom and took three paces round the room, and died because she was sick of shadows yet could not have reality."

"Let's give the Lady a ride," Brad said. "Another ride in a Jag one-fifty. We can give her that much reality."

Brad drew the car over to the left, against the nonexistent traffic, approaching the curb where the figure yet waited, with a thin flat package clasped under an elbow while the hand fumbled for something in a black patent-leather hand bag.

"Look," Brad whispered, "she holds her head down as though she could see into the bag. Just like any woman fumbling in her God-damned bag."

"Yes," Yasha Jones said, studying her posture.

But the car was almost at the spot now, and the girl's face, calm and clear, with the deep unquestioning blue gaze under the pale hair, with the damp lips ever so slightly parted as though in expectation, was lifted toward them.

"Hi, Leontine," Brad said. "This is Brad, Brad and Yasha."

"Oh, yes," she said, "I was sure it was you. From the car." She paused, smiling in pride. "From the way the car sounds."

"Gosh," Brad said, "that's wonderful."

"That's not anything," she said, shaking her head ever so slightly, and the high spots of color on the cheeks bloomed and mantled downward in a blush over her paleness.

"Well, get in," Brad said, "and we'll give you a ride. We quit playing tennis, it was so hot, and we'll give you a ninety-mile-an-hour ride out on the state slab to cool you off."

Yasha Jones got out of the car, and went to the curb to take the girl's arm. She held out her right hand to him, prettily. He took it and led her around the car and established her. He slipped into the back and reached forward to touch the door into place, with its small, solid, authoritative click of the latch.

"I like the way that door closes," she said. She let her head sink back against the seat. Her eyes, very blue, were open against the sky, as though they were reflecting the sky, but bluer than the sky.

"Yes," Brad said, letting the car drift down the street, "that door is a good solid job of coach-work. When you shut it you always get the sense that you have settled something important. You feel like a man of decision, who settles weighty matters without fuss. Of course, you have only shut a door. But in a world where so few matters can be settled, the illusion is worth something."

He suddenly stopped talking and looked at her.

Her eyes were closed now. The lips were again parted ever so slightly, in that characteristic expression of expectancy. With her head in that position the throat was arched back a little. The throat was white and clearly molded with, he observed, none of those tiny transverse lines in which powder so often tends to collect grayly, like infinitesimal lint. Under the whiteness of flesh you had the sense of the windpipe, some sense of the fine articulation sheathed in the softness, with the breath moving soundlessly in that dark. Where the windpipe entered into the darkness of the body, at the twin points of the clavicle, there were the twin indentations, like the prints left by the thumb of a sculptor. There were a few tiny drops of sweat, he noticed, on the temple toward him— as, he thought, there must be on the other side, too—just at the edge of that remarkable and beautiful piled-up disorder of pale hair. Those tiny drops of sweat— they were just fine he thought. They made everything really real. Then he thought how the wind would snatch that hair once they got out on the highway and hit ninety.

They were over the ridge now and away from the river. "Ten minutes more," he said, "and we'll hit Billtown—good old Billtown." Then by way of explanation to Yasha Jones: "That's where we turned off the slab, you remember, coming here. No houses, just some sort of drugstore and package-goods joint and handkerchief-size dance floor and bowling alley and car hops to bring out the set-ups for the non-athletes parked in the moonlight. All fancied up now. But in my day, it was not fancy. It was pine boards, pinball, pig barbecue and bootleg, and the only bowling alley was in the back seat of a jalopy. This being, I explain, where the local juvenile delinquents of Fiddlersburg used to forgather on Saturday nights in the dear dead days beyond recall. Now, I imagine, the trade is middle-aged delinquents. And not from Fiddlers-burg."

He paused.

"Anyway," he said, "there it is."

Automatically, he wheeled the car onto the highway, his eyes fixed on the yellow brick and chrome and plate glass of Billtown, set in a field of winter-raddled, ocher-colored broom sage from the last season. At the edge, a few tons of crushed limestone had been dumped to make a parking area. All the buildings were now hushed and withdrawn in the mid-after-noon blaze of May.

He turned back to Leontine. "Do any of the local juve-niles still go to Billtown?" he demanded suddenly, as though in anger.

"I don't know," she said softly.

He slammed the accelerator to the floor.

"Hold your hats," he said.

The Jaguar leaped forward, the motor sang with a steady whet-edged whine, the needle surged toward ninety, hit it.

"We'll hold this," Brad said. "No use being ostentatious. You can cool off at ninety."

The girl, not lifting her head, put both hands up to her hair. "Oh, my hair!" she cried.

"I'm sorry," he said. "Just some damned juvenile-delin-quent foolishness got into me."

He had lifted his foot from the throttle.

"No," she said, "oh, no! I like it—it's exciting, I never went this fast!"

"Listen," he said, and gave it the throttle again, "just let it blow your hair. You can put it back up."

Obediently, she was lifting the pins, putting them be-tween her lips as she collected them. Her eyes were open now, and very bright. She gave a toss of her head and the hair flung free in the wind. "Oh," she said, "oh," sitting straight in the seat now, laughing with a sudden, deep throatiness.

"Atta girl!" Brad said. "You look great with your hair whipping in the wind at ninety m.p.h. You look like an ad for superoctane. In fact, you both do. Distinguished film director and Lady of Shalott use—"

But the face of Yasha Jones was fixed straight ahead, up the white track that came flying at them out of the blankness of dazzle.

Brad looked up the slab, saying nothing.

"Her," the girl said, "I know about her."

"Who?" Brad demanded.

"The Lady of Shalott. She was in a poem we had at school. A poem by Alfred, Lord Tennyson. I made my mother read it to me all the time." She paused and again let her head sink back on the seat. But the wind was still snatching the pale hair straight back, whipping it. Now and then she would roll her head, ever so little.

"My mother," she resumed, "maybe you remember, she was a schoolteacher. I mean before she got married to my father, and she could still read awful good. With expression, I mean. She would read to me a lot."

"Did you like that poem?" Brad demanded.

"Yes, it made me cry, what happened to the Lady of Shalott, and what he said seeing her lie dead. What was his name?"

"Lancelot," Brad said. "He was a rotter, as the English would say."

"I liked 'The Wreck of the Hesperus,' too. That made me cry, too," the girl said. Then: "My mother, she's been dead an awful long time. When I was thirteen. But after a while I got hold of Books for the Blind. But they don't always have what you want. I never got hold of 'The Lady of Shalott.' "

She lifted her head a little, and the wind snatched at the pale hair. Brad looked at her, then fixed his eyes into the hot dazzle of distance. They whipped on, and no one spoke.

They came over a rise, and at ninety almost piled into a wagon and team going in their direction at a mean speed of a mile and a half an hour. But despite the fact that there was an oncoming Chevrolet, overage and bulging with towheads and not too expertly maneuvered by a fat farm-wife whose eyes were round with horror, Brad managed to squeak through just as the space opened between the left rear wheel of the wagon and the left rear fender of the Chevrolet. As they whipped through, the old Negro man on the wagon board—overalls, old black felt hat pulled down around the grizzled head like a baby bonnet—looked out at them with profound unconcern.

"Don't say the Black Man never strikes back at the oppressor," Brad said. "You give Uncle a wagon and a span of mules and he will move out on the highway and sooner or later will nail him a Confederate. It is not in Clausewitz and it is a tactic not developed in seminars at Sandhurst, but it works. Uncle and his simple equipment have accounted for more Confederates than all the campaigns of U.S. Grant and W.T. Sherman combined. Uncle damned near accounted for us, just now."

Leontine was fingering the square thin package on her lap. "I got a Book for the Blind now," she said. "It just came through the mail this afternoon."

Brad, still staring into distance, asked what it was.

"I won't tell you," she said. She laughed again, in that sudden, throaty way. She rolled her head a little on the back of the seat and the wind snatched the hair.

But Bradwell Tolliver was not looking at her. He was looking at the limestone bluff that, plumed with cedars, was just that instant heaving into view. Then he was looking at the Seven Dwarfs Motel.

At ninety miles an hour, he thought, *it doesn't take long to come forty miles. You get there before you know.*

He thought: *You get anywhere before you know.*

He broke the speed, bringing it down just enough to allow him to snap into the parking area of the Seven Dwarfs Motel, and, with a great spraying of gravel, snap out again, westward. The throttle was as near the floor as he dared.

Hard by the gasoline pumps, Jingle-Bells, in his trick pants and the jerkin out of fantasy, stared after the Jaguar.

After they had got back to Billtown and turned off on the side road to Fiddlersburg, the girl sat up in the seat and began to work at her hair. She held the pins in her mouth and, with a little frown of preoccupation, worked at the hair as though she were alone in her pine box of a room at home, in that white wooden box of a house, propped on high, thin brick piers, off the black ground.

When they drew up at the Purtle gate, Brad got out and came around to open the door for her. But she did not immediately move. "You know," she said shyly, then stopped.

"Yes?" Brad said.

"I wish you all would come in," she said. "I know you all are awful busy, but just a minute."

Brad looked at Yasha.

"I wish I could," Yasha said, and she turned to fix the blue deep gaze on him. "I sincerely do," he continued. "But I have some letters I absolutely must get off. Will you ask me again?"

The girl turned back to Brad, a slight shadow over her face, waiting. She waited with a peculiar passivity, a passivity that pulsed inwardly, as it were, with some certitude that if the waiting was long enough, the passivity passive enough, something would happen, whatever it was she was waiting to happen.

"You stay," Yasha Jones was saying to Brad. "I'll walk. As a matter of fact, I'd rather, if you don't mind."

Brad hesitated a moment, then said: "Sure."

Yasha Jones walked south down the road, not looking back. His arms hung down at his sides, and the third and little finger of each hand touched the palm, where the sweat was.

Walking along, he shut his eyes and saw the white highway again blazing at him. A ride like that, it was therapy, he thought. Maybe if he had Dr. Bradwell Tolliver give him the ninety-mile-an-hour treatment every afternoon, he would get cured. If he didn't get killed. And that, too, would be a kind of cure.

The sun was still high and strong. It filled the sky and poured over the wideness of the land. It poured over Yasha Jones, like a flood. Walking down the road, past the vacant lots, in the blankness of afternoon, Yasha Jones suddenly had the vision of himself, hatless and erect, the hairless head glittering in sunlight, walking down the road.

It was as though he saw himself in a film, moving down a road under the hot blankness of sky. It was as though he himself had made a film and was, at the same time, in the film. It was as though he, Yasha Jones, who had made the film, was watching the film being run off for him and, to no sound but the faint whirr of the projector, was watching that other Yasha Jones walk down that road. It was as though, while he watched the film, he realized that in making it he had lost the thread of meaning which the film had been supposed to have, and as a result, somehow, the film would never stop, and forever he would have to watch that man walk down that road, pressing the third and little finger of each hand against the sweat in the palm.

Her package in her hand, Leontine had led him into the

house—past the broken board in the second step, past the shrunken heap of flesh and unshrunken old bones in the wheel chair and the dry-skinned handshake, past that long glimpse down the road to the fake façade of Lorton's Hardware Store, where, one hot afternoon thirty years ago, the shadowy interior had been full of the smell of burnt cordite. She had led him into a little room off the living room, which, she said, her mother used to call her sewing room. It was there she said, her mother used to read to her.

In the middle of the hot cubicle, which swam with a green light from the pulled-down window shades over open windows, stood a rickety-looking card table. On the table was a reddish-blue tapestry cover of some kind, rather faded, with elaborate tassels hanging down. The scene on the tapestry cover had something medieval about it, lords and ladies and greyhounds, fading out. Bradwell Tolliver made mental note of the tapestry.

In the middle of the table, on the tapestry, was the Books for the Blind phonograph.

"Won't you have a seat, please," Leontine said primly. "You just take the big chair, won't you, and be comfy."

She was gesturing, with absolute certainty, toward a somewhat derelict Morris chair, upholstered in black imitation leather, brown cracks in the upholstering, here and there some gray stuffing visible.

"Thanks," he said, and sat in the chair.

"Lean back and get comfy," she said.

He leaned back.

"I like the word 'comfy,'" she said. "It sounds like it means. Don't you like a word like that?"

"Yes," he said.

"Shut your eyes," she said, in a hushed, yet throaty tone, "and I'll give you a surprise to make you wise."

She giggled.

"That's what children used to say," she said. "You remember how it was?"

"Yes," he said. "And you'd shut your eyes and open your mouth and they'd pop a nice passel of fishing worms right in."

"I won't do that," she said and giggled again.

He wished she wouldn't giggle.

"You got your eyes shut?" she said.

"Yes."

"No fudging," she said.

He lay back in the chair with his eyes shut. He heard a little snip of some kind from the table, then a surreptitious rustling of paper. He wondered what it was like to be blind. He heard a robin utter a couple of half-hearted notes from the hydrangea bush outside the windows, then give up. He wondered about Digby, who lived in this house. He wondered if Digby lay in his bed at night in the little pine box of a room upstairs, twenty-five dollars a month, and wondered what it was like to be blind.

He himself now lay back comfy in the chair, and wondered what it was like to be blind, and saw in the dark of his head how, in the dark, in the middle of the night, which to her would be clear as day, Leontine Purtle, in a white gown that glimmered in the dark, her pale hair down and glimmering, her bare feet soundless on the boards, would move down the upstairs hall, and lay her hand on a doorknob.

Hell, no, he thought, *not Digby!*

Rage flared up in him.

He would kill the square-headed, square-toothed, square-peckered son-of-a-bitch.

"You opened your eyes," Leontine was saying. "Oh, you promised not to open your eyes!"

He sat up in the chair with a start. "But—" he began.

"Yes, you did," she said, "I know you did."

"My eyelids must have rattled," he said. "If you heard 'em, my eyelids must need greasing." He stopped. "Oh, I'm sor—" He stopped again.

"You don't have to be sorry," she said. "I think what you said was funny. You don't think it bothers me to have somebody refer to my—to my handicap, do you? About how I would have to hear you opening your eyes because I couldn't see them. It was a joke."

He couldn't think of anything to say.

"Now lie back and shut your eyes," she said, sternly. "And don't cheat any more."

He lay back and shut his eyes.

He heard a soft click, a slight burring motion, the grinding little *beep-beep* of a voice cut off, then another. Then he heard the voice.

The voice was saying:

"On good evenings in spring, when the light began to hold late, Abraham Goldberg—Old Abie, with his stooped shoulders, pale brow, paper-thin nose and dark pained eyes—would come out of the tailor shop on River Street, and prop himself in a split-bottom chair to read. But his gaze would lift across the great bend of the river which slid past like molten copper, copper-colored with the spring burden of clay coming up from Alabama and with the reflection of the red sunset. What does an old Jew sitting in front of his tailor shop, alone in a lost town by the copper-colored, deep-bellied river, think as he stares into the red sunset?

I do not know. Now I shall never know.

All I know is that, when the time came for me to go away from that town and the burdened river, I did not tell you goodbye. But I am telling you now.

So, Abie, if you—"

"Cut it off," Bradwell Tolliver burst out, and sat up in the chair. "Cut the damned thing off, won't you?"

The machine stopped. The last indistinguishable word or two dragged out to a sigh, then into silence.

He turned to her now. She was sitting in the straight chair beyond the table, in her stillness which, somehow, was not a heaviness, but a waiting, her blue gaze steadily on him as though she saw everything and forgave everything.

"You were pretty cute," he said, and laughed. "Fiddling with that thing so it wouldn't give any title or anything."

"I wanted to surprise you," she said.

"You did," he said. He paused. Then: "You sure did. You filled my mouth with fishing worms."

"What do you mean?"

"Oh, nothing," he said.

"Don't you want me to play it?"

"No, I don't."

"Why?" she asked, mournfully.

"Damn it," he said, "it was so long ago."

He saw the cloudy, troubled look on her face.

"But you know," he said, with artificial enthusiasm in his tone, "I'm damned if I see how you got that thing started right off. No title, and all. To surprise me."

She sat up straighter and smiled, gratified.

"Oh, it's easy," she said. "I could of started it almost anywhere in the record."

"What?"

"I mean the number of times I have played it."

"You just got the damned thing this afternoon," he said.

"Yes," she said, "but you see I have had it a lot of times before. I don't know how many times I have played it. I could just pick it up and go on saying myself what came next."

"Well, don't," he said.

But the voice began, not the phonograph now, her own voice: " 'So, Abie, if you are now in any place where—' "

"I said I don't want to hear it."

"I think I could just say it all," she said. "I have played it so much. And that part where you go back to the grave, I could just cry. The first time or two I played it I did cry."

"I'll tell you something to dry your tears," he said. "I never went back. I just made that up. I had to end the story some damned way."

She was silent for a moment, her wide gaze on him. He had the crazy impulse to wink at her. To wink at her because it was a joke. Something, whatever it was, was sure a joke. And she would wink back, because it was sure a joke.

But she was saying: "That doesn't matter. That you just made it up. What matters is that it was in your heart to make it up that way."

He felt trapped. He even felt a constriction of breath.

"Listen here, Leontine," he said. "That is crap. You read it somewhere and it is crap. I've been in this business a long time, and the fact is when you are writing a story or doing a movie script, you hit some logic, and it is that logic, not the heart business, that drives you to a certain end. It is like chess, and—"

"Old Mr. Goldfarb," she said softly, "he left you his chess set—yes, that part of the story is—"

"To hell with Goldfarb," he said. "What I'm trying to say is—"

But she was looking at him from that serene, blue, forgiving distance.

He shut up.

"Do you know why I played the record so much?" she asked, finally.

"No."

"It was after my mother died. Maybe two years or so. I was just a kid and I was still awful lonesome and lost-feeling. Then they got me the Books for the Blind. I was about sixteen then. When I played your record I didn't feel lost any more, somehow. It was like I had never before known where

I was—I mean, in Fiddlersburg. Your record, it sort of made me know where I was. I know you didn't call the place Fiddlersburg, like you called that old Mr. Goldfarb another name, but it was Fiddlersburg, and I knew where I was for the first time. Then everything felt different. The voices on the street were different. It was like I knew that people were alive and something was going on inside them. And inside me, too. I had always felt sort of frozen inside, I guess—or clogged up like a drain pipe in the sink or something. And all of a sudden I wasn't. It ain't—I mean, it isn't—that way any more. That record, that story—it made me want to reach out and touch the world. I must of played that record a thousand times or—"

He rose abruptly from the big Morris chair. He found that pudgy, enclosing softness intolerable. He turned to her, and even to himself his voice, though low, sounded grating, outraged and angry.

"What's it like," that voice was demanding, "what's it like to be blind?"

Having said that, he stood there in the middle of the room, in the green light from the pulled-down shades, the constriction in his chest. He was afraid she would hear the difficulty of his breathing.

"I don't know," she said, finally.

He turned toward her.

"Oh, yes, I'm blind," she said. "I just mean I don't know how to tell you what it's like. If you're blind, it's—it's just being yourself."

She hesitated, her gaze on him.

Then went on. "Yes," she said, "suppose I asked you to tell me what it's like to be you. You couldn't tell me, I bet. What I mean is, it's just the way you are. Being you is like being blind."

He stared across at her. She sat calmly in the straight chair by the table, her hands folded in her lap, her gaze on him.

"I got to go," he said.

He took a step toward the door. She rose.

"Listen," she said.

"What?"

"You aren't mad, are you?" she asked, humbly.

"No," he said.

"Did I do something wrong?" she asked, moving from the chair. "About the record—the stories? It was because I liked them so much."

"You didn't do anything wrong," he said. Then burst out: "It's just—"

He stopped.

"What?"

"Nothing—I'm glad you asked me to come in. But I've got to go now."

He got to the door, put his hand on the knob.

"Thanks for the ride," she said. "I never went for a ride that fast before."

Bradwell Tolliver stood in the road with his right hand on the door of the Jaguar. But he did not get in, not right away. He stood there and thought what she had said.

What had she said?

She had said: *Being you's like being blind.*

Chapter

19

BRAD PUT DOWN THE TELEPHONE, not racking it, and went out into the dark garden. About halfway down the walk, he called: "Hey, Yasha! Brother Potts wants to come see you."

"Of course," Yasha's voice called back from the foot of the garden.

In a minute Brad came to join them, his huaraches making their dry, dragging sound on the old bricks, in the dark.

"He was sure steamed up," he said. He took a sip of his coffee, of his cognac, then resumed: "You could tell from his voice."

"Poor old thing," Maggie murmured. "I wonder if he's had some bad news about—"

She paused.

"About his cancer going to win the race?" Brad finished for her.

"About not being able to have that last farewell service," she emended.

"We should all arrange to go to that service," Brad said. "It is our chance to find out that the life we have lived is blessèd."

"Hush," Maggie said. "That wasn't a very funny thing to say."

Over in shadow by the tumbling gazebo, Brad was silent. Then, after a long time, during which the moon began to lift over the roof, outlining the TV aerial, he said, very quietly: "Ole Sis, you are right. It was not very funny."

He fell back into silence.

Yasha Jones was looking at the moon.

"Look," he said, "the moon is in the same phase as when I came here. I have been here through one whole cycle of the moon."

He continued to study it.

"Or," he said, "has no time passed at all, and we have been sitting here only the time of an eye-blink?"

"Oh, Yasha," Maggie exclaimed, laughing, "Squire Colts-hill told you! There is no time in Fiddlersburg."

He made no reply, staring at the moon.

When there came the sound of a car, Brad rose, word-lessly, and disappeared up the walk. He brought Brother Potts back.

Brother Potts, installed by the wall, where the moonlight fell on his pale, pained face, refused cognac, but accepted coffee. He hung on every word addressed to him, with that faint pecking motion of the head, like a scraggle-necked chicken pecking up corn, incongruously, in moonlight. He was awfully sorry to disturb them, he said.

"I hope you have finished the poem," Yasha Jones said.

He had something, Brother Potts said, but he didn't know how good it was.

"Read it," Maggie said. "We'd be awful happy."

"Privileged," Yasha Jones murmured.

Brother Potts turned his pained face from one to the other, beseeching.

"It happened so queer," he said. "I been working so hard

on it, but nothing came. Then tonight—blooey! Like something had broke in me—like a paper sack of water busting, the way kids do. That's why I called, and disturbed you."

"The poem," Yasha Jones breathed, "please."

"Yes," Brother Potts said, "but it's how the poem came." He paused, gulped, seemed to brace himself. Then: "You know Pretty-Boy—the nig—I mean the colored man who is to pay the supreme penalty?"

Yasha Jones began to sing, under his breath:

> "Where did you come from?
> Where did you go?
> Where do you come from,
> Cotton-Eye Joe?"

"The one who won't pray," Brad said.

"Yes, yes," Brother Potts said, with the pecking motion, "and what I can't bear in my heart is how people are making a game of it. There are good God-fearing church members who are betting whether he will pray or not. I have counseled with them, but some have laughed and said it is just one more hard-headed, mule-ornery, murdering blue-gum but he will crack when the time comes and they put him on the squat, they bet. I mean they are betting money, not just a way of talking.

"But it is worse than just betting. They stop Brother Leon Pinckney on the street and they ask him has his boy cracked yet. Some folks even ask him if he is not getting proud and stuck up because his boy is not cracking.

"It looks like something has got into folks, good folks. It looks like all this waiting to be flooded out is doing something to good people. They are turned inside out. For instance, some of 'em talk like they would like to get their hands on that boy and make him crack. One man—but he is not a professing believer, I must say—said he bet he could make him crack, but it would not be praying over him, it would be—but I just walked away.

"I been living in this town more'n twenty-five years, and in that time, lots of men up in the pen have paid the supreme penalty, but I can't get used to it. I have prayed with lots of 'em. I have seen some come happy to the Glory. But I can't get used to it, them waiting for the chair. I know the world is God's will, but I can't get used to some things."

He turned his head on his thin neck, and fixed his pained gaze on each face in turn, beseeching.

"Do you know what I mean?" he asked.

"Yes," Yasha Jones said.

"But I'm getting off the track," Brother Potts cried out, something near a wail in his voice. "I got to tell you what happened."

He was staring now at Yasha Jones, his eyes fixed there.

"I went to Brother Pinckney and asked him could I pray with Pretty-Boy. He was strange with me, not like he has ever been. He said to me: 'Don't we pray to the same God?' And I said, 'Yes.' And he said: 'Does not your Bible say that all rests in the hands of God?' And he looked at me.

"But I said to him, it was not I thought my praying would do anything special. But I could not bear for that boy to sit there and not know that some white man wanted to pray with him. I told him how last night after prayer meeting—last night being Wednesday night—eight people had stayed behind to get on their knees with me and pray for that poor boy. I told Brother Pinckney I wanted to go, but I could not go without his blessing."

Brother Potts stopped. He was staring into the moonlight now, blinking.

"He looked at me a long time and his face was like it was plaster and varnished that yellow-brown color." He turned to Yasha Jones, saying: "You see, Brother Pinckney is not exactly high yaller, but he is light-brown complected."

He seemed, suddenly, confused.

"What was I saying?" he asked.

"You said you had wanted Brother Pinckney's blessing," Yasha Jones said, very soft.

"Yes—yes—and Brother Pinckney, he looked at me. Then he said—you know what he said?"

"No," Yasha Jones said.

"He said, 'Oh, who am I to bind or loose!' And standing right there on the street—right in front of the Post Office and three o'clock this afternoon and people passing by—he just put his hands over his face. It was like he did not want to see what was there in front of him.

"I stood there and I did not know what to do. Then it was like when somebody is sick and you tiptoe out of the room. I tiptoed off. There on the street, in front of the Post Office. It was three o'clock, or near-bouts."

He stopped. The empty left sleeve was folded upward and pinned neatly to the left side of his coat, on the breast pocket. His head sank forward on the thin neck, and he seemed to be studying the coffee cup he held on his lap. Then, very carefully, but not so carefully that the spoon did not rattle in the saucer, he reached over to set the cup on the brick wall, above the river.

"I went up to the pen," he said, finally. "A guard took me to that boy, and stood outside the cell, not too far off. I got down on my knees, and lifted up my hand, and I began to pray. Then it happened."

His head sagged again, and he waited. Then he raised up his head.

"Listen," he demanded, thrusting his thin face forward at them, twisting his neck as though to show his face in the moonlight.

"Listen," he demanded again, "have you ever had a nigger spit in your face?"

In the silence, he stared from face to face, beseeching.

Then he said: "It is not a word a man ought ever to use. *Nigger,* I mean. I do not believe in calling a man by that word just because God made his skin of a dark complexion. But I had to say it that way—nigger—because that was the way it felt. My eyes popped open, and his face was right there not six inches from mine, and his eyes, they was popped wide open and bloodshot—they was so close I could see the little veins in 'em—and I was all tightened up and about to jump up and my feelings was churning around in me and I could hear the guard, him coming, and I heard him saying, 'The black son-of-a-bitch,' and I—"

He stopped.

"I'm sorry, Mrs. Fiddler," he said, "to be talking improper. It just popped out, the way it was."

"That's all right, Brother Potts," she said. "That was the way it was."

"But I didn't get off my knees," Brother Potts said. "Something held me down and I name it Glory. All of a sudden it was like I felt the spit on my cheek—it was my left cheek—and it was running down some. It was a good gob, to run down. And when I felt it, really felt it, I just stayed on my knees, not something I meant to do, just something that happened. I did not make a motion to wipe that spit. I let it run. And I was praying again, out loud. Me praying, the guard stopped and did not budge. You know what I was praying?"

He looked from face to face.

"I was praying," he said then, "for God to make me know that what happened was right because it was His Holy Will. I was thanking God that that spit was on my face, and I was not going to wipe it off, I was going to let the sunshine dry it, or the wind, in God's Holy Will.

"Then I got up. I lifted up my hands—my hand, I mean —and asked God's blessing on that boy. He was sitting on the cot now, looking at the floor. Then I came on out. I never wiped it off. I walked down through the middle of Fiddlersburg and never wiped it off. I went in my house and laid down on the bed. The shades were pulled down."

Brother Potts let his head droop. His eyes were fixed on his own hand, that lay in his lap.

After a while Yasha Jones spoke. "And the poem?" he said.

"I was laying there on the bed," he said, "I was not asleep, or awake neither. Then of a sudden, clear as a bell, I heard it. The words, I mean. I jumped off the bed and got me a pencil and tried to write 'em down."

"Can you say them to us?" Yasha Jones asked. "Or do you have to read them?"

Brother Potts wrinkled his brow, twisting his face in the moonlight. "I can say 'em," he said then. "The words that stuck."

"Please," Yasha Jones said.

Brother Potts lifted his face in the moonlight, the face suddenly smooth, and shut his eyes. He began:

> "When I see the town I love
>   Sinking down beneath the wave
> I pray I'll remember then
>   All the blessings that God gave.
>
> "When I see the life I led
>   Whelmed and sunk beneath the flood,
> Let the waters drown regret and envy—
>   Make me see my life was good.
>
> "God, make me know what I didn't have
>   Was the sweetest gift You gave.
> Oh, let me know such perfect joy,
>   When what I did have goes 'neath the wave."

He stopped and waited, in silence.

"Brother Potts," Maggie said, "it is pretty. Why, yes, Brother Potts, it is so pretty it makes my heart fill."

"Thank you, ma'am," he said, but his eyes were on Yasha Jones.

"Yes," Yasha Jones said, slowly. "It clearly springs from deep sincerity."

The smoothness had gone now from the face of Brother Potts. He shook his head from side to side, in a slight, shuddering motion. "But something happened," he said. "I heard the words as clear as a bell, and I wrote 'em down as fast as I could grab a pencil. But they just came to me one time, and it looks like when I got 'em on paper I had not got them down exactly the way they came. It looked like something had passed away out of 'em. Now what about that, Mr. Jones?"

Yasha Jones thought a moment, then murmured: ". . . c'ha l'abito dell' arte e man che trema."

"Beg pardon," Brother Potts said.

"I beg your pardon," Yasha Jones said. "Simply a line of verse written by the Italian poet Dante, came into my head. It is a line that has always seemed full of pathos to me. The idea is there—the vision, shall we say—but the hand trembles."

"I get the notion," Brother Potts said, mournfully. "It is like my hand must of trembled."

"Isn't that always true?" Yasha demanded. "Of all who try to live in the spirit? There is the vision, but—"

He spread his palms, upturned.

Brother Potts was shaking his head in the moonlight. "But if I could ask you a favor," he said, leaning his thin worried face forward. "If you could just help me fix it up a little. More like I heard the words, me laying there on the bed."

"Brother Potts," Yasha Jones said. "No one can restore the vision. But if we talk together, perhaps something of it may come back to you."

He rose abruptly, not moving his feet, his arms easy by his sides, rising from the ankles, with the easy elastic motion he had, like the motion of a dancer or fencer. Then added gaily: "But one can always mend the meter! Shall we go into the house to the light?"

They went together toward the house.

Brad stared after them.

"He's a hell of a tennis player," he said.

"You mean he is not any good?" Maggie asked, looking up the dark walk after the two figures.

"No," Brad said. "I mean he is good. He is beautiful and he is murder. He ran my ass off this afternoon. I got so pooped we had to quit."

A light came on in the living room, just one of the reading lamps, it seemed.

"I must have spent a couple of thousand on my serve," Brad said, "out on the Coast. But he must have spent a million—the way he ran me today." He looked out over the river now. "But I'm not in too good shape," he said. "Too much gut. And my wind could be better. Not that I'm drinking. It really got bad, one time out on the Coast. But I licked it."

He continued to stare over the moon-swept land westward.

After a moment, Maggie reached out, and touched his knee.

"I'm glad you did," she said.

"Thanks, Ole Sis," he said, and patted her hand.

He had not turned to her.

Then he said: "But I don't seem to be able to lick this."

"What, Brad?"

"This job," he said. "I have scaled the heights of Fiddlersburg, and now I am rim-rocked."

"I don't understand."

"It's what the old-timers say hunting mountain sheep out in the Rockies. You go up and up and risk your fool neck doing it and come out way up on top, and there he stands—the Big One, with horns like God—but he's way over yonder, out of range, and you're all rimmed in by rock—rock, nothingness, and vertigo. You are rim-rocked. All you can do is go down the way you came."

He paused, glumly.

"Maybe I've just got to go down," he said then. "The way I came."

"Oh, give it time, Brad," she said.

"I'm giving it all I've got," he said, "time and everything else. I've been working every morning, and I've been going

up right after coffee almost every night and working till all
hours. You've seen me go up there. You know, it's a funny
thing—"

He stopped.

"What's funny, Brad?"

"I have been a morning worker for years. Just that. If I
don't get on top of it by noon, it is a cinch that the vision,
as Yasha calls it, will not come. God hath turned away his
face, and that day is a dead duck. But when I wrote my first
stories—up at Darthurst—it was always late at night. I
might be studying or playing bridge and I would get rest-
less. I would sit up half the night, then, in an old wool bath-
robe and a turtle-neck, with the radiator getting cold, and
frost on the windowpanes, and me humped over that old
Oliver typewriter, and River Street would swim into my ken.
Here I've been trying it again at night. You know, sympa-
thetic magic. Or something." He laughed, shortly.

Then: "Maybe I ought to advertise for an old Oliver."

"You don't need it, Brad," she said.

"I need something," he said.

"You just need to relax," she said, "and be yourself."

"Huh," he grunted. Then he turned on her: "Do you
know what the Lady of Shalott, the beauteous Leontine, said
to me this afternoon when I asked her how it felt to be
blind?"

"I don't know what she said, but it does seem a strange
sort of topic for you to propose."

"It may be stranger than you think. Maybe I'll tell you
about it sometime," he said. "But you know what she said?"

"No."

"She said: 'Being you's like being blind.' Being me, that
is."

"I don't care what Leontine said," she said. "What I say
is, all you need is to relax and be yourself, your inside self."

"I need to take lessons from Brother Potts," Brad said. "I
need to get spit on by a nigger and hear the voices."

"Oh, don't call him a nigger," Maggie cried out. "Oh, the
poor wretched creature, and he beat that old woman's head to
pieces with a new claw hammer, and all he would say in
court was she made him do it, and he can't pray, and he's
going to die—"

"The word *nigger*," Brad said, "is not one I use or readily accept. But I appeal, in this instance, to Brother Potts.

He said you have to use the word to get the feeling. And if you don't get the feeling, you don't hear the voices, and—"

Maggie was not listening to him.

He got up and glowered dourly down at her. "You don't understand," he said.

"Understand what?" she asked. She looked up at him. "Understand what, dear Old Brad?"

"How this is different, this picture. It is like I am really rim-rocked. Paralyzed. But I've got to go for broke on this one, all or nothing. It is like nothing that ever happened matters if I swing it. But if I don't—"

He stopped. He shrugged.

"Sit down," she said, gently.

He said: "Damn it, I work, but nothing connects. I need a nigger to spit in my face."

"Sit down," she said again. Then, though he did not sit, she continued: "You've been very successful, Brad. I've read in the papers how you are one of the most successful writers out there. If you'd just relax now and—"

"And be myself," he finished for her, and laughed. "Yeah," he said, "I have come back to Fiddlersburg. I have come back to touch base. And mysteriously, mystically, I relax and am born again. Is that it?"

"Sit down, Brad," she said, even more gently.

He sat down. She reached out and took his hand and held it for a while. "Listen," she said, then. "I don't know anything about it, but why don't you make Brother Potts the center of your picture. Not that I know anything, but—"

Her voice drifted off, and she held his hand.

Finally, he said: "I'll think about it. Thanks, Ole Sis."

He stared over the river. After a while she patted his hand, then let it drop.

"Things certainly do change," he said, then.

"What changes, Brad?"

"Something just came to my mind, something I must not have thought of for a thousand years. Maybe never. Something that must have happened before you were born, even. Before our mother died."

"What?"

"Me standing and watching our father shave," he said. "You know how tough and black his hair and whiskers were. Well, he is standing there shaving, and I hear the scrape of the razor, a big old-fashioned razor. And I say to him, 'Fa-

ther, will you ever die?' And he looks down at me and grins—
yeah, grins, that is one of the funniest things I remember
—for you know what a cast-iron non-grinning old bastard he
was and—"

"Oh, Brad," she interrupted, "he wasn't always that way,
he—"

"Not to you," he said. "Not to me either in this recollection, so, by God, it must have been long back. Anyway, he's
shaving those bailing-wire whiskers off and I ask him if he's
ever going to die, and he grins down at me and says, 'I
reckon so, son, some day.' And I say, 'Don't fathers always
die before their boys?' and he says he reckons so. And I
say, 'Well, when I die, the first thing I do when I get to
heaven and get my wings is to fly around till I find you.'"

He paused, meditating. Then gave a laugh, quickly
chopped off.

"Yeah," he said. "Imagine what a hell of a time back
that must have been when I'd want to fly around heaven trying to locate the pleasure of his society."

He paused again. Then resumed: "Anyway, what I see in
my mind's eye is that old black-bristled booger just holding his
razor in the air and looking down at me, not grinning now,
and—"

"I think I am going to cry," Maggie said, quite factually.

"Wait till I get through, and I'll give you something to
cry about," he said, then paused. "There he is looking down
at me, the charming little tyke, and he is holding that big
razor in the air, and I say to him, 'And you remember, you
keep looking out for me, too. When I get there and start flying round, hunting.'"

She said nothing now, not looking at him, looking down
at her clasped hands in her lap.

"Now, damn it," he said, "you can cry. But I hope you
won't. For unaccustomed as I am to public crying, I might
cry myself." He waited glumly. Then said: "That episode, for
what it is worth, is what comes into my head. I leave it with
you, like a lock of hair or a pressed violet found in the family Bible. It is merely what, quite irrationally, comes into my
head. I have no theories as to why it should. Especially in the
light of my subsequent experiences with the old bastard."

He rose.

"I am going to work," he announced. "By the old Dart-

hurst schedule it is just about time for the vision. If there
is to be a vision. Toodle-oo."

He had taken a couple of steps when she lifted her head
and spoke.

"Wait," she said.

He waited.

"You know that book you started—the novel—before
you went to Hollywood?" she said.

He nodded.

"Well," she said, "if you want to use that—"

"You mean you and Cal—and the trial and all?"

"Yes," she said. "I don't mind now if you do. If that is
what will work for you. It won't matter now to anybody."
She waited. "It shouldn't have mattered to me then," she
said.

He looked heavily down at her, studying her lifted face
as she sat very straight in the chair.

"Thanks, Ole Sis," he said. Then: "But you see—you see,
I think I'll take a crack at your other idea. You know, Brother
Potts, et al."

He turned toward the house.

Watching him go up the walk, her heart was full of tenderness. When he had disappeared, she let her gaze move
over the garden, the tumbling gazebo, the river, the far land.
Far off, there was a single light. Some house, some cabin.
Something was there, far away.

She stared into distance and the whole world seemed
frail and beautiful in its drift of moonlight and field mist
and the far-off darkness of woods. She yearned to lean over
it all in protective tenderness.

She thought: *If only you could feel this way, always.*

". . . and when we got back to Nashville from our
honeymoon, we found an apartment on Grand Avenue—
which, by the way, isn't as grand as all that—an attic made
over to a sitting room and a tiny bedroom and a kitchenette,
and a sort of bathroom. It was in the house of a teacher at
one of those colleges around there—I don't which—I don't
know which—and the teacher had done the carpentering himself in his spare time and it was about what you might expect
he would do with beaver board and trellis strips nailed on the
joints, but his wife had tried to make up for things by splatter-

painting the floors in ten different colors and pasting flower decals on the lemon-colored doors. Except the bathroom door, which had a big decal right in the middle, a naked baby sitting on pottie.

"The wife of the teacher was from down in Mississippi, a large smiling woman—she couldn't stop smiling out of her acres of wonderful complexion—and there was always a damp stain under the arms of whatever dress she was wearing and she was forever waylaying me on the stairs or popping in on me in the apartment to push that smiling face at me and in a whispery, wet-lipped way, breathe on me and pry into how Cal and I got along in bed, or give me advice on contraception or how to achieve what she called the 'ecstasy of mutuality which is the music of the gods,' which she said she and Archibald—the teacher—had finally got the knack of and she wanted to spread the gospel.

"That was her finest phrase, that music of the gods bit, and I have often wondered where she got it, out of what handbook on love and sex. In fact, all her conversation, as she pushed that large, damp, breathy smile at you, was in that runny, melting marshmallow language you would find in a sex manual. At least, in the love and marriage book I finally got up the nerve to order from an advertisement which promised to send it in a plain wrapper, and did, and then I kept it hidden in the cabinet under the kitchenette sink, behind scrub rags and brushes and paper sacks for garbage, where Cal wouldn't find it. I was ashamed to show it to Cal, afraid he would think I was a goose or that I didn't love him or was reflecting on his wisdom. And on his M.D., too, for he was a real doctor from Johns Hopkins and ought to know everything, and therefore would tell me, or show me, or something, whatever there was to tell or show.

"Meantime, I had some awful sense of guilt and infidelity when I'd sit in the kitchenette—or even in the bathroom sometimes—reading the book and being afraid I'd hear his step on the stairs. Even though I knew being an intern was about like being in jail and you didn't just pop over home on impulse. But that guiltiness wasn't a patch on what it was like when spring came.

"The teacher's wife came one day with a big manila envelope. She did a lot of breathing on me and put out a lot of that marshmallow talk I couldn't make much sense of—

though I confess I was always trying to get at the facts that must lie behind that whisperiness and all that self-satisfied sweetness and sweatiness. Well, she drew it out of the envelope. It was that Fanny Hill thing, that dirty book. She left it with me. I stood there with the book in my hand, and she sort of tiptoed off, drifting off like a big rubber balloon wearing a pink dress, and got out the door but held the door open and stood there with a hand on the knob, and her face was peeking back in at me with that damp, whispery, inflated smile that seemed to say that she knew exactly what I would be doing in three minutes.

"And she was right. I did it. That is, as soon as she had gone and I had opened the door to be sure she wasn't squatting down to peek in the keyhole. As a matter of fact, I guess my feelings about her weren't too far wrong. She might have been peeking. A couple of years later, there was a fat scandal in Nashville, a sort of little sex circle where the members swapped around and even gave little exhibitions by candlelight—oh, dear God, by candlelight—and the teacher and his wife were involved. Since then it has occurred to me that maybe she was trying to recruit Cal and me for fresh blood, maybe. Anyway, the police got into it, and the teacher got fired from teaching whatever he taught and they had to leave town. But isn't it pitiful—that whisperiness and the runny marshmallow stuff and the ecstasy of mutuality and the marriage-manual gabble and the balloon shape and acres of wonderful complexion all over, and the wet lips and Fanny Hill, with illustrations, and whatever in her made her do whatever she did—oh, dear God, by candlelight—and it all winding up in a grubby police court in Nashville? You don't know whether to laugh or cry.

"But getting back to me, I could almost cry about me, too, if it weren't so funny, locking that door as soon as the sex balloon was gone, and piling upon the studio couch on my stomach to read about the fun Fanny Hill had, until I got ashamed of myself and stood in the middle of the floor, half nauseated, and I was staring out the apartment window, where soot from soft coal crusted the sill the way it does in Nashville, and I saw the upper part of a maple tree, with the buds just breaking, gold and pink, with the sunset light touching them brighter, and I heard the traffic and automobile horns going out Hillsboro Avenue, people going home from work as though it were just another day. I stood there and knew that I ought to hurry and go to the grocery before it closed, to get something for my supper. My supper, for Cal was on duty that night. But I couldn't move. The thought of something cooking in a skillet made me sick. I wasn't hungry. I wasn't anything. I stood there and wanted to die.

"It must have been that way forty times that spring, me finally going to get that book, moving like a sleepwalker, trying not to know what I was doing, then flopping there on the couch or standing by the kitchenette sink so I could chuck the thing into its hiding place if I heard steps—even though the door was locked—or locking myself in the bathroom, with that God-damned cute decal on the outside of the door, of a baby going potty. Yes, I'd go into the bathroom, I felt that guilty and dirty and awful.

"Then, it always ending with me throwing the book down and standing in the middle of the floor, and somehow it always seems late afternoon in spring, with the old soot crusted on the window sill and the maple buds out the window now turned into fat maple leaves and the flock of starlings making their ghastly racket in the tree, and dropping their gray droppings on all the leaves, and the sunset light pouring over everything.

"And, oh, yes, there'd be the traffic out Hillsboro, and the horns. It was a sound like all the world, everything, the past and the future, everything, going away from me, just falling away, and soon there wouldn't be a sound in the world, and it would be totally dark, and I would be standing there in the dark, not able to move.

"But I would move. I'd pick up the book, and go hide it under the sink.

"The funny thing, it wasn't all like that. It was as though I were two *me's,* or I lived in two worlds, and one was natural and easy, and Cal was sweet to me, and I loved him. It sounds funny to say that, but I did, and we had some good times together. Maybe if he hadn't been so busy. Or so desperately anxious to do well in his work. Or if we'd had a little money, we had just peanuts, and Cal's mother just had enough to make out in Fiddlersburg. Or if we'd been able to go out a little, see some people. Oh, a thousand *ifs.* It sometimes just seems as you look back on your life that life is a stalk with the *if's*—the possibilities—just falling off one by one, like leaves when the cold comes, and there isn't anything

left but the bare stalk and no *if's* left, just the absolute bareness of what it turned out to be.

"Maybe I was just lonesome, alone in that apartment so
much. I had a job in the Christmas rush at Cain Sloan's—
that's a department store there—but I couldn't get a real job,
just an odd or end. I was trying to teach myself shorthand
and typing, but it was slow. Some of my old Ward Belmont
friends were nice to me, a couple were having debuts that
year and Cal and I got asked to parties, but Cal couldn't get
off from the hospital but one time, and the only time he
made me go without him wasn't any good. I'd go to a girly-
girly bridge party now and then, but I felt more and more
different from those girls. I thought everything would be all
right when we got to Fiddlersburg. That was in my head.

"There was the picture, too, of what Lettice and Brad
were. How they seemed to exist in some sort of perfect freedom, like birds in the air, or dolphins leaping out of the
waves. I thought how, the summer before, in the evening,
they used to sit in the porch swing and hold hands and you
thought their hands were glowing in the dark. I felt that
when Cal and I got back to Fiddlersburg the magic might
rub off on me. I would reach out my hand to Cal in the dark,
and our hands would glow like that. When we got to Fiddlersburg.

"But when we made a visit at Easter, things were different at Fiddlersburg. I don't mean that Brad and Lettice
weren't nice to us, and weren't in love with each other.
Maybe I mean that they showed it a little differently—no, it
just comes to me now, maybe it was that Brad sort of showed
off a little bit about it, how he'd lay hand on Lettice. But
she was cute about it, she could turn almost anything into a
joke. But I noticed that Cal was different there. It was as
though he weren't himself, trying to imitate Brad. I didn't
like it. I felt embarrassed. But I reckoned it was because Cal
was drinking, something he never did, except maybe one or
two little ones when he wasn't on duty.

"The drinking—now there was a lot of drinking around
the house in Fiddlersburg. Brad was working—I don't mean
that. He had done a long story and sold it for a lot of
money, and he was working on another one. But there were
all-night poker games. Brad had been making a new gang of
friends, young engineers on the TVA dams up in Kentucky,

and people building the new plants up there, and some shady river-rat types, and Jibby Jackson, who came from God knows where, very handsome, and had married a nice girl with a million acres of river-bottom land. He wore expensive riding boots all the time and riding breeches, and white silk scarves, like a World War I aviator, and had a fancy convertible, and spent most of his time seducing high school girls in half the towns in West Tennessee. He was awful. Brad would laugh and say how awful Jibby was, then he'd say, 'But he's worth twenty-five thousand dollars to me, wait till I get him on paper!'

"I reckon that Brad, as a matter of fact, made more than that out of Jibby. Not a book. You know, it's Jibby in Brad's current movie. I saw it—the one called *The Dream of Jacob*. A man like Jibby who comes in and marries a girl like Rita Jackson and treats her badly and gets killed by an old colored man on the place who is devoted to the girl and won't say why he has killed the husband. Dear God, it was an awful movie! I sat there in the dark and flinched for Brad, I really did when I saw it. But I said maybe it wasn't his fault, they had done something to the way he wrote the script.

"But the real Jibby wasn't killed. He just drifted to nothing. He didn't know anything about farming. He threw money around and mortgaged Rita's land, and even with high wartime prices, lost the place and they moved away. She looked like an old woman by then.

"But what I was trying to tell is how things were different at Fiddlersburg, with the drinking and the all-night poker games. Oh, Lettice would play right along with Brad— the only woman there, I guess, when I wasn't there. Sometimes, just for fun, she'd put a green eye-shade on, and once stuck a cigar in her mouth for a joke. It was her way of keeping control of things, I guess. She was probably right, too. For once, later on that summer, when she wasn't well and didn't come down to play, some kind of a row happened, something nasty. I never got it straight.

"Things had changed. They must have been changing bit by bit all winter. Lettice and Brad didn't seem to belong in Fiddlersburg any more. They just lived there, and people came from outside and drank and played poker. Or bridge. Even from Nashville or Memphis, sometimes with girls.

"But Brad still had his swamp friends—the hunting and fishing friends. He would go off with them. Or sometimes take Lettice along with them. She was painting pictures of things in the swamp. And she was going to do a portrait of Frog-Eye, she said.

"She did paint it. You have seen it, in the room with the stuffed birds and animals. It's good of him—the way he used to be—so quiet-looking, like he is waiting, and that good eye staring out like it sees everything. Lettice and Frog-Eye—they got along fine. She would kid him, and . . ."

Chapter

20

BRADWELL TOLLIVER GOT UP from the table, and looked at his watch. It was 1:50 A.M., just the hour when, long ago at Darthurst, the radiator would be giving its last despairing clank, and the frost, gray as the film of cataract on an old eye, would thicken on the windowpane against the absolute glossy blackness of night, and he would lift his eyes from the old Oliver and see, hanging in the mystic haze of cigarette smoke, the vision of River Street.

But that, he decided, had been on Eastern Standard Time.

This was Central Standard Time.

He cut off the light and felt his way out of the dark

house. Standing in the road, which River Street became this far out, he looked up at the bulk of the house. Then he faced northward, toward town, and began to walk. The moon was westering now. Far off up yonder, the moonlight washed to whiteness the hulk of the penitentiary. It paled to nothingness the beams of the searchlights on the corner turrets. The moonlight flooded the land. In that light, River Street would float like a vision.

He stared up the road and moved steadily toward it.

In front of the Purtle house, he stopped. He stared at it, the white weather boarding, the darkened windows, the modest gingerbread scrolling on the porch, the high spindly brick piers lifting the house, so precariously, above the black ground and the clotting blackness of shadow; then, above it all, the black composition roof where some hard granules of texture caught, here and there, small, tingling gleams from the moon.

The front of the house was in shadow. The house was withdrawn, closed upon itself, dreaming inward with folded hands, sleeping. He thought of Leontine Purtle sleeping in that house. He thought of a room with the curtains closed tight, darker than dark, and in that dark she lay naked in her remarkable whiteness. She was sleeping, and she glimmered in the dark. He shut his eyes, and suddenly pressed his face into that fragrant softness that was her belly. In that soft, fragrant, absolute darkness he could see nothing. But he knew that her whiteness glimmered around him in the dark, around his thrust-down, blinded face.

"Jesus," he said out loud.

His lips were dry. The moon was westward. Somewhere on the ridge behind him an owl called. It called again, in that deep-throated, puffy, exhalation, far off.

He turned up the road, and moved on.

He moved up the road, past the fallen tree on the west side of the road, past the abandoned Tomwit place with its windowpanes broken, past the vacant lots where the stalks of old ironweed rose above the new-springing broomsage, the pale green of the broomsage now silvered in the pale light, past the church. He stood in the road, and looked at the cemetery, the tombstones bone-white in that light, the grass, on those few plots where it had been mowed, white with dew.

Nobody would have mowed the grass on the grave of

Israel Goldfarb. He wondered where the grave was. He
would come again. He would try again to find it. He thought,
suddenly, that he had to find it.

He moved on toward town, up River Street. He stared at
Perkins Dry Goods, where the iron awning hung over the pavement, and saw the wax dummy in the window smile de-
votedly at him. He stared at the Post Office, at the You'll
Never Regret It Café, at the old poolroom with the broken
glass door, at the window of the abandoned store where
warped and decaying cardboard announced old basketball
games, at the Lyceum Moving Picture Theater, where shreds
of the poster announcing the last attraction ever to be shown
there, the colors bleached out, still hung from the board by
the ticket booth. He went closer and stared at those fading
shreds. He could not make out what image had been
there. All he managed to get was:

AN AMER   I   PARI

The rest was faded, blurred, or torn away.

Then, all at once, he knew: *An American in Paris.* And
that was a thousand years ago. That had been in 1951. It had
taken four Oscars.

Well, he had taken an Oscar, once.

He reached out, seized a corner of the shredded poster,
and in that one motion, pulled off what he could. He held
the piece of paper in his hand.

He saw the moonlight on the river. He thought of the
water rising. It would cover River Street. River Street would
not be here any more. He wondered, what of himself—of
Bradwell Tolliver—would not be here, or anywhere, when
Fiddlersburg was not here any more.

He moved down the street. He saw, ahead of him, the
Confederate monument. The high bronze figure on the
block of stone, slouch hat, grounded rifle, stared northward,
down the river. He moved toward the monument. Somebody
was sitting at the base, in the shadow.

It was Yasha Jones.

"Forgive me," Yasha Jones said. "All I was doing was
spying on you. I was looking at Fiddlersburg, in the blankness of moonlight. Then I saw a human figure approaching,
in the distance."

"Yeah," Brad said, "I'm human."

"And I thought of a man who would rise in the night, just before the flood began, and go look at Fiddlersburg once more, in moonlight."

"You are right," Brad said. "That was what I was doing."

"But," Yasha said, "I was thinking of a man in what you call our beautiful moving pictures. I was thinking of *m-a-n* —a man—any man who rises in the night before the waters come. At first, the camera would show only the night sky. Then only the feet in the moonlit dust of summer. We would never show his face. He would not be recognizable. We would not know what man of all Fiddlersburg had risen. We should see, simply, the figure. The man would stare upward at the old high-water mark on the corner of Lorton's Hardware, and the camera would zoom in on the date, now nearly obliterated, April 12, 1924, and we could see the pores of the disintegrating old brick. Then the man would stare at a display dummy in a store window. He would touch the broken glass of the old poolroom door. He would tear off a last piece of a poster at the abandoned moving-picture palace."

Brad held out the shredded piece of poster. "It was *An American in Paris,*" he said. "Four Oscars."

Yasha Jones did not seem to hear.

"With the torn bit of poster in his hand," Yasha Jones said, "the man would sit at the base of the Confederate monument. He would sit in the shadow. We would never see his face. The camera, I think, would pan up—pan up toward the statue on the monument, then zoom in and—"

"What made you sit at the base of the Confederate monument?" Brad demanded.

"Pure accident," Yasha said. "But how often accident gives us the deepest meaning."

Yasha Jones fell thoughtful for a moment. "No," he added, "it was not an accident. Whatever an accident is. For how can one really define an accident?" He paused. "Unless," he said, "we have already defined it."

"What?" Brad demanded.

"That event," Yasha Jones burst out, with a kind of wild gaiety in his tone, "which gives us the deepest meaning!"

Yasha Jones stared up at Brad, his eyes glittering in the shadow.

"No," he said then, gravely, "this is more commonplace.

It was not an accident that I sat here. I suppose, on reflection, I sat here at the base of this monument because it gave me the angle of vision I wanted."

"You picked right," Brad said, "for it is the spiritual center of Fiddlersburg. I shall drop my own ass here."

He sat down on the flange at the base of the granite block. He jerked a thumb back over his shoulder, and said: "I wonder if they're going to relocate him?"

"Who?" Yasha Jones asked.

"Johnny Reb," Brad said, "his monument." He paused. "He's been standing there a long time now," he resumed, "holding off gunboats and Yankee investors and new ideas. Didn't do so well with the gunboats, but made up for that on the other two counts." He paused again. "He is all that makes Fiddlersburg Southern. He is all that gives us the dignity of our defects. He is all that makes paranoid violence into philosophic virtue. Take him away and Fiddlersburg wouldn't be anything but a wore-out bunch of red-necks and reformed swamp rats that had crawled out on dry land, and the dry land nothing but a few acres of worthless real estate. Take Johnny Reb away, and Fiddlersburg would be just one more benighted ass-hole in that splendid *derrière* which we call the hinterland of America. Fiddlersburg would be just like Iowa. But as it is, his blood hath sanctified our confusion, his valor hath—"

He stopped.

"Nuts," he concluded.

"There are Civil War monuments in Iowa," Yasha Jones said. "At least, I have been told that."

"Yeah," Brad said, "all over Yankeeland you'll find those wasp-waisted statues. Leaning on their rifles with their butts sticking epicenely out like a bustle in Godey's *Lady's Book*. But those monuments up there in Yankeeland—they don't stand for anything. Up there, a monument is merely an expensive roost for pigeons and a latrine for tired sparrows. Down here, the monument stands for something."

"What?"

"The answer is simple," Brad said. "Lies."

"Lies?"

"No," Brad said, "not lies. Better said, it stands for the lie."

"What lie?"

"That lie that is the truth of the self," Brad said.

He leaned forward, elbows on knees, big hands drooping, and stared at River Street in the moonlight.

Then: "I reckon River Street was always nearer to me than hands or feet. I reckon I always took River Street to bed with me. Yeah"—he paused, stirred his weight on the stone —"to bed. Yeah," he repeated, "a few years back I was gone on a Yankee girl. I don't mean my first wife, Lettice. She was *Mayflower*, but she was raised in New York and the street the dough had come from was Wall not State. I use the word *Yankee* more advisedly. Massachusetts Bay Colony and none of the Plymouth Rock hoi polloi, Boston all the way, Calvinism and the China trade, with a subsequent shift toward Episcopalianism and gilt-edged debentures, and tweed to obscure the figure, and flat heels, and Latin for pleasure, and brown hair pulled back and horn-rimmed glasses that weren't really needed and when she took them off, there was the glittering shock of glacier-blue glance, and hell on a horse, but where she really bloomed was in the dark. Everything else was a dream and that was reality. She was a night-blooming cereus, all right. She was a night-blooming cereus full of learned jokes, unpredictable giggles, gallant gaiety, and the poetry of that moment when spirit and viscera join hands in what we may call transcendental sincerity. I was gone, real gone, on her."

He stared at River Street.

"She was gone on me, too," he said.

Then he said: "Yeah, she was gone on me, too, and we were lying up there in the California moonlight, which was pouring over the Pacific like spook-fire, and pouring in the window, and we could hear the surf below. Do you want to know how this ravishing creature happened to be in a sty like California?"

"If you wish to tell me," Yasha Jones said.

"I do so wish," Brad said. "I so wish because I am a cad. She was the fairest flower of Yankeedom, but she broke reservation and married a Jew, a Harvard *summa* Jew. She even remained loyal when he betrayed his *summa* and went Hollywood, but then, whoever got rich on a *summa*? He had betrayed the fancy press his first book of poems got, too, but then, whoever got rich on a poem? He wrote two wonderful pictures. *Nothing for Love* and *The Sands of Kil-ja-pu.*"

"Brandowitz," Yasha Jones said, musingly, "Merl Brandowitz."

"Right," Brad said, "and you see I am a cad, for I am implying that it was Mrs. Brandowitz with whom I lay while the spook-fire of Pacific moonlight poured in that window. Only by that time Merl, having done two wonderful pictures, had become a wonderful lush, and she had left him, and now I, sitting here at the base of the Confederate monument, which is what makes Fiddlersburg Southern and stands for that lie which is the truth of the self, feel a deep need to tell you how we, Prudence Brandowitz, née Leverell, and I, lay in the important California moonlight, in the backwash, you might say, of our bliss, and she got to talking about some encounter with a woman we both knew, a great, beautiful, ignorant, rich fool from Alabama, full of Black Belt airs and graces, and Prudence began to giggle and imitate that theatrically sorghum accent, double distilled no doubt for California distribution, and suddenly stopped and tensed; I could feel her tense, lying there on my shoulder with my arm around her and my hand over one of those breasts, the glory of which the tweed ordinarily did its imperfect best to hide, and she stared at the ceiling and burst out, 'Oh, that ghastly Southern vulgarity—I simply can't bear it!'

"Now that female comic from the Black Belt was nothing to me. In fact, I loathed her. I found her embarrassing, humanly and historically. And Prudence Brandowitz was right on every count: she was ghastly, she was Southern, she was vulgar.

"But here the mystery begins. When Prudence Brandowitz, on whom, as I have said, I was real gone, and who was lying deliciously beside me in the wash of California moonlight, said what she did, my heart suddenly knobbed up, like a fist, and I heard, clear as a bell, that inner voice, which is the deepest *you,* saying: *Sister, you are through.*"

He was still leaning forward, elbows on knees, heavy hands hanging, eyes fixed on River Street in moonlight.

After a moment he said: "Well, not quite through, to be technical. My heart had knobbed up like a fist, and if you make a fist—just casually, even—it is almost like pushing a button, and the fist jumps, it's got to hit something. When Mrs. Brandowitz said what she did, my heart knobbed up and started a wild swing. It was as though all those hairy, flea-bit, underfed, iron-rumped and narrow-ass-ted, whooping and caterwauling, doom-bit bastards, on hammer-headed nags gaunt as starvation, who rode with Gin'l Forrest, had broke loose, and there was fire, rape, and unmitigated disaster, all the way to the Canadian border."

He waited, staring at River Street.

"I didn't say a damned word to her," he said then.

He waited.

"I ground her bones to make my bread," he said.

He waited again, longer.

"Then," he said, "I was lying there staring at the ceiling and not seeing it, and Brandowitz, née Leverell, had her face pressed against my right side, below the armpit, hanging on to me like I was a life raft in a stormy sea. Which I was not. I was the stormy sea. My heart, you might say, was a seething storm of rage and black despair. Ah, sweet mystery of life!

"But Sister was, indeed, through. I rose, put on my pants, walked out the door, never came back. She, being a straightforward, honest Yankee gal, finally wrote me a straightforward letter saying she loved me, she thought I had loved her, and what had gone wrong? But what could I answer to that?"

He waited, staring at River Street washed in moonlight.

"Especially," he finally said, "since I did not know the answer. Anyway—"

He did not go on.

"Anyway what?" Yasha Jones finally asked.

"Just something that occurred to me," Brad said, and shifted his weight on the stone. "You know, if I had gone back to Brandowitz, née Leverell, after that last great big old bang and that burning and raping all the way to the Canadian border, I might just have been impotent with her."

"Ah," Yasha Jones murmured, "the *lex talionis* of the soul!"

"Huh?"

"The law that fits the punishment to the crime," Yasha Jones said. "If the superego," he began, with a prim parody of classroom manner, "really incorporates the basic drive of aggression, as some have maintained, then the old superego perfectly knows how to make the punishment on the poor little ego the very mirror of the ego's aggressions, and so—"

"Do you go for that crap?" Bradwell Tolliver demanded.

Yasha Jones laughed. "It does sound rather out of place in this moonlight, doesn't it?" he asked. "But shall we say that

it is only old goods in a new package? As for the *lex talionis*
of the soul, Dante knew all about it, to wit, the *Inferno*. And
Sophocles, he—"

"Yeah," Brad said, "and me. Maybe I, too, am learning
something about your *lex talionis*. For my crimes I, who am
of Fiddlersburg, am sent back to Fiddlersburg to do a beautiful motion picture about Fiddlersburg."

He swung angrily toward the other man, in the shadow
of the monument.

"God damn it," he said, "maybe I can't do your God-
damned picture!"

"You will do it," Yasha Jones said, calmly. "And it will
be beautiful."

Brad rose, with heavy abruptness. "Maybe too God-
damned much has happened here," he said. "Do you know
what has happened here?" he demanded, glaring down at the
other man.

"Not all," Yasha Jones said, "but something."

"Maggie—has she been telling you?" He swung his arm
to point at the hulk of the penitentiary on its hill. The
searchlights at the corner turrets were bleached out by the
moon.

"Yes," Yasha Jones said, evenly, "she told me something."

"I knew she would," Brad said.

Far off, up in the darkness of the ridge, the owl called.

"Do you hear that God-damned owl?" Bradwell Tolliver
demanded.

"Yes," the other man said.

Bradwell Tolliver was silent. He was waiting for the
owl. The owl did not call again.

Then he said: "I knew she would. She would figure
she'd have to do it herself."

Yasha Jones looked up at his face, studying him. Then,
very quietly, said: "No, she is not one to pass responsibilities,
is she?"

"Listen," Brad said, "if you had seen her back yonder. At
the trial, I mean. Sitting there cold as ice, staring straight
ahead, at that room full of those drool-jawed Confederate
yaps, and every one of 'em in his mind ripping her Suspants
off under the hydrangea bushes.

"Yes, and did you know it was those very hydrangeas
there right now at the end of the screened porch? And for
nigh twenty years she's been sitting there on the porch, alone

in the summer night, watching them bloom in the moonlight." He stopped, glaring down at the man.

Then: "Can you see her sitting there? She may be there
right now, this very minute."

"Yes," Yasha Jones said.

"Not that I know how long a hydrangea bush lives,"
Brad said dourly. "But you can be damned sure if one of the
originals had died, Maggie Fiddler would have planted another one there just like it. She being Maggie Fiddler."

"Yes," Yasha Jones said.

For a moment, Brad said nothing. Then, with a sudden
motion of the head, like a horse shaking off a fly, or a dog
snapping at one, he said: "I guess that business about finished off Lettice and me, too. We didn't last too long after
the trial."

He waited, sunk into himself.

"I had come back here," he said, "figuring I was going to
live here forever. With Lettice and love her. I figured it was
the only place I could live, and be me. Write, I mean. But"—
and he gave a quick rasp of a laugh—"it did not work out."

He waited again.

"Yeah," he resumed, "and a dozen times on the Coast I
have thought of coming back here. Finding me some woman
around here. The right kind. And settling down."

He waited.

"Well, here I am," he said. "And for what?" he demanded.

Then answered himself: "To write a God-damned moving
picture."

Yasha Jones rose from the base of the monument, with
that easy, controlled, fluid thrust upward from the ankles. He
faced Bradwell Tolliver, and reached his right hand out and
across to lay it on the other's right shoulder.

"You are here," he said, "and you will do what you have
come to do. All that has happened here—it will flow into the
feeling. It will be the oil that feeds the wick where the flame
will burn. You will stand, in the end, in what Stendahl calls
le silence du bonheur. And in that silence you will make a
beautiful thing."

"You better get another guy," Brad said.

"What you make—it will not be exotic," Yasha Jones said.
"Ah, that is the danger—you don't know how exotic Fiddlersburg is! But there is something else here, too. Archetypally

human, archetypally simple, and therefore precious. No, I don't pretend to tell you about Fiddlersburg. But shut your eyes and think of the faces. The faces—how medieval they are! Think—"

"It is not the faces that are medieval," Brad said, "it is the heads."

"—think," Yasha Jones said, scarcely pausing, "of that hewn-out non-exotic simplicity. It makes you feel the chisel on stone. The story lies there."

He let his hand drop from Bradwell Tolliver's shoulder, and stepped back. He gestured up toward the nearest turret of the penitentiary wall. "What was the name of that guard?" he asked, "the one whom Mr. Budd ordered to shoot the sparrow?"

"Lem," Brad said.

"Well, here is an image that comes into my head. I have shut my eyes and seen it a hundred times. What it means, I do not know."

"Yeah?" Brad said.

"We see the rising waters, a long shot, picking up light westward. Then we pan to the turret, and the sky is moving beyond it. We zoom in, perhaps fifteen yards. We see Lem on the turret, rifle in hand, looking down into the prison yard. Cut to prison yard, the prisoners small below. Cut to Lem. We see his jaws work slowly on that quid of tobacco. Do you remember that rhythm?"

"Yes," Brad said. "Like death and taxes."

"Do you remember how the jaw stopped, suddenly, when the rifle came to his shoulder?"

"Yes."

"Well," Yasha Jones said, "we see Lem, staring down into the prison yard, that sleepy slowness, that lethal watchfulness. His jaws are moving in that rhythm. But he slowly lifts his eyes from the yard. Cut to the sky, the clouds are moving. Cut to Lem, but at a distance, perhaps sixty feet, and we see the head turning, caught with the motion of the clouds, the eyes leaving the prison yard, turning westward over the waters. We zoom in. Shoulders and head only. The jaws are moving. They stop. Freeze head, against sky. The sky is moving beyond the profile of that face."

Brad was staring heavily at him.

"Do you know what Maggie said?" he demanded. "Tonight?"

"No."

"Well," Brad said, "after you took Potts in the house to fix his meters, Maggie said that Potts ought to be the center of our beautiful moving picture."

For an instant Yasha looked into the face of the other man, almost as a doctor, on first coming to the bedside, looks into the face of the patient. "Christ!" he exclaimed suddenly, the excitement mounting. "Christ!"

Then he looked out over the river. "But," he said, "I don't know where you'd get your actor. You'd have to make him." He was looking off, wrapped in himself. Then he swung back to Brad, his eyes glittering in the moonlight. "But think of a face like that! That twisted mouth, that gaze of humble, uncomprehending pain. Just think—the moment when the Negro's spit strikes and glistens on the cheek! Think of the awareness dawning on that face, the—"

"I was working on the Potts idea all night," Brad said. He spat in the moonlit dust. "I got nowhere," he said.

"Christ!" Yasha Jones exclaimed, not listening to him. "It could be great."

"Yeah," Brad said, "it could be great. But I couldn't get down even one decent line."

For a second Yasha Jones stared at him.

"Wasn't it funny I couldn't?" the other demanded.

"Remember!" Yasha Jones then said, gaily.

"Remember what?"

"That it will come," Yasha Jones said. "It will come *dans le silence du bonheur.*

Chapter

21

YASHA JONES CONTINUED to sit at the base of the monument which was the spiritual center of Fiddlersburg. He sat there, he told himself, in the stillness of joy.

Yasha Jones had, for some years now, lived in the joy of abstraction—which means participation in all that is not yours, since you have lived past all that was yours. Having nothing, he had all. He had known how light falls on a leaf. He had know how a hand turns on the wrist. He had known how a heart fills with longing. But it had not been his heart.

For he was, he had told himself, past longing.

On August 7, 1945, Yasha Jones, OSS, on rest leave, moved down a lane four kilometers from the little beach town

of Kerglaw, on the south shore of Brittany. It seemed remarkable to him that he was not dead, because if Monsieur
Duval—with penurious black coat, frayed white shirt painfully mended, and pince-nez, the failing *pharmacien du village,* the unprosperous *notaire,* the harassed master of a village school—was dead, then how could Yasha Jones be alive.
He wondered, in fact, who Yasha Jones was, this stranger in
white shirt, yachting cap, blue shorts, faded blue espadrilles
on bare feet—like a tourist.

The lane was very deep, the close hedges above man-
height on both sides. The light soil had been worn down by
feet that had passed there for—he asked himself—how many
centuries? The Celts had walked down this lane, the Romans,
the Franks.

The yellow of *gênet* was long since gone, the white of the
blackberry blossoms, and the modest tints of the little hedge
flowers, but now there was still the honeysuckle, its scent almost suffocating in that green ravine. The sky swung intensely blue, at a vast distance, and, invisible in that glittering height, a lark was singing. Around him, in the lane, the
air tingled with the innumerable summer hum of insects in
the hedges. At a gap in the hedge he saw the sandy meadow
open, scraggly with gorse, and beyond, the squat, brutal gray
of the German blockhouses, profiled against the shimmering
blue of the sea. The French tricolor stirred idly above the
blockhouse on the highest dune.

A man came down the lane on a bicycle. He stopped and,
in French, asked if Captain Jones had heard the news. The
news, he said, was formidable. It would no doubt mean the
end of the war. The other war, the Pacific war, he corrected
himself. He offered to leave his newspaper for the Captain to
read. The man went on down the lane. Yasha Jones carefully
focused his attention on the date at the upper right of the
sheet, avoiding the black headlines that screamed for his attention. It was, he discovered, *Mardi, 7 Août 1945.*

Then he sat down, in the gap in the hedge, under the sky
that swung up there so high and so intensely blue, with the
sick sweetness of honeysuckle in his nostrils, read the big
black letters:

LA PREMIÈRE BOMBE ATOMIQUE
A FAIT SON APPARITION

LA VILLE D'HIROSHIMA EST ENVELOPPÉE DANS UN NUAGE IMPÉNÉTRABLE

Le Président Truman a annoncé la mise en action de la bombe dont la force est . . .

His eyes dropped down the column of black blurred print, came again to rest:

Le Président Truman a ajouté que la force de la bombe relève de la force élémentaire de l'univers, de celle qui alimente le soleil dans sa puissance.

He lifted his eyes and stared at the glittering blue of the sky. His head was throbbing with the light.

That night, Yasha Jones wrote his resignation, as briefly as might be consistent with courtesy, and addressed it to the Dean of the University of Chicago, Chicago, Illinois.

Somewhat later, Yasha Jones discovered, to his astonishment, that he could not bear the scent of honeysuckle. It reminded him, he decided, of the sickly-sweet odor that had filled the glade where, in the spring of 1944, he stumbled upon the body of the dead *Maquis*, a body that had been there a long time. In those later years when he attributed this aversion to honeysuckle to the scent that had filled the glade where the *Maquis* lay, he had forgotten the honeysuckle in the hedge in Brittany.

In 1946 Yasha Jones, being wealthy, was persuaded by a young man whom he had met in the service to finance the making of a documentary film on cancer research. At that time, in fact, he hoped to go, eventually, into bio-physics. But he planned to begin by studying medicine. He had been accepted at the Harvard Medical School.

But he never went. In the summer of that year, as he hung on the outskirts of the work on the documentary, sitting in the shadows of a Hollywood cutting room rented for the editing of the film, he discovered the human face. Rather, he discovered the image of the human face.

He flung himself, with total passion, into the study of directing. In 1949 his first independent picture was released.

He loathed it, but it was a success. His second film, released
ten months later, was a success. He loathed it. But his head
was already full of the third. He dreamed about it, with his
eyes wide open, as he walked down the street.

He was walking down Sunset Boulevard at five-fifteen,
just at the rush hour, automatically avoiding the bodies that
flowed at him down the sidewalk, when he saw her. She was
crouched in the street, some five feet from the curb, holding
the dog in her arms. The left hind leg of the dog was jerking
spasmodically, the blood was flowing out of the animal's
mouth over her yellow dress; her purse lay on the street,
with the catch open and odd bits of junk spilling out; and her
face, lifted toward the little crowd on the curb, was weeping
without shame. Yasha Jones stood on the curb and looked
down into that face lifted with its shameless grief.

A large man, young, in a mechanic's coverall, was standing on the curb beside Yasha Jones. He was laughing. He
would interrupt his laughter to say to anyone who would listen: "Jeez, and her cry-eng fer a dawrg!"

The man said it again.

To his surprise, Yasha Jones heard his own voice saying:
"I wish you would stop laughing."

"Fuck you, Jake," the big man said.

To his great surprise, Yasha Jones discovered his fist
traveling through the air to the man's chin. It barely grazed
the chin. The big man knocked Yasha Jones down. He was
still laughing.

Yasha Jones rose slowly, his right hand against the side
of his head where the man's fist had clubbed him. He was
studying the man's stance. *There ain't a man born*, the ser-
geant had said, *no matter how big the son-of-a-bitch is and
got a gun, you can't kill with your bare hands, specially if he
is flat-footed on a transverse line, and the son-of-a-bitch don't
know you can do it.*

The man was standing flat-footed on that hypothetical
transverse line, and he was laughing. Yasha Jones wished he
would stop laughing. If he did not stop laughing, it might
happen. "Please," Yasha Jones said, in almost a whisper,
"please go away."

"Fuck you, Jake," the man said, and laughed.

Yasha Jones, holding the side of his head, thought that it
might happen now. It had happened once before—it had had
to happen then, for the German sentry had surprised him in

that dark alley just off the Rue des Saints Pères, in Paris. In this instant now he remembered very explicitly, as though a strong ray of light cut into the dark to specify the scene, how, long ago, he had stood in the dark alley, and it was over, and he had risen from the darker heap huddled there. He now remembered the terrifying shudder of ecstasy as he had stood there over that dark heap. But he remembered how, finding himself in the grip of that ecstasy, he had been, suddenly, sick of himself; and of the world. Now standing on Sunset Boulevard, looking into the man's drop-jawed laughter, he felt the first pure spurt of that terrible ecstasy. He felt his hands lift, ever so little, on the wrists.

Then, suddenly, he was seeing the man's face. He looked at the other faces, face by face, that were grinning at him, all under the late afternoon light of summer in Hollywood, California, and that stir of ecstasy was gone. There was the cold glob of nausea in his stomach. He turned slowly from them all, thinking, *We live with faces, that is all we have, the faces around us.* And hearing the laughter behind him as though at a great distance, took two steps to where the girl crouched, with the dog in her arms, weeping. The dog's left hind leg was not jerking any more.

"It's dead now," Yasha Jones said.

He took her elbow and lifted her. Still carrying the dog, a nondescript parcel of bloody fur, she allowed him to guide her across the street to the parking lot, and establish her in his three-year-old black Ford coupe.

"Where do you want to go?" he asked.

"I've got to bury him," she said. She wasn't weeping now.

"You will miss him a lot?" he asked.

"No—no—" she said. Then: "You see, he wasn't mine. I never saw him before. Look"—and she laid her finger on the neck of the animal—"he has no collar."

Yasha Jones looked. "Yes, a stray," he said.

"That's the reason," she said, "the reason I've got to bury him."

"Yes," he said, not looking at her, staring into the westering sun as he threaded the traffic.

"I can't bear to see things hurt," she said.

His eyes were fixed into the sunlight, seeing the myriad glints of light on approaching chrome.

"I suppose I can't bear it, either," he said. Then added: "Not any more."

After a few blocks, she said: "I'm sorry to cause you all the trouble."

"It's nothing," he said.

"I'm sorry about that man," she said. "What he did to you."

"It's nothing," he said.

It was nothing, and it was everything. Three weeks after they had buried the dog on the dune, with a cairn on the spot, he married her—Lucy Spence, rather small but well developed, rather squarish face, small rounded determined chin, high cheekbones, nose small and well freckled, brown hair in braids coiled on her head, and a deep, warm, direct glance from brown eyes. She was twenty-three years old, had been born in Morning Star, Iowa, had gone three years to Grinnell College in that state, had brought her widower father to California for his excruciating arthritis, had buried him last year, and now worked as a secretary at Columbia Pictures, where she made ninety dollars a week. She was not a virgin, having had a sweetheart at Grinnell. In Hollywood, since her father's death, she had lived in a residential home for working girls, and had known no men.

Of Yasha Jones she knew nothing, except that he had some kind of job in pictures, was quiet and considerate and well educated, wore an unpressed seersucker suit, drove a three-year-old Ford coupe, lived in an epic disorder of books and papers, in a small nondescript bungalow in Westwood Village, where she had gone once for a drink and been kissed and where, just as she thought the manhandling was about to start and she would have to decide what she wanted to do about it, he had abandoned her on the couch, amid some of the disorder of books and papers, and begun to pace moodily about the room, to end by telling her to get up, he was taking her home. Early next morning, before she left for the office, he proposed to her by telephone.

She stood a full minute, clutching the receiver, hearing his breath, hard and slow, far off there in Westwood Village. Then she heard her own voice, thin and weak as though far away, much farther away than Westwood Village, saying: "Yes. Yes." For a moment she had thought that he did not hear. Then his voice said: "I am happy." Then, after another wait: "There is something I suppose I should tell you—"

She waited, her heart frozen in her bosom, for the shock of the revelation. But all he finally said, in that now strange, flat, detached voice, was that he was rather well off, and he thought, now that she was going to marry him, she ought to know. She didn't really hear the words, or rather heard only words. She burst out: "Oh, it doesn't matter, nothing matters, oh, my darling!"

For she had loved him totally from the start.

His warning had not been sufficient to forestall her incredulity at being whisked to a suite in the Royal Hawaiian in Honolulu, and then being whisked back to a house in Beverly Hills, very different from the bungalow. Gradually she recovered from that incredulity. It was more difficult to recover from the incredulity at the fact that he loved her totally, too.

Lucy Spence Jones was still herself in the middle of that big house, surrounded by the soft-footed correctness of people who were paid to open doors and to hand her things. Yasha Jones wondered if he, in some deep complication of spirit, had put her in that house, and in that life, to test her—or himself—to be sure that she was truly the Lucy Spence who had sat in the street and, while people laughed, had held that dying dog in her arms and lifted up that pleasant but not beautiful face with its naked beauty of shameless grief. He could shut his eyes and see that face lifted in the beauty of that sincerity. He could open his eyes and see the face, not in grief, but in the naked beauty of all the other sincerities, big and little, by which she, from day to day, lived.

He had never been in love. He had known and, in his detached, almost clinical way, enjoyed certain women. But his passion had been reserved for what went on in the laboratory at Cambridge, in England, or in the little room with the big blackboard, in Chicago; then that passion had been reserved for the daily task at the time when Yasha Jones thought of himself as already dead and knew that Monsieur Duval would die, he hoped in not too unpleasant a fashion, soon; then that passion had been reserved for the process of putting the image of a human face on celluloid. Now the passion was for this particular human face, the image of which he would never put on celluloid, and this, he told himself, was love.

His greediness for her very process of life seemed to be without limit. He wanted to know, and possess, every shift and flow of feeling in the present and every detail of her past life. Nothing about her was like anything he had known. Morning Star, Iowa, as it gradually rose into his imagination, was like nothing he had ever known. But in his imagination he knew every nook and cranny of the white frame house where she had been born, the size of the elms, where the jonquils grew, where the creek ran, the location of the Civil War monument, the color of the paint on her father's drugstore on Osage Street, the names of the neighbors, their peculiarities.

Now, in Beverly Hills, after dinner, on the terrace, with the Pacific lifting whitely in the distance, he would put his arm around her and say: "Tell me about Mr. Wiggleswait." He would feel the little shiver in her shoulders as she tried to suppress the giggle. Then the giggle would come. Then she would tell him about Mr. Wiggleswait. Or about Estelle Jarveen, who weighed three hundred pounds and had broken down the seat in the Jarveen backhouse and been stuck there all of a Thanksgiving afternoon, after the big dinner. Till they found her and then till they found Mr. Casky and he brought his tow truck with the hoist on the back. Lucy Spence would giggle, and then tell him.

Or she would tell him where the jack-in-the-pulpits used to grow.

They had been head over heels in love, and had never quarreled. But on the night of May 4, 1952, they quarreled while driving home from a party. Later, he could never remember how the quarrel started, or even what it was about, except that it had to do with money. He came to think sometimes that it was because she, in the middle of his house and his life, felt suffocated by money. But he wasn't sure; and in any case, money, of which he had a great deal, meant so little to him that he could not imagine its meaning that much to her.

Later, he came to think that she had been suffocated by love.

She was driving. She, always abstemious, had had very little to drink, but she was driving faster and faster, sitting forward on the edge of the seat, leaning over the wheel. They did not make a curve, crashed into a tree. The car being a convertible, with top down, Yasha Jones was thrown clear. He landed in a mass of shrubbery that broke his fall, but by the time he had collected his wits, and fought clear of the shrubbery, he saw flame at the car. He crawled into the wreckage, calling her name, and tried to pull her clear. Then hands were dragging him back. He could not see, for the flame and smoke about his head. Then while somebody sprayed the wreck with foam, he hung there struggling in the grip of two men, calling her name, being sure that he heard her calling him, trying as hard as he could to break away and plunge into the flame to save her.

But had he struggled as hard as he could?

In the hospital, where he lay for fourteen weeks, while the burned scalp and hands were being repaired, that question began to come into his mind. Later on, whenever he thought of the question, the palms of his hands would begin to sweat. Later, it worked the other way: the palms of his hands would begin to sweat, and then the question would come into his head. Later still, the sweat would come in the hands, but the question would not come into his head; and that moment of anguished disorientation, before the question could come into his head with its sharp focus on the specific guilt, was the worst of all. More and more, it seemed that the question would delay its appearance, that it had a life and will of its own, that it would hide and flirt and tease until, when it did appear, he would embrace it with desperate relief. In those moments the coming of the question seemed to be all that was left to him.

That, and his work.

For now that he had lost the meaning of his own life, he could see the meaning in other lives. Since the face of Lucy Spence, in which that flash of naked sincerity had opened life to him, was withdrawn, he found that he could detect on other faces, beneath all the smears and grime of experience, the gleam of lost innocence; could, in fact, evoke it, seize its image. Thus he entered upon his greatness.

He had paid the price for it. Having lost all, he could now have all. But no, he would think, it was not he who had paid the price. Lucy Spence had paid the price. She had died. She had called out to him in the flame, making him the gift, and had died.

Late at night, in the same room where he had slept with Lucy Spence—for he had felt, not thought, it part of his doom to continue to live in that big house—Yasha Jones might unlock the little desk he had installed beside the bed, and take out the inquest report on Lucy Spence Jones. It said what, over and over, the doctors had told him. She had been dead at the moment of the crash. She had not called to him from the flame. He could have done nothing.

All he could do now was to lie there and wait for the sweat to come in the palms of his hands. It was better to know why it would come, and wait for it, than to have it come and, for that moment of disorientation, not be able to know why.

This was the way of life Yasha Jones had come to accept. It had its own laws, its own rationale, its own deep necessity, its own reward. Even in those periods when he could flee from it into the arms of some woman of charm and beauty and, even, sincerity, he knew that the flight only confirmed that necessity. He knew that the time would come when, waking by the side of that charming stranger, he would feel the sweat start in his palms.

This was the way Yasha Jones had lived until that moment when, as the morning sun of California struck the white napery of his table and the sweet steam rose from the broken egg in the egg cup, he picked up the Los Angeles paper and saw the brief news story, how a little town lost in Tennessee would now, after its century and a half of unremarkable life, be flooded. He read the words, he shut his eyes, he saw the vision of Morning Star, Iowa, float before him; and he saw Lucy Spence, a child, walking down the street, under the elms, on a hot summer afternoon, on her way to her father's drugstore for an ice cream cone. Yasha Jones, who had never lived anywhere, or rather, had lived in a thousand places, felt tears rise to his eyes.

So now, in the middle of the night, at the base of the Confederate monument, Yasha Jones sat and stared into the moonlight of River Street.

Several years before, he had visited a tourist attraction in California, near Santa Cruz, called the Mystery Spot. It is simply a patch of ground, sloping, partially wooded, but there, presumably because of magnetic disturbances set up by a buried meteorite, the visitor experiences a profound disorder of the senses. A companion, stepping into a certain location, will suddenly seem to shrink; then shifting location, will shoot up to unusual stature. Perspectives shift, equilibrium is impaired, the gut goes cold.

The whole effect is somewhat like that brutal parody of

experience you find in the Fun House of a street carnival. There you pay twenty-five cents for this distortion of experience and of the self so that, when you come out, you can, with a gush of gratitude, take refuge in the old dreary categories of experience, and in the old dreary self. The Fun House is made by men, to provide men with this deeply yearned-for violation of, and return to, the accustomed. The Mystery Spot, made by Nature, accomplishes in a way more disturbing, because apparently more natural, the same result.

Yasha Jones sat there, at the base of the monument, and remembered the Mystery Spot, and thought that Fiddlersburg, too, was a Mystery Spot. It was a Fun House.

He wondered when he would leave this Fun House and go back to the accustomed categories of his life, which were his doom and in which he had been able to discover, he desperately told himself, something like *le silence du bonheur*.

He sat there, and observed how the structures of River Street shifted and heaved in the moonlight. He thought how, if you look at a thing, the very fact of your looking changes it. He thought how, if you think about yourself, that very fact changes you. He was afraid that if he moved he would hear, not silence, but a great roar around his head, like wind. He was afraid that, if he thought about himself, something would happen.

Chapter

22

"It happened around three o'clock," Mr. Budd said, "the spitten."

He leaned toward Bradwell Tolliver, under the high barred window of the Deputy Warden's office, and fixed him with a flat pale blue stare out of the clay-colored face.

"And by God," he said, "it wasn't more'n ten after five when we got the backlash. The guard who seen the spitten, he told somebody, the blabber-mouth bastard, and it was like set-ten fire in a cedar thicket, it must of spread that fast, and in the pen you never know exactly how. Hell, it could of happened in Siberia and in the pen they'd all knowed it by ten after five.

"But like I was 'bout to say, the boys was marchen up for grub, in line, toten them big cafy-teary trays. Some guy—

name of Bumpus, twenty years—had his tray all loaded and was marchen sweet as could be to his place. All of a sudden he stopped. He threw his tray up in the air and it hit the concrete, *whang*. Then he yelled: 'Hooray for Pretty-Boy, he spit on a preacher!'

"Then hell broke loose. The next guy—name of Lauray, seven years—threw his tray up, and *whang* it hit the concrete, and he yelled: 'Spit on a white man, you son-of-a-bitch!'

"So he slugged Bumpus because he figured Bumpus was in favor of a nigger spitten on a white man, even if he was a preacher.

"Then it blew up right general. Forty-five minutes it took to quieten it. Took some busted heads."

Mr. Budd leaned back, making the swivel chair creak with his heft, and stared at the ceiling.

"You know," he said, "I been in the business a long time. I ain't smart as some but I keeps my mind on my business. It is a way not to be dead. You set here and try to figger how things are goen to break. But sometimes it is like tryen to figger exactly how a sheet of plate glass will break if you hit it with a five-pound sledge.

"Now take this here thing. Pretty-Boy won't pray. The white boys started betten the niggers that Pretty-Boy would crack, maken book with ev'ything from reefers to five-dollar bills. We been tryen to hold it down, tryen to keep white boys and black boys apart, for it sure smelled lak trouble. There is big odds down town that Pretty will crack, but up here it is even money, fer the niggers got to back their boy. Now I figgered that if Pretty did crack, we'd sure have trouble. You know, white boys rubben it in, and all. But shucks—"

Mr. Budd shook his head in wry philosophy.

"Shucks," he repeated, "you can't never tell. Our trouble didn't start because Pretty cracked, but because he ain't cracked, and up and spit on a preacher and him white. Or you can say it was because Bumpus, who is a white man, starts yellen hooray for a nigger who spit on a preacher, the preacher white notwithstanden, and Bumpus not by his-self, plenty boys taken his side, so in a way them busted heads was preacher trouble, not what you might call race relations. Yeah, the Lord ain't had much success in maken black men white, but shore as green apples and cholry-morbus goes to-

gether, He ain't had no success maken preachers popular in
the pen."

Mr. Budd shook his head. He scratched the copper-wire
bristles standing out on his chin.

"The black boys," Brad asked, "were they mixing in?"

"Hell, no," Mr. Budd said. "They eats second shift."
Then: "Thank God, fer if they had been mixed up in this here
business, we would of had race relations and some of 'em no
doubt dead, and then the whole country would been down my
neck droolen sweet slobber."

Mr. Budd looked at his watch.

" 'Bout time," he said. "You see," he added, "we got a old
guy over there dyen of cancer of the gut, and the doc, he
takes keer of him. The doc, he sent me word to hold you half
a hour, the old guy was gitten it rough."

He touched the bell, and waited.

"Sort of surprised me when the doc wanted me to telephone you and get you to come," Mr. Budd said; and Bradwell Tolliver, hearing how the doc had for nigh twenty years
let nobody come but his ma and how he had never asked no
favors and how this was not visiting day, but it was OK for it
was the doc—Bradwell Tolliver was not sure he wanted to be
here at all.

For who was Cal Fiddler?

He was a memory who now was, as Yasha Jones had said,
nothing but a boy grown gray.

"The doc has lost his confidence," Mr. Budd was saying.
"He won't do no serious doctoren any more."

Bradwell Tolliver tried to see that face as he had seen it
long ago, in the courtroom down the hill. The sentence had
just been pronounced. The face, thin, handsome, high-arched,
had been pallid as putty, the eyes, staring from the face and
seeing nothing. Nothing, at least, that Bradwell Tolliver had
been able to see.

"But the doc," Mr. Budd was saying, "he takes keer of
that old guy like he was a baby."

As he followed the guard across the sun-blazing yard, he
passed the canna bed where, the other time, he had loitered
alone while Yasha Jones went into the infirmary. The cannas
were coming to bloom now. He had been in Fiddlersburg that
long. The God-damned cannas were coming to bloom.

. . .

Cal Fiddler dropped the head of the syringe into the little saucepan over the flame of the gas ring, and turned. He was —yes—like a boy grown gray. He put out his hand, and smiled. The smile was from distance. When, as a boy, he had smiled, the distance had been that of shyness. Now it was another distance.

"How are you?" Brad demanded.

Cal laughed—he seemed, Brad thought, to laugh more easily than he used to, twenty years back.

"You know," Cal was saying, "I'm going to answer your question quite literally. You see that syringe over there?"

Brad nodded.

"Well, taking care of my old geezer with cancer of the duodenum, I have lately squirted enough morphine through that thing to kill an elephant. I could have been saving out enough to kill me. There was a time I would have. Not now. That means I'm splendid, thank you."

Brad was about to say he was glad, but the other spared him that, saying: "You see, a man must be splendid when he has lived past his own death."

He studied Brad. "You're looking well," he said.

"I'm OK."

Still studying him, Cal said: "I'm glad you've made such a go of things. Movies and all." He stopped, turned inward, then added, as though to himself: "I really am."

"Thanks," Brad said, and saw the gray eyes looking at him from under the fine arch of the scarcely wrinkled brow, under the graceful crest of gray hair, and suddenly was seeing, in his mind, the face of Merl Brandowitz, the last time he had seen him, not more than three months back, in Hollywood, on the Strip. He had, for several years, assumed that Merl Brandowitz was dead.

At first, standing in front of La Rue's, under the marquee, waiting for a cab, he had made no association between Merl Brandowitz, whom he hadn't seen in seven years, and the skeletal figure in decent, well-mended black that was moving toward him, a crutch swinging, with methodical caution, under the right armpit, the left arm crooked up over the chest in some frozen parody of the way a woman holds a baby. Then the figure, hatless, stopped; the hair was gray; and the

face was looking at him. The face was gaunt, twisted and
pale; and a burned-down cigarette, with a single thread of
smoke rising calmly in the evening air of California, hung
from the left corner of the mouth. With eyes fixed on Bradwell
Tolliver, the stranger bowed his head a little, and his tongue
delicately detached the cigarette from his lips, let it fall.

"Hello, Brad," the man then said, and in that instant,
Brad recognized him.

As soon as Brad had said hello, the man said: "I read it
in the paper. It's great, being tapped for that Tennessee picture. And with the Wonder Boy."

Bradwell Tolliver, standing there on the Strip, said: "Not
all that great."

But at that moment, Bradwell Tolliver did feel great; for
his heart had suddenly flooded with energy, a promise of new
life, even as his gaze fell on the claw-stiff hand of that arm
crooked to hold the hypothetical baby. He felt some sense of
release, of justification, of redemption: that was the arm of
Merl Brandowitz. Somebody's arm had to be that way and, in
cosmic justice, it was not the arm of Bradwell Tolliver.

Then, startled, he saw Merl Brandowitz, propped on his
crutch, reach across with his right hand and touch the
crooked-up left forearm. "Had a little trouble," he said. "Own
damned-fool fault. Too much bottle. But we're making out
now. Got a job tutoring the golden lads of California who
want to go Ivy League. My *summa* is some use, after all."

He was smiling. The smile was twisted, but that was the
only way it could be. The face was twisted.

Brad was thinking: *We.* Had he said *we?*

"Yes," the man said, reading his mind, "Prue is back
with me. Hard to beat a Yankee girl. Give 'em a muddy track
and the long race, and they show up great in the stretch."

"Sure," Brad had managed to say.

"Well," the man was saying, "glad to have seen you.
Happy for you. Grab another Oscar. Onward and upward.
Excelsior. *Ad astra.*" He thrust out his right hand, off the
crutch.

"Thanks," Brad said, taking his hand.

"Prue was glad, too," the man was saying.

"That's great," Brad said and did not feel great, for all
at once he could see Merl Brandowitz, that very evening,
coming into the two-bit apartment and propping his crutch,
and Prudence Brandowitz, née Leverell, who was great on a

muddy track in the long race, was smiling at him; and his own heart was not flooded any more with energy and the promise of life.

The man moved two crutch-paces away, stopped, turned. He said: "If you think I've been trying to shit you, you're wrong. I meant what I said. About being glad."

The man had smiled and the smile had known every-thing, even about Bradwell Tolliver and Prudence Brandowitz, in perfect charity. The smile was on a face that was gray and ravaged under the graying hair; but the smile had been real, like moonlight falling over the ravagement and rubble of a bombed-out town, and Bradwell Tolliver had stood there on the Strip in Hollywood, with an image in his head of some town in Spain, bombed out, the be-Jesus bombed out of it, and they had got into it at night, in moonlight, with the stones white in that moon-drenched silence.

Now he stood, not on the Strip, in California, and not in the moonlit street of a bombed-out town in Spain a thousand years ago, but in this little room, in the pen, in Fiddlersburg, and watched the long white deft fingers of the slim man in the patched but clean white coat adjust the saucepan of boil-ing water, scrupulously, superfluously; superfluously, for that, he knew, was a way for Calvin Fiddler not to look, for the moment, at him.

Then Calvin Fiddler lifted his calm face, under the gray-ing hair, and said, quite evenly: "When you were here last month on the—the tour of our institution—why didn't you come in?"

"Oh, I don't know—I thought—"

"You thought I'd be embarrassed?"

"I reckon you might put it that way."

"A man in my position," Cal said, and laughed, "he has sort of come out on the other side of *embarrassed*. Like living past your own death, as I said. It is like coming out on the other side of yourself. It is like a picnic on the dark side of the moon. The side other people never get to even see."

"You ought to have been a writer," Brad said.

The other man touched the saucepan, inspected it; then not looking up, said: "Whatever I ought to have been, it now seems that I always knew what I would be."

"A doctor?" Brad said. "Yeah, that was all you ever said when we were kids."

The man in the white coat lifted his gaze, but not to the other. Instead, he looked out the window, over the yard, the sun-blazing gravel, the cannas coming to bloom. "We had some right good times together," he said. "When we were kids."

"We sure did," Brad said, and tried to remember.

"We sure had fun with that Erector set. And that chemistry set, back in that little room off the library, in our house, where—"

Cal Fiddler stopped. "I suppose," he said then, "that slip I made shows something—my saying *our* house. I guess I always thought of it that way, and didn't even know it."

"Well," Brad said, "people still call it that—the old Fiddler place." He paused, then continued. "I reckon I think of it that way, too, not as *our* house. All the years I always felt like a stranger there."

Cal seemed to be withdrawing into that distance.

"Remember," he said, after a moment, "that room—where you kept your taxidermy materials, and your stuffed birds and animals and your guns and tackle. The Erector set, too. You know"—and he paused meditatively, then went on— "I admired you, the way you could pull out into the swamp with those swamp people. Those times you let me come, with what's his name?"

"Frog-Eye," Brad said.

"Yes, I was so grateful I could have cried. But—"

He stopped, and returned his attention to the saucepan.

"But," he resumed, "it didn't do much good. All I found out was I couldn't talk to him. And the others like him. They looked at me some way."

"They looked at me," Brad said, grinningly, "and they saw that green scum dripping off my hair. My old man, remember—he had come boiling out of the swamp. Your hair didn't drip green scum, that's all."

Cal Fiddler was looking at him as though just discovering his presence. "Listen," he said, with an air of excitement, "maybe I was hell-bent on being a doctor just because I felt I couldn't talk to people. Not to any people, really. Couldn't get close to them. Maybe I felt if I made them well they'd be grateful, things would be different, and—"

"Hell," Brad said, bluffly, the very bluffness, he knew, a crust over something else, over an anger, an anger at an unspecified, undeterminable accusation. "You had gangs of friends in school. In college."

The other shook his head fretfully. "Oh, it's not that," he said, "it's something else, it's—"

"Everybody liked you," Brad broke in.

Again, Cal Fiddler was not listening. "It's funny," he said, "me wanting to be a doctor. You know what doctors have to do, and not get disgusted. But I was afraid of blood. I was afraid of anything slick or slimy or squishy. I was afraid of the dark, slick weeds in the river. You know, I used to sit there in that room—in *your* house—and watch you skinning an animal or bird, you just calm and natural, or cleaning a skull—and you know, I thought you were God."

He stopped.

Then: "Maybe I thought I had to be a doctor so I could be a man."

He turned, cut off the gas ring, and picked up a pair of tweezers from a pan of alcohol. "Don't know why I'm so damned careful with this. I could use rusty nails from a horse lot to punch the morphine into my old geezer and it would still be cancer that would win against tetanus. It would win against the Black Death. But I keep the squirter clean, anyway. A habit a doctor gets into."

With the tweezers he transferred the syringe head to a flask of colorless liquid, and closed it.

"Yes," he said, "speaking of habit, you can get used to anything. You ought to see the shape my old geezer is in. A real cancer-trap, and it is scarcely attractive. But I can do what I do and not give it a thought. That way anyhow, I'm a real doc."

Brad was not hearing the words. He saw before his eyes that little glassed-in room, off the library. "Listen," he broke in, his heart suddenly swelling, "that room—it's just like it always was! Even the Erector set—something half-built, a crane or something—still there. And the stuffed birds, well, they're moulting a lot but they're hanging on. Yeah, just like it was when—"

"When what?" the other asked, quietly.

"When I went off to school in Nashville, and left everything. I just walked out and—"

"Is that old coon still there?" the other asked.

"Yeah, that big old coon," Brad said, "pretty decrepit, but still there."

Cal was staring at him.

"You know," Cal said softly, "I was just getting ready a minute ago to say I owed my being able to be a doctor to you. I was just about to say how I owed it to you. And to that old coon. Did you know that?"

"No," Brad said.

"That day you were mounting that big old coon—remember?"

"I told you I remembered the coon," Brad said.

"I was sitting there watching you, you were cleaning out the skull, holding it upside down, between the forefinger and thumb of your left hand, and just scraping the brains back into the palm of your left hand. I was talking about being a doctor. Then you looked up. Don't you remember?"

"No," Brad said.

"I wish you remembered," Cal said.

"I don't," Brad said.

"If you remembered, then maybe I wouldn't have to tell it."

"I don't remember it," Brad said.

"Well, you suddenly looked up at me, a very peculiar expression on your face. 'Doctor!' you said, and sort of laughed. Then: 'Hey, Dr. Fiddler, give me your hand.' Before I thought, I had stuck out my hand. Quick as can be, you had dropped the skull and reached out your left hand, and squished the coon brains right in the palm of my hand, my right hand. I went outside. I went out and vomited. But of course you didn't know that."

"I must have been a great little friend to have," Bradwell Tolliver said, sourly.

"Well, it made me a doctor," Cal Fiddler said. "I must have thought of that a thousand times, my first year with the stiffs. But—"

He dropped the word, and waited as though it were a stone falling down a well and he were waiting for the splash down in the dark to know how deep it was. He suddenly lifted his head as though he had heard the splash, and now knew what he needed to know.

"But what?" Brad demanded.

The other turned back to face him. "It wasn't being a doctor I had in mind," he said, "when I said it looked like I had always known what I would be."

"What was it?"

"Me," Cal Fiddler said, and tapped his chest with a fore-finger. "Well," he said, and laughed, "don't look at me like I'm crazy. Sure, everybody becomes, tautologically enough, his own *me*. No, I mean I always knew how it would end." He scrutinized Bradwell Tolliver's face. "No, I don't mean neces-sarily in the pen. Though I might have known that, too. It was just that there was always something waiting for me. Some-thing dark and shapeless. Oh, I'd forget it for months, but it was like a cloud gathering in the sky, but you couldn't see the cloud, it was over the hill. It was like something around a corner.

"At first, when I was a boy, I thought it was just Fiddlers-burg, Father losing the place and all, taking to dope. So I thought all I had to do was to get away from Fiddlersburg. So I got away. Then it seemed like the only way to escape it— whatever it was—was to trick it, was to cut back on my track, to come to Fiddlersburg. It was as though I wouldn't be no-ticed here. I wouldn't be noticed in Fiddlersburg because my name was Fiddler. Protective coloring, like a field mouse hid-ing in dry grass, and that thing up in the sky looking down like a hawk wouldn't see me. So I came back to Fiddlersburg. And—"

He stopped. He was staring at Brad.

"And what?" Brad demanded.

The other shook his head as though denying something he seemed to see. "You sit in a place like this," he said, "and you think about the past because there isn't any future."

"That isn't what you started to say," Brad said. "You don't begin a sentence like that with *and*. Not in that tone of voice."

"All right," Cal Fiddler said. "I'll begin it over, with *and*. I came back to Fiddlersburg. *And* I found you there."

"Sure, I was here—" Brad began hotly.

"Sure," Cal said, very softly, "you were always there. You came to the school in Nashville, and you knocked me off the football team, you came to Darthurst and you knocked me off the team, then you—"

"It was just the freshman team," Brad broke in. "At Dart-hurst. Hell, I wasn't good enough for varsity."

"You didn't even go out for varsity," Cal said. "It was as though once I was knocked off, football didn't matter."

"Christ," Bradwell Tolliver said, softly, with slow, almost delicious marvel, "you really hate me, don't you?"

The other man was sitting on a stool now. He had suddenly sat down, staring at the floor. Now he lifted his face.

"No," he said. "Maybe sometimes I tried to hate you, but I didn't make it. You know, you had a perfect right to play football."

He fell to brooding. Not looking up, he then said: "I almost made it one time. Hating you, that is."

"When?" Brad demanded. He felt he had to know.

"Up at Darthurst when you used to make those jokes about Fiddlersburg. Used to boast about your father being a muskrat-skinner. Used to call me Mr. Fiddler of Fiddlersburg, and—"

"Christ," Brad said, "Christ, why didn't you tell me you took it hard?"

The other was staring up at him from the stool.

"I thought you ought to be able to guess," he said. "You were my best friend." He paused, meditating. Then: "You know, the funny thing, when your book came out. You know how I took it?"

"No," Brad said. His throat was dry as chalk.

"It's funny," Cal said, and rose from the stool, "but I took it as a sort of secret apology. As though you knew, after all, and were sorry, and I could like you again. It was as though you gave Fiddlersburg back to me."

He reached to touch Bradwell Tolliver lightly on the shoulder. "Hey," he said, looking into his face, "don't *you* take it so hard!"

"God damn it!" Bradwell Tolliver burst out. "I wish I'd never heard of Fiddlersburg!"

Cal Fiddler studied him. Then, very softly, said: "But you're here."

Cal Fiddler returned to the stool. He seemed to forget the other man. He looked out the window, where the sunlight blazed whitely on gravel. "It was very peaceful at my private little picnic on the dark side of the moon," he said, still staring out the window. "Until you came."

He rose from the stool, and wheeled. His face was, suddenly, white and drawn. "What made you bring that fellow here?" he demanded. "To Fiddlersburg?"

After leaving the infirmary Brad went directly to the Deputy Warden's office. He asked him how Calvin Fiddler, long back, had made that attempt to escape.

That, Mr. Budd said, had been when he himself was off killing Krauts, so it wasn't first-hand, but the doc had managed to get into the kitchen in the slack time in the morning, when the garbage truck, backed up to the kitchen had just been loaded, and he had near brained a fool guard with a big iron skillet, laid the body, unconscious and gagged with wet dishtowels, behind a range, taken the pistol off the guard—the guard having one, being a wall and not an inside man—then buried himself in the garbage. He had escaped off the truck, flagged down a passing car and put the pistol on the driver, gone ten miles with the driver, then tied him up in a ditch and made off with the car. When the car had a blowout, he took to the woods.

It had all been a mixture of luck and craziness, but when he made the woods the craziness took over completely, Mr. Budd said, for like a damned fool, he took time to wash the garbage off himself in a creek, even to wash his clothes. He was the kind of a man could not stand the garbage on himself too long. But anyway, where would a man like that go to? Tracking him had been easy. Taking him had not been too easy, though. They had orders not to gun him, unless he was armed. He was not armed, having thrown the pistol away long back, but he fought. You wouldn't think it, but he was strong as hell, nigh killed one of the guards with a hunk of rock. So there he was, Mr. Budd said, back in the pen, the only difference being he now had four more raps on him— nigh killing the first guard, kidnaping, stealing an auto, and nigh killing the second guard with that hunk of rock. And the extra raps put him under the Habitual Act, and that is for keeps.

Yeah, Mr. Budd said, back here and done used up his luck. Looked like he knowed it, too, and maybe didn't give a damn. Didn't even want no trial. Just said to the judge he was guilty, and the judge hit him with the mallet—for life. Hit him too hard, some folks said, but it was the same judge done tried him in the first place and now tied up with Milton Spire in politics. Yeah, politics. I hear tell they wouldn't ever killed Jesus Christ if'n it hadn't been for politics.

But as for that break the doc tried, Mr. Budd said, it would not have happened in his time. Things were run slack back then, and that was why the Deputy Warden before him had resigned with a bad case of lead poisoning of the kind

there ain't any medicine for. But, by God, Mr. Budd said, you
sure right now would not find no guard standing by himself
in the kitchen with his nose buried in a cup of coffee and nobody on the truck.

Anyway, when you get a guy like the doc had been,
young and clean and ree-fined and not raised for life in no
pen, you have got to take pains. It's the guys that are like that
that can go crazy and cause trouble. They cannot take it. A
pen is full of very tough guys who are not ree-fined, it looks
like they was raised to be in the pen, and some of them, they
hates the guy that comes in young and clean and ree-fined,
and they takes it out on him, or some of them, they likes him
too much, if you saw what Mr. Budd meant.

Sometimes a guy that comes young and clean and ree-
fined, maybe he will just start moving around like he was in
a dream, and his eyes not really seeing a thing. He is the kind
sits stunned from the start and there is no harm in him. But
you take one like the doc, he will go crazy, he will kill somebody, it don't matter who, or kill himself, or hide in garbage,
like the doc. He is high-strung.

Mr. Budd reflected a moment, rasping the copper-wire
bristles on his chin. Then he had reflected that his deceased
predecessor's mistake was double. For one thing, a prisoner
like the young Doc Fiddler might, if not broke in gentle, cause
trouble. For a second thing, it is dumb to risk losing a good
doctor, especially one from that Johns Hopkins, for they are
hard to come by.

The doc, Mr. Budd said, had lost his confidence, he was
afraid of real doctoring, and that fact, Mr. Budd said, he attributed to not being broke in gentle.

Bradwell Tolliver now sat on the stone steps outside the
penitentiary and looked out over the river. It was after five
o'clock in the afternoon. He would go home soon.

But he could not move yet, for the voices—the voice of
Cal Fiddler and his own voice—were yet in his head.

CALVIN: *You think we don't know. But up here in the
pen you do not need to hire Pinkerton. We get news up here
before the Associated Press. And Yasha Jones and Maggie
Tolliver Fiddler, I know they take long walks together. They
walk at night by the river.*

HIMSELF: *Now, how the hell—*

CALVIN: *And Bradwell Tolliver—yes, you—sits in his room at night working, and pretends he does not know.*

HIMSELF: *God damn it, I didn't know. But to tell the truth, I hope to God they are up to something.*

CALVIN: *No doubt. And no doubt they are.*

HIMSELF: *Well, it's high time. All these years, sitting there in that house.*

CALVIN: *And I've been sitting here. In this house.*

HIMSELF: *If only you'd divorced her—yes, in the pen or not you could, that's the Tennessee law, yeah, I looked into that long back. If only you'd made her go—*

CALVIN: *What do you know about what anything is like?*

HIMSELF: *Well, by God, if you—*

CALVIN: *Being a virgin. Being the one the senior class ought to have voted the most likely to stay pure, and ought to have put in the Darthurst yearbook, with that under the photograph. Then being a Johns Hopkins M.D. virgin. Being a twenty-six-year-old M.D. virgin in a white linen suit and coming into that house, which was not my father's house any more, and seeing her coming down the stairs wrapped half-naked in some fancy shawl that that fancy wife of yours had wrapped around her, barefoot on the stairs and one shoulder bare, and her eyelids painted purple as though she were an expensive whore who had just earned her money, and her mouth painted purple like a wound swollen or as though her underlip had been bitten by somebody and was swollen. But she wasn't anything but a little ignorant virgin girl, and she married the Johns Hopkins M.D. virgin. And I sit here. Can you know what it is like?*

HIMSELF: *No.*

CALVIN:*And no doubt you do not know what you did. That it was somehow you being in Fiddlersburg when you did not belong in Fiddlersburg. And that fancy wife of yours, who did not belong in Fiddlersburg. If you and that fancy wife had not been in Fiddlersburg. You would love up that fancy wife—oh, nothing rough, very subtle, very easy, very casual —and out of the corner of your eye all the time, you would be watching Maggie, and I would be half-drunk and I would try to love up Maggie. But do you know what?*

HIMSELF: *What?*

CALVIN: *I have looked in the eyes of that fancy wife of*

yours, even if I was half-drunk, and I swear to you there was
something in her eyes like despair. I am an expert on despair,
for I have lived past despair, and as an expert, I tell you—
HIMSELF: *And I'll tell you something, despair or not,*
the very day I drove that fancy wife of mine, as you call her,
over to Nashville to put her on the train for Reno, she had
pulled out of her despair, if that is what you call it and if
she ever had any, enough to reach over and say to me that
she—
CALVIN: *That what?*

Bradwell Tolliver sat there on the stone of the penitentiary steps and thanked God he had not gone on with that. He
had clammed up, thank God.

But then the voices:

CALVIN: *I was here in the pen on the other side of*
everything. I was on the other side of myself, and it was very
quiet. I was not alive and I did not have to live anything over.
But now you come back. You bring him here.
HIMSELF: *Damn it, you know why I brought him—to*
make a movie—
CALVIN: *I should think that no reason would make you*
want to come back here.
HIMSELF: *What do you mean?*
CALVIN: *You are you in Fiddlersburg.*

Bradwell Tolliver continued to sit on the stone of the penitentiary steps and stare over the river. It was just after five
o'clock. He heard a noise up the steps to his right, and looked
over his shoulder. Brother Leon Pinckney had just come out
and stood on the top step.

Brother Leon Pinckney was a large well-knit man about
forty, now running somewhat to flesh. He wore an old seersucker suit, a white shirt, and a black tie. The knees of the
seersucker suit were crumpled and dirty, and under each
armpit a big stain of sweat was spreading. The face of
Brother Pinckney was large, yellow, impassive, with a rather
small, somewhat flattened nose; the face resembled the face
of a Mongolian. Now the face was lifted, with the long rays of
the westering sun targeting on that yellow—that light brown
—flesh, and the face looked drawn and waxy.

Brother Pinckney began to descend the thirty stone steps.

He set each foot down as though it hurt him, or as though he were not sure of his balance.

Bradwell Tolliver saw Brother Pinckney stand at the top of the wide steps, staring into distance, and then descend the stairs. His heart was, suddenly, filled with a dry, angry envy of that man. He wanted to be Leon Pinckney. He wanted to be Pretty-Boy. He wanted to be any nigger. For he yearned for the simplicity of purpose, the integrity of life, the purity of heart, even if that purity was the purity of hate, that a nigger must have.

That would be, at least, something.

Chapter

23

IT HAD BEEN TOWARD SIX O'CLOCK when Bradwell Tolliver finally rose from the stone steps and, with a motion which, though he could not know it, resembled that of Brother Pinckney forty-five minutes earlier, went down. He sank into the Jaguar, released the brake, let it start rolling gently down the grade, switched on the ignition. The car drifted down into River Street. It was as though he, the driver, had let the reins fall from his hands, but the old horse knew the way.

The Jaguar drifted into the courthouse square, stopped before a narrow two-story brick building, flanked on one side by a low frame structure which had once been a dry-cleaning establishment, and on the other side by the decrepit remains of a Piggly Wiggly. In the two-story brick building, some gold leaf, against the interior blackness of a window, yet showed:

DR. AM S Q. FI DL R, M. D.

But Bradwell Tolliver entered the dark door of the stairway to the floor above.

In the obscurity his feet found the stairs. His feet felt the sponginess of the wood worn by many feet before him, the fibers rolling minutely loose under his tread. The little hall above was dark, but he saw the frosted glass of the door, with light beyond it. The lettering, in black, on the door indicated the office of Blanding Cottshill, Attorney.

He entered the little room that served as a waiting room and working quarters for a secretary. If there was a secretary now. With what little practice there was. Not that Blanding Cottshill had to worry too much about money, for that thousand acres of bottom land must still produce.

Brad stared at the typing table, at the machine with a black hood on it that made him think of the black hood that Mr. Budd had said he always made the sewing shop run up for the big doings when Sukie grabbed a man and turned on her juice. He thought, fleetingly, that he, as a writer, ought to go to Pretty-Boy's send-off, if he could work up stomach for it. He had seen men killed, he said to himself. He had even seen them executed. But up against a wall, with a blast of gunfire. This would be different.

The door beyond was ajar. "Come in," a voice was saying, from beyond.

There, in what now, after the shadows, seemed the blaze of late-afternoon light, sat Blanding Cottshill, his back to the windows, a stubby, big-headed man in white linen coat, blue shirt open at the collar and black tie loose, both coat and shirt a little the worse for the wear of a hot June day, the feet, in scuffed high brown shoes laced with thongs, propped on an old golden-oak desk. The man's arms were lifted stubbily and crossed behind to cradle the big head, with that thorny growth of white hair hedging the pink of the bald spot. The large blue eyes in that weathered face seemed, as always, about to squinch into distance, or into a depth of undergrowth. As always, the mouth was drawn to one side by a stubby cob pipe, long since defunct.

"Hello, Squire," Brad said.

"Glad to see you, Brad," the man said, and his gaze swung to the left behind the door, "and I'm sure that you know—"

Brad stepped forward and pushed the door back, and there, sitting solidly in an old leather chair, was Brother Leon Pinckney.

"Indeed, I know Brother Pinckney," Brad said, and stepped toward him, hand out.

Brother Pinckney rose, and gravely took the hand. His face was drawn and waxy. The yellow flesh, in that light leveling in through the window, carried the patina, the undergloss of half-dried perspiration.

Blanding Cottshill waved Brad to a large brown leather chair identical in form and decrepitude with that into which Brother Pinckney sank.

"Sorry I can't offer you a drink," Squire Cottshill said, "but as you know, I am very moderate, and for an aging, coon-hunting Southern lawyer, with merely a token practice in a moribund community, to keep likker in his desk drawer is one way to cease to be moderate. My only dissipation is the society of Brother Pinckney, who, as a man of God acting under the injunction to visit the sick and comfort the fatherless, extends his franchise to include a broke-down trial lawyer who, in between times of losing his cases, is dying of a thirst for cultivated conversation.

"In fact, in this room, you now see the only extant representatives in Fiddlersburg of the learned professions. Dr. Amos Fiddler—Cousin Amos and a man of scope—is long since dead of failure complicated by narcotics. Dr. Calvin Fiddler is, as we know, removed from active life. Dr. Tucker practices dentistry, an ambiguous profession which despite recent scientific aspirations—aye, achievements—is not associated with the reading of the New Testament in Greek, a habit of Brother Pinckney's, nor with the reading of Tacitus in Latin, a more modest predilection of my own. Besides, Dr. Tucker's mind is on how to escape from the hot-eyed attentions of Sibyl Parris, whose sexual insatiability, inflamed by the approach of the menopause, is undermining his health and whose craving for dope is driving him to bankruptcy or, even, Federal prosecution. So much for medicine.

"As for law, I am the last. When the county seat was removed, in expectation of the inundation of Fiddlersburg, to Parkerton, the five other lawyers resident here up and followed the court, rising majestically on black pinions to drift in high cortege through the intense inane, like a flock of buzzards that have spotted the wagon hauling off a dead mule.

"As for the cloth, we really cannot count Brothers Potts as dedicated to learning. He is merely a good man, full of suffering and befuddlement, doing his best to walk in the steps of the Master. He has no irony. And without irony—I mean an awareness of that doubleness of life that lies far below flowers of rhetoric or pirouettes of mind—no real conversation, conversation of inner resonance, is possible. Is that not true, Brother Pinckney?"

The yellow flesh of that broad face, on which the level light fell, looked stiff beneath the patina of half-dried perspiration. It was as though the flesh were dead, the body propped there in its massive immobility, with the flesh of the face preserved against decay by a coating of semi-gloss shellac on which the light struck. Then the head moved. It moved with a stiff, mechanical motion, nodding.

"Yes," Brother Pinckney said.

"You see," Blanding Cottshill resumed, "Brother Pinckney agrees with me. And well he might, for we are both keenly aware of the irony of our having conversation at all. According to the mores and folkways of our time and place, we are not supposed to have conversation, at least not our kind of conversation, and so we meet in a context of the irony of evasion. Further, the vast difference between our personal histories and the histories of the races to which, respectively, we belong, means that neither words nor things mean precisely the same thing to us. The exploration of this situation makes for a most delicious irony. Do we have meeting of mind upon the Pauline text of 'Know ye not that your bodies are the members of Christ?'

"But such ironies, however delicious, are incidental. For Brother Pinckney the fundamental one arises from the fact that he believes in God and demands human justice. Is not that true, Brother Pinckney?"

"Yes," Brother Pinckney said, in his husky whisper.

"As for me," Blanding Cottshill said, "I believe in nothing and yearn for human decency. So I do not know which of us lives in the more perilous balance. Let us take, for a current example, the story of Pretty-Boy Rountree. With a claw hammer of the value of six dollars he did with malice aforethought and against the peace and good order of the State of

Tennessee, beat the pore bleeding be-Jesus out of the head of
pore old Mrs. Milt Spiffort. All he could say in court was that
she made him do it. Now what was I, as the defending attorney, to make of this?

"You see, I believe the pore bastard's statement. But how
am I to explain to the jury of his peers the exact and subtle
nature of my belief? Can I give a history lesson? At what
date do I begin? Or do I sketch the metaphysical unity of
things? Or, if I could, what would be, legally speaking, the
relevance? So I tried to prove he was nuts. That failed. Then I
tried to get him off with twenty years. Brother Pinckney here
agrees that that was all I could do. Is not that true, Brother
Pinckney?"

"Yes," Brother Pinckney said.

"And as for Brother Pinckney," Blanding Cottshill said,
"now he, in trying to bring Pretty-Boy to prayer, confronts a
problem of some psychological subtlety. Since the white
folks of Fiddlersburg assume that God is white, for Pretty-Boy
to get down on his knees means that Pretty-Boy would be, at
last, apologizing to the white folks. But since the sophisti-
cated God worshiped by Brother Pinckney is merely a Purity
of Being in which, according to him, we must believe in order
to be, his God has no face and therefore the problem of complexion does not emerge. Do I interpret your theological position, Brother Pinckney?"

"Yes," Brother Pinckney said.

"Thus," Blanding Cotshill said, "we find a most complicated irony in Brother Pinckney's situation. If he—"

The big man with the yellow face that looked dead and
shellacked, rose from the depth of the big brown leather
chair, as from the inwardness of earth, or from mire, not
blundering up but rising with some steady solidity of motion,
as though being acted upon by a force from beneath.

Blanding Cottshill stared up at him. The mouth in that
broad yellow face, on which the sunlight struck, made a
small twitching motion, with no sound. It was as though the
man had to be sure he could make the lips work at all before
he trusted them to say what he was going to say. Then,
huskily, he said it.

"He prayed," he said. "He prayed today."

Blanding Cottshill stared up at him.

"Well, I'll be damned," Blanding Cottshill breathed.

Then added: "You know I'm cantankerous enough—

apologies to you and your vocation—to be sort of sorry he prayed. Looks like somebody ought to be able to hold out against Fiddlersburg—and the universe—to the end."

"He prayed this afternoon," the man said, "and I walked down the street, coming here, and five people stopped me, one after the other, in three blocks. Each one said to me: 'Has your boy cracked yet?' "

Brother Pinckney paused, waiting. Blanding Cottshill stared down at his unlit pipe. "What should I have said?" Brother Pinckney demanded.

"Damn it, how am I to know?" Blanding Cottshill said. He held the unlit cob pipe in his hand and looked down at it, then back at the man.

"Here is what I said," the man replied. "I said, 'He has found the peace of God which passeth understanding.' "

The man seemed, for a moment, to withdraw into the massiveness of his own flesh, his eyes veiling. Then he leaned over and delicately plucked the crumpled and stained seersucker over his right knee.

"Look," he said, "it is still damp. When he got through praying, he sat on the floor and I—I was sitting then on his cot—and he put his face on my knees and cried. He cried like a baby. The tears flowed out of him. I did not think they would stop flowing. He wet me through."

He plucked at the fabric. He looked down at the seersucker, marveling. Then he lifted his gaze.

"I've got to go," he said.

He offered his hand to Bradwell Tolliver, who rose and took it. Neither said anything. Brother Pinckney turned to the desk and offered his hand to Blanding Cottshill, who rose and took it. He had reached the door, his hand on the knob, when Blanding Cottshill spoke.

"Listen," he said, fretfully, playing with the cold cob pipe, "I talk too damned much."

Brother Pinckney shook his head. "No, Squire," he said.

"It's your own fault," said Blanding Cottshill. "I don't have anybody to talk to except when you come, and by then, I'm ready to blow the gasket."

Brother Pinckney, standing there with a hand on the knob, had again withdrawn into himself.

"What the hell are you thinking about?" Blanding Cottshill demanded, still fretful.

The other slowly lifted his head.

"I was just thinking," he said, "that if a white man had not gone to pray with Pretty-Boy Rountree and got spit on, then today Pretty-Boy would not have found that peace which passeth understanding."

"Well, what do you make of that?" Blanding Cottshill demanded.

The man pondered. Then said: "I don't know."

He opened the door, and for one last instant stood there.

"I am going home," he said. "I am going to pray for understanding. I can scarcely hope for the greater gift of the peace that passeth that."

He went out, softly drew the door shut behind him. They heard him fumbling his way in the dark hall.

Blanding Cottshill sat down again.

They sat there for five minutes before Blanding Cottshill stirred, and spoke. "He ought to get out of here," he said, again fretful.

"Trouble?"

"No," Blanding Cottshill said. "Not here, anyway. Maybe he ought to go somewhere where he can have trouble. He would not dodge trouble with the yaps. He's started an NAACP here, very quiet. But they won't be quiet about the school when the relocation is made. That'll be Federal funds anyway." He paused. "But it's funny he's here—a man with his education and all. Presence, too."

"Where did he come from?"

"That's the point," Blanding Cottshill said. "I know all about him. What I didn't know already, he's told me. His mother's folks were slaves, up-river, back from Savannah, toward Memphis, on a cotton plantation. His mother was raised on a farm around Jackson, then was up here on the Broadus place. His father, from Virginia or Carolina, was some kind of engineer-helper on a river tug. Met the mother, maybe even married her. Anyway, on one of his trips, he knocked her up, and pretty soon was gone for good. She broke her back with the kid, taking in wash and all, saving her dimes. Got him some sort of a start, gets him off and he gets himself a big education. So he turns preacher and comes right back where he started from. Once I asked him why. You know what he said?"

"No."

"He said back here it was easier for him when he got down on his knees to shut his eyes and see his mother's hand dropping a dime in the old broken coffee pot on the top shelf."

He waited and studied the cob pipe.

"So he is here doing God's work and waiting for a revelation. Meanwhile, he is my only intellectual comfort in Fiddlersburg. I got my hunting and fishing friends, some black, some white, but that is different. A man can't have only—"

Bradwell Tolliver got up. He took a couple of heavy paces about the office. He stared at the books that covered the end walls from floor to ceiling, then out the window.

"Well, what the hell are *you* thinking about?" Blanding Cottshill demanded.

Bradwell Tolliver swung toward him. "I want the record of the Fiddler case," he said.

Book
FOUR

Chapter

24

Q: Where were you on the afternoon of Saturday, October 5, 1940?

A: I was in my study—the room I work in—reading.

Q: At what time did you come down?

A: Around six-thirty.

Q: How come you know the time?

A: My wife called me at six. She called up from the garden and said it was six o'clock.

Q: Not what your wife told you—what you know of your own certain knowledge. Do you know what time it was?

A: I know what time my watch said—if that is good enough for you.

Q: Your Honor, may the witness be instructed to—

Judge: The witness is instructed to answer the question without comment.

Q: What time was it when you come down?

A: When my wife called me I had a few more pages to finish a book, so I did not go down right away. I finished the book, then I lay on the bed a few minutes, then I—

Q: Answer the question, please.

A: I am trying to answer it.

Q: I don't see how you laying on the bed answers anything, and how—

Defense Attorney: Your Honor, I object. I object to this irrelevant heckling of the witness. And may I, Your Honor, remark that a level of common literacy might enhance the dignity of this—

Bradwell Tolliver stuck a paper cutter in the place, closed the page of yellowing typescript, laid the massive black-bound volume on the table between the Remington Electric and the folder marked *IN PROGRESS*, turned off the big pivot fluorescent light, and went to the window. He saw the glow of the cigarette far off, down there in the dark by the darker hulk of the gazebo. Then, a few feet away from it, he saw the flare of a match. Yes, if tonight of this Year of Our Lord they were to walk by the river, it would be later. He felt as though he himself were groping in mist beside the river.

He sat down and stared at the black volume.

At one o'clock one Sunday afternoon in April, 1940, on the screened porch tacked on at the north end of the house, Bradwell Tolliver, sitting in a blue robe of Italian silk, by Sulka, a gift the previous Christmas from his wife, laid his fork down beside the half-finished waffle and looked out, beyond the random jonquils, over the mud-red river.

"Darling," his wife said, "if your waffle is cold, I'd love to make another."

"It's not that," he said.

He decided that it must be the booze. In a poker session from 8:00 P.M. to 5:00 A.M. a man could take on a little.

But he knew it was not.

"It must be because it's Sunday," he said.

He thought of Sunday, of the eternity of time it would take the sun to cross the sky to die. He thought of going fishing. But he could not stand the thought. He thought of all the books in the house, of the magazines yet in those brown wrappers, piled under the table in the hall. He could not bear the thought of reading. He thought of the unfinished sheet in his typewriter, upstairs. He could not bear that thought.

Then he thought, suddenly, that he knew what you did on Sunday afternoon in Fiddlersburg. You screwed your wife.

He thought of everybody in Fiddlersburg who had a wife doing that to her, at exactly four-thirty—not too soon, for that would just make the rest of the afternoon worse, and not too late, for you'd have to get up too soon for the cold supper—this inevitably in a room where the green roller shade was pulled down on the window and the April sunshine glowed aqueously through the green shade, and far off, on somebody else's premises, a hen would utter a peculiar puffy, garroted sound, like *cha-ark, cha-ark,* in contempt of the world. He could not bring himself to look across the table at that beautiful auburn-glossy head that, at four-thirty, would be lowered innocently and humbly to his right shoulder.

He could not bring himself to look across the table because he was thinking of the late Sunday afternoons when they had sat side by side in a bar in the Village, or hand in hand had walked among the dark, mist-wreathed warehouses on the Hudson, or had lain side by side on the bed in the room on MacDougal Street, while her muted voice told about herself, about her heart, about her body, about her life, in her aphrodisiac agony of expiation and surrender. Now it was Sunday afternoon in Fiddlersburg, and all he now had was, in love and innocence, herself.

"Christ," he said, out loud.

"Christ what?" she said, and reached a thin, strong, tanned tennis-player's hand across the table to lay it on his hand.

He knew that when he turned toward her she would be smiling with the little wrinkles at the corners of her eyes; and the fox-brown eyes would be forgiving him everything, in total indulgence, because she loved him.

"Christ," he said, and looked at her, "let's go to Mexico!"

"Mexico?"

"Not," he said, "because I love Mexico, but because I need a change, and everywhere else in the world the God-damned crooks are fighting their wars. Besides, I might get careless and knock you up in Mexico. We could call him Pepito. How would you like that?"

She would like it all right, she said. She didn't want to wait till she was ninety for her first pregnancy. It might be hard on the arthritis. She loved him, she added, as though irrelevantly.

They would go to Mexico in November, it was decided. That would let them enjoy Fiddlersburg, the speedboat and the guests they had invited this summer, and get Maggie out of that little hot-box of an apartment in Nashville for a few weekends of fun. And it was great, she said, that in the fall, when Cal had finished interning, they could turn over the house to Cal and Maggie just by themselves, and that the pair of 'em could really start living after Nashville. She would love to help them get settled, she said in the tone of an old married lady.

While she talked, he sat there and looked over the river and thought of Mexico. He began to feel better. Nothing specific, merely a faint lift of spirit. He looked at her.

"How about giving a guy a cup of coffee?" he said and grinned. The grin was broad, innocent, heavily boyish.

She grinned back. She rose, with a wide swoop of green silk sleeves, and poured the coffee. She leaned over and blew lightly into the crew cut, on the very top of his head.

He thought of being with her, in Mexico.

He thought how, long back when he had been getting nowhere with his writing in that hole on MacDougal Street, she had proposed that they go to Mexico, and he had refused because it would have had to be on her money. Well, he could afford it now.

But there was this day, in this place, to get over, to live through. He thought of all the people in Fiddlersburg getting up from Sunday dinner and having to live through the afternoon, through the comics and the war news, through the cold supper, through the coming of April dusk, through the evening service. He thought of the last hymn, far off, drifting over the night of Fiddlersburg. Then he thought of, or felt, that blind throb of energy which is the possibility of life, or of the self. He thought how it drives through day and dusk and dark.

Later, the image of Mexico gave the long summer its delight. With Mexico so surely there, floating high like a dream, aglow and beckoning, he could plunge into the world here, see it differently, feel it with fresh poignancy. With his own power to go, there grew the sweetness of pity, as it were, for what would be left and for, even, the leaver. Years later, on the Coast, on two or three occasions, he was to have an analogous feeling.

But on the Coast, it would not be Fiddlersburg that was being left; it would be a woman. When in that inner managerial room of his being, that room of locked door and cold indirect light like snow, it was decided that for the good of all concerned a situation should be resolved and losses cut, he would come out anticipating the tenderness and energy, the fusion of mutually generating pity and lust, which he would experience in that last encounter when the partner, though still uninformed, would sense a new quality of things and respond as to a promise of unsuspected revelation. It was as though only under the hanging sword-point of unperceived goodbye, could that partner achieve the final sincerity; or as though he himself, as he was candid enough to admit, could achieve a final sincerity only because he did perceive the hanging blade, by her unperceived. In any case, it was a great discovery.

But he never discovered why, in those periods of anticipation for a last meeting, some random image of Fiddlersburg would float into his head, some trivial episode of that summer when they had looked forward to Mexico.

In that special light shed by the floating vision of Mexico, the summer swung past. The guests came for the weekends. There were the local drop-ins, and the young engineers from up in Kentucky. Maggie came almost every other weekend. Cal came three times, and the first time had trouble decently controlling his pleasure at the prospect of being alone with Maggie in the house for the coming year.

"Hell," Brad said, "think nothing of it. You and Maggie fill the house with kids. I'm thinking of building us a kind of lodge on the ridge back there, where the cold spring is. Something we can lock up and walk away from."

There was the aquaplane, the gin rickey, the poker, the bridge. There was the fishing and the swamp. There were the hours of simply staring at Fiddlersburg, in an avid ritual of goodbye.

There was, even, work. He was deep into a story that might turn into a novel, and she was doing sketches of the swamp and Frog-Eye. She was planning a portrait of Frog-Eye. He would come to the house and sit on the porch by the hour, squatting on his heels, motionless except when he would reach down to pick up a glass of whiskey and water. He would wipe the edge of the glass on his sleeve, in the unconscious gesture of wiping the nipple of a communal jug, and then take a slow, fastidious sip, set the glass back down on the floor between his knees, and sink into his stillness, like a backwater in shadow unrippled by any wind.

Then in early September, the package came. And in the same mail, a letter from Telford Lott. This, Telford Lott wrote, was an advance copy of a novel to be published in October. It was going to create an international sensation, he predicted. And justly, for it was the masterwork of a master writer, who, in this, had at last discovered the deep truth of man's relation to other men, and had fused it with his own tragic sense of individual destiny. It was, he added, the book that, in his own way, Bradwell Tolliver might have written.

The book was called *For Whom the Bell Tolls,* by Ernest Hemingway.

Bradwell Tolliver stood at the edge of the high curb in front of the Post Office, under the corrugated iron awning, the letter in one hand, the unopened parcel in the other, and felt the world, the river, the flats beyond, the Confederate monument, the buildings of River Street, all heave and yaw in the ten-o'clock sun-blaze of August. A nausea was coldly clotting in him. His right groin hurt as it had, long back at Darthurst, when he had been kicked in a scrimmage. Fiddlersburg was rising and closing around him like a fog, like a trap. He could not breathe.

He stood there and hated Fiddlersburg.

During the next weeks, he must have picked up the parcel a hundred times, only to lay it down unopened. For a week it was on his work table, and he did not write a line. He put it on the mantelpiece, with other books and papers. It stared at him from the mantelpiece. He dropped it on the closet floor among old sneakers, waders, hunting boots, a cigar box of discarded tackle; and shut the door.

Work was out of the question. He could not read. He became short and sardonic with people. He walked much at night.

One night when he came in about two-thirty and began

to undress in the dark, Lettice spoke from the shadow of the
bed.

"Darling, tell me what's the matter," her voice said.

"Not a damned thing," he said.

"You know," her voice said, "we don't have to go to
Mexico."

"The hell we don't," he said, standing naked in the dark.
The hell they didn't.

On the morning of October 4th a long envelope came
from Telford Lott. There had been a leak, Telford Lott briefly
wrote, in a major review, and he was enclosing a copy, confidential. He knew how much Brad would be interested. Admiration, confidence, regards, he added.

Brad put the letter and the unread review in the wastebasket. He held out until 2:00 P.M., just after lunch. Then
he opened the original parcel.

It was a long book, 471 pages. By dinner, at seven o'clock,
Brad had read one hundred and eighty-five pages. Wordlessly
he poked at his dinner, then said he had to work that night,
maybe an idea was coming on. He started to the door, then
halted. He could not bear the thought of going to kiss her. Or
even pat her shoulder. She was, somehow, the cause of everything. He did not know how. But everything was the cause
of everything, and she was part of everything.

She was, in fact, a tall auburn-haired girl, some twenty-
seven years old, sitting in a green-checked gingham dress, at
a large table of damaged rosewood, offering him, beyond the
candlelight, a smile of puzzled humility. He went to kiss her.
There was nothing else to do.

He read until three-thirty in the morning; flung himself
down on the cot in his workroom, clothes on, light on; slept
till eight-thirty. When he came down for coffee, Lettice had
already gone to her studio. He sat at the rosewood table
while Sue-Ann the Negro cook served him, and felt as he had
that morning on MacDougal Street, long ago, when he had
waked late, poisoned by the likker, the politics, the asser-
tions and certainties of the evening before, to find that note
in her flamboyant scrawl:

Dear Old Mess—

gone to work—got sudden notion—see you
at 4:30—

I loved last night
I am going to love tonight
I love YOU
          L

P.S. write me something BEAUTIFUL

He saw the note, clear in his head.

That had been the day when he enlisted for Spain. Yes, that had been that day, and this was this day, and there was some appalling logic afoot in the world. He bowed his head over the coffee cup, not yet touched, and did not know what the logic was. But he knew that after the coffee, he would have to go upstairs and pick up that book.

He came down at two-thirty to eat something, standing in front of the Frigidaire, alone in the kitchen. The house was silent. He went back upstairs. On the way up, he remarked to himself how hot it was. It was like summer.

Late in the afternoon, he heard a car, then Maggie's voice below. Later Lettice called him. Then he finished the last page and lay on the cot and stared at the ceiling. He hoped that Lettice had finished that God-damned picture of Frog-Eye and Frog-Eye had cleared out. He thought of the drinks to come, the supper on the screened porch with Maggie and that engineer—hell, which one was it?—the bridge game, the badinage, the last insects of the season plopping with remorseless softness against the screen, trying to come in where the light was, like thoughts that made that insane plopping but could not get through to you. He thought of the men who had been killed in Spain. They had not had to find how everything turned out.

He got up. He washed himself in cold water, from the waist up. He pulled on a fresh white T-shirt, brushed his hair, and went downstairs.

Q: Who was on the porch when you came down?
A: There was Tut, and—
Q: Who?
A: Al Tuttle—they called him Tut.
Q: Is this Tut—or Al Tuttle—the person legally known as Alfred O. Tuttle?
A: I reckon.
Q: What are you reckoning for? Haven't you seen his legal signature?

A: Not that I recollect.

Q: Well, here it is on a check. Look at it. Do you recognize that signature?

A: Well, er—

Q: Turn the check over. Is that your endorsement?

A: I'd forgotten.

Q: What was that check for?

A: Cards.

Q: You mean gambling?

A: Yes.

Q: How many times did Alfred Tuttle come to your house? Before the last time?

A: Maybe eight or nine.

Q: Did he gamble every time?

A: I reckon.

Q: Were you accustomed to win?

A: I didn't keep books on poker. But I did on bridge, because—

Q: Were you accustomed to win?

A: I just told you, I don't know about poker. I was trying to improve my bridge, so—

Q: So your poker didn't need improving, is that it?

A: That's not it, just I was more interested in—

Q: How much is that check for in your hand?

Def. Att: Objection, your Honor! That paper is not in evidence.

J: Sustained.

Q: Your Honor, I will now offer this check as an exhibit.

J: Admitted. Mark it.

Q: Now, Mr. Tolliver, did you win a sum of money at cards the night you received this check—Exhibit M?

A: I guess so.

Q: Was it paid by this check?

A: I reckon.

Q: How much is that check for in your hand?

A: One hundred and thirty-five dollars and sixty cents.

Q: Well, I consider that a good night's work. Was that the only time you ever won money from Alfred O. Tuttle?

A: Look here, this is made out to me, but that doesn't mean I won it. I was banking, so all the settlement was made through me.

Q: Your Honor, I'd like to come back later to this piece of business. Now I'd like . . .

.   .   .

He put the thick black volume on the table and thought
of Alfred O. Tuttle, a big, uncomplicated, scrubbed-looking
lad, with long legs and excessively big hands, hands clearly
made to quiet a horse or scratch a bird dog's ears, raised on
a poverty ranch in Colorado, by a widowed mother to whom
he wrote a letter of confession and apology when he lost
$135.60, knowing how much she needed what money he
could send, saying he would try to stay away from tempta-
tion, using the word he remembered from the white church
under the shadow of the Rockies; but he hadn't stayed away
from it, and had come back once more, then once more and
got shot.

His mother had sat in the witness stand. That son-of-a-
bitch of a prosecutor had brought her, in a black dress and
with red, work-raw knuckles, all the way from Colorado to
cry on the witness stand when the letter was read and then
identify it.

Q: What is your name?
A: Frog-Eye.
Q: I mean what is your legal name?
A: Gomp.
Q: Gomp? Gomp ain't a name.
A: Hit's mine.
J: If there is any further laughter I will clear the court.
Q: Gomp what?
A: Gomp Drumm. Lak my pappy. He was Willyby Drumm.
      Now Pap—
Q: Stick to the question, please. Mr. Drumm, where were
      you on the afternoon of October fifth?
A: The Fiddler place.
Q: Why were you there?
A: Gitten my pitcher painted. 'Cause I'm so purty.
J: Order! Order!
Q: Who was painting your picture?
A: Let-tuce.
Q: Who is it you call Let-tuce?
A: Brad's woman—right thar she sets.
Q: You mean Mrs. Tolliver?
A: I mean that 'un setten right thar with all that shiny red
      ha'r on her haid, and them long limber legs.

Q: Well, tell me, Gomp, how long it takes to paint a pitcher. How long?

A: Wal, we was foolen 'round, it looked nigh all summer.

Def. Att: Your Honor, I object. I move the first part of the answer be stricken as not responsive.

J: Strike it. The jury will disregard the reference to "foolen 'round." Proceed.

Q: Well, Gomp, how long did it take to paint that pitcher of you?

A: Lak I said, nigh all summer.

Q: How come, Gomp?

A: Lak I said, we was foolen 'round.

Q: Foolen 'round? What do you mean by foolen 'round?

Def. Att.: Object! Object! Your Honor, I object that . . .

Bradwell Tolliver, twenty years later, with the thick black volume in his hands, thought: *The son-of-a-bitch.*

That s.o.b. Melton Spire, he had made his career out of the case—Congress and all. He rose, laid the volume on the table, stood there working his fingers.

He went and looked out the window. The cigarettes still showed. So he found a flashlight. No use in making Maggie think Mother Fiddler was on the loose and come boiling in here. He did not want to see Maggie. He did not want to see anybody.

He found his way downstairs, not having to use the flashlight, went down the hall, into the library, beyond the library into the room of his boyhood—the room where, among the pasted-up maps from the *National Geographic* and the Erector set and discarded tackle and rusting guns and examples of taxidermy, mangy or moulting, the portrait had been left. He turned on the flashlight.

The stuffed coon leaned mournfully over a nonexistent riffle. The owl—an enormous barred owl—stared with hauteur into the darkness beyond the beam of the flashlight. The shrike had long since lost confidence in its own ferocity, and seemed ashamed. The beam found the portrait.

The head of Frog-Eye came out of the darkness, forward thrusting, the color of red clay, the nose flat, the wide under-lip pendulous and aggressive, with no chin below, only a bulging muscularity of throat, the left eye near shut, the other glaring wide. It was the head of a frog, not green but

red, set on the torso of a Greek god shirted in bold tatters of
blue-checked gingham. Frog-Eye crouched there in the black
skiff, paddle across knees, eye glaring out, that eye the center of a world of green leaf and shadow and mottled gleam
on black water, all the items that, one by one, seemed to
rise from and then lose identity in the unmoving swirl
around that angry center of animal omniscience, the eye.

Brad stood a long time before the portrait. The ray of
the flashlight seemed to be dimming. Then he remembered.

The prosecutor had asked: "Did you see Bradwell Tolliver turn on the phonograph?"

And Frog-Eye had answered: "Yes."

And the prosecutor: "After he turned on the phonograph what did he do?"

And Frog-Eye had blinked, grinned, and said: "I had
done drunk me a gallon of likker. I had done et me them
san-iches they give me. So I laid on the floor and I went to
sleep. I ain't seen a thing."

He hadn't seen a thing.

Standing there in the middle of the night, in front of
that eye that had seen nothing, Bradwell Tolliver felt a great
gush of gratitude. He cut off the light. He stood in the dark
and loved Frog-Eye, who had seen nothing.

But he knew that, after a while, he would have to grope
his way upstairs, where the thick black volume was.

Q: At what time did the dancing start?
A: About eight o'clock.
Q: Did you start the dancing?
A: To the best of my recollection.
Q: Answer yes or no.
A: Well, yes.
Q: Who was it you started dancing with?
A: My wife.
Q: What was she wearing?
Def. Att.: Your Honor, I object. Of what possible relevancy—
J: Mr. Spire, what is the purpose of that question?
Prosecuting Attorney: Your Honor, I intend to connect it up.
   I aim to show that when a grown woman is dancing around
   with tight pants and a little short jacket and a naked mid-
   dle—
Def. Att.: Your Honor, I object.
J: Objection sustained.

Q: Well, Mr. Tolliver, was it you made Alfred O. Tuttle dance?

A: Yes.

Q: Who with?

A: My wife.

Q: Anybody else?

A: Yes, with my sister.

Q: Yes, with your own sister, the wife of Dr. Calvin Fiddler and—

Def. Att.:   Your Honor, I object.

J: Objection sustained.

Q: Did you make them keep on dancing?

A: I don't remember.

Q: So, you don't remember?

A: No.

Q: Did they dance several dances in a row?

A: I don't remember.

Q: So, you don't remember that, either. Were they dancing what folks called "intimate"?

A: I'm damned sure they weren't, if by "intimate" you mean—

Def. Att.:   Your Honor, I object.

J: Objection sustained.

Q: You said you didn't know whether you made them keep on dancing. Is that right?

A: I just don't remember.

Q: You mean you were drunk?

A: I had some drinks—

Q: Do you mean you were drunk? Is that it? So drunk you can't remember?

Def. Att.:   I object, Your Honor, I object . . .

Bradwell Tolliver cut off the big pivot light, swung it to one side, and went to the window. He leaned on the ledge, thrust his face close to the screen, and looked out.

No, he had not been able to remember. He could not remember now. All he could remember was what they had said in court. But he couldn't remember.

He stared into the night. It was a summer night, no moon, but the sky throbbing with stars. The pervasive crepitation of insects filled the night, like the ringing of the ears in fever. If you shut your eyes the air brushed against your cheek as sweet as flesh.

He opened his eyes and thought how that night, long ago, had been like this, but then the air had been heavy with the desperate sweetness of the death of the season. He wondered how he could now remember what that night had been like, when he could not remember what had happened. He thought of the people on that porch that night while the phonograph played and their bodies moved in shadow. In their pathos, like the pathos of dolls, they had been dancing— he had that vision suddenly in his mind—and he had not known, and did not now know, what was happening to them. He had not known what was happening to himself.

Now, he looked down. There, far off at the end of the garden, were the cigarettes glowing in the dark. He tried to hear the sound of voices. He could hear nothing.

". . . made the Tuttle boy get up and dance with Lettice, and then grabbed me. As we danced past, he switched off one of the floor lamps on the porch and Lettice said, no, we were going to play bridge, but Brad laughed, the way he laughed sometimes when he was drinking, and said the hell we were, and danced to cut off the other lamp. That still left a good deal of light from the living room, so he danced me in there and cut off most of that light, leaving the porch very dim. Then he danced back out and got faster and faster, flinging me around and making me dizzy, now and then giving that grinding kind of laugh. In between the laugh and the music I could hear, now and then, how heavy his breath was.

"As soon as the record was over he put on something else, I forget what, and danced me over to Lettice and the Tuttle boy, who were just standing now, and he grabbed her with one hand and with the other shoved me right against the Tuttle boy—I was sort of dizzy, I guess—and said, 'Shake this wench up, Tut,' and danced off with Lettice. The boy began dancing with me slowly and carefully, as though he were afraid to touch me. He was tall and awkward, and had awfully big hands. My hand was lost in his, and I remember when he first put his right hand on my back, carefully as though he might break something, it almost scared me, for just a split second, it was so big.

"Brad had Lettice off in the shadows dancing slow with her, and I heard her whisper something, then louder, 'Oh, you idiot!' but half laughing then, and they danced across

what light there was from the living-room door, Brad with his
face down, and I could see his mouth against her shoulder,
bare, where he had pushed back the jacket she was wearing.
They danced past the drink table, and even in the shadow I
could see him grab a glass and take a great gulp, and heard
Lettice say, 'Oh, Brad, you've had enough, you old pig!' But
then he danced her off into the shadows, where they danced
quiet and slow, sometimes not even moving, till there was a
sort of quick scuffle, and the record stopped.

"He didn't let her go then, just hung on to her wrist like
a policeman and dragged her to fix the phonograph, then
jerked her into a whirling dance. Then they were in the
shadows again, swaying there, and when they danced across
the light from the door again I saw what made me embarrassed, what I hoped the Tuttle boy did not see, it would
have made me so ashamed. I saw that Brad had got his hand
down back under the waistband of her slacks, and you knew
he was dancing with his hand on the bareness of her behind,
under that tight purple cloth. Oh, I forgot to tell you what
she was wearing. It was a hot night, like summer, and she
wore slacks, cotton, purple with a gold stripe down the seam,
and a gold and green sort of jacket, short enough to show
some of her gold-colored middle.

"But the Tuttle boy must have seen Brad's hand. Anyway, I was feeling, suddenly, the bigness of that Tuttle boy's
hand on my own back, and the fact that it was so terribly
still and rigid made me sure he had seen what Brad's hand
was doing.

"Once Lettice jerked away from Brad and went and sat
down in the swing. He started for her, but the record finished. He put on a new one, took a big gulp at the drink table, and headed back for her. I could see his face.

"It was a really hot night and his face was sweating,
and the white T-shirt was sticking to his big shoulders—
back yonder, twenty years ago, Brad had a wonderful build
—and the sweat on the hair-tips of his crew cut caught the
light behind him from the living room and made a haze of
furry prickles of brightness round his head. He was staring
at her and he moved toward her with a motion that made
you think of a heavy stone, a boulder, that had just begun to
slide downhill, and was slowly grinding things under it but
was going to go faster and faster. There was a grin on his
face, a kind of grin that you might say was not directed at

anything, a kind of a blank willfulness. I remember thinking for a second, the grin was like a baby grinning when it reaches out for something and is bound to have it, if the baby weighed one hundred and ninety pounds.

"Then all at once I thought of stone grinning, if there were a kind of life in stone that could grin and didn't recognize any other kind of life than that stone-life, or recognize anything that might happen except what that sliding heaviness was going to make happen. That blankness, and that stubbornness, that inevitableness on his face—I saw it all in just a second really, the light from behind and one side, and in that second I was sort of frightened by it. At the same time I knew why Lettice got crazy about him, just the blankness, something like a stone sliding down, that might slide over you, a sense that something had to happen in a certain way and it had to be that way.

"No, that's not right. Now that I think about it, I'm sure that's not what made Lettice crazy about him, something else very different, maybe the opposite. But whatever he was inside, what I saw was outside, and I saw him moving at her, his face like that.

"Then his face was blacked out, all of a sudden. He had leaned over her, into the shadow of the swing. He had jerked her up and was whirling her around and around, and her hair was flying. For a second or two, it was as though she had given in, in some way, her head fallen back with the whirling, her eyes closed and her hair whipping back like wind. Then I saw her eyes open, and though she was smiling, I saw a sort of bright tenseness under the smile. I guess she had decided to ride through with it, whatever the messy, awful 'it' was, and keep control that way, the way once or twice, I had seen her put on the green eye shade at the poker table and take a cigar, clowning to keep control of something. But she wasn't clowning now, just riding it through.

"Back some time before that there had been a movie with Fred Astaire and Ginger Rogers, who were wonderful dancers. But what am I telling you about movies for? You know all about movies. Anyway, they danced a dance called the Continental, and Brad and Lettice had the old record and used to dance it by the hour. About as well as Fred Astaire and Ginger Rogers, it seemed to me, with some tricks of their own. By this time, that night, Brad had put on 'The Continental,' and he never changed it, just flipped the needle back up near the beginning, and took a gulp of a drink, even out of the bottle now, and grabbed Lettice, or sometimes me, to whirl me.

"It seemed that all this was going to go on forever. Or rather, it seemed that it didn't have anything to do with time passing, for there was nothing but that same record over and over, saying, 'the Continental—the Continental,' just that one crazy word, like when you take ether, and you were being whirled and flung but your feet somehow always with the music as though you were tied to the music with a million invisible cobwebs and could never get away, just more and more wrapped and tangled to the music and always in time with it. When he was dancing with Lettice I might see them moving furiously in the light; but in the shadow they might get so quiet that, once or twice, I got sort of light-headed and sick.

"Now and then, in a blur, I'd see her face dance by. There was still the control. That smile was still there but it was pale and flickering. You could see the sweat on her temples, it was such a hot night, that last night of Indian summer, and a strand of her hair, looking black from damp and that bad light, was plastered across the left cheek. I saw her lips parted and how she was breathing through them, and suddenly I thought how she was involved too, how all that struggling with Brad to make him behave, the shadows and that record with the one crazy word over and over, had got her involved, too, caught in the very thing she was trying to keep control of. By this time she had broken the heel of one of her sandals, and had kicked them both off, and was dancing barefoot. That made everything worse. It made her seem small somehow, even if she was a tall girl, and defenseless. Defenseless and involved.

"Just then Brad shoved her at the Tuttle boy and grabbed me, and just as Brad grabbed me, I saw in a flash, how carefully the Tuttle boy tried not to let that big hand of his touch the bare skin at the small of Lettice's back, and noticed, too, how he was a lot taller than she was, and how she looked even smaller now and more defenseless, dancing with him who was so tall and had such big hands, and I noticed how grim and suffering his face looked above her, not like his face at all.

"In that flash I thought, or felt, how it must be for him to have a big beautiful girl like that, all agitated and breathing and damp and confused and struggling inside herself, and angry too, just shoved into his arms, and the moths batting the screen to get in and the last big pale hydrangeas pressing against the screen out of the dark, and that Frog-Eye lying over there asleep on the floor in the shadow, now and then making some soft blubbery, breathy sound, like mud settling, and that insane record going on and on. I felt my clothes sticking to me with sweat.

"I was, all at once, afraid. Of what, I didn't know. So, even while Brad was flinging me around, I jerked my hand free from his and began to beat him on the chest and tell him to stop, he had to stop.

"For a minute he paid no attention to me, just grabbed me tighter and flung me around, with that blank, willful grin on his face, like stone grinning, and his breath heavy and short, but I jerked my hand loose and began hitting him again. Suddenly he stopped, stared right into my face, gave a throaty short laugh, swung around, and still dragging me, grabbed Lettice and pushed me at the Tuttle boy. The Tuttle boy began to dance with me, in that stiff way, and for a second I thought that that was all Brad wanted, just to switch partners because I had been hitting him.

"But no, he was dragging Lettice toward the living-room door. She was holding back, for a second leaning back and looking over her shoulder at me, then lifting her right arm, the back of her hand wiping back the hair that had got plastered to her cheek and forehead, then shaking her head in a way to shake the hair loose and at the same time say, no, no. I saw the light from the living room—what little light there was—fall across her face. Her face looked white in that light.

"Then Brad had pulled her arm, twisting it a little, in that blank, stone-grinning playfulness, not saying anything, just staring at her with that grin that never changed. As the Tuttle boy danced me past, I could see her being drawn across the living room, her left arm straight ahead of her as though it were a rope Brad was pulling her by, her bare feet moving on the rug. I saw him draw her up into the darkness of the stairs.

"The Tuttle boy and I were turning and moving in that crazy music that wouldn't stop. But it would stop in just a minute, I told myself, and I wouldn't have to dance any more, and I could say good night somehow, and run upstairs, and shut the door and lock it, against what God knows, and fling myself on my bed alone in the dark and try to forget all that had happened, and try to go to sleep and forget that I had ever been born.

"But then it happened. Brad must have scraped it—the record, that is—the last time he shifted the needle back to the start. The record, all at once, was stuck. Stuck in one groove and going on and on, with just that one word: 'the Continental—the Continental—'

"The Tuttle boy had stopped dancing. He stood there and held me in that careful, rigid, distant way. I heard him breathing, like a sick man. I heard the moths batting with that awful softness at the screen, out of the dark. The stuck record was yammering it over and over, that crazy word: 'Continental—Continental—Continental—' That was all it was saying, and I stood there absolutely stiff, as if I were afraid to move, and I felt how he was holding his body back from me so it wouldn't touch me anywhere, except for that big hand laid stiff, and so careful, at the small of my back, and I felt the sweat collecting under my hair, and two or three big drops ran cold down the nape of my neck. My breath would not come, and I thought I was going to faint, with my head full of an enormous reeling blackness. I thought I was going to die if I couldn't get a breath.

"Then that Tuttle boy made a sound like a painful, breathed-out groan. It was as though something had given way. He was sort of slumped in his height. I knew this, even if I did not dare look up. Then, in a sort of grinding whisper, he was saying: 'That God-damned record—if the record hadn't got stuck—if it hadn't got stuck . . .' "

Chapter

25

BRADWELL TOLLIVER STARED into the dark. He saw two tiny glowing points that were cigarettes, down by the black dark of the gazebo. He leaned into the dark and did not know what had happened to anybody. He did not know what had happened to himself.

Late Sunday afternoon—October 6, 1940—he woke up with a dog-killer of a head. Under the twisted sheet, he was naked except for the sweat-stiff T-shirt. His clothes were in a heap in the middle of the floor. He shut his eyes against the sunlight.

He had not managed to get up before Lettice came in. She was wearing a dark-blue linen dress, and against that color her arms looked long, small, and golden. Her face was streaked white under the suntan.

"Hello," he said.

"Listen," she said, "you've been lying up here all day like a swine in his mire. And I'll just say it once and for all, if ever you again even begin to behave the way you did last night, I am going to mix you a very big double and offer it to you in a very wifely fashion, and when you throw open your filthy maw to gulp it, I am going to cool-cock you, as Frog-Eye would say, with an empty bourbon bottle laid against the side of that thick skull."

He managed a rueful grin.

"And just wipe off that boyishly charming grin," she said, standing in the middle of the floor, shaking. "I mean every word I say, and poor Maggie, she's ghastly sick—no, it's not a hangover, drinking doesn't run in the family, thank God—she's just sick and shivering. Wouldn't let me call Cal. I've finally knocked her out with a veranol."

She looked at him as though freshly discovering him.

"And you," she said, "get up and get dressed, and do try to stay out of my sight the rest of the day."

She wheeled and marched, heels clicking, to the door, opened it, and with hand on knob looked back at him. "You wouldn't tell me," she said, suddenly mournful in distance, "you wouldn't even tell me what brought it all on, what was chewing on you. Oh, what was chewing on you!"

Then, before he could say that nothing was chewing on him, God damn it, she was gone.

For the next three days, while he moved in the shadow of the unrecollected, which was always there but would always slip back with invincible adroitness just out of eye-range no matter how quickly he turned his head, he scarcely saw Lettice and Maggie. He was left alone to hate the sights and sounds of Fiddlersburg, while Lettice sat by Maggie in a darkened room. Maggie wasn't much better, but all she would permit was a call to tell Cal that she had had a little upset and would stay the week, and would expect him the next Sunday, when he was supposed anyway to bring a load of stuff in the car. She hated to make him do that packing, but she'd go back, sure, on Monday and finish dismantling the apartment on Grand Avenue.

On Thursday afternoon, late, Lettice came into Brad's

workroom. She shut the door, and moved toward him. She adjusted a straight chair near his table, sat down, lighted a cigarette, and with the V-shaped mark sharpening between her brows, as though she were straining to read in a bad light, looked directly at him.

"We played hell," she said.

He looked out the window. It was raining. Then he turned back to her.

"What do you mean?" he demanded.

"The less you remember, the happier you will be," she said. "Our little Dionysiac, goat-footed revels of last Saturday night—we really fixed it, we put Maggie and that Tuttle boy right on the grass under the hydrangeas."

She let her body sag, her head dropping forward, her knees tight together, her bare arms stretched straight beyond her knees, the hands loose, the smoke uncoiling slowly from the dangling cigarette. "I could cry," she said.

He looked out the window, where it was raining. The rain, pervasively and ceaselessly treading and shuffling the surface of the river, made it a dark, misty gray. The rain itself seemed to be a steady falling of the very grayness of the sky, as though that grayness that filled all space westward were an unending deliquescence of the very substance of the sky, of the nature of things.

He looked out the window and did not know what he felt. He felt angry. He felt deprived and outraged. He felt full of pity. And, strangely, he felt, too, a sudden crazy, abstract lust. In that moment, he thought of Mexico. It would not be raining in Mexico. He looked at her.

She was leaning forward, with her head bowed, her hair falling heavily on one side.

"She's no slut," Lettice was saying. "She's just a little girl full of ideals. And according to her, the Tuttle boy was about as shaken up as she was. He hadn't meant to get into something with a nice married girl. He's sort of a Church-of-Christ-Christer," she added, "in his Rocky Mountain way."

She looked down at the smoke uncoiling from her cigarette.

"You know," she said, "after he'd done it, it seems she was just stunned and he sort of tried to fix her clothes, wipe off her face with his handkerchief, brush her off—you know, like fixing up a kid that's had a tumble—and him all the time saying over and over, 'I'm sorry, I'm sorry, I'll never see you again.' "

She took a drag from the cigarette and ejected from her mouth a sudden, ragged cloud.

"Christ," she said, "think of her there stunned as a doll and those great big beautiful hands of his trying to brush her off."

She smashed the cigarette butt in the tray.

"I could cry," she said, "Goddammit."

She lighted another cigarette.

"You know," she said, "I heard that damned record."

"What record?"

" 'The Continental'—it was the only thing you, in your drunken frenzy, would play. I was lying up in bed and I suddenly heard that record and knew it was stuck—had been stuck some time. And I just knew something was wrong. I should have got up right away then and gone down. I knew I should, damn it—I knew it deep inside—but you—"

She stopped.

"But me what?" he demanded.

She looked at him in a quick, probing way, and then turned to smash out the cigarette she had just lighted.

"Forget it," she said, studying the cigarette.

She swung back toward him and fixed him in the eye.

"Well, I didn't get up, and so it happened," she said, "so I had to do something to try to pick up the pieces, didn't I?"

"Sure," he said.

"So I did," she said. "I told her about us."

He heard the words, but they seemed to have no meaning. He knew, suddenly, what they meant; but their meaning was in a vacuum of no-relation, and therefore had no meaning. He looked into the distance of rain. He had, fleetingly, the image of himself, far off, yonder on the flat earth, crouched naked and alone, under the unending grayness of rain.

"I had to do something," Lettice was saying, "to keep her from feeling so alone. She was on the verge of writing a letter to Cal and just running off. I told her I wasn't going to advise her about telling Cal or anything else. She knew what things might do to him, and she had to decide what she had to do. But I told her about that Basque major, exactly why it happened. And I told her—"

She was looking at him with a strange, soft, enveloping look.

"Told her what?" he demanded harshly.

She leaned to lay a hand on his, on the table, with that soft, glowing look on him. "Oh, what would I tell her?" she asked. "What?"

"I told her," she said, "how happy we have been."

She got up suddenly. She said, matter-of-factly, she had told Maggie that she, or Brad, would talk to Cal. After, of course, she had had her own session. They had a nasty responsibility, she said, and couldn't dodge it. Maybe, too, it would draw some heat off Maggie.

She stood in the middle of the floor, pensively. "You're Cal's best friend," she finally said, "but maybe I ought to talk to him. It might be more of a shock to him, being the kind of Southern gent he is, to hear a lady tell it—have her just lay the turkey on the table and ladle out the cold stuffing."

She went to the door.

Hand on the knob, she said: "You know, he's an M.D. and all that, but I don't think he knows much about—"

She made a wide gesture that took in the world outside, where the rain was, and the room, where the man's heavy-lidded gaze was fixed on her.

"—about the way things are," she concluded.

As she closed the door, she was, all at once, smiling back at him from the hall, with that look of enveloping softness, like misty light.

He looked at the closed door and felt experienced and competent. He knew how things were, he told himself.

And now, nearly twenty years after, he stared through the screen into the summer dark where the two cigarettes glowed, and thought that he did not know how things were.

". . . for when you have all at once done something you had no reason to think you were capable of, it is like finding out that the *you* you thought you were isn't you at all. If the thing is something you think is terrible, that is bad enough, and at that time I thought the terribleness was just in the thing I had done. But I've had a good many years since then to think things over, and I have decided that the worse terribleness under that terribleness is that you don't know

any center of *you* any more, you don't feel *you* any more, and
you are sick because everything is sliding out of focus, out
of equilibrium, as when those canals go wrong in your ears.

"I remember the first day this thought ever came to me,
that there was this deeper terribleness. It was long after the
Tuttle boy was dead and Cal was in the pen for good. All
the time I had been hanging on to the thought of the terribleness of the thing I had done, for it seemed that the terribleness
was all I had to live for, and you have to live for something.
But when I discovered the deeper thing under the specific terribleness of what I had done, it seemed that I couldn't live at
all. For how can you live if there is no *you* to do the living?

"But to go back, in that week before Cal came, when I
was first beginning to live in the specific terribleness of what
I had done, Lettice came and told me what she did—about
her and that little Basque major or whatever he was. She
just wanted to make me feel not so alone. But the effect on
me was something else too, for I had felt that she and Brad,
their being in love, was so solid—the dream come true, the
promise to me, like I told you—and all at once here she was
telling me that the very night when Brad took me out from
Ward Belmont and I was dancing with him, thinking of him
and her, she was in bed with that little Spaniard.

"Now I've told you how that happened, and you seem to
understand it, but I don't mean to imply that Lettice was letting herself off easy. She was trying to say to me, even if
she had to suffer everything over again to say it, that you
have to make your *you* out of all that sliding and broken-
ness of things. I suppose something of that came over to me
then, but at that time the main effect was to make me feel
that there wasn't anything except more of that sickening sliding without any center which I didn't have any name for.
So when I went out Saturday afternoon, to go down town for
the first time that week, all of Fiddlersburg, people and things,
actually seemed to float and slide.

"But I felt I had to get out and try to pull things together to get ready to face Cal the next day. I drank a lemon
Coke at the Rexall store, and I remember staring over the
top of my glass into the mirror back of the soda fountain—
oh, you know that kind of fly-specked, smeary, cracked mirror, with a big wooden ceiling fan barely stirring the air
above you—and I was seeing my face in the mirror and wondering if that was me. In a funny way it made me feel worse

to find out that what I had done didn't make any difference in the way I looked. In a way that makes you feel that nothing in the world is real anyway. Then I bought a movie magazine, just like a little Ward Belmont girl, which was what I looked like, and went out the door. It was just after three-thirty. It had turned off clear again, and the sun was blazing, and after that damp dark of the Rexall store, I blinked my eyes.

"In a town like Fiddlersburg, there used to be, and still is, a sort of Saturday afternoon gang of loafers, maybe a truck driver who fancied himself as a dude and had got himself a Saturday shave and haircut and put brilliantine on his hair, and sported a white shirt. A couple of no-good farmers squatting on their heels while their wives scrimped at Piggly Wiggly then waited after dark in an old pick-up truck with the children asleep on the boards on an old quilt. And one of those awful old men with blear eyes and purple wattles like tumors hanging off their jaws, the kind of old men who hang around half-drunk and tell dirty stories to little boys. And two or three grown boys with those knives you call frog-stickers in their pockets, the kind with snap blades. You know, just awful and sad.

"In the old days on Saturday afternoon they'd start out in the barber shop, drinking and shooting dice. Then they'd all squat against the wall outside, spitting and talking and annoying people. After dark they'd wind up in the back of the poolroom. Now that there's no barber shop or poolroom in Fiddlersburg, that sort of gang, what's left of it, hangs around the restaurant drinking, then winds up in an alley shooting dice under a street light, or they get into some abandoned store and play cards by two or three of those big square flashlights—what you call frog-gigging lights, or jack-hunting lights, for it's the kind used to take deer at night, illegally.

"Anyway, when I came out of the Rexall store that Saturday afternoon a thousand years ago, I didn't actually see those men squatting against the poolroom wall. They were there, like rocks or trees, part of Fiddlersburg. For a second, I stood there blinking in the light. The street was empty. I blinked again. Then it wasn't empty.

"The car—it was an old black convertible with the top down—was just suddenly there, dead stopped, in the middle of River Street, as though it had been called up out of noth-

ing when I blinked my eyes. In the seat of the car, sort of
humped over the wheel the way a tall man sometimes does,
with both the big hands gripping the wheel and about hiding it, was the Tuttle boy. He did not have a hat on, he was
wearing a khaki shirt open at the throat, and he was staring
at me. At that distance I could see how blue his eyes were in
the brown face. I could see the expression in them. It was
blankness and surprise, and you knew that in just a second it
was going to be something like pain. I saw him swallow. His
tongue came out and touched his lips. You knew his lips
were dry, like wind burn.

"Then I was moving, very slowly, in the blazing sun,
setting my feet down on the ground, moving straight toward
that car that seemed to hang there and shimmer in the
blazing light that filled the empty street . . ."

Cal, with the load of plunder from the apartment on
Grand Avenue, was expected early Sunday afternoon. Maggie was in her room. Brad and Lettice were waiting in their
little upstairs sitting room, reading the Nashville *Banner* and
the Memphis *Commercial Appeal*. They heard a car drive up;
there was a movement downstairs in the hall, then in the
library; there was the sound of the front screen; then the car
again started up. Brad went to the window.

"It's Cal," he said, "he's dashing back down town, load
and all. Must have forgotten something."

He came back, propped himself on the couch, and studied the paper. After a moment, he remarked that it looked
like the RAF was really knocking the *Luftwaffe* out of the
air. "Now," he said, "maybe we won't have to get mixed up
with any of the crooks."

Lettice, making no reply, rose and came to kneel on the
floor by the couch. She let her head sink against his chest.
She slipped a thumb and a forefinger into the top of his
white T-shirt and began to twist the hair. He said for her
to stop, it hurt. She said that he had hurt her, he had been a
drunk beast that Saturday night a week ago, she still had a
bruise to prove same. He said he was sorry; and really felt
sorry—or rather, felt a flicker of terror that the unrecollected had, again, adroitly slipped out of range of vision and
was waiting. He said again that he was sorry.

There was plenty to be sorry for, she rejoined, with the
way the world was and with Maggie hiding out today worse

than before, waiting for Cal; but there was one thing not to be sorry for.

He asked what.

"Pepito," she said, giving the twist of hair on his chest a sudden yank.

"Hey," he protested, feeling the yank, not really hearing the word, snapping to a sitting position.

"It seems," she said, looking up at him, "that Pepito has come to our house to stay."

"Huh?" he demanded, staring at her, and got his bare feet to the floor.

"And oh," she said, laying her arms loose across his knees and looking up, glitteringly, into his face, "oh, I do hope he likes it at our house."

"Well, I'll be damned," he breathed. Then, slowly, as the notion dawned, he looked straight at her. "If—" he began, paused, and resumed, "if it's last Saturday night you're talking about, and this is Sunday, how do you know? I thought—"

"Listen," she said, "I'm always regular as a clock. They can set their clocks by me. Western Union calls me up to set their clocks. And now I'm off."

"But—" he began.

"But me no *buts*," she sang, gaily, "I don't care what you or any old doctor says, I just know it in my bones. And don't gape," she said in mock severity, "for there was just one possible time and you—you old dear darling sodden pudding-headed wreck—you have nobody to blame but yourself. I told you as soon as you dragged me upstairs. I struggled with you. I told you I wasn't fixed. You were so difficult. You about ruined that new outfit of mine. You tore it off. You hurt me, you bruised me, and you know how I bruise. You—"

She stopped. The mock severity had become something else. The flesh of her face, all at once, seemed drawn tight on the bone. She wasn't looking at him.

Then she shivered as with a sudden chill; but tossed her hair back with a quick motion of the head as though dismissing something; and, with the dismissal, again smiled glitteringly up at him.

"Listen," she said, "a lot of things have happened in this world and not one of them is Pepito's fault. There are plenty of things I'm sorry about, but I'm just going to be so glad

about Pepito I could die, and I can't wait for him to come
busting into Mexico yelling for his breakfast, for we are going right on to Mexico, otherwise he wouldn't be Pepito, and
I am going to love him all my life and be happy. And—"

She smiled up at him with that glitter, and reached up
to pat his cheek, like making a promise to a child. "—Brad,
oh, Brad," she demanded, "aren't you happy?"

"Yes," he said.

He was thinking, yes, a man could be happy, there was
a secret and he was about to know the secret. A sudden energy filled him. He felt like a man who has just recovered
from sickness. Hell, he couldn't wait to get at that typewriter tomorrow.

"Oh, Lettice!" he cried out.

Just then the telephone rang.

Bradwell Tolliver sat under the big fluorescent light at
his worktable and remembered the voice of Sheriff Purtle,
long ago, on the telephone. All that voice had said, in its
flat way, was to come down to his office, please, there had
been some trouble.

Bradwell Tolliver looked down at the big black volume
in his lap.

Q: So you was saying, Dr. Fiddler, that the news about your
     wife come as a surprise to you? A shock? Is that it?
A: Yes—yes, sir.
Q: And you was saying—right here in this witness stand
     and under oath, so help you God—that it was such a big
     surprise and shock you just went and got that pistol and
     went and shot that poor, defenseless, unarmed man like it
     was a dream, like you couldn't help it? Is that what you
     said?
A: Yes, sir.
Q: Now I'm just trying to get it all straight, Dr. Fiddler.
     And now I ask you is that what you expect these gentlemen
     sitting right here in this jury box to believe? Is that it?
A: Believe? Believe it or not, it's true.
Q: That's not answering the question. But now I'll put it this
     a-way, Dr. Fiddler. You say Sam Gudger and Albutt Sullins
     teased you and funned you about seeing your wife get in
     that car with Alfred O. Tuttle. Is that right?
A: Yes.

Q: Yes, and they funned you about that car going off up
the ridge, and her in it. Is that right?

A: Yes.

Q: And Jack Kelly saying he had seen that car parked off
the ridge road, back in some bluckberry bushes and ast
had you give your little girl written permission for recess
time. Is that right?

A: Yes.

Q: Now you being a doctor, did you recognize that all
those persons had been drinking?

A: Yes.

Q: Now listen here, Dr. Fiddler, here's what I'm getting at,
if you hadn't knowed pretty durn well in your bones what
was happening and transpiring all summer up there at the
Old Fiddler place, you wouldn't of cared what those
drunks said. You never would of got worked up except
they teased you in public. You didn't care much what you
sort of knowed so long as it was private-like. Ain't that
right, Dr. Fiddler?

A: What are you driving at? What in God's name are—

Def. Att.: Your Honor, I object! I resent any implication of
any previous infidelity. Unless the Prosecution can tie that
up with direct affirmative evidence, this is merely a device
to inflame the jury.

J: Objection sustained. That is a double question, Mr. Spire.
Break it up. You may proceed.

Q: Well, I'll put it this a-way. Dr. Fiddler, you went up to
the Fiddler house on the afternoon of October thirteenth,
and got a gun you knew was there and did not even speak
to your wife, to ask her had she been up to something?
Was this because either you knowed something in your
bones or suspicioned things—things going on with your
wife and them folks up there at the Old Fiddler place
when you were off in Nashville doctoring? Is that why you
went out in cold blood and shot a man to death on drunk
hearsay?

A: God damn it!—I—

Def. Att.: I object, I object!

A: God damn it, I killed him! Isn't that enough for you?
Isn't that enough?

"... and in the middle of all my guiltiness, right at
the trial, there was something else mixed up, too. I was bit-

ter because Cal had simply taken the word of those men, and not even confronted me, and had just rushed off to do it. It was only later on I began to get the feeling that everybody was caught in some sort of web, you might say.

"Back at Ward Belmont when I first went there, there was a saying the girls used. They would say some girl was a gone gosling, meaning she had fallen in love, or flunked out, which was hard to do at Ward Belmont, or let some boy push her over the line, or almost anything drastic that could happen to you. It was a country saying, and I suppose it was sort of funny to hear those little girls with all their carefully citified airs using that expression for what happened to one of them. But I was enough of a country girl to know, and I almost never heard the expression without seeing in my mind the picture of a little fluffy white gosling on a pond in the sunshine, and a snapping turtle under the black water just grabbing a little foot and pulling it down. It always made me shiver.

"Well, that Saturday afternoon when I was moving toward that car in the empty street, in the bright sun—just setting my feet one after the other on the ground and moving toward all that was going to happen to me—I heard, way off, a voice saying, 'If you touch a finger to the door of that car you are a gone gosling,' and I had that same shivery picture in my head, even as I kept on moving, like in a trance, feeling as though I were floating on the water in the sunshine like the gosling, and waiting for those jaws to clamp and pull me down to the dark.

"And the Tuttle boy, he was just back in Fiddlersburg on a fishing trip with two other engineers, camping down-river, and never even knew I was in town. And just for some reason, some reason he couldn't do anything about, like a spool on a string he got drawn back up River Street, and just stopped, and he was a gone gosling. And Cal—oh, poor Cal —he was a gone gosling, for something those awful drunks said just pushed a button he probably didn't even know was there in his head, waiting.

"I had been living with and loving—if that is what I was capable of—a man I didn't even know and certainly didn't know what he needed and wanted in order to live. To find out, all of a sudden, that I had never known the man I was supposed to know best—that was just another thing that gave that sickening sliding feeling of the world with no

center. And then I had to think, too, that he didn't know me
either. I wondered what kind of picture of me must have
been in his head for him to do what he did without bothering
to find out, to ask me, what I had really done. That picture
in his head—was that all of me, the real me?

"Then quite a time later, after the trial, after Lettice
was gone, and even Brad, off to the war, or rather, to the
training camp, I discovered some of the stuff Cal had
brought down in the car that Sunday from the apartment in
Nashville. Brad and Lettice had just stacked it away in a
closet. There, in the bottom of a red tin ten-cent-store wastebasket, wrapped carefully in some dust rags, with a mop
head on top, was the marriage manual I had got sent to me
in the plain wrapper. There was, too, that stupid book of
Fanny Hill.

"I sat there on the floor with those two books on my lap,
in the big empty house in the middle of Fiddlersburg, where
I felt like a stranger now, and wanted to cry. But it was too
crazy and funny and pitiful to cry—Cal, that Sunday morning, finding those books under the kitchen sink in that apartment in Nashville, and knowing they were mine, and wrapping them up in his careful way, and wrapping up in his
head some picture of me—and of himself, too, I guess—
and driving on to Fiddlersburg to have some drunk loafer
push that button and make him do what he did.

"Well, that was part of it too. Those books.

"I sat there and thought that there was something worse
even than being that gosling on the pond and feeling that
first sudden illogical grab of that snapping turtle under the
black water. The thing worse was to feel what I felt sitting
there on the floor—not the blankness, the illogicality no—
the crazy tied-togetherness of things . . ."

The trial, which packed the house for three weeks, despite bad weather, and drew reporters from big towns like
Louisville and Nashville and Memphis, ended in early March.
Three days after the sentence, while Blanding Cottshill was
preparing the appeal, Lettice had the miscarriage. She had
stayed by Maggie, night and day. Now it was Maggie's turn.

Brad would go into the room where Lettice lay, looking
like an old woman, with a smile that struggled to come up
to him as though wavering up through murky water; and he
would feel that there was no place for him in that room. He

felt as though he himself were standing to receive a sentence. He would go back downstairs and read the war news, or turn on the radio and wait for the next newscast.

For now the war news was all that interested him. Several nights he dreamed of Spain. What it had felt like. Now and then he would go into town on some necessary errand. He conducted his business in flat monosyllables. If he met an eye he stared it down. One Saturday afternoon the loafers were on the street, squatting in front of the barber shop. He walked close, so that some of them had to draw back toward the wall, or pull in a leg. He hoped one might speak to him. Or try to trip him, pretending an accident. How he hoped that!

He would kick a face in.

Lettice got up, still weak. In the afternoons the three of them would drive out for air, to see spring coming on, not through town, out south. At night they sat around the damaged rosewood table and put food into their mouths. Now and then they spoke words. One night Brad said that they should all get the hell out of Fiddlersburg, forever. Maggie burst into tears. They knew that she got no answers to her letters to Calvin Fiddler, now behind the bars on the hill.

That night Lettice told Brad he did not understand that Maggie had to do things her own way. She said that she herself was going to stay with Maggie as long as she needed her. He made no reply, walked to the radio and turned it on and waited for the war news.

He spent more and more time in his workroom, reading detective stories, or on the river with Frog-Eye, or in the swamp. Frog-Eye was the only person he saw. Sometimes they would quit fishing and tie the skiff up in the shade of some black backwater and wordlessly pass the jug of rot-gut. One evening Brad came home, went to the bathroom off his workroom, vomited, and went to lie on the cot. He did not come down for dinner.

But he had had only a couple of shots of rot-gut the July afternoon when, bored with the river and with Frog-Eye, he came home earlier than usual, to find Lettice on the floor in the hall, by the table, a great stack of still-wrapped copies of the New York Sunday *Times,* a mass of magazine wrappers, and two piles of magazines around her.

"What are you doing with that crap?" he asked.

"I couldn't stand it any longer," she said. "I'm sorting it out."

"Is that why you've been crying?" he asked, and leaned over and picked up the magazine open on her lap.

The magazine—a copy of *Time*—was almost a year old. The little article his eye found was headed "Liquidation Sale." The article, based on the testimony of Loyalist refugees, reported the executions in Spain, by Stalinists, of various types of dissidents in the Republican army—"POUM, anarchists, Catholic liberals, *et al.*" The last victim named was "an eminent medievalist, a Catholic, a major of infantry twice decorated for valor, Major Ramon Echegaray."

He looked down at her.

"So that's it?" he said.

"Oh, Brad," she said, "don't be like that. You know how I feel. It's just that things are so pitiful."

He held the magazine and stared down at her. Some powerful feeling was swelling and dawning in him. He did not know what it was. He would have to wait.

"Don't look at me that way," she said, beseeching.

He said nothing.

"It's just it's so pitiful," she said. "If you just knew how small and sick and angry he was, and his brown legs just dry tendons on bone, the skin so dry, almost like the scales on a chicken's leg, and the red scars on his right side just barely healed, and you knew he was going to die, you smelled it, and how weak and fierce he was, just struggling for one second of life. Oh, don't you see? I would rather have died than do what I did, but since it happened, oh, let me be sorry—let me be glad, even, that maybe for a second he—"

He leaned and carefully dropped the magazine, open, on her lap. He lighted a cigarette.

She looked up at him, watching him inhale the smoke, then hold back his head and exhale it toward the ceiling.

"Maybe," she said bleakly, "maybe we shouldn't ever have come to Fiddlersburg. Maybe it was just a dream I had of being with you in the dark, out of the world."

He took another deep drag of smoke. He exhaled it toward the ceiling, waiting.

"We have played hell in Fiddlersburg," she said.

Her long fingers began to smooth, very meticulously, the pages of the magazine open on her lap.

"If you had only kissed me," she said.

"Hell," he said, "I've kissed you a million times."

"Just now," she said, "when you came in the door and found me crying."

She began crying again.

"What are you crying about now?" he wanted to know.

"All right," she said, through her tears, touching the open magazine on her lap, "I am crying about him. And about Maggie and Cal and Alfred O. Tuttle, and you and me— and oh, my Pepito!"

He stood there frozen, with a rageful bliss blindly swelling in him. He was discovering the great and terrible secret of the world, and discovering that he had the strength to bear it.

That night Lettice offered to let him go to Reno, and she could stay with Maggie as long as needed. Brad insisted that she go, he would be staying in Fiddlersburg, he had work to do. So it was agreed, and for three days they lived in a strange, delicate peace, like the beauty of age, while she packed or sat with Maggie. On the drive to put her on the train in Nashville, Lettice asked him to stop on the way and make love just once more so she could remember how things had been before the bad began. In a sardonic trance, he got a blanket out of the trunk and went back into a grassy glade by a stream, under a cedar bluff. It was very confused and numb and strange, but in the end like plunging into the black center of things, where nothing equaled nothing.

Whether the episode was a victory, or a defeat, he was not quite sure.

He stayed on with Maggie, trying now and then to persuade her to leave Fiddlersburg, to get a divorce. They would quarrel. When just after a Sunday dinner, the news of Pearl Harbor broke, he paced the house in excitement and elation. On Monday he drove to Nashville and enlisted in the Marine Corps.

Eight months later he was in the hospital with a broken knee. At Camp Pendleton, in California, waiting to be shipped out, he was standing one morning behind a truck, stowing his platoon aboard for the range. Some idiot already on the truck dropped a rifle. The butt caught Lieutenant Tolliver just above the right knee cap. After five months of hospital treatment, he was back in Fiddlersburg.

By this time Maggie had acquired Mother Fiddler. Old Mrs. Fiddler had not spoken to Maggie during or after the trial, but now had come down with a serious stroke. The doctor said that her mind would be permanently impaired. So Maggie snatched her from genteel penury on a back street of Fiddlersburg and installed her in the same room to which she had come as the bride of Dr. Amos Fiddler, in 1910. Maggie was, Brad told her, when he got home and discovered the situation, a fool. It would have been all right to pay money now and then anonymously into the old girl's account, but there was no use in hog-tieing yourself in perpetuity.

Fiddlersburg, he found, was as it had been long back. He talked with people on the street. The war had, as it were, washed the slate clean. The trial seemed forgotten. But he had not forgotten it. He was, in fact, writing a novel about it. When he had done some hundred and fifty pages, Maggie stumbled on the manuscript, on his table. She was badly shaken. She told him she could not bear his writing about all they had been through and selling it for money.

By this time he had reached a point in the novel where he could not bear to think about it. But he could think of nothing else. As the novel got better and better—and he knew it was getting better—some blank fear was growing in him. At the same time, he could not stop the thing, he had hold of the tail of a tiger.

As he stood there, with the manuscript lying on the table beside them, and stared down into Maggie's anguished face, he realized that, if he was caught in the cleft stick of the novel, he was also caught in the cleft stick of Fiddlersburg. He could not bear to think of leaving Fiddlersburg, but at the same time he could not bear to be here and see Maggie doing what she was doing, the blank trips to the penitentiary, the unflagging care of the old woman, the erect carriage of the head, like victory, when she walked down the street. All that did something dark and uncomfortable to him. Fiddlersburg was another tiger and he had hold of that tail, too.

Staring down at her, he was now feeling how mysteriously appropriate it was for her to stumble on the manuscript this very morning, to speak to him in that sad, bitter way.

For at this very moment he had in his pocket a telegram

from his agent saying that there was a firm movie offer of
$60,000 for the title story of *I'm Telling You Now,* plus, if
he wanted it, a contract of $1,750 per week, minimum guar-
antee of thirteen weeks, for work on the script. Yesterday
afternoon he had wired back confirming the sale, but after
a sleepless night he was now no closer to a decision about his
going to the Coast—which he knew, somehow, meant leaving Fiddlersburg forever.

Suddenly, with a sense of breaking out of bonds, he said,
OK, OK, to hell with the novel if that was the way she
wanted it. She began to weep, and clung to him. She thanked
him, over and over. He kept patting her on the shoulder,
saying, OK, it was OK.

He had not told her about the telegram. And now he did
not. Not telling her was a reprisal, undefined, for the dark
accusation which her life had become for him. When he left
Fiddlersburg, a week later, he told her only that he had sold
the story.

". . . all those years, waiting and not knowing what I
was waiting for, having Mother Fiddler to take care of, going
up the hill all those times—whatever it was, it wasn't trying
to make up for something. How could I ever make up for
anything? And believe me—you've got to believe me—I
wasn't feeling grand or proud about giving up anything, for
I guess I know as well as anybody that renouncing—to use
that horrid word for giving up—can have something nasty
and weak about it, something vain, and slimy like something
left too long in the icebox, not something that is just honestly
spoiled in the fresh air. And as far as Mother Fiddler is concerned, maybe I took her on just so I'd be stuck, just so I'd be
trapped into whatever it was I wanted to be trapped in. And
I know enough to know that the way I lived all those years
wasn't what they call normal. Maybe it all was crazy.

"But maybe that craziness was the only kind of normal
for me. Maybe it was just what I had to do in order to be, in
the end, myself. No, not to *be* me—to *become* me, if I could.
Me, in Fiddlersburg.

"I have read about the people in the city of Pompeii
when Vesuvius blew up and the ash fell, how some of them
were caught just as they were, like that soldier on guard.
And how, though after nearly two thousand years the bodies
weren't there any more, you could pour plaster into the

space where the body had been and then get an exact statue of that person at that very moment when the ash fell.

"I used to feel that I was in Fiddlersburg like that, that if the ash fell—or maybe it had fallen already—somebody a thousand years later could pour in the plaster and get, you might say, the shape of my life. There wouldn't be any me in that hole, just the emptiness—maybe there had never been any real *me*. But there would at least be the shape of a life. At least you could live, I used to think, so that the world around you would hold, if nothing else, the shape of your emptiness. I might try to be that much of a *me*.

"No—don't touch me.

"Don't touch me, I might be awful. I'm nearly forty years old, and I've lived half my life this way, by myself. And sometimes I think all my recollections are false or are a—a hallucination—something I dream up because of what I am, and—

"No, don't touch me, I might be awful, like a starved cat smelling fish, and I don't want to be awful like that. Or maybe worse, just blank. Like a rag doll, nothing but old rags inside. Old rags and lies, and I couldn't bear that, oh—

"—oh, hold my hand.

"Oh, Yasha, Yasha, please hold my hand."

Bradwell Tolliver cut off the fluorescent light on his table and again leaned on the ledge of his window staring into the dark. Now he could see no glow of cigarettes down there in the dark. Mist was rising among the river growth on the flats beyond. Loneliness enveloped him, like mist.

He thought of that yellowing typescript of the novel he had begun long ago, now lying in a trunk in California, and he shivered as though with cold. He thought of the things that he knew had happened in Fiddlersburg. He thought of the things that must have happened in Fiddlersburg but that he did not know about, for they always slid out of his range of vision as soon as he turned his head.

He wondered why he was here, in Fiddlersburg, in the middle of the night.

It was to make a movie.

"Christ!" he said, out loud, and laughed. "It's only a movie."

He swung from the window, switched on the fluorescent light, waiting for the first small glow to burst into a glare.

He saw the big black volume on the table. He picked it up, hefted it, tossed it in a flat trajectory, slowly spinning on a level plane, over to the overstuffed chair. When it struck, some of the sheets splayed out, heavily and evenly.

"Wheel and deal!" he cried, in the empty room, and felt energy, like omnipotence, swell in him.

He swung, and his eyes fell on the folder by the Remington, marked *IN PROGRESS*. He opened it, seized the typed sheets there, crumpled them in his two hands, feeling his hands very strong in the act. He laughed out loud. "You too, Brother Potts! There you go, old Pottsy-Wottsy," he exclaimed, and dropped the wad in the wastebasket, and laughed in loud glee.

He swung his gaze wide around, dominating the room.

"By Christ," he affirmed, "I'll fix 'em a movie."

He knew he knew how to do that.

"Dawns lewr see-lawnce," he sang out, with an exaggerated West Tennessee accent, *"dew bun-her!"*

Chapter

26

IN FOUR DAYS AND FIVE NIGHTS, in a withdrawn fury of effort, seeing nobody except briefly and silently for dinner, soaked in coffee, taking no exercise except the interminable pacing of the room and a nightly walk over Fiddlersburg somewhat before dawn, sustained by his strange, angry sense of power, he finished the eighty pages of the treatment. At 3:30 A.M., July 1, he stood outside the door of the room occupied by Yasha Jones and held the manila folder in his hand and felt great. He knew that there wasn't a bolt out of place or a nut loose.

He let his mind run over the thing, not the content, just the wonderful clean shape of it, and felt delighted with that shapeliness. It was, he thought, like running your hand down the neck and into the musculature of the shoulder of a good horse, or running your fingers over the glossy flank of a girl. It was a kind of delight, he thought, that existed by itself without reference to *before's* or *after's*.

He slipped the folder under the door of the room occupied by Yasha Jones.

Christ, he thought, *it is July.*

He went back to his room, did a few push-ups and squats, shaved—as he had not done for three days—took a soak in warm water, took a Seconal, drew the curtains, and went to bed.

He woke late, dressed, went down, feeling fine but rather floaty, and ate a prodigious breakfast. While he was dawdling over the third cup of coffee, cigarette in hand, mind deliciously blank, Yasha Jones came in. He was wearing the black Japanese kimono. The good part of his tall skull —the part without the scar—gleamed as though it were a metal carefully rubbed and tended.

"Quite a marathon you put on," he said. "How do you feel?"

"Fine," Brad said.

"Let's go up and talk," he said.

"Fine," Brad said. He looked out the window, over the garden. The day was going to be a scorcher.

The day was a scorcher, and he now stood in the middle of it, on the lost patch of brick pavement outside the gate of the Fiddler place, at twenty forty-five. He looked at his watch. It hadn't taken long.

Brad thought: *It doesn't take long to say something stinks.*

But Yasha had done his horsing around, first.

"It is expert," Yasha Jones had said. "You have done nothing more expert. In my time on the Coast I have seen nothing more expert. But," added Yasha Jones, "it is not you. It is only that *you* who is an expert."

"I told you," Brad had retorted, "that night down by the monument—I told you, damn it, maybe I wasn't your guy."

"I remember," Yasha Jones had said, "and you said that maybe too much had happened here, and I said that no matter what had happened, you would come out on the other side of it and do a beautiful thing."

"*Dawns lewr see-lawnce*," Brad had begun, in heavy
burlesque, twisting his mouth.

"It is true," Yasha Jones had said, soberly, "and it will be
true. The time will come when there'll be no need to tell what
happened—or need not to tell it. You'll be free then to let
your feelings move into the vision of life which Fiddlersburg
could be. But look, Brad—"

He had stopped.

"I'm looking," Brad had said, "and all I see is that object
on the table which you think stinks."

"But, Brad," Yasha Jones had resumed, oblivious, it
seemed, to the words just spoken, "what you have here now
is not freedom in a beyondness of what happened. Nor is it a
plunge into what happened to find freedom. It is, to be blunt"
—and he had touched, with a long forefinger, the folder on
the table—"a parody of what happened."

"OK," Brad had said, feeling something dry and crumbling in him, "it's a parody."

"Let's look at it simply," the other had said. "Old man
in decayed house—the aristocrat, shall we say, rather like
your friend Blanding Cottshill, but poor, crippled, in wheel
chair. Son in prison, rather like Calvin Fiddler. Daughter-in-
law—rather, I suppose, like Maggie—taking care of old man,
who understands her and what has occurred. Old man's first
obsession, to persuade son, due out soon, to accept the wife.
Second obsession, to hold old life together—i.e., house—for
son's return. But the dam will flood them out. Old man
fights back. Won't move. Government engineer tries to persuade him. Falls for girl. Waters begin to rise. Trouble in
penitentiary. Then—"

He had paused, again touching the folder.

"Then the prison break. The husband, crazed by ru-
mors—"

He had stopped.

"Now listen, Brad," he had again begun.

"You listen," Brad had said. "Strangely enough, that
prison break is exactly the way things have a way of happening."

"It doesn't matter what way things have a way of happening," Yasha Jones had said, almost impatiently.

"What do you mean, it doesn't matter what happens?"

"In that sense," Yasha Jones had said, "what matters is

the feeling. Where, in this"—he had touched the manuscript
—"is the feeling we want? Where is Fiddlersburg?"

"Oh, I'll feed you some minor characters," Brad had
said, "if that's all you want. A dime a dozen. I'll put platoons
of darkies on River Street all singing 'Suwanee River.' I'll put
a whiskey-ad colonel weeping at the base of the Confederate
monument while the rising waters lap his bony old shins.
Anyway, you are a director. You are a great director. You
have a camera. You are great with a camera. Flesh out the
feeling with that famous camera."

Yasha Jones had fallen into thought. "You were working," he said, after a moment, "on a story line based on
Brother Potts. May I see that?"

"It stunk," Brad had said, and laughed with crazy glee.
"It stunk, and I tore it up."

That thought had, at the time, seemed terribly funny.
Now, as he stood at the gate, in the middle of the day which
was sure a scorcher, it did not seem so funny. Nothing
seemed very funny.

It hadn't seemed very funny, either, when he had felt
the overmastering impulse to turn on Yasha Jones and de-
mand: "Did you see *The Dream of Jacob?*"

Then, before the other could reply, he had plunged on:
"Sure you saw it and didn't like it, that's why you've never
mentioned it. Well, God damn it, why did you hire me?"

And Yasha Jones had said: "I did not want you for *The
Dream of Jacob.* I wanted you because you are, in the end,
you."

"OK, I'm me," he said and turned to the door, and Yasha
Jones had stepped to him and laid that hand on his shoulder
—yes, he had even laid on the hand—and said: "Remember,
Brad, I can wait."

Slowly Brad had looked down at the hand, which was a
reproach, an affront, an accusation, and which was unen-
durable. He had drawn out from under the hand. He had
said: "Yeah—but maybe I can't wait."

And he had gone out the door.

And standing outside the closed door, on the other side
of which Yasha Jones was standing, he had demanded of
himself: *Can't wait for what?*

He had not known.

·   ·   ·

Now at the gate, he looked down at the thick black volume he held in his hand, and thought that there was at least one thing he had known he couldn't wait to do: to get that damned thing out of the house. It had been lying there four days and five nights on that chair where he had flung it, and he had seen it lying there.

He looked at his watch. It was 1:05. Englishmen, mad dogs and Bradwell Tolliver stand in the midday sun. For fifteen minutes he had stood there. He got into the car, and with hardly a suspiration of the engine drifted up River Street, and when he was where he was going, got out of the car and climbed the dark stairs and stood before the golden-oak desk on which the booted feet of Blanding Cottshill were propped, and laid down the big black volume.

"Sorry I sort of beat the thing up," he said. "I—I dropped it."

The man in the coarse blue work shirt, with the black tie hanging loose at the open collar, glanced at the volume, from which some sheets splayed out.

"Couldn't matter less," he said. The man's blue eyes fixed on Brad, and suddenly squinched, as though he were peering into brush or the shadow of trees. "I don't think I'd particularly enjoy reading it again," he said. "Why did you read it?"

"It just seemed something natural to do," Brad said.

"You and that Jones fellow putting that in your movie?"

"No," Brad said. "We aren't, in one sense, putting anything in our movie. It's just a general feel—you know, a sense of things—we're after. That's why I read the damned thing. To whiff the peculiar effluvium of Fiddlersburg."

He sat in one of the decrepit leather chairs and heard his voice saying that, and savored the dry, crumbly feeling in his chest, the sense of loss.

"You know," Blanding Cottshill was saying, pointing the cane stem of his cob pipe at the black volume, "that thing was a watershed for a lot of us. The trial. Sure, for poor Cal and Maggie and Old Lady Fiddler, and you too, and your wife. But for me, too. I'd been Governor if it hadn't been for that. Probably in U. S. Senate right now. Not that I gave a deep damn. I'm not really ambition-bit. Just something maybe natural to do. Playing a role. A *persona*, old Prof Willbrough used to say in Latin Twenty, back at Washington and Lee."

He stared at the black volume.

"You know," he resumed, "back in my time, after I got back from France and making the world safe for democracy, there must have been down South here ten thousand young squirts a year graduating from college or medicine or law— even those squirts like me that went up East for law—I went to Yale—who didn't want to do a damned thing except what I actually did, and a lot of 'em did it too, or the equivalent. A farm up-river, an office on the square, in Fiddlersburg in my case, folks squatting on their heels under the maples, swapping talk with you, the hunting and the fishing, training a bird dog, breaking a colt, maybe fooling with politics, watching the seasons change and your kids grow up and get ready to do what you were doing. I reckon a man figured it was a way of feeling all of a piece, in himself and with things around him."

He pointed the pipe stem again at the black volume.

"Then that," he said.

"Yeah," Brad said, "that."

"You know," Blanding Cottshill said, "when the trial started I was sure it was in the bag. According to the local folkways and mores and the unwritten law, it was in the bag. Sure, he shot the guy. But let the prosecution establish everything and then put on the stand that nice, clean-cut, fine-grained, soft-spoken young physician—local boy, too, who's come back home to serve his own people and not gone to Chicago to get rich—and let him just look 'em trustingly in the eye and say how it was such a shock to him it was all like a dream. Which, by God, it was. And still is."

He paused a moment, staring at the black volume.

Then said: "It was in the bag. But Cal blew it. Melton Spire gave him the needle and he couldn't take it. He blew it. Maybe—" He stopped again, and again stared at the black volume. "Maybe," he resumed, "he didn't even want to be out, be free. Maybe he wanted to be locked up, in the pen, where nothing matters."

Brad leaned at him. He felt the painful stir of some feeling, some idea, that he could not define. "You think that's it?" he demanded. "Do you think that's what he really wanted?"

"Hell, how do I know?" Blanding Cottshill retorted, as though in anger. "The point is, that fellow Spire was too smart

for me. He outsmarted me on every point. He made everything backfire. Unwritten law, and all.

"Now if it had just been Maggie alone, we'd have swung
it. She is pretty, she even has a kind of beauty, and she is
the kind that makes you want to protect her. But Lettice was
mixed up in it too, and when that jury was looking at Lettice
and those legs, they did not think of protecting her. They did
not think of protecting anybody. They looked at those legs
and went into a drooling trance, every man-jack of 'em, and
got sick just honing after those legs and thinking how they
could latch around. You could look at their faces and know
what was happening. I know, because I had a touch of the
disease, too.

"But here's the point. They suddenly realized those legs
weren't for the likes of them. And that delicious nausea
in the pit of the stomach could turn into a hot ball of hate.
They had to take it out on somebody. They had to revenge
their own deprivation and the death of ambition and the defeat of boyhood dreams, and the knowledge that when they
got home to their wives the aforesaid wives would, no doubt,
have legs like sausages and would be full of household problems and would smell like old buttermilk. Well, vengeance
was theirs. There was Cal Fiddler, throat ready for the
knife. Yeah, there's something about poor old Cal that in-
vites punishment.

"Well, Melton Spire had it all figured out. He got all
that anger and deprivation and vengeance pointed at Cal. I
tried to head him off. But by the time he got through they
weren't just taking it out on Calvin Fiddler, they were trying
all the Fiddlers that ever lived, because they had a big house,
and Old Lady Fiddler because she came from New Orleans
and held her head up, and me because I'm a cousin of Amos
Fiddler and because I own a thousand acres of bottom land,
and you because your mother was some kind of a cousin of
mine, and you had a father who came boiling out of the
swamp and grabbed off all the local real estate and then gave
the darkies the white-folks' Methodist Church he foreclosed
on, but chiefly because you could read and write, and your
wife because she had those legs.

"Yeah, Melton Spire—he had the town folks hating us—
you and me especially—because we consorted with swamp
rats and our colored friends more than with some of 'em. And
he had our swamp companions and colored friends hating us

because he got the notion over that we laughed at 'em behind their backs. Yeah, that page he read out of one of your old stories, it didn't help any."

"God damn it," Brad burst out, "what I meant was—"

"Take it easy," Blanding Cottshill said. "It was twenty years ago. Sure, I know what you meant. But by the time that half-literate yap had got through, I don't know who could be feeling all of a piece in himself and with things around him. Except Spire, of course, who had found the secret and was on his way to Congress. Yeah, he had found the cracks—for all of us, all right. But you know—" he said, and paused.

Then: "You know, you got to be honest. There were cracks in Fiddlersburg already, he just tapped and made 'em show up."

He stopped.

"God damn it," he said then, "there are always cracks. Even in a loving family. The question is just how much humanness you can get over the cracks. To hold things together."

He stopped again. He was breathing heavily.

"It killed my wife," he said. "You know it—it killed her off. But I hung on here. For one thing, my boy loved the farm, and I was really building it up for him. Then Arnhem. He was a paratrooper. They shot him out of the air."

He stopped.

Then: "I reckon it was Tad getting killed did it, made the cracks start to moss over, some. Made people feel sorry for me, I guess you'd say. So I kept plugging away out at the farm. Was going to make it a model. Had a lot of experiments going. Got farmers to come out and take an interest. Hell, I was making money, too."

He stopped.

"I was going to leave the place to the state," he resumed, "a model experiment farm. Name it for Tad, you know. Now they're going to flood the whole damned thing."

He stopped.

Then: "Yeah, I plugged along. Had some friends—hunting and fishing friends and a few of the other kind, too. But folks die off on you. First thing I knew, the only person I really liked to talk to was Brother Pinckney. In our bootleg conversations."

He stopped again.

"And?" Brad asked.

"Yeah," Blanding Cottshill said, "and I practiced me some law, too. Even if I didn't have to make a living at it. After that"—he pointed at the black volume—"there was a time that folks with folding money didn't want me. So I got in the habit of taking cases for folks without folding money. You know, swampers and scrabble-farmers, and colored folks. I got in the habit. Still got it. Now, mind you, I don't have any theories. It had just got to be more fun. Besides, I got a streak that makes me want to make myself a little un-popular now and then. To feel real. Yeah, there have been times when I have seen some fellow on the courthouse steps bracing himself to say something to me. I just look 'em in the eye. For you know—"

He grinned, somewhat sourly.

"You know the gossip," he said. "About me and Ro-selle?"

Brad nodded.

"I know they gossip about me and a colored woman. To hell with 'em all. It's the old-time religion. It was good for Paul and Silas, and I reckon Grandpa too, and it's good enough for me."

He stopped, resumed: "She's a fine woman, and she's good to me. Fine-looking, too, sort of tawny-color. And if any son-of-a-bitch on the courthouse steps ever says 'nigger lover' to me—well—"

He fell into thought.

"But you know," he resumed, "if folks know you really don't give a damn, they hesitate to monkey with you. They are afraid of you in the clutch."

He grinned, less sourly now.

"So I sit here on slack days and read Tacitus. And Sue-tonius. Got to recover my investment, all those nights at Washington and Lee I sat up sweating over Prof Will-brough's classes. I sit here now and read how Rome went to hell. Fiddlersburg is going to hell. The country looks like it's going to hell in a hand-basket. So it's a sort of satisfaction to read about Rome.

"But take President Eisenhower now—you know, Ike is a mighty poor sort of Emperor Galba, and Harry wasn't really cut out for Nero. And here, in Fiddlersburg, I look out the window and I see some pore misguided boogers doing the best they can—according to their dim lights. And I see Brother Pinckney walking down River Street because it is

only in Fiddlersburg he can shut his eyes and get that vision
of his mother's old hand dropping that dime into the busted
coffee pot on the shelf. So what you might call the pathos of
the mundane sort of takes the edge off my grim satisfaction in
my reading matter."

He grinned, with a trace of real gaiety now, and paused
to load his pipe.

"And now," he said, "they're going to flood us, and that
will solve a lot. Maybe they should flood the whole country,
Maine to California."

Brad got up.

"I enjoyed the chat," he said.

"Chat, hell," Blanding Cottshill said, "it was a signed
and sealed confession, but further the deponent saith not."

"Well, deponent," Brad said, "I still enjoyed it. But I
got to go."

He did not know where he was going.

Blanding Cottshill was, he discovered, looking at him
with those blue eyes squinched in that way he had, as though
looking into brush, waiting for movement.

"You," Blanding Cottshill said, "did you come back to
Fiddlersburg to be made whole? All of a piece in yourself
and with the world around you?"

"Hell," Brad said, "I'm here to make a movie."

He went to the door.

"So long, Squire," he said.

"When I asked had you come back to be made whole, I
wasn't talking about *now*," Blanding Cottshill said. "I was
talking about *then*."

Blanding Cottshill pointed at the black volume on the
desk.

"How the hell do I know?" Brad demanded, and in out-
rage stared at the man.

Chapter

27

He stood in the square, under the windows of the office from which he had just come. The sunlight glittered on the upper maple leaves as on tin. Between the maples the light struck the grass, sparse and uncut, going brown already. There were heavy wooden benches under the maples; and on the benches, he knew, were carved the initials of men who, over the years, had sat there, waiting; but nobody was there now. The courthouse door was, he could see, locked with a big padlock. One window was broken jaggedly, where a stone had passed. The clock, above the maples, was frozen at 8:35.

Eight thirty-five when?

He stood there and did not know where he was going.

And, he thought, did not know where he was. For he looked around him and did not know what Fiddlersburg was.

So he sank into the driver's seat of the car and crept around the square and back down to River Street and turned left. Somewhere in his mind was the image of himself, out on the state slab, whirling into the heat dazzle. You could do that, anyway. Then he saw her.

"I'll be damned," he said under his breath, "the Lady of Shalott," and let the car creep down River Street.

She was standing in front of the Rexall store in some rig that seemed worse than usual, a broad-brimmed straw hat stuck on top of the glorious haystack of hair and tied under the chin with a blue cloth of some gauzy kind, and some kind of blouse that might have been made out of a flour sack except for the big blue polka dots, and an electric-blue skirt, too long and not even. She wore, he could see now and wished he couldn't, high-heeled white shoes, very pointed. She held a swatch of electric blue over her left arm, and that must be the jacket of the electric-blue suit. A small straw suitcase was set beside the white shoes in which she stood and which, now that he was closer, he wished even more she were not standing in.

"Hi," he said, close now, the motor like a whisper, "you going away?"

"I'm waiting for the bus," she said, "for Parkerton. I'm going to visit my girl friend. But the bus, it's late."

"You don't need the bus," he said.

The improbable clear rose-pink bloomed and mantled on her cheeks. "Oh," she said.

"Yes, girlie," he said, gaily, "you just get in here and I'll whirl you there in nothing flat."

He got out, came to seize the suitcase, and reached up a hand to help her off the high curb.

"I'd love to—it's just I'm afraid you all are too busy— I don't want to interfere—"

"It's me, just me," Brad said. "And it may well be that, unbeknownst to myself, I have just taken a vow never to be busy again. Get in, girlie."

She got in, settling herself decorously, putting the white very high-heeled shoes down side by side on the rug, folding her hands in her lap, on the white patent-leather purse, sitting there in her deep, velvety, unglimmering darkness. He examined the scene, closed the door, went to his side. But he had scarcely got into motion before she said, "Oh—oh, I hate to say it—but could you go by home a second? I forgot something."

They went by home. He stood by the car, waiting for her to come out. The porch was empty. Sheriff Purtle was not there in the bright wheel chair, under the jigsaw scroll-work. So he didn't have to go and say hello.

She came out, they moved back up River Street, took the turn for the ridge road, wordlessly.

Finally she said, in a small voice: "You aren't mad?"

"No," he said. "Why the hell should I be mad?"

"Men don't like it," she said, "when girls are always forgetting things."

"It killed time," he said.

Up the ridge road, he held down the speed to the minimum the grade permitted. The Jaguar lounged upward in its indolent power. The patches of shade and the patches of sun flowed slowly over them.

"Brad—do you mind if I call you Brad?" she said.

"I don't mind," he said.

"That day you came to my house," she said, still in that small, defenseless voice, "and I played the record—were you mad then?"

"No," he said.

"I never even heard from you—or Mr. Jones—after that," she said. "Not that I expected to—it was just you sort of felt mad. When you left, and—"

Her voice was trailing off to nothing. He did not look at her face, but he did see the hands folded, palms upward, in perfect stillness, on the purse in her lap. He saw how absolutely white was the skin of her inner wrists. The veins there were small, intricate, and blue.

"I've been busy," he said. "Till last night I hadn't had a night's sleep in five nights."

"The movie?"

"The God-damned movie," he said, and stared up the winding road; and the shade and sun flowed over them. To the left was a sage field. To the right were the woods, the dry, hot, unbreathing woods of July, shelving deeper and deeper inward, in a dappling of sun and darkness. The woods were full of the tinny, merciless iteration of the locusts, like Time passing through your head.

"Have you finished it?" she asked.

"It is a stand-off," he said.

"What do you mean?"

"I mean I have finished it," he said, "and it has finished me."

"What do you mean?"

"I mean," he said, "that I wrote what is called a treatment—that is the story you later make the scenario from—and I showed it to my dear colleague and employer, and he says it stinks. He says, in fact, that it is expert."

"But that—" she began.

But he interrupted: "Take that hat off."

Submissively she leaned her head a little; untied that strip of gauzy blue rag that held it; laid it on her lap.

"But expert," she began again, "that's a nice thing to say."

"Not the way Yasha Jones says it," he said, and laughed. "So I guess I have finished it, and it has finished me, at least as far as trying to be a non-expert, and I'd better get the hell back to where I can at least try to be an expert."

He paused.

"And so I reckon it has finished me with Fiddlersburg, too."

The sun and shade, in slow flickerings, flowed over them.

"You mean," she said after a little, "you're going away?"

"Yes," he said.

"You could start again," she said.

"Listen," he said, "if a man gets his leg shot off, it is not much use to start again to grow a new one. He had better get a fancy prosthetic limb from the Veterans Administration, and practice a lot and learn to do the rhumba with it, and give exhibitions in hospitals to hearten the inmates in their infirmities, and he will get his picture in the papers. He will be an expert."

He laughed, staring up the road.

"Yeah," he said, "an expert is a man who can do something on an artificial leg almost as well as you can do it on a real one."

After a moment she said: "Doesn't Mr. Jones want you to start over again?"

"Yes."

After a longer moment, in a thin, distant voice, she said: "I've got to start over."

"What do you mean—you?" he demanded, not looking at her.

"I can go everywhere," she said, "in Fiddlersburg. I know where I put my foot. I know every second where I am. But in Lake Town, where they're going to relocate us—"

She stopped.

Then: "You ought to make that movie. So folks can see it and know how a place like Fiddlersburg was. So they can know how it feels to be drowned out and leave. You ought to make it."

"Damn it!" he said, gripping the wheel. "I told you why I won't."

She let her head sink a little. Then, in a voice even thinner and more distant, she said: "I couldn't see the movie anyway. But you know—"

She paused.

"Know what?"

"I can put on the record. I bought my own new record like the one in the Books for the Blind. It came yesterday through the mail. Now when they put us in Lake Town and I want to remember how it used to be in Fiddlersburg, I can put on my own record."

He stared up the road.

"Are you mad?" she asked.

"No," he said.

"You sound mad," she said. After a moment, she said: "I don't want you to be mad."

He said nothing.

"If you are mad," she said, "I can't ask you a favor."

"What?"

"You remember how I told you about the first time I heard your stories, on Books for the Blind—how it made me feel I knew about Fiddlersburg for the first time—and about how people are." She hesitated. "Well," she began, her voice thin and shy, "it did something else, too. It made me feel like I could live, too. Like people do. That record, it made me want to reach out to other people. Reach out and live." She hesitated again. Then, even thinner and shyer: "You aren't mad I'm telling you this?"

"No," he said, harshly, "no."

"When we're relocated," she said, "in Lake Town, and I want to play my record—if—"

"If what?" he demanded.

"My friends," she said, beginning over, "the people I like, I know what their faces are like. I mean I have touched their faces with my fingers. It is like seeing, in a way. What I mean is, if when I'm relocated and turn on the record, if I could remember—"

She stopped.

Then: "You're mad."

"No."

"It just takes a second," she said.

She waited. The car was scarcely crawling now. He did not look at her.

"If only you would," she said.

He drew the car to the side of the road. He stopped it with an unnecessary jerk. He swung his gaze around. There was the stretch of road, on the left the sun-glare on the sage field, on the right the dark and dappled hollowness of woods.

"All right," he said, in a grinding voice.

She was over there, in that expensive seat, sitting straight, hands on lap holding the edge of the straw hat with blue gauze. Awkwardly, he leaned over and thrust his face out. Her eyes were as though on him, very blue and calm. Her fingers released the edge of the straw hat on her lap and rose with a very slow, very gentle, groping action, toward the spot where the face must be.

He waited for the fingers to find his face.

They found it.

With a hand on each side, the fingers framed the width of the face. They found the ears, traced the shape. They found the jawbone, then moved upward symmetrically on each side, over the cheeks, in small, cool, firm but feathery dabs of contact. The fingers traced, on each side, the curve of the brow, then the arch of the eye sockets. He shut his eyes, and the fingers, as light as breath, showed him the shape of his own closed eyes. The fingers were dropping, touching the mouth, the chin.

With his eyes closed he was, suddenly, aware of that metallic, unremitting grind of the locusts.

He jerked his eyes open.

Her eyes were shut. Her face was slightly lifted, the expression pensive, unruffled, calmly inward and distant and intact, the lower lip slightly damp. She did not seem to be breathing. He thought she must be holding her breath. In the middle of the sun-blaze and stridor that filled the world, the shade of a tree lay across her face and the closed eyes.

A sound like a groan wrenched up in him. He thrust himself over and seized her and pressed his mouth upon hers. The tips of her fingers were still on his lower cheeks and chin. Then, his arms were around her body in an untutored and desperate embrace, and he was pressing his face between her breasts, his lips on the dry fabric of the blouse. Now her fingers were lightly touching the shape of his skull, under the unluxuriant, cropped hair.

The white patent-leather purse and the hat had slipped to the floor.

Pressing his face against that thin, dry fabric, his eyes shut, he tried to hear the beating of her heart. Once, in his darkness, he heard the clatter and hammering of some wreck of a car drawing near, passing on. He thought of the eyes staring from that wreck, the red eyes of some scrabble-farmer, the yellow-muddy eyes of some old Negro. He heard the locusts, and they would not stop.

He spoke the words into the fabric, which was now damp from the pressure of his lips and his breath. "You've got to," he said.

She made no answer. The fingers were moving slowly and lightly on the shape of his skull.

"You've got to," he said again, harshly.

After a moment he heard the voice, far off, incredulous and slow, as though in meditation.

"I never thought," she was saying, "I never thought it would happen. Happen to me."

Abruptly he jerked his head up, and stared into that calm gaze.

"Listen," he said, "will you go with me somewhere? Now? Will you, now?"

She was turning, reaching her right hand toward him. It found his left hand. She took it in both hands, carefully straightened out the fingers, applied the palm over the V of flesh exposed where the blouse dipped between the swell of the breasts, and pressed it there. She was smiling at him, like the slightest movement of air brightening on still water.

·   ·   ·

When they got to the state highway, Brad pulled over beyond the drugstore entrance of the amusement center called Billtown, and left the motor running while he dashed in. When he came back out he took the wheel, without a word. And she said nothing.

There was Jingle Bells. There he was, red leg and yellow leg and fairy-tale jerkin and all, doing something to a gasoline pump. Bradwell Tolliver wheeled in far to the right of the pumps. With no alacrity, Jingle Bells approached. "Yassuh," he said, idiotically.

"I'm taking my wife to a doctor in Nashville," Brad said, getting out of the car. "But she's having another attack. She's got to lie down. Right quick, please!"

"Yassuh," Jingle Bells said, "but you gotta go to the office. Mr. Burrus, he's—"

"Lie back," Brad ordered Leontine, "just lie back a minute."

At the office door, forty yards off, he glanced back. Leontine was lying back. He could not tell whether her eyes were open or shut. Jingle Bells was wiping the windshield with a motion of infinite care.

Mr. Burrus, squat as a hop-toad, fat, yellow as jaundice, bald with a few black hairs plastered with sweat to the yellow skull, lacking the energy, it appeared, to wipe away the drop of sweat that quivered in the middle of one lens of his spectacles, managed to push a registration card and pen toward the customer. Bradwell Tolliver scribbled something that looked like *Redfill Tellfer, Los Angeles,* and pushed the card back.

"Fourteen dollars," Mr. Burrus said.

As Mr. Burrus picked up the ten and five, Brad said, "Give me change for the dollar, please. My wife's having an attack, and I've got to call Nashville and tell the doctor we'll be late."

"It's fourteen," Mr. Burrus said, "no matter if'n you don't stay fifteen minutes."

"You've got the fourteen," Brad said. "All I want is change, please. To telephone."

Eventually, he got the change. The coins were slick with the exudation of the palm of Mr. Burrus. He went to the pay phone on the wall and put a coin in and faked a call to Nashville, added forty cents and when he got the nonexistent office, explained the situation to a nonexistent secretary, and hung up.

When he turned from the phone, Mr. Burrus said, "We got ice and set-ups."

"No, thanks."

"The ice is free," Mr. Burrus said. "You pays for the set-ups."

"No, thanks," Brad said, and with the key in his hand, nearly ran toward the car, where Leontine waited in her darkness, and Jingle Bells was wiping the windshield with his infinite care.

Brad handed the key to Jingle Bells, told the girl to lean on him, led her to Candy Cottage, just after Gingerbread House, and when Jingle Bells had unlocked it, introduced her there; and while Jingle Bells busied himself adjusting the Venetian blinds and turning on the air conditioner and the TV and the pink-shaded bed light, he pushed a chair to the bedside and made her sit.

Did they want the bag in, Jingle Bells asked, and Brad said, no, all he wanted was to get the lady comfortable as soon as possible, please, and Jingle Bells said, "Yassuh, cum-fer-bul."

Then he pointed to a chrome box on the little table beside the bed, a box with a red button and a slot, above which red letters declared *Quarters Only.* "Yassuh," Jingle Bells said, pointing. "Dar 'tis. Awful cum-fer-bul."

"What?" Brad demanded.

"Ain't you seen de sign out dar? Sayen how we got de fust in de South? Massage bed. 'Lectric. Dey sort of jounce and slounce. Wiggle and waggle. Git out de kinks. Ain't you seen de sign?" Then not waiting for a reply: "Know what dey calls hit? De Lazy Man's Dee-light! Hee-hee."

He gave his idiotic, handsome grin.

"For Christ's sake," Brad said, then controlled himself.

"Jes a quarter," Jingle Bells was saying. "Hit jounce and slounce and—"

"For Christ's sake," Brad said. Then: "Thank you, thank you. But my wife—"

"Make her cum-fer-bul," Jingle Bells said. "Hit 'lectric and—" Then reading Brad's face, he stopped. He took a deep breath and began again: "We got ice and set-ups. The ice, hit is free."

"No, thanks," Brad said, and thrust out a dollar bill.

When Jingle Bells had gone he stepped to the door and threw the bolt and, for an instant, leaned his forehead against the door. That fool, he kept thinking, what had that fool done, coming in here. His heart was going in a jumpy, hollow way. After a moment, not turning, he adjusted the Venetian blind to blank the big window. Then he turned.

In the middle of the green carpet, by the low, department-store *moderne* bed of yellow wood, on which was a pink chenille spread made pinker by the pink-shaded bed lamp, Leontine Purtle, who had risen from the chair while his back was turned, was standing, motionless, her hands folded at her waist. Beyond her, across the room, the poorly adjusted TV set was flickering black and white and uttering voices which sounded as though coming, distantly and desperately, from mouths slowly settling into mud.

For an instant he could not believe that he, Bradwell Tolliver, was here, in this room, in the Seven Dwarfs Motel, in Tennessee, with that afflicted and scarcely known female who waited so patiently in that electric-blue skirt, standing in those white, high-heeled shoes, much too pointed. Then, not looking at her, he crossed the room to cut off the TV.

As he leaned toward the TV set, he heard her voice. "Where are you?" it said.

"I'm just turning off the TV," he said.

He started toward her, got nearly to her.

"Brad," she said then, softly.

"Yes?"

He had stopped there. Something had made him stop there. He could hear the purr of the air conditioner.

"Do you mind?" she was saying.

"What? Mind what?"

"Mind—I mean, mind going, while—"

She stopped.

"Oh," he said, "sure."

"It's just—" she began.

"Oh, my darling!" he cried, "don't you fret."

He felt tears spring to his eyes.

He went into the bathroom, and shut the door. He stood there, thinking how he had called her his darling. He began to undress, still thinking how he had called her that. His motions felt slow and numb, his heart bruised, ripe, and full, like fruit ready to drop.

He stood, naked now, at the basin, and leaning toward the mirror, touched his fingers to his face. In the mirror he watched his fingers explore the face. He shut his eyes and felt the fingers moving on flesh and wondered what the fingers were telling him about that face.

He opened his eyes and saw the face and thought of all the things and the years that were behind that face. He sat down on the edge of the tub and stared down at the bathmat of the Seven Dwarfs Motel, pale green with a brown-clad dwarf fishing, but he did not see what he was staring at.

For Bradwell Tolliver, at that instant, was not here. He was leaning on the window ledge of his old room at home, a thousand years ago, a boy—how old? fourteen, fifteen?— in the middle of the night, staring into the spring moonlight that fell over the silver river and all the land beyond, where drifts of white mist tangled the hedges; and his heart had been sore with tears of delight that could not be shed.

But now, as again he touched his fingers to his face, he knew where he was. And who he was. There had been a promise in that moonlight that spread over all the world westward without end. Where had that promise gone? For one instant he seemed to hear a pounding noise, muted like hooves, far off, on hard turf in the dark; but knew, all at once, that that was only the beating of blood in his head. Slowly, he decided that there must be a way toward quietness.

Something could be redeemed. Everything could be redeemed.

He rose and ran water into the basin and picked up a pale green washcloth with a brown dwarf on it, and began, slowly, to wash himself. He was thinking, with deep calmness, what life could become. He could marry Leontine Purtle. He could build a house high up, looking westward over the lake. He could take care of her, and when her foot was set on the strange stone, her hand would be in his.

When he came out of the bathroom, she was in bed, lying on her back, very still and straight under the pink chenille, as though trying to be as small and inconspicuous as possible, her eyes closed. The pink bed lamp was on. He approached the bed, very quietly as though not to wake a sleeper, and folded back the pink chenille. Then he saw how neatly her clothes were folded and stacked on the chair be-

yond the bed. So she would know exactly where everything
was. He was overwhelmed by pathos and protectiveness.

He looked down at her. Under the single sheet that,
drawn very even, scarcely molded her form, she looked
smaller than he had imagined. Her hair had not been let
down. He leaned over her and drew out the pins and spread
the hair evenly over the pillow. While he was doing this, she
began to smile, but with eyes still closed; it was a faint, inward smile, like that of a sleeper who smiles in a good
dream. He came to the left side of the bed, the side he preferred, and slipped himself, carefully, under the sheet.

He lay on his back, not touching her yet, not even near
her, thinking of drifting, side by side, down a gentle current.
He knew, as clearly as though he could see the actual fact,
that her arms lay by her sides, palms upward; and after a
minute, he reached over to take her left hand and drew it to
him and laid the palm over his mouth. He began to kiss the
palm, very gently. The fingers were light on his face. Under
their touch he wanted to drift. If you just drifted you would
drift into some calm place where you would lie side by side,
out of the current, and the current would go past and carry
with it everything that had ever happened, like the trash
and plunder sluiced away on the crest of a freshet.

After a while he rose on his right elbow, carefully replaced her hand by her side, and as she lay in that gentleness, he leaned over and began to kiss her mouth. There was
just the liveness of the mouth. That was all he wanted now.
He looked down at the parted lips, which were waiting for
the next kiss. He brought his own mouth close, but not
touching, and held his breath, and let her breath, while she
lay motionless, play against his mouth.

When he had stopped kissing her, he lifted his left knee
and drew the sheet taut like a tent and with his right arm
anchored the cloth over their heads. They were inside the
tent, and the world was outside. In the pale light that filtered
through the cloth, he looked at the body lying there, with all
its slendernesses and fullnesses and roundness and taperings
and whiteness, motionless except for the slight rise and fall
of the bosom. Under the tent he reached out his left hand,
touched a forefinger to the upper swell of the right breast,
and traced the curve down the narrowing, gracile sweep of
the waist to the swell of the right hip. His hand was shaking. He felt that his breath was not coming right.

Then he saw the scar. It was, clearly, the scar from an appendix operation; expertly done, old, healed. There was only the faintest line and slightest pucker against the motionless perfection that glimmered opalescently in that dimness. Suddenly, even to his own surprise, his left hand was laid across the scar, and the fingers and thumb had thrust cruelly into the belly, grasping a handful of that softness.

"Oh!" she cried out. "Oh!"

And reflexively her right leg had jerked up, the knee swelling to its roundness, the lower part of the leg out beyond at an angle, heaving the right hip up as though she were about to thrust herself toward him, under the tent.

Even as he said, "Oh, my darling!—oh, I'm sorry, I'm sorry," everything was changing. Time was, all at once, a succession of breathless instants, totally separate, brilliant, mindless, mindlessly fulfilling themselves like a dream, in a separateness that had no meaning beyond the individual instants: until the meaning exploded coldly into consciousness at the instant when that first long, slow, unremitting, dilating penetration and thrust, which had been as effortless as a dream, struck the diaphragm.

In that cold burst of awareness in which everything had exploded into meaning, he felt his erection sag. "For Christ's sake," he was saying.

And she was saying: "Don't you like me—don't you like me—"

Then, saying that, with the hint of a wail coming into the words as the breath suddenly seemed to give out—the wail being, as it were, the answer to the question that in the wail ceased to be a question—she was desperately arching herself up to receive his full weight inwardly, and was bringing the soles of her feet up to touch his lower thighs in a motion that feathered and then gripped, then did it again, then again.

It was, he knew in that flash, all going to be OK.

He got his right hand into a mass of that loose hair and drew it down under her neck, drawing her head back so that the throat bulged whitely upward. He got his left hand under her right knee and slipped it until the knee hooked in his bent elbow to cant her at that slightly cross-grained, chiseling, arrogant angle. He hunched his head down and set his mouth against the white bulge of the throat.

OK, he would rock her to sleep.

He realized that she was saying something.

She was saying, oh, slower, slower, oh, slow.

"Who the hell is running this show, girlie?" he demanded.

It was well after five when they came out of Candy Cottage and passed Gingerbread House, toward the Jaguar. Jingle Bells was leaning on a gasoline pump. Nobody else was in the parking area, where now some shade crept over the blazing gravel.

By the time Bradwell Tolliver had established the girl in the car, Jingle Bells was carefully polishing the right headlight. Brad came around the front of the car. "Thanks," he said, and automatically reached toward a pocket.

But Jingle Bells was grinning at him, not idiotically now, and was whispering: "Tell me, Mac, how do you like blind tail?"

For an instant Brad froze, staring at him, at that direct, non-idiotic grin.

"You bastard," he said, "you bla—"

He did not finish what had been about to be said. Jingle Bells, with a motion like a flick of a cat's paw, had knocked him down.

Lying on the hot gravel, Brad reached to touch the numbness of his right jaw, glared up at Jingle Bells, who still wore that non-idiotic grin, then scrambled heavily to his feet, and started forward.

Jingle Bells danced back in his boxer's crouch, grinning. "Skip it, Mac," he was saying, in that teasing whisper, in which there was no trace now of that idiotic accent. "Skip it, Mac—I'm high-rated in Golden Gloves, Mac."

And before the other's heavy, methodical advance, Jingle Bells fell back, gracefully weaving with the tiny tinkling of bells.

"I'm telling you, Mac," he was whispering, "you better skip it. You're too old, Mac—you're old."

Bradwell Tolliver slowed, stopped. Then, after the second in which he had been frozen to immobility, he moved again, veered off to the right, past the poised figure, and moved steadily toward the office. Jingle Bells fell in behind him, a little to the left, whispering.

"You can't get me fired," he was whispering. "I'm already through. My time is over at six P.M., I take my pay, I'm long gone for Chi."

Brad kept moving, the gravel crunching under his weight.

"Oh, you can call the Sheriff, Mac," Jingle Bells was whispering. "Sure, he'll take me in. But listen, Mac, lynching is out of date—in a progressive state like Tennessee. So they'll try me, Mac. In a court, Mac, and I'll subpoena that blind tart and—"

Bradwell Tolliver turned on him, but the other danced back, dropping into the crouch, grinning.

"Easy, Mac," he was whispering. "Let us have no *bêtise,* no *stupidaggine*—pardon me, I mean no Southern chivalry— for really now, your friend Leontine—"

Bradwell Tolliver stood heavily, and stared blankly at him.

"Sure, everybody knows Miss Purtle," Jingle Bells said. "Lots of boys, it would seem, like blind tail. And you, Mr. Tolliver—sure, I know your name too—just tell me, Mr. Tolliver—"

Bradwell Tolliver looked into the grinning, very handsome face that was now leaning toward him in conniving intimacy, bright as gold where the leveling sun rays struck it. Then he swung his gaze away, over the expanse of blazing gravel where shade was encroaching, over the bluff beyond where late sunlight struck the high limestone and cedar, over Gingerbread House and Candy Cottage and all the rest of the fantasy, over the big sign where Prince Charming in pajama tops was forever leaning over his well-endowed young companion, over the sign advertising the electric massage mattress and the Laz-ee Man's Dee-light, about which Bradwell Tolliver now felt he knew a good deal, over the sign where the enormous minstrel-show black face was forever uttering the words:

BREAKFAST SERVED IN COTTAGE
TENNESSEE SMOKED HAM AND RED GRAVY
YASSUH BOSS!

He turned, began to walk back toward the car.

But Jingle Bells was at his left shoulder, with that whisper: "I'm just curious, Mr. Tolliver. Tell me now, man to

man—you know, across the color bar and all that jazz—just
tell me—"

Then Jingle Bells wasn't there any more. Brad was now
nearing the car, where Leontine, seated, was leaning, to the
right, gripping the door, very white in the face, calling softly,
over and over: "Something's happening! Oh, I know something's happening—what's happened, what's happened?"

Then as she caught the crunch of his foot on gravel:
"Brad—oh, Brad—what is it, what is it?"

"Calm down," he said quietly. "It was nothing much. Just
an argument about change. And"—he paused, stepping into
the car—"they were right."

He swung the car off the gravel, on the cement, west.

"Yeah, change!" he said. "Yeah, that's a great one."

He repeated the word *change,* and began to laugh. As
he laughed he felt like both the laugher and the laughed-at.
But he was glad that somebody could laugh.

Mortimer Sparlin, who was Jingle Bells, stood and
watched the white Jaguar whirling away, westward. He
stood there in the late light of a summer day in Tennessee,
in the last flush of his exaltation, feeling blood beat in his
ears, his stomach feeling empty and light as air, a strange
acrid-sweet, metallic taste, like the odor in night air after an
electric storm, in the saliva that he kept swallowing. When
the car had disappeared, he walked toward Candy Cottage
and entered. He clicked the bolt behind him.

He flung himself, face down, across the twisted sheets
under the pink light. He had not noticed the object lying
damply on the far pillow under the pink light, the object
which Bradwell Tolliver had bought at Billtown and had prepared but had found no occasion to use.

Mortimer Sparlin closed his eyes, and knew that the exaltation was gone. He did not know what was left. He pressed
his face into the sheet where the odor of flesh and the occu-
pations of flesh faintly lingered. He thought of falling into
blackness, for he did not know what was left.

Yes, he did know what was left: the fear. The fear was
not of anything in the world. It was of something in himself,
and he did not know its name. He did not know what it was,
but lying there, he knew that it was in him. He thought:
Something is going to happen.

He heard the purr of the air conditioner, like the sound

of something in distance getting ready someday to happen. He heard his heart hammering.

Mortimer Sparlin, twenty-four years old, of winning personality and personal dignity, as all his letters of academic recommendation declared, was an extremely able student of the romance languages. After a degree with honors at the University of Chicago, he had come for a year at Fisk University, the famous Negro institution in Nashville, and the home of the Fisk Jubilee Singers, who have performed before crowned heads, because a professor there had done certain work that interested him and, incidentally, because he wanted to know what it felt like to be a Negro in the South. Now he knew.

It felt like being himself.

But that was all over. In two weeks he would be flying to Rome on a fellowship at the University of Rome. He had thought that everything would be different in Rome.

Now, lying on the bed, under the pink light, his face pressed into darkness of the now-stilled electric massage mattress, he was shaking with the thought that he himself would not be different in Rome. In Rome he would be himself, and that was what was happening to him and would happen to him forever, and, oh, he was not sure that he could bear it.

As they rolled westward toward Parkerton, at an easy sixty, she, breaking a silence that had lasted since they swung away from the Seven Dwarfs Motel, said: "Brad."

"Yes?" he said, squinting into the low sun.

"Brad," she said, shy and hesitant like a child asking for praise, "Brad—I sort of fooled you, didn't I?"

"You sure did, girlie," he said.

After a little she drew closer and leaned against him, awkwardly because of the bucket seats. She drew his right arm around her shoulder and drew the hand down and got it into her blouse. She laid it on her right breast. She parted the forefinger and the second finger and slipped the nipple between them. Then she pressed the fingers together, then released them. She did it three times. She was very methodical.

"You can play a little," she said, whispering, "if you want."

The hand lay there for a moment.

"It's hell driving into this direct glare," he said then. "Maybe I better keep my mind on my business."

While he gripped the wheel with both hands, she still leaned against him.

"Maybe," she finally said, "maybe you could come and get me in Parkerton, to take me home. On Friday."

"That's swell," he said.

"I'll give you the telephone number of my girl friend."

"That's swell," he said.

After a little she lifted her head and straightened up. "Don't you like me any more?" she said.

"I like you just fine, girlie," he said.

His voice was, at that moment, thick with emotion, because Leontine Purtle was Leontine Purtle and Bradwell Tolliver was Bradwell Tolliver, and that was all there was to it. He even hoped that she would believe what he said.

Chapter

28

ABBOTT SPRIGG, with his belly against the inner edge of the counter of the You'll Never Regret It Café, was reading the theater section of the Sunday edition of the New York *Times.* He habitually kept the current issue under the counter and when there was no customer, as there usually wasn't, he pressed his belly against the counter and devoutly read, over and over again, what was printed in the theater section.

That is, he would read it if Old Man Sprigg, his father, who owned the café and did the cooking, did not see him and invent something for him to do. Or worse, come out and say how you would think a fellow who had been up there in New York City with all them Yankees and fruiters and found he was no good, would not want to be reminding his-self of how he was no good by paying out hard money to buy a paper to read about them as was. Or Old Man Sprigg might look at the belly that strained under the once-white jacket and ask who, outside of a circus, would pay money for a ticket to see a tub-o-guts full of chess pie and beer, the chess pie and beer being all the profit of the You'll Never Regret It Café which he stole and et up, get up there on a stage in New York City and show off.

But now Old Man Sprigg was back in the kitchen, sitting on a stool with his head propped forward against a chopping board, and Abbott Sprigg was reading the theater section when Bradwell Tolliver came in and ordered a hamburger, rare, and a beer. "Have one yourself," Brad invited, and the fat boy drank a beer with him while the hamburger was cooking.

Abbott, with the offhand air of one pro talking it over with another pro, said that he had just been reading in the *Times* how costs off-Broadway were inhibiting the artistic spirit. "Now, when I was working," he said, "there was real artistic spirit off-Broadway. There was integrity."

He lifted his head and stared down the counter, through the glass, out into River Street, where the summer dark was coming on. The face he lifted was strangely double: there was the face of a handsome boy, with dark, glowing, anguished eyes and very glossy black hair and skin pale and smooth as marble on the brow, but over it was hung, somehow, the face of a fat man with cheeks and throat sagging, the color of warm tallow. Now Abbott Sprigg held his head up with an air of heroic conviction, and the glowing eyes stared out of the tallow, into a distance.

"Yes, sir—integrity," Abbott Sprigg repeated, almost in a whisper.

The hamburger was ready. Brad had another beer and invited Abbott to join him. Abbott, with the new bottle in hand, leaned his belly against the counter and spoke in a low tone. He said that when he left the West Tennessee State Normal at Memphis and went to New York to go on the stage, he had started out in the wrong spirit. He said he had always tried to impose himself on a role. He said he was glad he had had to come back to Fiddlersburg and stand behind the hash counter, for here he had watched the people come in day after day. He said he had at last learned what it took to be an actor. He said it took humility. He said it took com-

passion. He said he knew that now. He repeated the word
humility several times. He repeated the other word several
times, too.

Brad ordered apple pie and coffee, and Abbott Sprigg
came back and leaned closer, pressing the belly even more
painfully against the inside of the counter. He said—now in
an absolute whisper—he wondered if Mr. Tolliver would
speak to Mr. Jones about him. He wondered if Mr. Jones
could let him read a scene. He wondered if, when they made
the flood movie, Mr. Jones would give him a test.

Brad wished the bastard would not lean so close and
breathe so hotly. He could not look at the bastard because
the bastard's eyes, behind their dark glossiness, were full of
naked pain. So he drank his coffee and said nothing.

Abbott Sprigg was saying that when they flooded out
Fiddlersburg, his father was not going to work any more. His
legs were bad from standing up so much. He was old enough
for Social Security. He said he himself had come back from
the stage in New York just to be of some comfort to his father
when his mother passed away, but as soon as his father retired he was going to start over in New York. Now he knew
what it took to be a great actor. It took humility. It took compassion.

Brad got up. He had not said a word. He picked up his
check and paid it. He looked, then, at the fat man-face in
which the dark, glossy, beautiful boy-eyes were near to tears.
All at once, like a wave of nausea, the pity was in him.

"Listen," he said, in a voice that sounded like anger,
"I'll do what I can. I'll speak to Yasha. Let's hope for the best.
So long."

"Oh, Mr. Tolliver," Abbott Sprigg was saying, moving
down the counter, trailing him toward the door, "oh, Mr.
Tolliver! I'll really try! I'll give my all, Mr. Tolliver—I won't
let you down, Mr. Tolliver—"

Brad saw that now the eyes were really glittering with
tears. He felt he had to do something to get out of here. So
he thrust out his hand, over the counter, and they gravely
shook hands. Before it could start over, he made the door.

He stared at River Street, in the last dusk, and lighted a
cigarette. He wished that that pity, which was like nausea,
would go away.

He did not know that, in the long perspective, the pity
would be totally superfluous. He could not foresee the day

when, several years later, he himself would pick up the theater section and read a lead article about a new comic who
was scoring a great hit on Broadway. It was an actor who,
"exploiting fatness and fecklessness, in a deep awareness of
the frustration and courage to be seen in the daily world
around us," had, according to an eminent reviewer, developed "a heart-wounding, heart-warming blend of laughter
and tears."

Not being able to foresee that, Bradwell Tolliver looked
back once into the lighted blankness of the You'll Never Regret It Café, made his way to the old steamboat landing, unlocked his boat, got the outboard into operation, and swung
out into the river, downstream.

By now he was not thinking of Abbott Sprigg. He was
thinking of Bradwell Tolliver.

He was thinking how Bradwell Tolliver had left Leontine Purtle with her ghastly divorcée girl friend, who had
lived in Chicago and wore black lace stockings and waved
that ghastly fake-jeweled eight-inch cigarette holder; and
how he would never see Leontine Purtle again.

It was night now, starlight but no moon. The shores
were dark, and the river, on each side toward them, black;
but the mainstream, sliding slick and unmarred ahead,
seemed to gather and give back what light there was, like a
blade in shadow. Brad looked back over his right shoulder
and saw the sparse lights of town, and above them, on the
hill, the black bulk and the searchlights of the penitentiary.

Then he faced downstream. Far off, to the left, he could
make out now the reach of deeper darkness that was the
swamp woods. A little later he spotted the glow. It seemed to
be hanging in the darkness of the woods. He began to cut
in. He drew in slow, and lay quietly rocking some yards off.

"Hey!" he hailed. "Frog-Eye!"

"You, Brad?" the voice came out of the shadows to one
side of the glow.

"It's me."

"Come on," the voice called, somewhat thickened and
blurred.

Brad swung gently to the shantyboat, tied up, stepped
aboard. The woman crouched beyond the glow of the home-
made brazier—an old dishpan with holes punched in the
bottom and set on bricks. She was gently shaking the skillet

over the heat. The grease made a popping sound. Then Brad
discovered Frog-Eye, a shadow propped in the shadows of the
shanty itself.

"Hello," Brad said to the shadow that was Frog-Eye.

Then turning toward the woman: "Smells good."

"Cat," she said. "Cotched him this af-noon."

"Cain't you cook hit no faster?" Frog-Eye demanded.

"Hit's nigh done," the woman said.

"Set and eat some catfish," Frog-Eye invited.

"I'll set," Brad said, and squatted against the shanty,
"but I've done et."

The woman put a slab of catfish on a big tin plate,
poured some fry-grease over it, put on a corn pone and a tin
fork, and brought the plate to Frog-Eye.

"Set hit down," he commanded, and picked up a jug
from the shadow beyond him. He turned to Brad. "Mebbe
you done et," he said, "but you ain't done drunk, you kin still
walk. Heah."

He passed the jug over.

"Don't care if I do," Brad said, with the word *care* shad-
ing toward *keer*. He took the jug, stuck his right thumb
through the handle, rolled it over the crooked elbow, slowly
elevated the elbow, and drank. It was not quite as much like
ignited coal oil as he had feared.

"Pretty good," Brad said, and passed the jug to Frog-Eye,
who drank, belched, said, "Hit'll grow ha'r on ye," set the jug
by, picked up the tin plate, slipped a switch-blade from a
pocket, snapped the blade out, and with the point dissected
a chunk of catfish. Ignoring the fork, he deftly speared the
chunk and got it to his mouth. He broke corn pone into the
fry-fat. To get this he used the fork.

The woman brought him a tin cup of coffee and set it
by him. Brad declined coffee. The woman went back to
crouch beyond the brazier. Brad slapped at a mosquito.

"Fix the fahr," Frog-Eye ordered.

The woman began to lay on damp wood. The glow died
down somewhat. In the motionless air the smoke hung
around them, curling idly in the remaining light. Back in
the swamp there was the grind and whirr and tingle of the
myriad life of that darkness.

The woman, crouching by the fire, was opening a tin
can. When the time came, she brought it to Frog-Eye and

took the empty plate. Frog-Eye wiped the blade of his knife on his trousers, and speared a half of a peach from the can, got it into his jaws. Then he drank some of the juice.

The woman, again by the fire, was eating now, crouched and abstracted.

"How's the kid?" Brad asked her.

She did not seem to hear, moving her jaws in a small, slow motion, staring into the brazier.

After a moment, Frog-Eye said: "He ne'er taken a-holt."

He had given up the knife for the tin fork now. With that he got a half-peach to his mouth. The woman was now looking at them across the smoke-threaded glow.

"If'n they make hit acrost one summer," she said, "mebbe they make hit. But he got the flux." She returned her gaze to the brazier.

"Got a piece of peach left," Frog-Eye said to her, "and some juice. Come git it."

"I done had a sufficiency," she said. "Thank you kindly."

The whirr and tingle came out of the swamp darkness. Now and then, back in the darkness, a bullfrog made its deep-bellied, bronze-hollow sound, then the grumbling gum-grind like the ocean, far off, grinding the shingle. Frog-Eye passed Brad the jug. Then Frog-Eye, in turn, took a deep drag.

"Hit'll make ha'r grow," he said, and belched.

After a time in which no one had spoken, Frog-Eye passed the jug again. The woman rose and moved silently, on bare feet, to lean over the side and wash the tin plates, cups, and skillet in the river. Then she said she reckoned she would lay down. Frog-Eye said for her to fix the fahr. Having done so, she slipped past them, silent as the coiling smoke, into the interior darkness.

By midnight, the jug made a hollower sound when you sloshed it. Frog-Eye had slid a little further down the shanty boards against which he had been propped. He held the knife in his right hand, and now and then would push the button and watch the steel flick out to catch what light there was. Now, when the fire needed fixing, it was Brad who fixed it.

Once, when he came back to squat by the shanty, he said: "I been reading about the trial. The record they took down in court."

For a moment Frog-Eye did not seem to hear. Then he flicked the blade out, and staring at it in the new glow of the brazier, said: "He give it to her under them bushes."

"That was the testimony," Brad said, shortly.

"Hit was them big fla'hr bushes," Frog-Eye said.

"Hydrangeas," Brad said. "That late in the season they were still blooming."

Frog-Eye passed the jug; Brad drank, then Frog-Eye, a long deep drag. Frog-Eye set it by and stared across at the smoky glow. His hand held the switch-blade, and now and then the button was pressed and the steel leaped forth. But Frog-Eye, staring at the glow, did not look down at the blade.

After a while, not turning, speaking in a voice thicker now, more blurred, he said: "That-air music, hit got hung some way that night, and hit kep on sayen the same fool thing, over and over. You and yore woman, you done gone by then, you draggen her off. But him—that feller what got kilt —what's his name?"

"Alfred O. Tuttle," Brad said. "They called him Tut."

"Tut," Frog-Eye muttered, as to himself, and seemed to slide a little further down the shanty wall, staring at the glow of the brazier.

"That-air music," Frog-Eye said then, "hit got hung some way, and that feller stopped dancen 'round with her, with yore sister. They jes stood thar. Then he give off a moanen lak he was sick, er sumpen. He was a-holden her, but not to grip. Hit looked lak he was 'bout to fall down."

He was silent again, seemed to slide lower, still staring.

"Yeah?" Brad said, very softly.

"He ne'er taken her to grip," Frog-Eye said, in the cloudy, slow, distant voice, "not fer me to see, no-way. He jes sort of taken her arm, up toward the shoulder, and hit nigh looked lak he was picken her up by the arm lak hit was a hantle. Hit was nigh lak he was picken up one of them teacups by the hantle and toten hit careful not to spill. Looked lak her feet wasn't more'n touchen the floor. He taken her to the door. It was lak she sort of floated in his hand. He taken her down to them bushes. I knowed he war slippen her the bizness. I knowed he warn't in no shape to wait. But she ne'er made air sound. Naw—naw—"

His voice drifted off. He sank in upon himself, shutting his eyes.

"Yeah?" Brad whispered. "Yeah?" He felt as though something was pressing on his chest.

Frog-Eye roused.

"Yeah," Frog-Eye said, "I crawlt acrost the flo'hr, then I hear'd 'em. But nuthen to brag on. Jes rustle and breath, not no man-noise ner woman-noise. But hell, I ne'er seen 'em. Not I keered, to speak on, fer—"

Brad heaved up to his knees and reached over and seized the man by the shoulder and shook him.

"Look here," he commanded, "look here—in court you swore you were drunk and sound asleep, passed out. You swore you didn't see a thing."

Slowly Frog-Eye turned his face to him. The glow of the fire made the sweat on the face gleam red. Then the wide frog-mouth, chinless and with the pendulous flesh below, twisted into a grin of slow cunning, and the bulging eye narrowed.

"Yeah," Frog-Eye said, "but that was in that-air co'ht."

He sank again upon himself.

"You were awake?" Brad demanded, shaking him.

Frog-Eye slowly turned his head.

"Shore," he said, "I was a-layen thar. Lak I was sleepen. But I was squinchen out and I seen. Yeah," he said.

He paused, turned his gaze to the glow of the brazier, then resumed, the voice more blurred, more misty, more distant.

"I seen folks dancen," he said. "I seen 'em a-prancen and switchen they butts. I seen that red-head one sashayen and a-switchen her butt. She had a butt on her."

He paused, resumed.

"I seen you dance her nigh me. I seen what you done nigh me in the dark. I seen you a-foolen with her. Her pullen off and you grabben fer a soft holt, and foolen. Yeah."

He was sagging down the shanty wall. Brad shook his shoulder.

Frog-Eye stirred, his eyes opened.

"Yeah," Frog-Eye said, "I seen you a-foolen. One of them times nigh me the music was stopped, and I hear'd her breathen."

He was no longer looking at Brad.

"Yeah," he was saying, "and I seen you a-draggen her off. I knowed what you was aimen to do. Did'n look lak she hankered, a-pullen back. But you—you was hell-bent or bust a hame. She was bar'foot now. I seen her a-goen bar'foot, you a-draggen. A-goen in."

He resumed: "Then that feller what got kilt. Him and the little one. I crawlt acrost the floor, and hear'd, but shucks, she warn't nuthen to me. Did'n have no butt on her. Did'n have them long limber laigs. Them long limber laigs, they gits on a man's mind."

He stared at the sinking glow.

"They was long and limber-lak," he was saying, and the voice drifted off.

"Wake up, damn it!" Brad said, kneeling over him, shaking him.

"Yeah," the blurred voice began, "and I crawlt acrost the flo'hr and in the house. I taken off my shoes and set 'em down by the pee-anny. It was dark up them stairs and I did'n aim to make no racket."

"You—" Brad began, staring down at him. He wet his lips with his tongue and began over. "You," he said, "you came up there?"

"Hit gits on a man's mind," Frog-Eye said. Then rousing himself, he turned and looked directly into the other's face. "Don't hit?" he demanded.

Brad turned his face away, toward the dark river.

"I come down the hall," Frog-Eye was saying. "Hit was dark. I ne'er knowed what do'hr, but I felt along. I did'n aim to make no racket. I ain't ne'er one to make no racket. I would come to a do'hr and open hit. I come to the one. I opened hit."

"God damn it!" Brad said, swinging back at him, seizing him, shaking him. "You opened that door?"

The face, duller and more distant now, the big eye glazed and not glaring, turned upward at him. "Hit gits on a man's mind," the voice said.

"You—" Brad began, again.

But the face had fallen away. The voice was coming from a depth.

"I opened the do'hr," the voice said, "and thar was some light. Hit come in the window and I seen. She was layen on her back and a sheet acrost. You—you was layen thar on her arm, layen crooked on yore side. Yore arm was laid acrost her belly, on top the sheet. You was gone out, drunk and a-sleepen. You was puffen heavy with yore mouth open.

"I was standen thar. It was lak I did not know how I had done got thar. I looked down and I seen my knife in my hand. I seen the blade, and hit shinen in that little light comen in. I ne'er knowed what I was aimen to do. Hit comes on a man and he doan know. Hit was them long limber laigs gits in yore haid.

"I stood and hit looked lak I was a-comen in. I mought of had to cut or stob. To of cut or stobbed you."

Brad heaved to his feet, and stood sweating in the shadows of the shantyboat. He heard the man's breath below him, in the darkness. The body had now sunk down so far that only the head was propped against the boards of the shanty. Brad leaned over the body. "Why didn't you?" he demanded, whispering.

He shook the man, and the bulging eye, like the eye of a frog, came open to stare up at him, a dull glitter in the dimness.

"Why didn't you?" Brad demanded.

"Yeah," the man said, with an effort, "yeah. Must of been a cloud come off the moon. Of a sudden, light come strong in that room. The light laid of a sudden acrost her face. Hit looked lak I was comen on in, but the light come and I seen her eyes was open and tears comen down. Of a sudden, I knowed I was not goen in."

The voice stopped. The head had slipped entirely off the shanty wall. That eye, which was like a frog's, was closed. But, very dim and drowned and sad, the voice came again. "Naw," it said, "naw—I ne'er went in."

Brad stood there sweating. Then the voice came again, more dim and sad: "If'n I went in—I mought of—I mought of cut or—"

The voice died off.

"God damn it," Brad cried out, "I wish you had!"

He struggled with the constriction in his chest and got control.

"I wish to God," he said, now, in a dry whisper, "I wish you had stabbed me to the hollow."

There was no answer. The man's breath down there was a heavy, puffy sound, like a bubble in mud. Brad lifted his gaze to the woods. He heard the whirr and tingle of the life of the swamp darkness that seemed to fill the world.

He looked up at the sky. The Bear had now sunk below the darkness of the swamp woods. Vega, west-northwest hung high and bright. That whirr and merciless grind swelling from the swamp darkness seemed to fill the sky up to all the stars.

He stood there sweating because now, suddenly, he could remember all the events of that night which he had never before, over the years, been quite able to remember. He saw them all in his head.

The woman came out of the dark of the shanty. Looking down at the man, she said: "He done out?"

Brad nodded.

"I can't tote him," she said. "Nights it gits him a-fore he gits inside, I got to let him lay. Keep the fahr goen fer the skeeters. Hit is all I kin do."

"I'll help get him in," Brad said.

They managed to get the body inside and to a bed. Brad stood in that intenser inner darkness and breathed the fetid air and thought he was going to faint. Then he pulled himself together. "I better get on," he said.

"Naw," the woman said, "you ain't in no shape fer the river."

He was trying to pull himself together.

"You kin lay yander on the cot," she was saying.

"Thanks," he said, "thanks, but I'll just sit in the air awhile."

He made the door, got out, lowered himself against the boards of the shanty. The woman stood in the dark door of the shanty and looked down at him. Without turning his head he knew that.

"One thing you find out," she said.

"What?" He still had not turned his head toward her.

"The world," she said, "hit is swole with trouble. Hit is swole lak a blood blister. The world, hit ain't nuthen but a muckle and a lavish of trouble."

She had gone back into the shanty. Again without turning, he knew that. He looked up at the stars and tried to name what stars he could. But that grind and whirr and tingle from the dark swamp seemed now to come from inside his head.

So, after a while, he reached for the jug.

Chapter

29

WHEN BRAD NOSED HIS OUTBOARD in by the slip the next day, it was going dusk. He locked the chain, and walked up the old stone ramp. A man in a white suit—the whiteness sudden against the dingy and unlighted buildings of River Street—stood at the top of the ramp, staring westward, beyond the river, where the last color was fading in the sky.

"Hello," Blanding Cottshill said, "how you making it?"

"Terrible," Brad said. "I've been drinking with Frog-Eye."

"That would be a lifework," Cottshill said.

"I was just drinking with him one night," Brad said. "But it nigh killed me. The stuff he drinks. I couldn't stir till afternoon. Then I just stirred to vomit."

"It's about all he does now," the other said. "A shame, too." He paused, then resumed. "Yes, one of the best shots I ever saw, but he shakes so much now he couldn't hit a barn. You know that big fancy duck shoot I told you about? Well, I give another kind of shoot just for my own special pleasure. Say the twenty best guns I know, any kind anywhere. Irrespective. Hell, I've had a brace of senators, a banker, a retired admiral, and Frog-Eye, all cozy. Even three or four colored. Put 'em off at another table to eat, though. A sort of alcove. Put 'em in a couple of separate blinds, too.

"But Frog-Eye—I've had to drop him. Drunk before they rowed us out to the blinds."

He was looking out over the river now.

"Did you know," he said, "they've closed the gate of the dam? Nobody can tell it yet, but the water is rising. It rises so slow."

Brad looked at the river sliding past, in midstream yet showing some last red of the west. He said nothing.

"This fall," Blanding Cottshill was saying, "it'll be my last party."

"Where are you going to relocate?" Brad asked.

"Been thinking about Scotland," he said.

"Scotland?"

"Wonderful grouse shooting. Stag. Fine fishing."

"Sounds fancy," Brad said, and wished his head would stop throbbing.

"No, it's just I like those Scots folks. Ever since I was liaison with a Scots regiment in 1918. Been back three times."

He fell into thought.

Then: "Anyway, I think I'll clear out of here. Not get mixed up in things. In all the changes. When they open Lake Town there'll be big trouble about mixing whites and blacks in the school. Federal money in the school and all that. They're laying low now, waiting for Lake Town. And you know—"

He stopped.

"Know what?" Brad asked.

"They'll be asking me to take the case."

"Who?"

"Who you think? Brother Pinckney *et al.*"

"Would you?"

The man was studying the sky. He seemed not to

have heard. Then he said: "It's not I give a damn about being popular. I am not in the popularity business. And it's
not I'm afraid of any son-of-a-bitch. It's just I feel old, all of a
sudden. Just I don't want to get mixed up in things any
more." Then he added: "Maybe it's just I'm mixed up inside."

He paused, meditating.

"You know," he resumed, "a man can be mixed up more
than he knows."

He turned and looked up at the darkening hulk of the
penitentiary, where, just at that instant, the corner searchlights had come on.

"You know what night this is?" he demanded.

"No."

"This is the night they give the juice to Pretty-Boy. Unless," he added, "the Governor commutes."

"Will he?"

"Hell, no. Hasn't got any grounds. Pretty killed the pore
old woman. He beat her head in with a claw hammer. A new
hammer that was just lying to hand there in the store. Then
he couldn't stop beating. It is bloody murder. But if you are
a lawyer, you go through the motions. Like I tried the head-
doctors. Pretty is not crazy, not in any legal sense. He is
simply crazy in an extra-legal sense. It is the same extra-
legal sense the whole God-damned world is crazy in. But
Pretty, being provincial, is just Tennessee-crazy. So Tennessee, being Tennessee-crazy, is going to burn him."

He turned suddenly on Brad, as though in anger.

"You know why I'm standing here?" he demanded.

"No."

"Because I am trying to get myself ready to go up there
and tell the pore murdering, tear-drenched, blood-stained,
irrelevant and immaterial, illiterate banjo-picking black bastard goodbye."

After the other had gone, Blanding Cottshill continued to stand there a long time. He knew that he had a long
time to wait. He stood there and wondered how long the
time would be seeming to Pretty-Boy. He wondered if Pretty-
Boy would make it, as they said, unassisted.

For he was thinking how, after Brother Pinckney had
brought Pretty-Boy to prayer, there seemed to be nothing in
Pretty-Boy. Except the tears that would come out until the
eyes were dry. "Look at my trousers," Brother Pinckney

would say to Blanding Cottshill, late every afternoon when he came by the office, "they are soaked with tears. Every day, like today, he holds my knees and weeps."

Brother Pinckney, sitting there one afternoon, in the office above the deserted square, had said: "I do not want to blaspheme, but I have removed something from him and given him nothing. There is nothing left except the tears that soak my trousers until no more will come."

Remembering this, Blanding Cottshill stood in the gathering night and tried to get ready to go up the hill. Finally, he began to walk up. If he went in his car he would get there too soon. He comforted himself with the thought that if Pretty-Boy made it to the chair it would be quick once he got there.

Halfway up the hill, he stopped. He seemed to need the breath. He thought how he was getting old. He looked over the roofs of the town, south, up-river, over the land, and thought how this fall would be his last duck shooting up yonder at his place. He stood there and felt a flicker of that elation you feel as the ducks come in, high over the black woods, out of the buttermilk sky of dawn, uttering their cry. He felt his eyes swim with tears. There was, he thought, nothing so beautiful.

Then it was different.

It was, suddenly, all different, and what he saw, in his imagination, in a dawn sky, was the swell-out of parachute silk. He saw the dawn sky bloom full with that whiteness, and he thought his heart would break; but not with joy.

For they had just picked him out of the sky. Far below, the guns had boomed and they had picked Tad Cottshill out of the sky. Blanding Cottshill saw the astonishing face in the air. He saw the body hung in the harness. And he cried out, asking was it quick, was it quick, oh, God, was it quick? Was it as quick as Pretty-Boy?

After a time he moved on up the hill. He was thinking that he did not know whether he would have a duck shoot that fall. He was thinking of blood. He was thinking of all the blood he had seen in his life.

Then he stiffened himself, a short man with wide square shoulders and a too-big head, a white-clad figure in darkness, moving on up the hill. *God damn it,* he said to himself, *I know the way the world is. I have lived in it.*

Further on, as he ascended the stone steps to the big

gate, it occurred to him that he would not have to live in that world forever. He tried to sort out what he felt about that fact.

Bradwell Tolliver had driven south on River Street to the edge of town before he stopped. He drew the car to the side of the road and thought of Blanding Cottshill going up the darkening streets toward the pen. He thought how he himself had had the notion of attending Pretty-Boy's send-off party. He could still make it, he reflected. There was plenty of time. Mr. Budd would let him in.

He felt a sudden flare of excitement at the idea of going. He owed it to himself. It was a thing he had never seen. Not this kind. He ought to see it. He was a writer, wasn't he?

Writer, he thought.

And thought: *Shit.*

And thought: *On all writers.*

Then he turned and looked back toward town. In that long perspective there was a space far beyond and well above the roof of the Rexall store, where, under the night sky, you could see the shadowy hulk of the prison; and there under a light blazing down in darkness from above the arch of the great doorway you could see, even at this distance, the wide, stony sweep of stairs reaching down to the upper road. Now he fixed his eyes on that space. That lighted space seemed to float in air, above the dark roofs.

It was a long time before he saw, in the night, a patch of white that would be Blanding Cottshill enter the space. The spot of white waited a long time before it began to go up the stone steps toward the great door, under the light. The light beat down on the long steps the patch of white was ascending; but above the light, filling the sky, there was dark- ness. At last the patch of white disappeared into the dark doorway.

Brad Tolliver sat there in the Jaguar and was over- whelmed by rejection and envy. He felt rejected by life. He envied the man who had a reason to go up the hill and up those stone steps and enter that dark door. He had no rea- son.

As he drove on slowly toward the house, he grew gradu- ally aware, as from a distance in which sparse snow was falling, that, in the moment of excitement when he had thought that he himself might go up to the pen, the face he had seen, in his mind, with the black hood poised over it, was not that of Pretty-Boy at all. Beyond the falling snow of his inner vision, the face he was now aware of was the face of Jingle Bells. But even though the black hood, held by anonymous fingers, was poised above the face of Jingle Bells, that face was grinning triumphantly at him through the streaky whiteness of falling snow.

Slowly, he lifted his hand to touch the soreness of his jaw, where the fist of Jingle Bells had been laid.

Well, he thought, *just getting knocked down by a nigger doesn't bring on the vision.*

It seemed, in fact, that Brother Potts was right: you had to arrange to have him spit in your face. Then you had to refrain from wiping the spit off. You had to let it dry there, in God's sun and wind. He should have taken the whole matter up with Jingle Bells. With that thought he felt like laughing.

Then he didn't feel like laughing.

He felt tired and weak. He thought of the likker he had drunk last night. He thought of lying on the boards of the shantyboat and staring up at the stars and trying to name their names. Well, he'd go on to the house now, and get something to eat out of the Frigidaire to settle his stomach, and go to bed. He did not want to think beyond the going to bed. He did not want to think of morning and the getting up.

Now the cemetery was on his left. He thought how he had not located the grave of Old Izzie Goldfarb. He thought of Izzie Goldfarb sitting in the split-bottom chair in front of his tailor shop on River Street, a thousand years ago, looking westward with his face calm and the last light striking the thinness of the skin over the thin bones of his face. He wondered why he had not found the grave.

He would make one more try, he decided, tomorrow.

An owl kept calling up yonder in the woods, on the ridge.

When he entered the dark hall, he saw light falling through the wide arch of the dining-room entrance, toward the back. But it was far too late, he knew, for anybody to be back there. It must be near ten now. But he did not look down to inspect the luminescent dial of his watch. He did not want to know how long it would be until midnight.

He stood in the hall and felt the emptiness of the house.

The emptiness was palpable, like a dense but invisible fog that condenses coldly on the cheek, in darkness. The night was hot, it was a night in July in West Tennessee, but he stood there and felt that dark emptiness of the house weigh down and condense coldly on his cheek, like fog.

But the house couldn't be empty. For one thing, the old lady was bound to be upstairs, and Maggie never left her alone; if Maggie went out, Irene, the cook, or somebody, stayed. There was bound to be somebody upstairs. Then he thought that the old lady herself was just another kind of emptiness. She was part of that invisible fog that filled the house. Irene, too—she was just part of that emptiness. He knew her name, Irene, but the name was all he knew—that and the brown thumb on the white plate proffered him, the thumb with the too-white half-moon in the nail. All at once he remembered that the name meant peace. *Irene* meant peace. Then, with a dry twist of the mind, like lips twisting, he was thinking, hell, peace was emptiness too, wasn't it?

He went down the hall and entered the dining room. The bracket lights on each side of the mantel were on—that was all the light there was—and the crystal prisms glittered. Despite that light the room was full of emptiness, too. He felt like a diver who, with monstrous gear—the helmet nodding like a nightmare, the trailing cords and pipes, the shapeless, swollen gray body, the lead-weighted feet—enters a chamber long submerged. It was as though emptiness were not a negative, it was a positive, and it was like a flood that had filled the house. He felt how it was, how the house, the town, maybe the world, had been flooded long back, and here he was, in that gear out of nightmare, moving in painful, lead-footed retardation into that room.

Then he saw it.

It was a big envelope, propped on the mantel, boldly across the face of the bronze d'oré Louis XVI clock. A bud vase, or something of the sort, held it in place. Though at that distance he could make out nothing, he knew that the name on the envelope was his own.

When he held it in his hands he did not open it, not immediately. He read the name, which was his own. It was, he knew, in Maggie's hand.

To the right side of the clock, a satyr, all gilt, sat on a gilt stone and piped on a gilt pipe. To the left side, a nymph, gilt in her delicious nakedness, trailing a gilt scarf in the terror of her flight, was about to be overtaken by another satyr, gilt too. Looking at the gilt figures, Bradwell Tolliver felt as though a sudden eclipse had blotted out a sunlit green meadow.

In looking from one side of the clock to the other, in that moment of delay before he opened the envelope, Bradwell Tolliver had, he realized, made his eyes drop to avoid the face of the clock. Then he remembered that he did not have to avoid the face of that clock. The clock had been stopped for years. He couldn't think whether it was broken or just nobody gave enough of a damn to wind it.

The clock said 4:22, but nobody, nobody in the world, knew what day it had stopped, whether it had been daylight or dark. He thought of the clock on the courthouse down town, and thought that nobody knew what day it had stopped either, whether daylight or dark. The world was full of clocks that had stopped, and nobody knew or cared.

Pretty-Boy—they would stop his clock.

He opened the envelope and took out the sheet of white typing paper. In Maggie's hand, in pencil, it read:

Dear Brad—

I am going away tonight with Yasha. We will be back tomorrow or the day after. I reckon it is foolish to go away—we could stay right here—but you will understand.

I would have told you before if there had been anything to tell. It was a long time happening and I was afraid to believe it was happening. Till today, in broad daylight, and it was like going blind from too much light.

Maybe I am still afraid. Maybe I am afraid that I can never be anything except what I have been. But, Brad, you are my own dear Brother. Will you please help me hope that everything is all right? Help me be happy.

Love,

Maggie

P.S. We waited till now—it is 9 o'clock—hoping you would come in so we could tell you face-to-face. I have arranged everything for Mother Tolliver. Irene will stay and take care of her so you won't have to bother.

M.

He looked at the date on the top of the letter. It said July 2. That was yesterday. Well, they weren't back yet. Hell, he probably wouldn't see 'em for a week. She had some time to make up.

Holding the sheet of paper in his hand, Bradwell Tolliver lifted his head and felt an elation seize him. For a moment, it felt like joy in her joy, and this fact in itself was a joy, a reduplication in a sudden bright clarity, like a mirror. He stood and marveled at that fact of his joy in her joy.

Then something happened. There was still the elation, but now it was not the out-going joy in her joy, it was the in-going joy of vindication. By God, he had tried, hadn't he, to make her break out, kick over the traces, do something! That was what they had quarreled about, long back, when he came home with the busted knee, out of the war. Well, she had kicked over now. She was human, too.

He felt the vindication. It was relief. Her whole life had been, for nearly twenty years—no, forever—one long accusation. The fact that she had never said a word to him, that was the worst accusation. Her whole way of being had been accusation, louder than words. And worse, far worse, than words, for words would specify. Her accusation, not specifying, was, therefore, total. Whatever it was. It had always been there.

But it couldn't be there now. For she had kicked over the traces.

Yes, and even she had had to get out of the house to do it. She hadn't been able to take on Yasha Jones in this house. In this house she would have lain in the dark, on a bed, and been frozen, and if the body of Yasha Jones had pressed upon her, and within her, dividing her, that would have been only, merely, part of the weight of darkness and emptiness that filled the house and cut off breath, emptiness entering emptiness, darkness entering darkness. It was vindication and relief to think that she, even she, had had to escape from the house.

Then he was standing there and shivering in the hot night of July in Fiddlersburg, and thinking that he, he himself, had never, in spite of all the years of flight, escaped from the house. He felt the weight of emptiness and darkness now, above him and around him in the house. Then he thought, suddenly, that the light was dimming in the room.

He looked at the bracket lights, on each side of the

mantel, first one then the other, at the bulbs within the dangle of crystal. He was sure that the light had dimmed. And he thought: *They're giving it to Pretty-Boy. That's the jolt for Pretty.*

But—that was impossible.

It was not on this circuit.

No, it was just that big, old, outdated Frigidaire out in the pantry switching on.

Anyway, the time was not right. It could not yet be midnight, the hour of the juice.

As far as the dimming of the light was concerned, he then remembered, they wouldn't dim even in the pen, even at midnight. That was superstition. Without foundation in fact. If anybody, in the pen or out, had to wait for lights to go dim to know that Pretty-Boy had got the jolt, they would never know.

Just then, thinking that, he noticed that the sirens, far off yonder on the hill, were screaming. He realized that they must have been screaming for some time. He had been hearing the noise without knowing that he was hearing it. It was as though that far-off screaming on the hill had been part of his own feeling, and had had no existence in the world outside. Even now, if you let your mind wander away from it, it was more like a feeling inside than a sound outside.

Then he heard the closing of the screen door, at the front of the hall.

Chapter

30

RIGID, with the sheet of paper in his hand, Bradwell Tolliver knew that the footsteps were coming down the hall. Then he identified the footsteps, the footsteps of two people.

He had a vision of Maggie's face, an instantaneous flash. It was as though her face were floating in the darkness of air, the face shining like light muted in alabaster. She was smiling at him.

In that instant as he heard the steps approaching down the dark hall, he felt as though a cry were mounting in him. The cry was a cry of yearning; he yearned for that joy in her joy to come back to him. He felt that as soon as she appeared in the door that cry, which was now stranglingly suppressed in him, would break forth.

Then she, with Yasha, was standing there in the broad archway that gave from the hall, she in a short-sleeved dark gingham dress, he in creaseless flannels and a seersucker coat. It was a hot night, and the dome of his skull looked slick. Brad studied them as they stood there, with the blackness of the hall behind them.

They stood there as though they had, just that instant, strolled in from the evening in the garden, down by the ruined gazebo, simply as though it were bedtime and they had just come in. The only thing that was different was that they were holding hands. They did not stand close together—they seemed too shy for that—but their hands reached across the space to make contact.

Brad stared down at the clasped hands, then into their faces. It was as though he were waiting for them to speak. But he was not waiting for that. He was waiting for something to happen in himself.

Maggie began to smile at him. But the smile seemed weak and without message. It was as though the smile were bleeding off at the edges, its force draining away into the surrounding darkness of the hall faster than it could be renewed from within her.

"We wanted to tell you," she said.

"That's OK," Brad said. He was waiting for it to happen: the joy.

"We waited last night," she said, "but you didn't come in."

"No, I didn't come in."

She dropped Yasha's hand and came toward Brad. She stood before him, then reached out and touched the sheet of paper he held, then withdrew the touch.

"I meant it," she said.

"Meant what?"

"That you are my dear Brother," she said.

He looked down at her face—how calm it was!—and felt the cry of yearning mount in his throat to the point of pain. If he could utter it, that joy in her joy would come true. The sirens, he realized, were no longer screaming off yonder in the dark.

"Kiss me," she said, and offered her cheek.

He leaned to kiss her. The touch of her cheek made him know that his lips were cold, cracked, and harsh. The lips, he discovered, had no sensation in them. They were something affixed to his face. He thought: *The lips aren't mine.* He lifted his head. His tongue, he was aware, had come out to wet the lips as though they were his and were real.

It had not happened. The cry had not been uttered. That cry was still locked deep and strangulated in him, trapped in its pain. The joy had not come. It would never come.

He stood there, still holding in his hand the sheet of paper which was her letter, and knew that the lips were going to say something. He felt something piling up and throbbing inside his forehead, he felt a thickening in the chest, and he knew that the lips were going to say it. They were going to say whatever it was that was piling up inside his forehead and thickening his chest. He felt the lips move.

The lips were saying: "Yes—yeah—I know. I know now."

The others were staring at him.

He thrust past his sister and went to stand directly in front of Yasha Jones. Behind Yasha Jones was the darkness of the hall.

"You thought I wouldn't know," Bradwell Tolliver heard the lips saying, and he waited, hypnotized and appalled, ignorant and, at the same time, fulfilled in a knowledge that was swelling beneath the ignorance. He waited for what the lips would say next.

"Know what?" Yasha Jones demanded.

Bradwell Tolliver felt the laugh hack up through his throat, felt the flesh of his face twist appropriately into the foreordained expression, felt the lips drawn back stiffly to emit the sound.

Then the lips were saying: "You assumed that I would not know why you rejected my story. My story for our beautiful moving picture."

"For God's sake!" Yasha Jones burst out, then stared at him. Then in a controlled, careful tone: "I rejected the treatment because I did not, and do not, think it worthy of your best talents. If I did not think those talents great I would never—"

"Be that as it politely may," Bradwell Tolliver heard his lips saying, "you scarcely seem to think that I have much talent for even elementary inference. In 1944 I began a novel that was concerned with—that was suggested by, shall we say—certain events in Fiddlersburg. And my sister, discovering this—"

He was delighted at the calmness of the voice that was coming from his lips. It was as controlled and careful as the voice of Yasha Jones had been. And he was delighted at the logic of what he was about to say. He did not know what he was about to say, but already he felt the calm awfulness of its logic. Already he felt—rather, some part of the self that had nothing to do with what was being said, felt—the delight of a mathematician in the elegance of a demonstration. Enraptured, he heard the words the lips were uttering:

"—and being distressed at what she considered a public exploitation of a private shame, persuaded me to—"

"Oh, Brad!" she had cried out and was coming toward him, across the room.

He turned toward her, with exquisite courtesy, feeling the courtesy as exquisite.

"Oh, Brad," she said, standing before him, "I was wrong, I was foolish, I was weak, and I'm sorry I did it. But I've told you I'm sorry and now—"

"Don't be sorry," his lips were saying, "for you sent me away from this garbage dump which is Fiddlersburg to learn the craft of making beautiful moving pictures, and I was well paid for same, and now at last have earned from Yasha Jones—your, I assume, prospective husband—the encomium of *expert* with all the rights, privileges, and contempt thereto appertaining. Yes, and that fact—being an expert— is why I am again being sent packing from Fiddlersburg. But there's another reason, too—for though Yasha Jones alleges that I, being crassly deafened by the clamor of mere factuality, cannot catch in darkness that delicate beat of the mothwing of feeling which is truth, the real reason—

He leaned at her.

"—the real reason, it is you!"

Her eyes were staring wide at him, and it seemed a long time before, even in that small, wintry voice, she could say: "Me!"

Then, in a smaller voice: "Me?"

"Oh, yes," he said gaily. "And how logical! Because of the subject of my treatment."

"But I told you," she said, "I told you I was sorry about stopping you then—back then—but now I don't care what you put in a story."

"Sure," he said, "that's what you told *me*. But what did you tell him?"

And he whipped a forefinger toward Yasha Jones.

"But—" she managed, "but I didn't tell him anything."

"Tell—the word *tell*," he said calmly, and stared down at her from a dispassionate distance. "Let us drop that word," he began. "Let us, my dear Maggie, substitute *indicate, suggest, communicate.* I did not even mean to imply that you proposed, consciously that is, to—"

"Brad—" she said.

The word was scarcely audible, but he stopped.

"Brad," she said, in that whisper, "you are my dear Brother."

She was standing before him with her arms hanging down by her sides, against the dark-colored gingham, the palms turned slightly forward, her face lifted, the light glinting on her hair drawn smoothly back, showing a few strands of gray. Her eyes were wide, and full on him. The face, with the light falling from behind it, looked very still. But then he saw that the lips were quivering. He saw the tears gathering in the wide brown eyes that stared up at him.

Then he heard the voice of Yasha Jones. The voice said: "Brad." Hearing it, he felt, with a burst of relief, that a cord had been cut. He could turn toward that. He could turn from the face of the woman who was staring at him out of those eyes in which the unshed tears were bright.

Yasha Jones had come fully into the room, and was now standing by the rosewood table, his back to the mantel. The light from the electric fixtures there gleamed on the bare skull. "Brad," Yasha Jones said, again.

Then, as Brad turned toward him, he said: "We shall use your treatment. Let's make that definite."

"Going to bail her out, huh?"

"There's nothing to bail her out of," Yasha Jones said.

"A concession, is that it?"

"Not a concession," Yasha Jones said. He paused meditatively. "No," he resumed, "not a concession. That would be insulting. But watching you now, in this strange, deep—forgive me—irrational anger, I have realized that perhaps your deepest feeling—the feeling that now finds form only in anger—may emerge on the basis of the treatment you have prepared, when you have developed it. All right!" he exclaimed. "All right—not elegy, but anger."

Bradwell Tolliver felt absolutely cold, absolutely paralyzed. He felt the blood beat in his head, but the sound was

far away, as in the darkness of a cave. He felt, suddenly,
blank and deprived. He tried to speak, but his lips would not
move. He felt that if they would move, if they would only
move, then they might say something to break the icy spell
that bound him.

Yasha Jones was saying: "There will, of course, be
changes, developments. There always are from this stage.
But they will be your own. We'll have plenty of time for—"

There was a slight sound, and they turned toward the
archway to the hall.

For ten seconds, in absolute silence, they stared at him.
Maggie had slowly raised her hands to her face, a hand symmetrically to each side, the fingers just touching the cheek
on each side, to frame the face from which the eyes stared
at the man in the gray denim coat. She made the first sound.

"Cal," she said.

There was no intonation. The word was a flat sound in
the air.

But the man in the gray denim coat did not turn to
that sound. He stared at Yasha, who was now standing in
the ample space between the rosewood table and the east
wall, ten feet from him, facing him. He ignored the others.

The man ignored, too, the nickel-plated revolver held
loosely in his own right hand. The hand hung loose at the
end of the slack arm, hanging out of the tube of gray denim
encasing that arm. The hand seemed to be no part of him.

The sirens, far off in the dark, were screaming again.

"The sirens are blowing," Brad said, and looked at the
man in the gray denim coat.

Calvin Fiddler cocked his head as though to listen into
distance. His graceful crest of gray hair was the color of
the denim. The high-arched face, lifting as though in cour-
teous attention, was gray, too.

The sirens stopped. There was silence. Then the silence
was not silence, but was the small grinding sound of the
July flies in the trees out there in the dark, like a nail file
delicately and insistently busy on a nerve end. Calvin Fiddler was again staring at Yasha, whose face was slightly
shadowed, for the light from the wall brackets at each end
of the fireplace was behind him.

"You said you'd have plenty of time," he said to Yasha.

"Yes," Yasha replied, and took a casual step toward him, as though to engage in conversation.

"Don't come any closer," Calvin Fiddler said. "I don't want you any closer." Then added, as though in explanation: "I reckon I never did like people coming too close."

Yasha did not take another step. He stood quite easy under the gaze, but Brad could see that his knees were bent, ever so little.

"You're a physicist," Calvin Fiddler was saying.

Yasha laughed, in deprecation. "A student of physics," he said. "A long time back."

"Don't fancy physicists have to think a lot about the nature of Time?"

"So I'm told."

Calvin Fiddler studied him. Then said: "But I'm only a doctor—" He paused, shook his head slightly. "Was a doctor," he resumed. "And doctors aren't scientists like you, they are not long on theory, like you pure scientists. But—"

Yasha had moved, ever so slightly.

"Don't come any closer," Calvin Fiddler said.

He seemed to fall into an inner depth. Then shook himself. "But—" he resumed. Then stopped.

"But what?" Yasha Jones asked, softly.

The man lifted his head, coming out of himself. "But," he said, "even if I am not long on theory about Time, I have had plenty of it. I had near twenty years to think about it."

"Yes?" Yasha asked, and leaned in attention.

"Don't come any closer, please," the man said, a note of pleading in his voice.

"You said you had plenty of time to think about Time," Yasha said, with interest. "What did you discover?"

"Only what you may think a truism," the man said. "But it is not. Listen, and I'll tell you that time is the measure of life and life is the measure of time, and if you have not sat all day and all night and tried to measure those—those incommensurables—to measure them by each other—then you don't know anything about them. And not anything about yourself."

Yasha Jones was nodding ever so slightly, in grave, abstracted agreement.

"Do you know what I mean?" the man demanded, his

gaze probing the face of Yasha Jones. The light from behind
gleamed on the high bald skull, which was slick with the
heat of the night.

"Yes," Yasha Jones said, finally.

"No, you don't," Cal said peevishly, as to a stupid pupil.
"You don't know a damned thing. If I could only tell you.
No, if I could invite you into my private laboratory, which is
vulgarly called the pen, and let you submit yourself to the experiment which I—"

He stopped, and pondered.

"I think we all know something of that laboratory,"
Yasha Jones said softly, "and it is not called the pen. It is
called—"

Far off, the sirens were screaming now.

"The sirens are blowing," Brad said.

Calvin Fiddler listened for a moment. The sirens
stopped. He turned again.

"Called what?" he demanded, of Yasha.

"The self," Yasha answered.

Calvin Fiddler shook his head, again peevish, saying:
"Listen, if you have sat day and night and tried to measure
against each other those things that are not commensurable,
you yearn for that one instant when—to twist the way the
Bible puts it—the incommensurable shall put on commensu-
rability."

He leaned at Yasha, demandingly. "Do you know when
that is?"

"When is it?"

"At that instant when both of the incommensurables
cease to exist but have not yet begun their nonexistence.
Tell me, Mr. Jones—yes, Mr. Yasha Jones—don't you, even
in your uninstructed way, don't you yearn for that moment?"

Calvin Fiddler's eyes glittered. His body stiffened. "Answer me!" he commanded, harshly, his courtesy gone.

Then he recovered himself. He seemed embarrassed,
overwhelmed, by his own discourtesy. "I'm sorry," he said. "I
talk too much." He paused again. "I didn't come here to
talk," he said, brusque again.

All of a sudden Bradwell Tolliver was laughing. His
body shook with laughter, his mouth opened in the heavy
face that was streaked yellow with fatigue and nausea, the
sound came out of the mouth, and he pointed at Calvin
Fiddler. Then, pointing at him but addressing Yasha Jones,

he managed to say, in the midst of his laughter: "And it all comes true—Yasha!—it all comes true!"

Calvin Fiddler was staring at him in a painful curiosity.

But the laugher, with the sounds rattling like phlegm from his throat, paid him no attention. "Yeah, Yasha Jones," he was managing to say, "you threw my story away, you said it didn't matter what way things have a way of happening—wasn't that what you said?—but what do you say now, Yasha Jones?—for it's all coming true!"

Yasha Jones said nothing.

It was the other—Calvin Fiddler—who caught up the words, echoing them, to himself, as though trying to interpret them to himself, in a voice that was, somehow, both bemused and agitated, saying: "True—coming true."

Then he looked down again, in a painful curiosity, at the right hand, which held that nickel-plated object. For a second, the July flies, out in the dark, were quiet.

Then he jerked up his head, and burst out, "Yes, yes—a coming true!"

Then he leaned toward Yasha, speaking in a harsh, quick voice that was, however, low and confidential, saying, "Yes, Mr. Jones—back yonder when I first found out about you and Maggie—that was just a coming true of something I had always known would come true, and twenty years ago that Sunday morning when I was riding up from Nashville to Fiddlersburg with all that junk piled in the car and that painted tin wastebasket with that stuff crammed in it, with that—"

He stopped, seemed fuddled, then went on: "But you wouldn't know about that."

"About what?" Yasha Jones asked, softly, leaning a little.

"All right!" Cal said, very excited now. "All right, let it all come true! Now! Now!"

Bradwell Tolliver looked down and saw the nickel-plated revolver quiver.

"Cal," he said then. His voice was casual.

Cal looked at him.

"Cal," he said, "remember back yonder when we were kids? In my workroom with the Erector set, and the stuffed birds and animals? Don't you remember?"

Calvin Fiddler nodded, slowly.

"Well," Brad said, "remember that time I was stuffing that big old coon?"

Calvin Fiddler nodded.

"Well," Brad demanded, almost in a whisper, leaning, "which hand was it I smeared full of those slimy old coon brains?"

The man with the graceful lock of gray hair over the gray face looked down at his hands, first at one then at the other. He fixed his gaze on the right hand. He turned the palm somewhat upward, and let the fingers go loose. The nickel-plated revolver lay loose in the palm as he looked down.

It was then that Bradwell Tolliver heaved his bulk at him, with a clumsy, fatalistic, uncoordinated motion, like a brick chimney undermined.

Bradwell Tolliver had not forced down the hand with the nickel-plated revolver before there was an explosion. Then, as he did force it down—or rather, as his weight, as he hung spasmodically to it, dragged it down—there was another explosion.

Then he let go.

Before the scream could get out of Maggie's mouth, before Yasha could make more than one leap toward him, Calvin Fiddler had let the revolver slip from his hand. It lay on the floor by the body. He was standing there, staring down at the body, when Maggie's scream did come, when Yasha leaped. But Yasha stopped at the end of his second leap and, with hands out as though to grapple, was, in that instant, frozen to stillness.

For Calvin Fiddler had suddenly dropped to his knees by the body. He rolled the head slightly—the body was lying on its back—and thrust his right thumb firmly under the jawbone, where the blood came out. "A fountain pen, do you have a fountain pen?" he kept demanding, idiotically.

Then Yasha Jones found the pen—a cheap plastic ballpoint—in his seersucker coat.

"Break it," Calvin Fiddler commanded. "Break it, I want a tube. Hurry!"

Mixed with the sound of the July flies was a faint wheeze and gurgle.

Yasha worked at the pen. The strong, thin, brown fingers worked methodically. Something got unscrewed, he inspected what he had, he put the other end into one side of his mouth and bit. He had a tube now. "One end is jagged," he said.

Clumsily, with his left hand, the man crouching there got the smooth end of the tube into the hole in the left side of the wounded man's throat.

"Get down here and hold it," he ordered.

Yasha Jones crouched to hold the tube, but Maggie was at his side, saying, "No, no, I'll hold it—oh, I've got to hold it."

"No, Maggie," Calvin Fiddler said, very calmly, "let him hold it. You know more about local things, so you get on the phone and get a doctor and an ambulance as soon as possible. Listen carefully now. Explain that the injury is a penetrating wound of neck. Mass of venous bleeding. And a tracheostomy. I need an emergency set of instruments and suction machine. And hurry that ambulance. Can you remember that?"

"Yes," she said. "Yes—tracheostomy."

"Tell them to have hospital emergency ready. Tell them to get here fast. There's no telling how long we can hold on."

She ran toward the pantry, where the nearest telephone was.

"The other wound," Calvin Fiddler said to his assistant, "the way he's lying it looks like the femur is broken. Some venous hemorrhaging, but not decisive. When Maggie gets back she can apply a tourniquet."

It was not until Maggie had risen from adjusting the tourniquet that she saw the old woman standing in the shadow of the hall a couple of paces beyond the door. Maggie knew, with perfect certainty, that she had been standing there a long time.

She went out to her in the shadow. She put her arm around her. Not resisting, wordless, the old woman allowed herself to be led away.

Book
FIVE

Chapter

31

"RECKIN I'M WALKEN YOU TOO FAST," the guard said, and slowed his pace.

"Maybe," Brad said. He stopped, planted the ferrule of his stick firmly in the gravel, let his right leg go lax. He felt the sun—hot enough, even if it wasn't yet summer—come through the fabric that hung so loose on him now, and prickle his skin. His bones seemed, for a moment, to be floating free inside the flesh, as though the bones had got too small for the flesh, even as the flesh had got too small for the clothes. Despite the sun, the bones felt cold.

He had, he thought, been a damned fool not to hire a driver in Nashville to bring him out here, instead of getting the U-Drive-It.

Then, in the inner darkness of himself, as the black beast heaved at him from some corner of deeper darkness, he thought: *Why the hell did I come here anyway?*

Then thought: *What was there ever here for me?*

And with that thought, even while the sun burned on his shoulders, he felt now, deep inside, the very breath of that blackness blowing cold on his innermost soul.

But he had learned that you can learn to live with anything, and had, in the long months, come to a grim acceptance of that black beast with cold fur like hairy ice that drowsed in the deepest inner dark, or woke to snuffle about, or even, as now, might heave unexpectedly at him and breathe upon him. No, he had come to have more than acceptance; in the long nights in the hospital in Nashville, with nothing in the white cell of a room but the night light, as dim and cold as a bit of fox fire, and no sound, not even the swish of a starched skirt in the corridor, not even the sibilance of a rubber sole on tile, he had even come to have an affection for that black beast. For in the hours before dawn the beast, weary with its own heaving and snarling, would lie down beside him and snuggle, as though trying piteously to warm itself from whatever warmth there was in Bradwell Tolliver.

So now, propped on his stick, by the canna bed—the canna leaves still pale, slick as cellophane, and just coming to shape, no buds yet—with the April sun prickling his shoulders under cloth, Bradwell Tolliver swung his gaze over the big courtyard, over the brick walls, the squat corner towers, the sky itself; and wondered why the hell he had, in fact, come.

And the guard, an unformidable, pot-bellied, middle-aged man in greasy blue, chewing a toothpick, was saying: "You gonna be cripple for good now?"

"No," he said, "the doctors say it'll get all right."

"How many times he shoot you?" the guard asked. "Three, warn't it?"

"Twice," Brad said.

"One kin do it," the guard said, and sniggered, and took out the mangled toothpick from his lips and inspected it. "A guy shoots you," he said, "and now you goen over and buddy up with 'um." He sniggered again.

With what might have seemed an excess of caution, as though propping up a too loosely charged croker sack, Brad let himself down on the bench across from the canna bed. The guard swung his butt around, about to drop it down to the bench.

"You needn't wait," Brad said. "I know the way."

He took off his old panama hat and lifted his face to the sun and closed his eyes. After a moment he heard the feet of the guard on the gravel, moving sullenly off. With the sun on his eyelids, he saw the color of his own blood against the light.

The room faced south and the light of an April morning poured into it; the man's back was toward the light. Bradwell Tolliver could not, therefore, see the face as clearly as he wished. The graceful crest of gray hair was, he decided, grayer—nearly white now—but he wanted to see the face. He sat there and wondered if he wanted to find—or if he was afraid to find—a change in that face that had, after so many years, become merely the face of a boy gone gray.

He controlled the impulse to reach up and touch his own face. There was no use, anyway, to touch it. He needed to verify nothing. He knew how the flesh now sagged at the jawbone, how it was tensed back at the corners of the mouth and the eyes.

He sat there and thought how every man is an index to you and you are an index to every man. Index faces index. But the indexes are incommensurable, he thought, remembering what Cal had said that night about things incommensurable. He stared at Calvin Fiddler.

Calvin Fiddler: who sat there smiling in a timid, embarrassed, boyishly appealing way, holding his hands flat on his knees, moving the long fingers ever so slightly on the white duck of his trousers. Bradwell Tolliver wished that Calvin Fiddler would say something. But he himself could think of nothing to say. They had shaken hands, and said hello—just that, hello—and sat down into that silence which was the completeness of their knowledge of their history. Or was it, Brad asked himself, the silence of their complete incapacity for that knowledge?

"Look!" Calvin Fiddler suddenly said, and jumped up from his chair, and gestured about the bright room. "Look what I've got here. Bet there's not a better little lab at Johns Hopkins."

"It's swell," Brad said.

"And come see the dispensary," Cal said. And led the way down a corridor, and into the next door, where they admired the dispensary, and then back into this room of bright glass and chrome, where the sunlight poured.

They stood there for a moment, again trapped in that silence. Then Cal, making an abrupt, aimless gesture quickly broken off, merely an abortive jerk of the right arm, said: "I guess you know why I was showing you round?"

"No."

"Because," he said, "I couldn't think of anything to say." For a second he sank into himself. Then: "It's funny, after writing you, getting you to come up here, feeling it was terribly important, I don't have anything to say. Maybe I ought never have asked you to come."

"Well," Brad said, "I'd have come anyway."

And he knew, all at once, that he would have.

"Why?" Cal was asking.

"To thank you," Brad said, grinning heavily. "For saving my life."

"It's a funny world," Cal said, "where a man shoots you and then you thank him for saving your life."

Then Cal was staring, probingly, into his face: the diagnostic stare, the stare of judgment. It was a look Brad had never seen on that face.

"But," Cal then demanded, that probing stare still there, "is that really why you would have come?"

Brad felt himself diminished under that probing stare, and did not know why.

"Listen," he said, gruffly, "there's only one way I can answer your question. Let us be objective. Let us make our minds innocent. This scene—between you and yours truly—is, as we say in my shop, mandatory. It is a must. The necessary confrontation. Symmetry calls for it. An inner logic demands it. Let us, poor human puppets that we are, surrender to the symmetry, to the inner logic, and words will spring unbidden to our lips. Meaning will evolve from—"

He stopped, abruptly.

"Christ," he said. Then: "I know that this is not a story conference. I know that this is the real thing. It is L-i-f-e."

"The only one we've got," Cal said, very softly.

Brad stood there in his heaviness. The leg was hurting.

"Sit down," Cal said. "You oughtn't to crowd that leg."

Brad sat down on a chair. He watched the other man move to a table and fool with a pair of scissors there.

"How's Maggie?" the other man suddenly asked, fooling with the scissors.

"She's fine," Brad said. "They're living on some isle of Greece. In the Aegean. Yeah, in a shepherd's hut and reading Sophocles. At least, Yasha is reading Sophocles—in the original, I warrant—while with one hand Maggie fans the fire of twigs with a dried gull's wing to make it burn and with the other stirs the soup with, very probably, a spoon fashioned cunningly from a billy goat's horn. By the way, she's pregnant."

The man toying with the scissors laid them down, then lifted his head and looked calmly across at Brad.

"I'm glad," he said.

"But to come back to the great Yasha," Brad said, "he's going to do a movie down there. Something pure in feeling and classic in form."

He heard the tone of his own voice and wished that he could not hear it. It was a tone that had once belonged to a certain world. He could not remember what that world had been.

But the voice, in that same tone, as though to spite him, went on: "You know, a sunlit masterpiece against the glitter of the wine-dark sea."

"Your movie," Cal asked, "what's happening there?"

"Got shelved," Brad said. "Then, after it looked like I was out of the woods and—"

"—and therefore, I," Cal interrupted, not looking at him, again gently clicking the scissors, "wouldn't get the chair for Mad Dog Fiddler's Murder Number Two." He paused, letting the scissors dangle from a finger, thinking. "No," he said, "it would have been Number Three."

"What?"

"My mother," Cal said.

"What the hell are you talking about?" Brad demanded.

"She died in her sleep. Two weeks later."

Cal turned full at him. "You know," he said, "when Mad Dog Fiddler claimed his first victim, twenty years back, the old lady just couldn't take it. God knows, she'd had plenty to take already, those last years, with my father on the morphine, then his dying near broke. But when I came back,

everything was going to be hunky-dory. Well, it was not
hunky-dory, and she just went dotty, dotty enough not to
believe I had done it, it was all a plot, and I would soon be
proved innocent and the guilty parties brought to book.
That was what was going on all those years in that poor old
head. But you know one thing?"

"What?"

"Sometimes even dottiness won't save you. So this time
when she stands in the dark hall and really sees me do it—
bang, bang!—she up and dies the way she would have died
twenty years ago if she hadn't struck on that artful dodge of
going dotty to keep what she would have called her faith in
her only son. So her dying now was—to use that happy
phrase you gave me that night—a coming true."

He stopped, then studied the scissors dangling delicately from a finger. Then, as though apologetically remembering his manners, he burst out: "But your movie—we were
talking about your movie!"

"Nothing much," Brad said. "When Yasha pulled out, it
got shelved, like I said. But just yesterday"—he was aware
that his left hand had lifted stealthily toward the inner coat
pocket to verify, as it were, the fact—"I got a wire from Mort
Seebaum—he's the producer—saying he's keen on my treatment, full-steam ahead."

"That's fine," Cal said. "Really."

But his attention seemed to wander. He looked out the
window, up at the bright sky. "The water," he said, at last,
"they say it's rising." He turned back and stared at Brad.
"Did you see it rising?" he demanded.

"Yes," Brad said.

"How high is it?"

"Not up to River Street yet."

Calvin Fiddler fell again into thought.

"They tell me," he said, after a moment, "that the house
has been knocked down. Ready for burning. Did you see the
house?"

"No, I just came over the ridge and directly here,"
Brad said. "But I thought I'd go down and take a last look."

"I wish I could go with you," Cal said. Then added: "It
might make me feel—feel free."

A bird uttered a petulant note under the windows where
the sun poured in, and Cal turned to listen. "There are
some bushes under these windows," he said. "Snowball

bushes." He paused, resumed. "They are, in fact, the only
cover bigger than a canna leaf in the whole pen. You don't
want cover in a pen. From the wall you want to be able
to interdict—you're a soldier, that's the technical term, isn't
it?—all lines of approach." He paused again, again resumed.
"Those catbirds, they come back every year."

He went to the window and looked out.

"Maybe," he said, after a moment, his back to the room,
"maybe I feel free enough without seeing the end of the
house." He waited awhile, his back still to the man sitting
there. "You know," he finally said, "as soon as I shot you—
no, maybe I ought to say, as soon as the gun went off in
my hand, for that was the way it seemed to me—"

He stopped, then swung back to face Bradwell Tolliver.

"What I mean is this," he said. "As soon as that gun
went off I knew that that—not shooting Yasha Jones—was
what everything had been moving toward, forever. To use
your phrase again," he said, "that, too, was, I reckon, a
coming true. And—" He paused. Then: "And when everything
has finally come true, maybe that's when you can feel free."

He stopped, sinking into his thought.

"But," he said, looking suddenly at the other man, "I'm
sorry about that last coming true. About shooting you."

"I reckon you had your reasons," Brad said. The room
felt cold to him. He felt the sweat drying on his body under
the cloth. Everything in the world seemed far away.

"Oh, it wasn't any particular reason—" Cal began.

"I bumped you off a football team," Brad said, and
laughed with no mirth. "Twice."

"No, not that. Not any particular reason, not even that
you took my house, took Fiddlersburg away from me, took
Maggie away from me—no, I don't mean just in the end at
that party on the porch, I mean long before, when I'd see
you and Lettice together, the way you treated her, and Maggie
would see you together, and I would watch Maggie's face, and
I would know that that was a way of taking Maggie away
from me, too—and you took—"

He stopped.

"Listen," he said, "I was in medical school, in Johns
Hopkins, and I read in the paper you'd gone to Spain, to fight,
and I almost blew it that term, busted out I mean, because
it seemed like one more thing you would have and I wouldn't.
The believing in something. So much you could go and kill

for it. Or get killed for it. No, it was just that you could kill or get killed, period. And I couldn't. Oh, I was going to be a healer. Maybe I hated you because I was stuck with being the little healer."

Under the windows behind him, the bird called again, in peevish reiteration, like a small rusty hinge. Calvin Fiddler seemed to be giving his full attention to that sound.

Then he said: "I don't mean I hate you now. I don't. Maybe I asked you to come here so I could look at you and be sure I don't hate you any more."

He paused, shook his head, fretfully.

"No," he said, "that's not the reason. For listen—listen here—that night when the gun went off in my hand and whatever it had been all those years came true, right then as I stood there and looked down at you on the floor—no, at a body, a thing that didn't seem at that instant to have any relation to you, to have no *you-ness* about it—right then at that instant, everything was different. You know—"

He paused thoughtfully, moved to the table, picked up the scissors again, and fooled with them.

"You know," he resumed, "it had got so I was afraid of doctoring, even the simplest thing. There was a man up here with a ruptured appendix and they couldn't get a doctor in time, and I just let him die because I didn't have the nerve— or something. Night after night, I'd lie up here in my cot and shut my eyes and try to see the pages of my old medical books, the way I used to before an examination. Well, at night, here in the pen, I'd see them clear as could be, just read them off in my head. But when daylight came it would all disapppear. Like mist in the sun. It would be like I was ready to bust the exam."

He withdrew into himself, letting the scissors dangle.

Then: "But as soon as that gun went off, it was different. I stood there and looked down and saw the wound in the throat, and at the same instant I saw a page in the book—the big old chunky, falling-apart, red *Anatomy,* by Piersol, the book my father had used, the book I always used because he had used it. Yes, I saw the page right there in my head, clear as day, and it said: 'Digital compression may be used in a case of stab wound or in the treatment of aneurism by making pressure backward and outward beneath the anterior edge of the sterno-mastoid muscle at the level of—' "

"Lucky you saw it," Brad said. "For both of us."

"Back then," Cal said, shaking his head, "I didn't think so. When I was waiting."

"Waiting to know whether I was going to die or not? Whether you might get the hot seat?"

"Don't misunderstand me," Cal said, not fooling with the scissors now, looking straight at him. "I didn't want you to die. It was just that I wanted to die. Even that way."

Bradwell Tolliver heaved up out of his chair.

"Do you want to die now?" he demanded hoarsely, glaring at the other man. "God damn it, do you want to die now?"

Bradwell Tolliver stood there, his breath constricted, and the question hung in the air between them; and outside the window the sky was blue with infinite distance, and one puff of white cloud hung there, and a catbird called under the window, and he did not know what answer it was he wanted the other man to make.

"Sit down," the other man said, very calmly. "Sit down, and I'll tell you."

Brad sat down.

"I was in solitary," Calvin Fiddler said. "I didn't know whether you'd live. They told me nothing. I thought I might get the chair anyway, I was present when that guard got killed in the break, I thought they might get me on that. Just a month ago they executed Bumpus—his name was Bumpus, he was a big raw-boned, red-necked bastard that I saw through the pneumonia four years ago, not doctoring him, for I'd lost my confidence by then, but carrying the bedpans and doing the nursing and all—well, it was his statement, they tell me, that kept me clear. But I didn't want to be clear. I wanted to die."

Brad stirred heavily in the chair.

"No, be quiet," Cal said, "and I'll tell you. Now in solitary, you begin by thinking you can detach yourself. That there is, somehow, a *you* different from, and above, that thing that they have put into solitary. You don't see, theoretically speaking, why you can't simply lie down, the way you'd throw an old coat down, and close your eyes, relax— die, perhaps—no, let the coat die and let the silence flow over, and the real *you* will ride on that flood of silence like a chip on water. Withdrawal of stimuli—what's so terrible about that! Why isn't it bliss? But then you find out."

Brad stirred again, opened his lips to speak.

"Be quiet," Cal said. Then: "You shut your eyes and think that all you have known in the world outside you is, quite literally, unthinkable, not to be thought. I'll illustrate. Suppose when you were twelve years old somebody had told you exactly what you would be at twenty-five—really be, I mean—what you became. It would have been not merely unbelievable, but unthinkable. Or at twenty-five told you what you would be at forty-five. It would have been unthinkable.

"In solitary you decide, well, I'll just shut my eyes, for only what you can think can truly exist. But then you shut your eyes and that thing that was unthinkable—it really does come true. It blazes up around you like a brush fire. It blazes up like spilled gasoline. It blazes in the dark inside your head. You realize in that flash that there is no *you* except in relation to all that unthinkableness that the world is. And you yourself are. So you begin to cry."

He took a step toward Bradwell Tolliver, and leaned over him. "Have you ever cried?" he asked quietly. "I mean that way?"

Brad moved his lips, as though trying to frame an answer, But the other suddenly drew back.

"Hush!" he said, as though in anger. "Don't answer me. Listen. And I'll tell you. I've got to make you understand what happened. If you won't understand then I can't be sure what happened. And I've got to be sure. You see, if I can't be sure—"

He couldn't go on. He sat down. All at once, he looked tired, but calm again.

"But then," he said, "after the unthinkableness of things, which is what makes you want to die, suddenly you feel different. I felt different. It was like knowing that life, which I myself had never had, for a nerve had got cut, or a wire short-circuited—like knowing that life, which is a sort of medium in which the *you* exists, like a fish exists in water, is beautiful. This is the queer part—that the *you* lying there crying and wanting to die suddenly knows, at the same time, that life is beautiful. Beautiful—that's the only word I can find for it, and it was funny to have that word suddenly coming true, for it had always been just a word to me, for I wasn't exactly a sunset-watcher. Too wrapped up in my own innards to look outside, I guess.

"Anyway, now it was just like seeing life like in a mirror—but nothing there before the mirror to be reflected. You might say the only thing reflected was just the possibility of something. It was as though a ghost, invisible to the direct look of your eye, could be seen in the mirror as an image, a reflection, of some sort of—of misty beautifulness."

He sat in the chair, withdrawn for a moment, and then shook his head. "That doesn't seem to say it," he decided.

Then he leaned and looked directly into Brad's face. "But if you yourself haven't had that beautifulness but you know it is there, and you are happy about the mere fact that it exists—then you have to find a way to say it."

He rose from the chair. He was very excited. He was shaking. "That's it," he said, and his tongue came out to wet the dry lips. "Yes, that's it!"

"That's what?"

"That's why I had to see you, why I had to make you come here. So I could—" He leaned toward Brad, his voice sinking as though to impart a secret. "You see, when you learn something like this you have to say it. But there was nobody here to say it to. And—"

He stopped, moved to look out the window at the sky, then back at the other, then resumed: "And when you—you, Bradwell Tolliver—get up and leave, there will never again be anybody else to say it to."

He began to walk about, deep in thought, as though the other had already gone, had been gone for a long time, and he were alone. But he seemed very calm now. He went to the workbench at the end of the room, and inspected some liquid there in a large, closed glass tube. A thermometer was sealed inside the tube.

"I've got an experiment going," he said, not looking around.

"That's great," Brad said.

"I'm doing all the doctoring in the pen now, but I've got time for this, too," he said, gesturing at two other contraptions down the bench. "I've got three going. But all on the same problem. I always had a yen for this kind of work."

"Bet you would have been great at it," Brad said.

"Guess if it hadn't been for Fiddlersburg—I mean for

feeling I had to get back here, to the place where my protective coloring could really protect, but didn't protect—I guess
I would have gone into research. Well"—he laughed—"I've
got it both ways now. Fiddlersburg, and research."

He turned back to Brad.

"Come here," he said, "and I'll show you."

Brad crossed over.

"It's the liver I'm interested in," Cal said. "Lots of un-
solved questions about the liver. Even now, from all I've been
reading lately. You see . . ."

His voice trailed off.

"Excuse me," he said, "I don't want to beat your ear off.
It would be just technical stuff. I guess you wouldn't understand all that crap."

"No," Brad said, "I guess not."

Cal came close and laid a hand on his sleeve.

"But the other," he demanded, "you understand that?"

"What?"

"What I said about being in solitary, and then—" He
stopped, he seemed embarrassed and abashed; but pulled
himself together and continued: "About things suddenly being different. You understand that, don't you?"

"Yes," Brad said, "sure."

Later, making his way across the prison yard, past the
canna bed, out to attend the farewell service for Fiddlersburg, Brad wondered what, in the tangle of things, Calvin
Fiddler would feel if he knew that a member of the legal
firm that handled the affairs of Yasha Jones, had paid a visit
to Nashville, to the office of the Commissioner of Correction,
to arrange an anonymous gift to improve the medical facilities
of the Fiddlersburg Penitentiary.

Chapter

32

BRAD SAT ON THE NEWLY SPRUNG GRASS of April, on the rising
ground of the cemetery, and stared across the road toward
the church. The crowd there was too big to get inside, and
so at the last minute they were rigging up the pulpit out-
doors. They had pulled a big flat-bedded truck sidewise to
the church door and brought out the pulpit to set on the
truck. They had even wrangled a piano up there, too. On the
cab of the truck, beyond the piano, you could see:

JACK McCOOMB
Cattle, Timber and Gen. Hauling
Fiddlersburg, Tenn. Tel. 401

Now they were tying boughs of dogwood in bloom, and
redbud, about the chassis and the cab, hiding the name of
Jack McCoomb. They were setting potted plants, palms and
century plants, along the edges of the truck bed. The men,
in their blue serge of Sunday, and their white shirts, looked
very peculiar working around a truck.

Over to one side, other men were setting up trestle tables. Women were spreading white cloths over the rough
wood, and the white cloth glittered in the sun, white as the
dogwood blooms. On the cloths the women emptied big
baskets, laid out the baked hams, the platters of fried
chicken, the chess pies, the angel food cake, the devil's food
cake, the coconut-delight cake, the ambrosia. After the
sermon and the songs and the tears, they would all eat.
Then they would weep again, and go away.

Over by the church Brad saw the wrecking crane. Tomorrow, men would dismantle the stained-glass windows
and bring out the yellow-varnished pine pews; then, on its
cable at the end of the boom, the great iron ball would, with
pensive deliberation, swing, and the brick wall would totter,
would hover and cream like a mounting wave, would hang
in the air for that split-second which, seeming out of time,
would seem forever, and then would disintegrate; and the
bricks, with their sharply, suddenly, anguishingly individu-
alized shapes, would slide redly down the blue air, as though
down a chute. A few whacks, and it would be nothing but a
pile of broken brick. That would be tomorrow, and tomorrow
Bradwell Tolliver would be far away. And, he told himself,
he would not come back.

He lifted his gaze beyond the church and the crowd,
over the river. No, not a river now, already a lake. The water
was brimming among the black stalks of old ironweed at
the lower end of the Murray pasture, down beyond the
Negro church that once had been the white Methodist
Church, back yonder before old Lank Tolliver had foreclosed the mortgage. Westward, farther off, the water spread
out over all the flat land. The hedges marking those far
fields stood in water. The trees, far off yonder, lifted their
bright, cloudy burden of new leaves, like a glittering haze
of green, shot and dappled with pale gold, above the black
trunks and the far glint of water. The water was shallow
yet, you could tell that. Only a few inches in some places.
But it was rising. You could not see it rise, but you knew it.

Far away, beyond that westward expanse of water, the land heaved up. Not long ago, that heave of land had been wooded, a line of green, or purpling darkness, in the distance, beyond the flat land. He had once known those far-off woods, the depth and gloom, every foot. Now most of it had been cut off, only here and there a clump. As he gazed off yonder toward what would be the west shore of the lake he could catch, now and then, the glitter, like a heliograph, of the sun striking the chrome or glass of some automobile passing on the new highway there. They had been building that highway for three years. But only now had they removed the screening woods.

He looked about him. Here and there, the earth showed raw, the black of humus streaking the clay-red of subsoil. Most of the graves here were empty now. The coffins—or what remained of a coffin, or what remained of what had been in a coffin after nothing remained of the coffin—had been carted off to Lake Town and put in the new cemetery. The tombstones, too. The bodies, or what remained of the bodies, of Lancaster Tolliver and Lucy Cottshill Tolliver, had been carted off. Maggie had, of course, seen to that.

The part of the cemetery to the south, and backing up toward the ridge, was the oldest part, the part where for generations nobody had bothered any more to cut the grass or brush. There the wooden board with the name carved by a hunting knife had fallen and flaked away, a century and a half back. There the name carved on stone, stone long since fallen, had been mossed over, and if you scratched off the moss, the name to appear would, as like as not, be Grimshaw or Grinder or Hanks or Shankins or Mountjoy, or some other name long since died out, or withdrawn into the swamp or hill cove, or absorbed into the general blood stream, or left on the land merely in the designation of a creek or crossroads. But even back there in that part of the cemetery, in a few spots, some raw earth showed.

Yes, there was the raw earth, for somebody off in Memphis or Chicago, somebody with a damned nice realty operation or the vice-presidency of a bank, and with a daughter who had been Queen of the Cotton Carnival or who had had her coming-out party at the Crystal Room—or even the Casino Club, if he really had it made and had married right—had heard, somehow, about Fiddlersburg, a name he hadn't thought of in forty years, and how it would be flooded.

So this man, whoever he was, had waked up in the middle of the night with a weight on his chest and a sense of suffocation. And the first thing next morning, he had told his secretary to take steps to have great-grandpa or great-great-grandma removed. He might, even, not have wanted his secretary to know about it, and so had piously made the arrangements himself.

But no Goldfarb, anywhere, had, it seemed, waked in the night with that pressure on the chest. Maybe there were no more Goldfarbs. Or maybe they had changed the name. Or maybe they had, simply, lost their money. Anyway, when Brother Potts' farewell service was over this morning, Bradwell Tolliver would, at last, rise and locate the grave of Old Izzie. And he himself would have the body removed to Lake Town, and dry ground. With that done, he would have balanced his books and would be ready somehow, though he had not said how, to go on his way.

And his way would lead straight back to the office of Mort Seebaum, and Mort's Filipino would press a button, and the doors of the wall bar would slide soundlessly open, and Pedro would set up two Scotch highballs, and Mort Seebaum, after the first swallow, would give a belch as soft as a black velvet pad in Tiffany's window with the Kohinoor lying in the middle of it, and they would get down to details. But the big detail was already set: $125,000 plus 7 percent of the net. His agent had already arranged that. Mort had screamed; but it came high, the Tolliver Touch. For three pictures now Bradwell Tolliver had had participation.

Brad was aware that his left hand was, again, lifting stealthily to verify the telegram in his inside pocket. But he made the hand sink back down, to lie, palm down, on the fresh grass. It sank down, obedient but disheartened, like a dog rebuked. Hell, he knew the damned telegram was there.

He knew it; but, after a little, the hand lifted from the grass, unnoticed, as it were, and reached the pocket.

But what it discovered and, on a sudden impulse, brought forth, was not the telegram; it was a long heavy white envelope, clearly of American manufacture but plastered with stamps exotically non-American. He looked down at his name written there by, he knew, the hand of Maggie Tolliver Jones, who was far away on an isle of Greece. The letter, plastered with those exotic stamps, was yet unopened.

He had been at a movie all yesterday afternoon, had sat in the dark watching images on a screen, and when he got back to his suite at the Andrew Jackson, he was too tired, even, to glance at his mail. He had ordered a little chicken soup sent up, had taken the Seconal, had fallen into bed. He had felt pretty good when he got up this morning.

He wished that he felt pretty good now.

Then, at the edge of the crowd over there, he caught a glint of sun on metal, and realized that the glint was from the chrome of Sheriff Purtle's wheel chair, and then, with a strange, numb, sinking delay, like a great stone slowly sinking into mud, he realized that the woman pushing the chair, trying to work it in closer to the pulpit, was Leontine. He was trying to decide how this made him feel, when the crowd opened, and the chair and Leontine were swallowed up.

He continued to stare across the road at the crowd, which had—so effortlessly and naturally—absorbed, accepted, the chrome-bright chair, its burden, and the girl. He stared at those people, at the men who were hanging the snowy dogwood on Jack McComb's truck, and he remembered how he had felt one day, long back, in a drugstore, on Sunset Boulevard. That was back in the days when he was just getting acquainted with Suzie Martine; had, in fact, only seen her at a few parties; had asked, once, for a date but had been turned down. Now coming out of the studio, feeling great, having just got the last bugs out of a script that was great, he suddenly had an image of her in his head, of her narrow, closely modeled, chalk-white face with the scarlet lips so disturbingly mobile and glistening, and the sloe eyes so black, sly, and teasing, and the barbaric frizzle-top of black hair, blacker than night above that chalk-white face, the hair crisp and smelling of musk; and had thought, hell, he might try her again.

So he had called her, and she had said, sure, yes, how delightful, she'd love it.

His hand still on the telephone, he had sat in the telephone booth in the drugstore, feeling great and remembering that tightly organized, ingenious, highly educated, acrobatic-looking little butt on Suzie Martine, the famous set designer, as she walked away from you across the room, and trying to decide how those eyes would be if they suddenly lost their slyness and popped wide to expose the full velvety blackness, and thinking how cruelly cat-sharp were the scarlet nails of her small long-fingered, phthisic-white hands, and how they might sink into flesh, your flesh, but you wouldn't notice at the time, and thinking of the Fiji-black frizzle of hair with the smell of musk, and wondering how inky-black and prickly-crisp the hair would be on the *mons veneris*, set off by chalk-whiteness around, and seeing the discreet gleam of the orchidaceously blossoming, brown-petaled, self-offering, immolation-inviting, crimson-winking, crimson-hearted slash.

He sat with his hand still on the telephone, for to remove his hand would be to break contact with Suzie Martine. His eyes, at that moment, were unseeingly fixed on the people, ordinary people, old, young, middle-aged, the nameless people with the nameless needs and desires that had brought them here to move up and down the aisles of this drugstore and stand staring at some object of need or desire. But, all at once, he did see them.

He saw them all, with appalling clarity, in the smallest detail, the twisted seam in a fat woman's stocking, the plum-colored mole on an old man's cheek. He saw them through the glass of the telephone booth, in that clarity that comes over the green world of summer when the purple thunderheads pile high but the full sun yet strikes from the sky with a mythic light, before the blast. Trapped in that glass box, in its icy glitter, he could not breathe. He felt that he was doomed to stay there forever, while the air got thinner and thinner. He could call out, but nobody, not one of those people outside the glass, nobody in the world, would hear.

Now sitting here, in Fiddlersburg, on fresh grass in the April sun, he looked down at the crowd across the road, and that feeling came back to him. It was like the gust of an owl's wing, in dark woods.

Then it was over.

He lifted the envelope in his hand. From the heft of it, Maggie must have written a book. He was tired, but he might as well read it now. While they were still horsing around across the road, getting things ready for the big weep.

The letter said that Maggie was well, and Yasha too, and the picture he was working on was really the kind he ought to make, he said he would never have made Fiddlersburg right, he thought now he had the idea he had always been hoping for, and on the island the stone glittered white in the sunlight and you could not believe how purple-blue the sea was, nor believe how happy she was. This was, though, just a scribble to say she loved her wretched old muskrat-skinner of a brother and wanted him to be well again, and wanted to thank him—please forgive her—one more time.

Brad looked up from the letter. So they were thanking him again. They had come to the hospital, after it was certain that everything would be all right, to say goodbye, and Yasha had thanked him, gripping his hand hard, and Maggie had thanked him, and cried. He had managed to say something, in a confusion that they, no doubt, took to be manly embarrassment. But the confusion had been something else. You do not know what to say when somebody thanks you for an act you have performed but do not know the motive or the meaning of.

Now, looking up from Maggie's letter, he stared at the crowd across the road, and knew, even now, that he did not know the meaning of the act for which she thanked him. It was one of the things he did not know the meaning of.

So he looked down again at the letter. It went on to say that Maggie was sending this scribble to enclose a letter that was addressed to her but was really for him. She hoped the letter would make him happy. It had, she said, made her happy—in its way.

He opened the enclosure. *Dear Maggie, dear little Maggie,* it began: and with old familiarity, the bold decisive stroke of ink on white paper leaped up at him, and shivered like black fire.

Well, he reminded himself, this was Fiddlersburg. He was, oh how appropriately, in Fiddlersburg, to receive this letter. He wondered if she—if Lettice Poindexter Tolliver, or whatever her name was now—knew that soon there would be no more Fiddlersburg. Would she sleep easier for that knowledge, sink more handily into that inwardness of self which is sleep, if she knew—wherever she was, whoever it was she lay by in the dark—that soon water would seal over Fiddlersburg, with no trace?

Anyway, the letter was now saying that last July she had been terribly disturbed to read about what happened. Then she had feared that even a letter would be an intrusion, but now that everything, as she had read in the papers, had turned out for the best, and Maggie had married that wonderful man who clearly knew how wonderful Maggie was, she would write to say that she held Maggie, and them all, in her heart, and in her prayers.

Yes, prayers—and that may sound funny to you. It
sounds funny, sometimes, to me, too. I even sort of giggle
at it as a kind of a joke, but it is a happy giggle, like a little girl stuck off in boarding school and awfully lonely—
how well I remember that part!—when she gets a surprise box from home with lots of revolting, nauseous
goodies. Only I never got a box from home, I got a check.
That sounds self-pitying and mean-spirited, and I imagine it is, so forgive me. My mother did what she could
perhaps, and I would not judge her. I only hope that thirteen years ago when she was killed in an air crash (a private plane, and she had no right to be with the man
whose plane it was) she had even a second to know God's
goodness. I wish I had been able to tell her that I wanted
to love her, even if not worthy to love her. Oh, dear little
Maggie, how hard it is to be worthy to love anybody! But
you have no reason to know that, with your true and loving heart.

But I'll tell you about myself, a little. After what
happened there in Fiddlersburg, and I left Brad (do write
me a little about him—no, everything, and make everything good!), what might have happened to me in my
wicked foolishness, I don't know, except that . . .

"Why, hello, boy," the voice said.
It was the voice of Blanding Cottshill.

"Yes, sir," Blanding Cottshill said, standing there in a
baggy old brown suit, blue work shirt, and black tie, a setter
at heel, "it's sure fine to see you around."

"It's fine to be around," Brad said, and started to push
himself up to shake hands.

The other laid a restraining hand on his shoulder. "Take
it easy, boy," he commanded, and dropped down beside him,
squatting on his heels like a farmer stopping for a conversation by the roadside. The setter came and lay down in
front of him, nose on forepaws.

"You're looking better," Cottshill said, "better than
propped up in that hospital bed."

"Listen," Brad said, a thickness suddenly in his throat,
"I want to tell you how much I appreciated those trips you
made to Nashville."

"Balls," Cottshill said, and from under the white eyebrows, thorny as a bramble hedge with frost on it, gave him

a steady look. Then said: "We old Fiddlersburgians got to stick together."

The music had begun across the road. Miss Prattfield was playing the piano up there on Mr. McCoomb's truck. The people were singing.

"The funeral of Fiddlersburg," Cottshill said. "Yeah, and when Fiddlersburg is under water, God-A-Mighty will jerk our passports. We will be stateless persons. We will be DPs for eternity and thence forward. We will have no identity."

He looked across at the crowd for a while.

"I have spent most of my life here," he said then, "and you know, you look back on things in a place like Fiddlersburg, and there's some sort of mysterious logic to 'em. What happened to anybody here—say, to you or Maggie or Cal or me—might, in a way, happen to anybody anywhere. But in Fiddlersburg everything is different. Things are tied together different. There's some spooky interpenetration of things, a mystic osmosis of being, you might say. Take Pretty-Boy even, he—"

"Pretty-Boy," Brad broke in, "I'm glad he made it."

"What?"

"I mean that they didn't have to carry him, or anything."

"Yes, he made it," Cottshill said. Then: "Mr. Budd, he's got his points. All hell broke loose that night. All the doing of that hickory-nut-headed, old red-neck Bumpus. Because Pretty-Boy prayed. Bumpus, you recollect, was the fellow had started the trouble celebrating the fact that Pretty-Boy had spit on the preacher. But Pretty-Boy lost his grip and prayed. And it looks like that was what that intransigent, murdering orneriness in Bumpus couldn't stand. Pretty-Boy had betrayed him. He thought that somebody ought to hold out against God and the State of Tennessee. So it was his idea to get those two dismantled revolvers sent in, piece by piece, in angel food cakes baked by loving hands at home. And his idea to work Cal up to the break, and his idea to get that terrorized trusty to stall the truck of cons coming in late from the prison farm, right in the big gate, and his idea— but hell, you know the rest.

"Boy, was Budd's professional pride hurt. Not that it was really his fault, not having the staff to check every morsel of angel food cake that comes in. And something came

over the stools—rising waters or blue funk. Anyway, Budd
was fit to be tied. He was in the middle of it, frothing at
the mouth, aiming to quell it with his bare hands.

"But what I was going to say, Boots Budd has his points.
As soon as they had a chance to pick up Cal—sure, they
guessed where—and had put the dogs on the three guys
that made the woods, Budd turned up for Pretty-Boy. He was
off schedule, but he took plenty of time for what you might
call the moral support. He was there in the cell with his hand
on Pretty-Boy's shoulder while Brother Pinckney prayed the
last prayer, and then—"

"Did he cry this time?"

"No, Pretty didn't cry. It was what you might call
dry praying, and then he proceeded under his own power.
Brother Pinckney on one side, Boots Budd on the other.
Just one time, at the door, it looked bad. But Budd,
in that top-sergeant way of his, sang out, 'Pick up them big
feet, Pretty, we're marchen in!' And in he marched."

Over across the road, the crowd was singing "Let the
Nearer Waters Roll." The notes of Miss Prattfield's piano
sounded very pale and thin and lost in the bright air. Each
note, alone in the air, would sound pale the way a match
flame looks pale, almost invisible, in bright sunshine.
Brother Potts was standing over yonder on the truck bed,
singing.

When the singing was over, Cottshill stirred, patting the
setter. After a moment, he said: "Looks like Brother Pinckney has out-foxed Brother Potts."

"How do you mean?"

"Word was out that Brother Potts, as soon as the sermon was over, was going to announce he was going down
yonder"—he nodded down the road toward the Negro church,
once the white Methodist Church—"to pray with the colored,
there being supposed to be a colored farewell service this
morning, too. Brother Potts was going to go traipsing across
the vacant lots followed by whoever was worked up enough on
this, the last official day of Fiddlersburg, to follow him to pray
with the colored for God to grant mercy and reconciliation
and what-all might be necessary to undo the work of History.
But," he hesitated, grinning, "you observe that the colored
folks are not there. Nobody is there. Brother Pinckney has
out-foxed Brother Potts."

High on the truck bed Brother Potts was praying now. He

was holding aloft his one arm and squinching his eyes and praying with the sunshine over his lifted face.

When the prayer was over, Cottshill said: "No, Brother Pinckney was not going to let Brother Potts, or any of us white folks—just in case two or three got that hopped up—make it easy for himself just by walking over there and praying together in the open air. He was not going to let anybody just clean out his system so easy, not merely, you might say, of his nigger-constipation but of everything else in his colon-congested self by using the nigger-purge as a substitute for other and more appropriate, and perhaps even more painful, cathartics. You see, my friend Leon Pinckney is a very deep fellow, and he knows more about you and me than we do. He knows that white folks are human, even if they are white folks, and he knows, therefore, that we like the cheap and easy way to feel good. Like praying with colored folks."

Brad looked at the other man. He was staring out over the river.

"You," Brad demanded, "would you have followed him down there? To the nigger church?"

For a moment the man did not seem to hear. Then, with eyes still fixed into distance, he said: "You mean, assuming I was a praying man." He laughed, then stopped abruptly.

After another moment, he said: "You never know till the time comes."

Brother Potts was preaching now. His voice, pale and far away, was saying that they had all lived here in Fiddlersburg together. It was saying that they should all pray to God to know that the life they had lived was blessèd.

Blanding Cottshill, a hand on the head of the setter, said: "Maybe what I said wasn't the reason why Brother Pinckney called off his farewell service and blew town. Maybe it was not merely because he wasn't going to let any of us white folks get purged pure by praying with him. Leon is a deep one, but he is also an honest one. So maybe he just didn't think he himself was quite ready yet to pray with any of us white folks."

Suddenly he stood up. "Is anybody ever ready to pray with anybody?" he demanded, harshly.

He stood there straight and stiff as a post. His breath was heavy. He gave a couple of gasps, as though stricken. He seemed to be trying to say something, but could not.

Then he said it.

"She left me," he burst out then, his voice a choked cry, his eyes on the stained and brimming river. "Roselle has left me."

He slowly sank back down on his heels. After a moment he again laid a hand on the setter's head.

"Just went," he said, "and I don't know where. Left a note saying it was not because she didn't care about me. Saying it was because she did. That was all."

He waited.

"That was all," he resumed, "except the misspelling. Just one word, though. *Becose* for *because*. It was just that one pore little piece of misspelling that seemed to hit me. Isn't that funny—how that one little thing hit me harder than the big fact?"

"Did she know you were going to Scotland?" Brad asked.

"Scotland—hell," Cottshill said. "That was just a notion. What the hell would I do in Scotland? Murder a few animals? Sit in the gun room of some drafty ruin of an abbey drinking whiskey with some handsome-headed, frosty-polled mackerel-eyed old laird who half the time wouldn't even remember my name? Get a thrombosis in bed in some quaint old inn in the middle of the night and be found dead next morning? Hell, I wasn't ever going to Scotland. After Fiddlersburg where can a man go, anyway? And feel real?"

He seemed to fall inside himself. The hand stopped moving on the head of the setter.

"No," he resumed, "I've gone and bought me another farm. In Benton's Valley. And that's that."

And with those words, he again stood up, again abruptly. This time he stared down, almost angrily it seemed, at Brad. "Do you know why she left me?" he demanded.

"No."

"She left me," he said, "because she didn't want me to be worrying about what might happen to her. About what some Ku-Klux cretin might do to her."

"But what—"

"Christ," Blanding Cottshill said, in his painful unfocused anger, "can't you figure it out?"

"Figure out what?"

"I never said a word to her about it, but she figured it

out. She figured it out long before I did. She had figured out
I would take that school case. In Lake Town."

He was looking across the water, breathing heavily. For
a moment he seemed to have forgotten Brad. Then he said:
"Remember that time—the time I told you about Roselle?"

"Yes."

"About the old-time religion? About the exact shade of
color? About the tawny?"

"Yes."

"Well, would I have been talking about a white woman
in just that way?"

Having uttered those words, Blanding Cottshill was impelled, it seemed, to get himself off immediately. His face
was preternaturally flushed, his blue glance flickered as
though he were in a fever. But he managed to control himself enough to ask when Brad was leaving, and what was
happening now about the picture, and to say, when Brad
told him about the telegram from Mort Seebaum, that it was
fine, boy, fine. He even managed to slap Brad on the shoulder
and say that it would make a great movie.

He wrung Brad's hand, and was gone, a stubby brown-
clad figure, with a too-big head fringed in unkempt white
hair, the setter at his heels, moving up River Street, up yonder where nobody was now.

Chapter

33

Brad watched the man a long time—long enough for him to pass from sight up River Street. He wondered where Blanding Cottshill, moving now under the brightness of April, would be going, in that empty town where, already, some of the buildings were only rubble. Then he knew. Blanding Cottshill would go, one more time, to sit in the office, and look out over the deserted square, where the stopped clock of the courthouse cupola would now be presiding, for the last season in all time, over maples coming to fresh leaf.

Well, Blanding Cottshill had earned that much.

Brad looked down again at the letter in his lap. He read again the sentence which said that Lettice Poindexter did

not know what, after she had left him, might have become
of her in her wicked foolishness, in her triviality, except—
Wicked foolishness, he thought.
Triviality, he thought.
He could make no sense of the words. Not in relation to
Lettice Poindexter. He sat there and wanted to tie those
words to her. Everything would be easier if he could. But he
could not.
So he read on: how the war had come in time for her,
how she had studied nursing, how she had been sent to the
Pacific to a hospital in New Guinea, where it was tough.
But she had made it,

. . . for I'm a pretty tough gal, really, and what I saw
saved me. I was so foolish I had to see a lot, when
smarter people need to see only a little to imagine the
rest. Well, if you see what can really happen to human
bodies and human souls, it changes you. It changes you
to realize that a body has a soul living in it—even if the
word soul still sounds strange and empty to you. It
changes you because that fact makes you realize that
bodies are precious. Precious in a way you never even
thought.
But I don't mean in a way to make you make a lot of
fuss about your own body. Remember, Maggie, what a
silly fuss I used to make about the one I had—lying out
there naked and oiled in the sun to get the right shade of
tan absolutely all over, like a chicken basted on a spit,
and taking those exercises to keep that waist I was so
proud of—"Save the waist and save all!" that was my
motto, remember?—and plucking my eyebrows by the
hour and putting all those expensive perfumes on me to
hone Brad up. Oh, what a fool I was, Maggie, about that
silly old me! And don't think I don't know now that nobody can just keep his wicked foolishness private, and I
flung mine around something awful. But I did love you,
Maggie, and I'm sorry.
Anyway, you ought to see funny old me now. That
waist is long gone, darling. I'm a big, heavy, slow-footed
old dame (170 pounds by golly!) and my hair is mostly
gray, and cut short, for I barely have time to wash it,
much less fool with it, and I have varicose veins on my
legs and have to wear elastic bandages, which aren't exactly fetching, and my hands are raw from scrubbing
things, and I wear usually a sort of gray cotton smock. I

suppose, in an upside-down way, I sound pretty pleased with myself, as though I had just been named Miss Universe at Atlantic City—or wherever they pick her out.

Brad let the sheets of paper lie in his lap, and shut his eyes and saw the big, heavy-footed woman, with cropped gray hair and raw knuckles and elastic bandages on her legs; and he felt sick. But he was seeing, too, a tall girl with auburn hair pulled back and tied with a strip of white rag, a smudge of grime on her left cheek, a bushel basket filled with junk in her arms, the red nail of one forefinger broken off in the quick—the girl standing at the foot of cellar stairs with a shaft of light from above falling across her face. Seeing himself trying to make her give up the basket, then managing to get it and set it down, spilling half the trash. Seeing her face in comic despair as she cried out, "Oh, look, you're spilling that trash, how'll we ever get this place fit to live in!" Seeing himself get his arm around her waist, and her twisting her face away, saying, "Oh, you sex-mad, blue-bottomed baboon, how'll we ever clean it up!" But all at once she was in his arms, in the gloom of the cellar in the old Fiddler house, in Fiddlersburg.

Well, they had managed to clean the cellar up, clean the house up. They had lived there. And now he sat on the grass, and the image of the slim-waisted girl, with the broken red fingernail, standing shallow-breathed in the cellar gloom, with a streak of light falling from above across her face, and the image of the heavy woman with elastic bandages, were one image. As he sat in the darkness of his closed eyes, the world reeled. He clutched the grass, and the world rocked. What had happened to the world?

He opened his eyes.

A speedboat was coming powerfully up-river. The hollow, angry, jazzing buzz grew in the air. The wake creamed back in its approaching V. The boat—a big Lyman Islander, he decided, twin-powered—came on. But now, behind, there was no tall, golden-skinned girl riding water skis, laughing in joy, like an advertisement, while the auburn hair was snatched back on the breeze. But then he remembered that, back in those days, it would have been an aquaplane, anyway.

The boat drew past. Out of that diminishing sound you

could again hear the voice of Brother Potts over there, across
the road, even if the words remained indistinct.

Brad looked down again at the sheet of paper:

But I'm getting ahead of myself. After the war I had
to find a way to live, and somehow—it's a joke on me, as
I said—I woke up one day a Catholic and one of the lay
workers in a home for old people here in Chicago. The
sisters, after I convinced them I meant business, let me
put my trust income into the place. And let me help. I do
a lot of scrubbing, about all I know how to do, since
tennis and French and riding and dancing don't seem
much use here, and I'm happy.

Really happy, Maggie. What I do is not a penance.
What you did, as I learned from the papers, for Cal's
mother, that wasn't a penance for you, was it? A necessity maybe, but that kind of necessity, it's a joy, isn't it?

I don't mean there's only one kind of joy. God wills
many kinds of joy, and there might have been a joy with
Brad. If we hadn't flunked out. No, if *I* hadn't, for I
should have been able to help him when he needed . . .

Brad lifted his eyes from the page.
Help, he thought.
He hadn't needed any help. Then or now.
But his eyes found the line:

. . . needed it. Maybe that was what drew me to Brad—
the fact that even if he was strong he needed something,
seemed vulnerable, and . . .

Vulnerable, he thought, *shit*. But his eyes found the
line:

. . . vulnerable, and even his not being so tall maybe had
something to do with it. Anyway, if I had just realized,
we could have lived a life together, and had Pepito—all
my Pepitos—and been happy, even if I got old and slow,
for we might have loved each other.

He stopped reading. He did not look back at the sheet.
He was thinking of Central Park, of a pigeon skirmishing the
gravel by an *NYC-SD* can, of the head and torso of a nameless woman framed in leaves, rising and falling in a decorous
but gradually accelerating rhythm, leaning a little forward
as though loosening the reins at the approach to the jump.

He was thinking of how smoky the late light of afternoon had suddenly seemed, slanting across the far towers and the Park. He was thinking of the blatting anguish of a horn, far off in the doomed city, rising from the pervasive hum and moan of traffic.

Now, sitting here on the spring grass in Fiddlersburg, he was in the grip of lust, for he saw the face of Lettice Poindexter, as he had seen it later that June afternoon all those years ago, as she jerked her head back and the eyes shut in the moment of spasm, the face with lineaments strained and pure, like a saint.

. . . got a bad start. But all starts are bad, I guess, or in-complete anyway, for we are only human, and it wouldn't have mattered if we—if *I*—had taken the trouble to learn what there was to learn. For I've read somewhere that people, in the Middle Ages, used to believe that the Devil likes to surprise a man and woman in the act and then they would be caught together forever, *more canino* the book said. (Yes, I fooled you, I did learn a little Latin at Shipley.) And I suppose the truth of that old belief is that that is like what happens to people who don't try to make something of what they start with.

Oh, why couldn't I have learned that much, and made Brad happy! I don't want to live in a regret, but I feel that it would be wicked (am I wrong?) to deny the possibility of that joy, but at the same time I am grateful to God for all that has led up to this joy I now have. But how do I put these things together? Here is where you have to pray. To know the *nowness* of God's will.

For you see, a person wickedly trivial like me has to get everything the hard way. A person dumb like me has to be prodded to what they call the Leap of Faith. And now, for the first time in years, I remember a terrible nightmare I once had. I told it to Brad the next morning, back in Fiddlersburg, and I remember the terrible look on his face, worse than the nightmare. No, I won't tell it to you, it's too embarrassing and messy—no, I'll tell you anyway, for if I tell . . .

But Brad did not have to read it. For she had told it to him that morning long ago, in Fiddlersburg, before they got up, a spring morning with bird song in the garden and sun-shine flooding into the room and her naked body lying stiff as a ramrod under the sheet which drew taut while she stared at the ceiling and told him.

In the dream she had waked up, she told him, in a foreign-looking, very elegant hotel room, the kind of hotel her mother used to live in, in France and Italy—and leave her alone in, for weeks at a time, with the Nanny. In that dream room, late at night, not a child now but grown, she woke up. In awful loneliness she found her way through an elegant suite, all mirrors and ormolu, out into the hall. There was only a dim light, and somehow she knew that the whole enormous place, perhaps even the whole world, was deserted. In this anguish of loneliness she wandered, in her nightgown, her feet bare, down the hall: that morning so long ago, at the very moment of telling about it, she could, she said to Brad, still feel the carpet under her bare feet, real as life.

She turned a corner and there they were. But she wasn't surprised. It was as though, that second, she realized that she had always known how, in that deserted, enormous hotel, all mirrors and shadows and soundless carpet and gilt, they would somewhere be waiting. And there they were.

It was as though she had known what they would look like, like Italian *bravi* of the time of the Renaissance, three thugs dressed in doublet and hose, the doublets velvet and gaudy but streaked with grease, poniard at belt. There was the tall skinny one with the high thin head and big bony hands, the short one that limped a little, the burly middle-sized one with broad shoulders and round thick-skulled head. But she could not see their faces; nor had expected to. They wore masks, as for a carnival, or a murder. And she knew which it was to be.

For she saw that one of them, the tall one, had a rope, and she went goose-pimpled at the thought that they might garrot her, or merely draw her off her feet under a lintel to dangle there as long as it would take. But no, by God, if it was going to be a murder, it wasn't going to be that kind of a messy one. Whatever it would be, she took charge, crying out commandingly, in a foreign tongue, but what tongue she couldn't remember after the dream was over, if indeed any tongue she had ever heard, saying, look here, you guys, follow me, I'll show you! And she marched in the lead, expecting every second a loop over her head.

She marched them through the grand silent halls and lobbies, through the great dining salon, with white napery glimmering in the dark and roses in silver vases dimly perceived, on through the pantries, into the cavernous kitchen. There one pale, penurious electric bulb burned. The stoves were spotless, cold, and bleak. In racks the great rows of copper pots gave back a sober gleam. But the plaster of the walls was stained. There were cracks in the ceiling. Yes, she seemed to have known what she would find up there—iron pipes running across, water pipes or heat pipes. Their long shadows, patterned upward by the light of the single bulb, were big on the ceiling, swelling away to merge into the general dimness beyond.

She pushed a stool up to a long table, a table with the wood pale and the grain raised by long scrubbings with brick and lye soap; and without too much care for decency scrambled up onto the table. Her bare feet felt the raised grain of the wood, the thin nightgown was sticking damply to her skin now, she shivered with fear and excitement. But she turned on them as they stood down there, and in that language she knew in the dream, ordered them to give her the rope. The tall one obeyed. Then, at her command, he passed up the stool.

They watched her silently, the three black masks tilted upward in a mathematical row, while she, with difficulty on account of the rope, mounted the stool—yes, by God, she'd at least take charge, it was her funeral, wasn't it?—and tossed one end of the rope over a pipe and got it looped there. She got off the stool—it was a rather high one—and stood there a moment to make her calculations. She would have to jump from the height of the stool set there on top of the table to get a jerk that would, she hoped, make it sudden. She had to be careful to give all the fall possible and yet not let her feet reach the floor.

Yes, Brad remembered her telling him all that, very systematically, that morning long ago; and now, sitting on the grass, while the words of Brother Potts came indistinctly from across the road, he remembered how at that very moment in the telling, she had interrupted herself, had raised herself on an elbow, and staring at him, had said: "What makes your face that way? Why, your face—it looks terrible! It's only a dream, you silly!"

And he, in that instant of long ago, feeling deprived of her and of himself, betrayed, jealous, and impotent, had said, in a grating voice: "Get on with it!"

She had reached over to hold his hand, which he had

known was as cold as a dead catfish, and which, somehow, he could not make clasp hers in return, and she had got on with it.

So now he looked down at the sheet of paper in his lap, turned it, looked at the next, found the place that he knew he would find. She was telling it again, getting on with it:

. . . and got it fixed as near right as I could tell. Since the first time, on account of the rope, I had difficulty in climbing up on the stool, I now hung the rope around my neck. Anyway, I wasn't going to let their dirty hands— whoever they were—do it. In that very instant, light as cats, they had jumped up on the table, not making a sound, and stood there looking at me. They had jumped up absolutely together, like puppets jerked up by one string, and they stood in a perfect row—tall, middle-sized, short. I stood there with my fingers still touching the rope, like a girl fingering a necklace, feeling the rope rough on the skin of my neck, and looked at them, and saw the eyes gleam in the slits of the black masks. Then, suddenly I got afraid I hadn't calculated right—for the length of the fall, that is—and instead of climbing right away up on the stool I turned to look over the edge of the table to the floor to verify my estimate. Then it happened.

Maybe it was just as well it happened that way. No, I can't say that exactly, since it didn't really happen at all, only in a dream, but even at that instant in the dream, as it was happening, mixed up with my anger at being cheated after all my planning, there was some sort of relief that now I wouldn't run the risk of being stuck up there on that stool afraid at the last minute to jump off it, just standing up there shivering and sweating.

Anyway, it happened. I had, as I said, turned to look over the edge at the floor. And one of them—somehow I knew it was the middle-sized one—goosed me. So hard I jumped clean off.

I jumped off, and they were laughing fit to split, slapping their thighs. And in that second, mixed with what else I was thinking, was the fear that now, just from the table top, there wasn't enough fall to do the job, so I'd be left dangling and clawing.

But all at once there wasn't any floor. I was falling into dark, and the rope was rough on my neck, but it kept coming on, longer and longer and longer, as I fell. It seemed that I fell forever, waiting for the jerk.

Then I woke up.

Twenty years ago, she had told him that, on a spring morning, holding his hand in what he had known was desperate hopefulness, and had waited for him to say something. He had found nothing to say.

God dam it, he now thought, *what the hell was there to say! Then or ever!*

He looked down at the sheet:

How did I ever get started on this, Maggie? But I couldn't stop telling it. Because, I suppose, it is what my life came to in the end. After I had failed to make sense of it, and of myself. I had to be forced, by all the terrible things that had happened, to jump. If you are that dumb, you have to be goosed to—it sounds blasphemous but I'll say it—goosed to God. Yes, if you're so dumb that—

He clambered to his feet. He leaned on his stick, and felt giddy. He found himself laughing. "Goosed to God!" he cried out loud, and kept on laughing, and didn't know why.

The speedboat that had gone up-river was coming back, close inshore. The angry, hollow buzzing grew in the air, grew angrier. The bright sunlight that filled the sky seemed, all at once, to vibrate with that powerful, jazzing, buzzing angriness. The mouth of Brother Potts, over yonder on the truck bed, moved, but in that hollow buzz you could not hear a word.

Then the speedboat had passed, going on to Kentucky. Behind it, the waters, roiled, lifted in undulations and fractured planes of violet slashed with gold. The water seemed to lift and become violet air and golden light.

"Goosed to Glory," Bradwell Tolliver said, and thrust the sheets of paper, crumpled, into his side pocket, and again found himself in the grip of that wild laughter.

Then he stopped laughing. He slowly began to realize, as you realize the first dull beginnings of a headache, that now, for the first time in all the years, even in the years of the contact and the clutching, of the blending of hopes and the mixing of breaths, Lettice Poindexter was real to him. She had really existed. Somewhere, in her way, she existed now. He marveled, slowly, at that fact. And he wondered, in a slow, powerful, painful way, why he had not, at some time in all the years, realized that fact. And why, at some time, he had not even had the thought of going across whatever thou-

sands of miles might be necessary, to tell her: to tell her that
he knew, at last, that she was real.

But he had not known it. Therefore how could he have
gone to tell her?

Then he wondered if the fact that he had not known she
was real meant that he himself had not been real.

The giddiness was gone, but he felt slow and dull. He
leaned heavily on the stick. God, would he be a crip? No, Dr.
Harris had said, no, he would be as good as ever.

As good as ever, he thought, and a black shiver shook
him, even in sunlight, as he thought of all the acts he would
again, over and over, perform—the lying down and the getting up, the cleaning of teeth, the washing of flesh, the scraping from the chin of the blindly growing bristles that would
continue to grow for a time after his death, the opening of
the mouth to make sounds, the opening of the mouth to put
food in, the pissing and defecating, the insertion of his own
flesh into a warm orifice in the flesh of another body, which
might emit a sigh or even make a sound resembling, by
chance, the sound of his own name.

He looked across the road, and saw the people, and
thought that these things that he had done and would do were
what they did, and they endured it, and now stood in the
April sunshine, and they now were singing. What strength
did they have that he did not have?

So his left hand slipped to the inner pocket of his coat
where lay hidden the telegram from Mort Seebaum.

But before the fingers could touch it, fondle it, verify its
existence, he had, inwardly and irrelevantly, cried in protest:
But I have done good things!

He had, he carefully enumerated to himself, done kind
things, tender things, generous things, had worked hard, had
been loyal to friends, had given money to worthy causes, had
been no coward, had risked his life, had—

At that instant, he saw again, in scrupulous clarity, a
dead body he had once seen, in Spain, the face calm amid
the white stone of the wall the mortar blast had found. He
saw the face now and wished it had been his own face. If it
had been his face, then people would have known why he
died, they would have had to believe.

Believe what?

What would people have had to believe if he had died,

last July, from the slug fired through his throat by Calvin Fiddler?

They would have had to believe nothing.

He looked across the road where the crowd was. Brother Potts, pale and thin and sweating in the face, stood high on the truck bed and called out to the people and lifted his arm to implore them. Brad strained to hear him. He heard him: "—and the Psalmist says: 'The floods have lifted up, O Lord, the floods have lifted up their voice.' And the Psalmist says: 'Let the floods clap their hands.' But O my friends, help *me* to rejoice. Help me now. Oh, sing with me, and help me now —for I am weak and full of sin and error. Help me to know the life I lived was blessèd. If I don't have that, what do I have? Oh, sing with me!"

So Brother Potts lifted his twisted face, and closed his eyes, and held his one arm toward the blue sky, and the sunlight poured down over his face. Miss Prattfield was playing the piano, and the people were all singing the song Brother Potts had written:

> "When I see the town I love
>   Sinking down beneath the wave,
> God, help me to remember then
>   All the blessings that You gave.
>
> When I see the life I led
>   Whelmed and drowned . . ."

Bradwell Tolliver heard them singing. He thought how Brother Potts would go to the hospital tomorrow, and would not come back, and how, never again in passionate April, would he be forced to stand in a dark kitchen and eat cold pork and beans from a can clamped under the sawed-off nub of his left arm. And then he thought how Brother Potts had won his race against the rising waters. Brother Potts had done what he had set out to do.

And with that thought came the thought that everything he himself had ever done, the good and the bad, had been like the grimace and tic and pose and gesture of the crazy man, who, by repeating the empty form, tries, over and over, to re-establish the connection that had existed before the weight of ice broke the wires.

My God, he thought in anger.

My God, he thought, at least a man didn't have to twitch and jerk and pule and mutter and twist his fact in craziness and call it all something else. At least a man did not have to lie.

At least.

With a sudden motion he thrust his left hand into the inner pocket and seized the telegram. He dropped the stick. He grasped the telegram in both hands and tore it across. He carefully laid the yellow halves one on top of the other, and tore again. He let the pieces flutter away from him, to the grass, while the people across the road sang on to the end.

He stood there and heard them. For, over the years, he had run hither and yon, blaming Fiddlersburg because it was not the world and, therefore, was not real, and blaming the world because it was not Fiddlersburg and, therefore, was not real. For he had not trusted the secret and irrational life of man, which might be the truth of man, and which was both more and less than the moment when, as a boy, in a skiff on the swollen river, he had seen the winter sun setting red beyond the black swamp woods, or that moment when he had seen the leather-dry, leather-brown hand of an old woman, in Spain, hold out bread to him, or that moment when he had seen his father lying in the black swamp mud, asleep after weeping. For he, being a man, had lived, he knew, in the grinning calculus of the done and the undone.

Therefore, in his inwardness, he said: *I cannot find the connection between what I was and what I am. I have not found the human necessity.*

He knew that that was what he must try to find.

But he knew that now, at this moment, he did not need to try to find the grave of Israel Goldfarb. And knew that Old Goldfarb would not have him try to find it. For Old Goldfarb was waiting for the waters that would come over him and over all the nameless ones who had lived in this place and done good and done evil.

No, he would not have to find the grave now. He would leave here and go wherever it might be he would have to go. He might, some day, even go back to the office of Mort Seebaum. He might even, some day, come back to Fiddlersburg—rather, to the edge of the waters that would cover Fiddlersburg.

For this was his country.

But then, even as he felt a sudden, unwilled, undecipherable, tearing, ripping gesture of his innermost being toward those people over yonder, who soon now would eat the ham and chicken and cake and chess pie, and after the goodbyes and the weeping, would go away, he thought: *There is no country but the heart.*

And for a moment he mistook the brightness of moisture in his eyes for the flicker of sun, far off, on the chrome and safety glass of cars passing on the new highway, yonder across the lake.

$\mathcal{V}$oices of the $\mathcal{S}$outh

Hamilton Basso
  The View from Pompey's Head
Richard Bausch
  Real Presence
  Take Me Back
Robert Bausch
  On the Way Home
Doris Betts
  The Astronomer and Other Stories
  The Gentle Insurrection and Other Stories
Sheila Bosworth
  Almost Innocent
  Slow Poison
David Bottoms
  Easter Weekend
Erskine Caldwell
  Poor Fool
Fred Chappell
  Dagon
  The Gaudy Place
  The Inkling
  It Is Time, Lord
Kelly Cherry
  Augusta Played
Vicki Covington
  Bird of Paradise
Elizabeth Cox
  The Ragged Way People Fall Out of Love
R. H. W. Dillard
  The Book of Changes
Ellen Douglas
  A Family's Affairs
  A Lifetime Burning
  The Rock Cried Out
  Where the Dreams Cross
Percival Everett
  Cutting Lisa
  Suder
Peter Feibleman
  The Daughters of Necessity
  A Place Without Twilight
Candace Flynt
  Mother Love

William Price Fox
  Dixiana Moon
George Garrett
  An Evening Performance
  Do, Lord, Remember Me
  The Magic Striptease
  The Finished Man
Reginald Gibbons
  Sweetbitter
Ellen Gilchrist
  The Annunciation
  In the Land of Dreamy Dreams
Marianne Gingher
  Bobby Rex's Greatest Hit
Shirley Ann Grau
  The Hard Blue Sky
  The House on Coliseum Street
  The Keepers of the House
  Roadwalkers
Ben Greer
  Slammer
Barry Hannah
  The Tennis Handsome
Donald Hays
  The Dixie Association
William Humphrey
  Home from the Hill
  The Ordways
Mac Hyman
  No Time For Sergeants
Madison Jones
  A Cry of Absence
Nancy Lemann
  Lives of the Saints
  Sportsman's Paradise
Beverly Lowry
  Come Back, Lolly Ray
Clarence Major
  Such Was the Season
Valerie Martin
  A Recent Martyr
  Set in Motion
Willie Morris
  The Last of the Southern Girls
Padgett Powell
  Mrs. Hollingsworth's Men

Louis D. Rubin, Jr.
  The Golden Weather
Evelyn Scott
  The Wave
Lee Smith
  The Last Day the Dogbushes Bloomed
Elizabeth Spencer
  Landscapes of the Heart
  The Night Travellers
  The Salt Line
  This Crooked Way
  The Voice at the Back Door
Max Steele
  Debby
Virgil Suárez
  Latin Jazz
Walter Sullivan
  The Long, Long Love
  Sojourn of a Stranger
Allen Tate
  The Fathers
Peter Taylor
  In the Miro District and Other Stories
  The Widows of Thornton
Robert Penn Warren
  Band of Angels
  Brother to Dragons
  Flood
  World Enough and Time
Walter White
  Flight
James Wilcox
  Miss Undine's Living Room
  North Gladiola
Joan Williams
  The Morning and the Evening
  The Wintering
Christine Wiltz
  Glass House
Thomas Wolfe
  The Hills Beyond
  The Web and the Rock